the MAP to YOU

RACHEL STOCKBRIDGE

www.rachelstockbridge.com

ISBN (paperback): 978-1-7352494-2-1
ISBN (ebook): 978-1-7352494-3-8

For information on bulk purchases for educational, business, or promotional use, please contact your local bookseller or write to hello@rachelstockbridge.com.

First Edition: January 2022

For the fighters.
You matter.

the
MAP
to
YOU

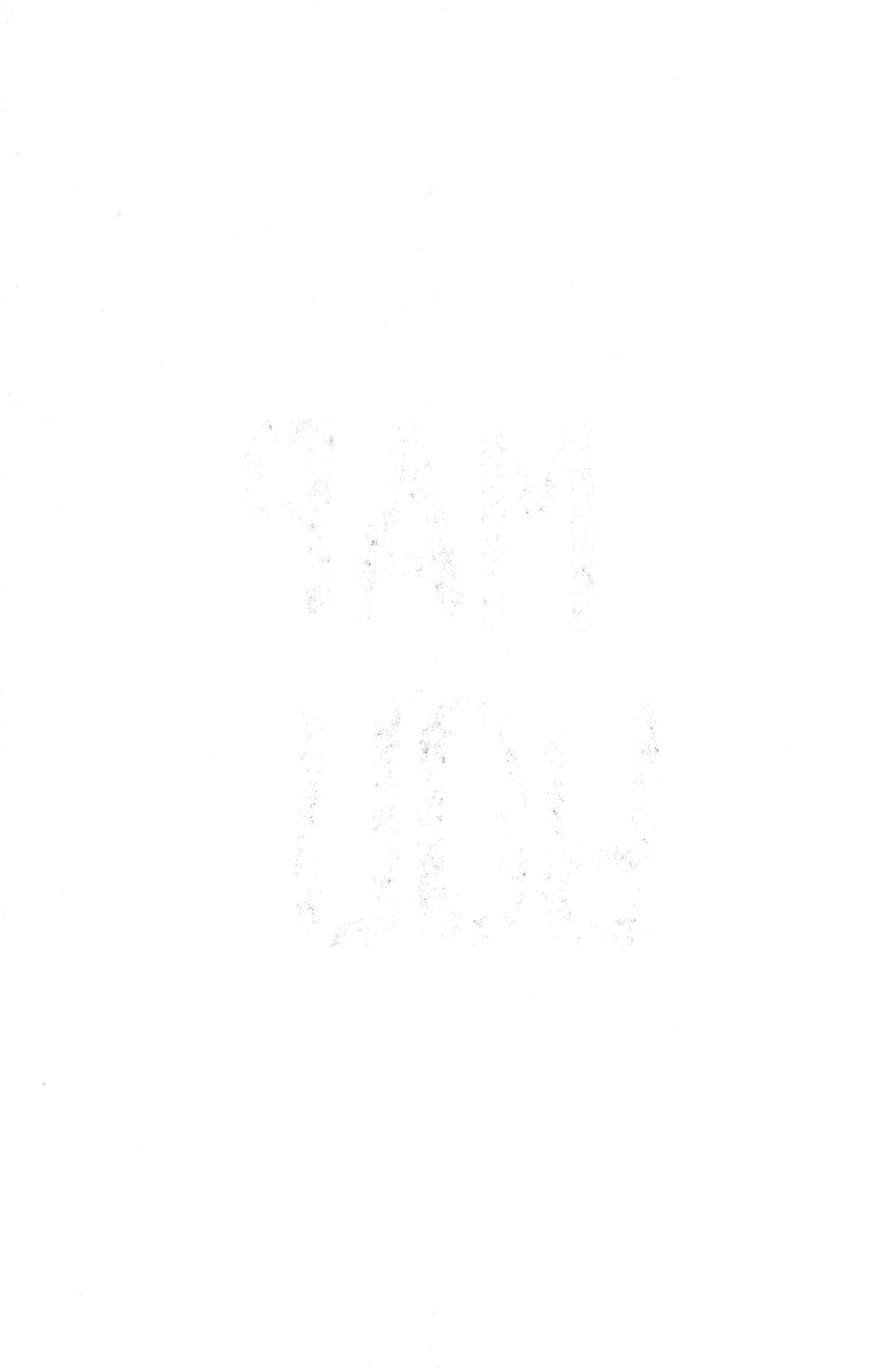

PROLOGUE

Greenwich Village, New York
Ten months ago

Kinsey held her head high as she walked through the door of her newly-assigned dorm, dragging a suitcase in her wake. She was not going to let her suitemates see she was falling apart.

As far as any of these girls were concerned, Kinsey and her last roommate simply couldn't get past their incompatible schedules. No need to mention the *incompatibility* was due to the fact that Kinsey had been dating the roommate until last week. Or that they'd split when Kinsey had run back to get her tablet between classes and caught her girlfriend of over a year in bed with another woman.

It seemed easier to lie and be angry than let anyone feel sorry for her. Being angry wasn't going to win her any new friends here, but it would hurt less than explaining again and again why she and Evie broke up. And if everyone here hated her for being too sharp, well . . . that wasn't a situation Kinsey was entirely unfamiliar with. She could handle a little bit of hostility if it meant being left alone.

A couple of colorful blankets were strewn haphazardly over the couches in the small common area. A laptop and some textbooks littered the coffee table. It smelled like warmed-over curry, and there were dishes in the drying rack on the kitchenette's counter, a few more in the sink. But the dorm's small common area was quiet except for the sound of Kinsey's one remaining friend wrestling a laundry basket through the door behind her.

Kinsey came to a stop, her resolve to be strong already crumbling without an audience of strangers to shore it up.

"Isn't anyone home?" Beatrice asked as the door swung shut.

"I bet they heard I was coming and ran for the hills," Kinsey grumbled.

"If they knew you were coming, they would've thrown you a welcome party," Beatrice retorted with a steely look in her eye that precluded debate.

Beatrice had taken over the logistics of the move when it became clear Kinsey wasn't up to it. Part of the "Get Kinsey Back On Her Feet" checklist Kinsey suspected her freckled, oddball best friend had drawn up within seconds of Kinsey turning up at her door post-breakup. Beatrice had too much on her plate already and was even shorter than Kinsey, but she'd insisted the two of them could accomplish the move themselves. *If ants can do it, so can we!* she'd declared with her trademark optimism.

Kinsey hadn't bothered to point out that ants usually had the benefit of hundreds of their colleagues helping out when they moved stuff. Once Beatrice made a plan, it was going to get done. With or without a colony of insects to pick up the slack.

Beatrice deposited the basket on the couch and cupped her hands around her mouth. "Halloo!"

"Bee," Kinsey complained.

Beatrice wrinkled her nose with a little grin. "Too soccer-mom-dropping-you-off-at-camp?"

"I can make my own friends, mom," Kinsey said, in what she hoped was a gently teasing tone. She didn't really mind. Being relentlessly goofy was Beatrice's way of helping Kinsey keep herself together. It wasn't like any of Kinsey's other friends had stuck with her the past week. They'd all taken Evie's side.

Kinsey knew she'd never had the nicest personality. But she thought at least Evie understood her. She thought they loved each other.

And then she'd left her for that scrawny, hippie track-and-field girl.

Kinsey clenched her teeth and dropped her suitcase by the door. "They're probably all in class," she said, checking the paper in her jacket pocket again for her room number. The suite was laid out more or less the same as Kinsey's old dorm, with three bedrooms and two bathrooms off the common area. She slipped between the couch and the tiny kitchen as she made her way toward her new room. "Or, you know, out doing New York things."

"Probably. Hey, throw me your car keys," Beatrice said. "I'll go down for another load while you figure out where you want everything."

Kinsey, not trusting her tossing skills, aimed for the couch. Beatrice scooped the keys up and jangled them cheerily.

As Beatrice pulled the front door shut, Kinsey dug her room key out of her purse and let herself into her new abode. Dumping the purse on the bare desk next to the door, she examined her new roomie's half of the space. A vintage poster for the '96 Olympics was tacked up on the wall, along with a sprawl of photos and a couple of San Francisco postcards. The bed was covered with a rainbow quilt and a ton of pillows. The desk at its foot had a dinged-up and be-stickered laptop charging in the midst of a crowd of books and assorted decorative clutter and—

Oh no. Medals. Sports medals.

She was afraid to look at them too closely in case they turned out to be track and field awards. She didn't really get sporty girls at the best of times. The early-morning thing especially. And the running around and sweating thing. And the weird intensity.

She could have gotten past all that. Even the early-bird thing, despite being a die-hard night owl, herself.

But if she'd gone through all this just to end up rooming with the woman her girlfriend had left her for . . .

Kinsey pressed a hand over her heart, trying to still its frantic thumping. No. No no no. She was *not* having another breakdown over something this stupid. It wasn't going to be the same girl. It couldn't possibly be the same girl. Fate wasn't that cruel.

She gripped the doorjamb until her knuckles went white. Where the hell was Beatrice when she needed her?

"Hi there," said a voice from behind her that was definitely not Bee's.

Kinsey spun around, desperately dragging scraps of proverbial armor around her, hiding her nerves behind a hostile glare. She was *not* going to look weak in front of her new suitemates, no matter who they turned out to be.

A cute, tallish white girl stood by the couch, balanced on one leg while she stretched the other behind her back. She was in black running pants and a purple tank top, her wheat-blond hair in a high ponytail, an elastic headband keeping her bangs out of her face. Her phone was strapped to her upper arm, the earbuds looped around her neck. Not the hippie Kinsey had discovered screwing Evie last week. Thank god.

The girl grinned—a bizarrely chipper reaction to being glared at by a short Asian person in her living room—and dropped her leg. "You must be my new roomie. Kinsey Han, right?"

"Um . . . yeah?" Kinsey crossed her arms, willing Beatrice to come back soon. The unnervingly bright smile made her feel strange and off-kilter. She didn't like it. She wasn't enough of a people person for this.

"Sasha Deforest. Sue and Preeta are in there," the stranger said, motioning to another room, "and Trish and Val are the Room A girls. They'll trickle in eventually. We like to think we're all pretty friendly." She pointed to the suitcase by the door. "You need a hand with anything?"

"This isn't going to work," Kinsey blurted out, unable to remove the reflexive bite from her tone. She couldn't explain to this tall, outgoing, put-together blonde that she was about two seconds from losing her weak hold on her emotions.

"It isn't?" Sasha's pale eyebrows jumped halfway up her forehead, her gaze traveling to the suitcase again. "It doesn't look *that* heavy—"

"We're not going to be good roommates," Kinsey clarified. She thought she'd be doing better today. Like she could just shake off the cheating, and the fight, and the fact she'd lost all her friends but one and march on. But she couldn't. And she hated herself for it. This whole thing was a bad idea. She should've just sucked it up and moved back in with her parents upstate. She'd wrecked things with them, too, but she was their only daughter. They had to at least wait a couple of weeks before saying *we told you so.*

"You're some kind of . . . athlete or something, right?" she pressed, using the first excuse that came to mind. "I'm not."

"Oh, of course," Sasha said, her eyebrows somehow climbing another few millimeters. "I forgot that athletes were prohibited from interacting with the artsy crowd. Think of the social upheaval! The anarchy in the streets!"

"How do you know I'm an art person?" Kinsey asked, her own eyebrows lowering to mask her confusion. Most people would've been on the defensive by now. Or at the very least, losing patience with Kinsey's prickly tone. This woman seemed completely unfazed.

"The cute skirt was a clue." Sasha nodded at the array of paint swatches that patterned Kinsey's skirt as she crossed to the fridge. She dug out a couple of water bottles, one of which she tossed to Kinsey, who surprised herself by catching it smoothly out of the air. Sasha grinned and jumped up on the counter, the heels of her sneakers thumping against the lower cabinets. "But you're also in my Humanities II class, and I remember you saying you were into hand lettering or something when everyone was doing the first-day-of-class bio stuff. It *was* lettering, right?"

"I—Well, yeah." Now she mentioned it, Kinsey thought Sasha looked vaguely familiar. Though she couldn't place where she sat, much less remember whatever she'd said about herself at the start of the semester almost ten weeks ago. Kinsey looked down at the bottle in her hands, mentally going through the faces of the other students. It was a large class. Kinsey usually sat in the second row. With Evie. Distracting each other with whispered jokes and secret touches. Until last week when—

She scrunched her eyes shut, taking a mental squeegee to the image behind her eyelids.

Sasha took a swig of water. "I'm still not sure what this alleged athlete/artist tension has to do with rooming together, though."

"I'm one of those artsy people who does their best work at two a.m.," Kinsey said, forcing herself to focus on the problem at hand. "Athletic people are the early-to-bed-early-to-rise types. Ergo . . ."

"First of all, I take exception to the blatant stereotyping," Sasha said, the amused grin on her face completely at odds with her words. "Even if it's true, in my case. But more importantly, I think we can work it out. I'm usually up before my alarm anyway. And you'd have to reroute a marching band through the apartment to wake me once I'm out. As long as you're not planning on hosting dance parties in our room late at night, we should be cool."

Kinsey crossed her arms, overwhelmed by anyone being this nice to her when she was being a defensive bitch. Her new suite-mates were supposed to dislike her the second she opened her mouth. That was the *plan*. They weren't supposed to try to fix problems she'd more or less invented because she wasn't good at friendly small talk and was too emotionally drained to try.

Sasha's smile softened as she searched Kinsey's face. "Hey, are you okay? You look kind of—"

"Don't ask me if I'm okay," Kinsey snapped. The thin protection of her proverbial armor was disintegrating, and she couldn't look weak in front of this weirdly canny, self-assured athlete. "Just . . . don't."

Sasha's head cocked thoughtfully to one side, but she didn't get a chance to say anything else. Beatrice had returned, arms loaded with so many bags she could barely see over them. Sasha hopped off the counter to take some of the load and introduce herself, all sunny smiles and helpfulness.

Sasha was early to humanities the next day, taking her usual seat near the back of the classroom. She hadn't seen much of Kinsey since helping move her stuff in. Mostly Sasha's doing, truth be told. Despite the assurances to Kinsey that rooming together would work out just fine, Sasha wasn't so sure.

Thing was, Sasha had been *very slightly* in love with Kinsey since she walked into the classroom that first day. She couldn't help it. Kinsey was gorgeous, for one thing. She was petite and curvy and seemed to have an endless supply of quirkily patterned skirts and blouses. Her eyes were big and dark, and her black hair was cut into a neat but swoopy bob that complimented the meticulous '40s bombshell makeup. And under all that, she had this tough sort of fearlessness about her which made her that much more attractive.

Of *course* Sasha had developed an instant, devastating crush. It didn't matter that Kinsey was already deeply in love with Evie Calhoun, either.

It wouldn't. Sasha had been the queen of one-sided infatuations since middle school. She seemed incapable of falling for anyone who wasn't straight, taken, or entirely oblivious to Sasha's existence.

Kinsey was into girls, at least. But one for three was poor progress on Sasha's part. The clearly-already-taken problem was bad enough, but Kinsey hadn't even remembered they took a class together.

Probably not her fault, Sasha thought, scrolling idly through her Instagram feed, chin in hand. Sasha hadn't exactly tried to get Kinsey's attention. She wasn't quite *that* deluded. Plus, she sometimes missed classes when her team had an out-of-town soccer game. It would have taken some kind of miracle for Kinsey to remember her name.

Sasha hadn't really minded the one-sided crush prior to yesterday. She was used to that kind of thing by now. But it felt like a cruel twist of fate to have Kinsey sleeping *in the same room*. Like some kind of punishment for only being attracted to girls she couldn't have.

Sasha glanced up as a few more students trickled in. She was beginning to regret showing up early. Every time the door cracked open, she flinched in anticipation, in case it was Evie, with Kinsey trailing after her, the two of them hand-in-hand and making doe eyes at each other.

It really was Evie this time. Her dirty-blond hair was clipped back from her face by a few bobby pins, and she scanned the room with a tight expression that didn't match the way she'd hooked her thumbs through the belt loops of her skinny jeans. Though for the first time all semester, Evie didn't have Kinsey with her. Instead, another white girl walked beside her, all willowy limbs and bangles and long, flowing skirts. Sasha was pretty sure the willowy girl was on the track and field team. Her name was Hayley. Maybe Bailey. Tended to sit near the windows, about halfway back.

Hayley hesitated at the door, face twisted in worry as she looked around too. She whispered something to Evie, who made a dismissive gesture, then brushed a lock of hair behind Hayley's ear and—oh.

Oh. Jeez. Suddenly Kinsey's mid-semester dorm-change and her touchy mood yesterday made sense. Sometime in the last week, while Sasha and her team were away in Connecticut, they must've broken up.

Evie touched Hayley's cheek as she finished the kiss, took her by the hand, and led her to the place where Evie and Kinsey usually sat.

Sasha straightened, tapping a finger on the scuffed-up sticker beside her computer's trackpad. Evie and Hayley—or Bailey, or whoever—looked awfully cozy. Lots of staring and giggling. And only Hayley seemed worried about being caught. A worry that was quickly fading, the longer she and Evie cuddled up.

Sasha was no stranger to the low-grade heartache of seeing her crushes preoccupied with someone else. That was painful enough. She couldn't imagine what it would be like to walk into class after a breakup to find some other girl practically in your ex's lap.

She didn't have Kinsey's number to text her a warning. She wasn't sure it would do any good to slip into the hallway and catch her outside, either. They didn't actually know each other that well, despite Sasha's involuntary habit of logging away every scrap of information Kinsey gave about herself in class. What was Sasha going to say that Kinsey wasn't likely to know about, anyway?

But before Sasha could work out what to do, it was too late. Kinsey marched in, jaw set, a worried-looking Beatrice close on her heels.

Kinsey stopped short the second she saw Evie and the other girl. Her hands made tight fists at her sides as the color drained from her face.

Hayley saw her first and drew back, having the grace to look ashamed of herself.

Some of the more bored-looking students were shifting their attention to the unfolding drama at the front of the classroom. Evie began to turn—

Sasha put two fingers in her mouth and whistled—a short, piercing note that could've caught the attention of teammates a whole soccer field away. Almost everyone in the half-filled classroom whipped around to stare at her.

Everyone except Kinsey and Evie, who were watching each other with expressions so charged, Sasha could feel the static from the back of the classroom.

Yeah, Deforest. You definitely have a chance, there. For sure.

"Up here!" Sasha beckoned at Beatrice and pointed at the empty chairs beside her. "Saved you seats."

Beatrice's shoulders sagged in relief, as though she was glad to have someplace to go before the confrontation came to a head. She hooked a hand around Kinsey's arm and ushered her to the back of the classroom where Sasha sat.

Evie glared after them for a few steps and then turned her attention on Hayley again, with a more exhibitory flair than before.

Real classy gal, that one.

"Thanks," Beatrice breathed, depositing Kinsey in the seat next to Sasha and bracketing her in on the other side.

"No problem," Sasha said, flashing a smile.

Kinsey wouldn't look at Sasha. She may not even have registered that Sasha was there. She just put her bag on the table and stared down at her knuckles, white from clutching the avocado-patterned canvas.

Sasha wanted to say something sympathetic, but Kinsey had told her not to ask if she was okay yesterday. Same rules probably applied here. So Sasha made small talk with Beatrice around Kinsey as they waited for class to start, as though she hadn't noticed any tension at all.

Kinsey said nothing, but her hands slowly unclenched, and she eventually got her laptop out and set up in front of her. Though she stayed slumped in her chair for most of the class, using the laptop to block her view of the blatant canoodling in the second row.

Sasha had started to hope that the roomie situation wouldn't be as agonizing as she'd feared, based on how infrequently she and Kinsey had run into each other so far. Sasha had classes and soccer practice keeping her out most of the day, and she suspected Kinsey was sticking close to Beatrice when she had time to kill. If Kinsey stayed up as late as she said, it was really only the one class Sasha had to worry about. And hey, her crush couldn't get any *worse* if they never talked, right?

But when Sasha returned from her last class of the day, instead of opening the door to an empty room, she found Kinsey lying flat on her back in the narrow sliver of space between her desk and Sasha's bed, hands over her face.

Sasha hesitated in the doorway. She wasn't entirely sure what the appropriate thing to do here was. She'd known a few people who'd gone through nasty, emotional breakups, but never a roomie who she had a massive, one-sided crush on.

She didn't have a whole lot of personal experience with this kind of thing, either. The last girlfriend Sasha had wasn't really a girlfriend at all. It was more of a friends-with-benefits situation. But light on the friends part. Or the benefits, really.

"Should I call 911?" Sasha asked, at a loss for what else to say.

Kinsey didn't move. "Go away," she said, voice strained, like she was trying not to cry.

Sasha bit her lip, hand still on the doorknob. She could get Beatrice up here. They'd exchanged numbers after class, before Beatrice whisked Kinsey off to help her recover from seeing Evie and Hayley together. Beatrice would know what to do.

But Sasha couldn't just leave this woman she was half in love with crying on the floor, heartbroken and alone. Shaking her head, Sasha dropped her bag on the foot of her bed and slipped out into the kitchen.

Moments later she returned, bearing supplies.

"Here," she said, holding out a carton of ice cream. "I hope you like mint chocolate chip, because it's all I have."

Kinsey peeked through her fingers. Her usually immaculate makeup was smudged, her eyes wet and puffy. She scowled at the offering, but Sasha wiggled it at her in good cheer.

"My cousin swears this is the best way to get over an ex."

"Isn't that kind of cliché?"

Sasha grinned. "Some things are cliché for a reason."

Slowly, Kinsey sat up, wiping her eyes, and accepted the ice cream and one of the spoons.

Sasha breathed an inward sigh of relief and sat down on the floor across from Kinsey, legs crossed, back against her bed frame. "To be strictly accurate," she went on while Kinsey pried the lid off, "he says it's the second-best remedy."

"What's the first?" Kinsey grumbled, shoveling out a wedge of ice cream. "Watching sucky sad movies until you lose all faith in humanity?"

Sasha shook her head. "Revenge filet mignon."

Kinsey froze with the spoon in her mouth, wide, mascara-smudged eyes turning to Sasha. "Revenge what?"

"Filet mignon." Sasha flipped her spoon around her fingers, trying not to let her grin get too big. "It's possible that one's a little Trevor-specific. He's a chef."

"How does one go about making revenge filet mignon?" Kinsey asked, passing the ice cream.

"Oh, you know," Sasha said, digging out a spoonful before handing the carton back. "Throw all your anger and sadness into making the perfect filet mignon, invite everyone but the ex to a dinner party to partake, video the whole meal, including testimony from the diners confirming its perfection, and then send the video to the ex with a message saying something like *eat your heart out, Greg.*"

"He never really did that," Kinsey said incredulously.

"Hand to god," Sasha said, holding up her hand, spoon and all. "He served revenge filet mignon a year and a half ago, after his boyfriend told him he'd met somebody else while Trev was studying in France. The filet was delicious. Greg—he was a big foodie—was devastated. And Trevor felt a hell of a lot better."

Kinsey stabbed at a chocolate chip with her spoon. "I don't think that would work in my case. I can't cook."

"I bet there's a hand lettering version of revenge filet mignon," Sasha offered.

"Is there a sports version?"

"Sure. It's called revenge soccer-ball-to-the-head."

Kinsey stared at her.

"We jocks are not always the most subtle of creatures," Sasha went on, smiling to make sure Kinsey knew she was joking. This was what she did when her friends were upset. Talk, and embellish stories about her cousins, and poke fun at herself until the other person felt better, or wanted to talk, or told her to shut up and leave. Whichever came first. "We solve most of our problems by throwing our entire body at it. Doesn't work so well when finding bugs in computer code, but other than that . . ." She shrugged.

"So what would the hand lettering version be?"

"I don't know, but I bet it's less likely to get you arrested for assault than the soccer version."

Kinsey lifted a shoulder. "Might depend on what surface you're lettering on."

"What, like your ex's face?"

Kinsey didn't smile, but there was a little spark in her eye, like a pinch of glitter shining through her dark, nearly black irises. "*That* might count as assault. Or vandalism, if you wrote something on their door."

Sasha laughed. "Aw, man, that would be *amazing*. Wait until they're out, then cover the entire front door with a beautifully lettered insult? That might be better than the filet mignon scheme. Are you sure it'd count as vandalism?"

Kinsey didn't respond. The glitter had faded as quickly as it appeared, and a line of tears was building up in her eyes. "I'm such an idiot," she whispered. "I can't believe I thought I . . ." She dropped the spoon in the ice cream tub and pressed her hand over her eyes.

Sasha rubbed the back of her own neck, jaw tight. She wanted to march down to Evie's dorm and give her one hard punch straight to the mouth. What in the hell was wrong with that woman, tossing Kinsey aside like last season's trendy latte flavor?

"You wanna watch a movie?" she suggested, with the abrupt, upbeat bounciness of a Labrador puppy. *Real subtle, Deforest.* "Not a sucky sad one. I'm thinking something with a ridiculous amount of gratuitous explosions. *Sharknado*, maybe. We can get Beatrice over and make popcorn and cackle at the improbability of sharks in tornadoes until you feel better."

Kinsey wiped her eyes and lifted her gaze to meet Sasha's in a stare as unimpressed as a cat. Sasha half expected her to take a warning swipe at her nose.

"I . . . I guess I could do sharks," she said thickly.

"Great," Sasha said, getting to her feet and offering Kinsey a grin and a hand up.

It wasn't like Sasha had ever had a real shot at a romantic relationship with Kinsey anyway. And it felt like a step forward, to be making friends with one of her hopeless crushes instead of making heart eyes at them from afar for months at a time. Maybe she could even get herself out of crush mode, if she could just . . . stuff her feelings down for long enough.

Gingerly, Kinsey put her hand in Sasha's and allowed herself to be helped to her feet.

Sasha squeezed her fingers reassuringly—just for a split second—before letting go and turning for the kitchen. "You call Beatrice up and I'll make the popcorn."

ONE

Greenwich Village, New York
Present day

February team building for the NYU women's soccer team meant paintball. Since twenty-some competitive women were likely to terrorize anyone playing for fun, their coach had arranged to clear a paintball place out for the afternoon.

They had split into two groups with Sasha, as team captain, heading up one while Nova, their first-string goalie, took the other. The women gleefully tore the place up for a few hours, then decamped, bruised and exhilarated, to a nearby bar to bask in the afterglow.

Sasha ordered a 7-Up and a basket of wings and retreated to the fringes of the crowd. Her paintball team had pushed themselves pretty hard and she wanted to sit down for a few minutes before someone dragged her off to play billiards or *Space Invaders*. Nova seemed to have gotten the same idea—she was sitting alone at a booth in a quiet corner, nursing what looked like a glass of plain cranberry juice.

Sasha collapsed onto the opposite bench with a huge sigh. "I think I'm getting old," she said. "I don't remember paintball being this exhausting."

"You do kind of remind me of my grandmother," Nova said. She motioned to Sasha's temple. "I think you've even got some gray coming in. You sure you're only twenty-one?"

Sasha chuckled. "Pretty sure." She slid the basket of wings to the center of the table to share. "I can't help but notice you aren't very paint-splattered."

"I prefer to let my minions do the dirty work," Nova said, taking a wing and lifting it in thanks. Her curly black hair was pulled away from the warm mid-brown of her face into a thick bun—her go-to hairstyle for soccer games. "Let the soldiers get all sweaty, and then I waltz in and save the day when things look dire."

"You're such a goalie," Sasha said, shaking her head.

"Meanwhile, I bet you're covered in bruises because your innate striker brain has you convinced the best possible strategy is to charge headfirst into the fray and hope for the best."

Sasha grinned. "Hey, we won, didn't we? Can't be *that* bad a strategy."

"Luck, Deforest," Nova said archly. "Pure luck."

"Sure, sure."

Sasha was selecting a wing for herself when one of the other girls slid into the booth beside her, forcing her to scoot closer to the wall to make room.

"So I was thinking," Viv said, setting two beers down on the table and turning to face Sasha more directly. "You're single. I'm single. We both like girls. What d'you say?"

"Uh," Sasha said with an awkward laugh. Viv was a decent player, though she got frustrated too easily on the field for Sasha's liking. When Viv got frustrated, she had a tendency to go rogue, which almost always started chain reactions of aggravation and discord in the rest of the team. Sasha had spent about a third of game time last season trying to keep Viv in line, or at least mitigate the effects of her anarchy. She was a little less intense off the field, but still.

Sasha threw a help-me look at Nova, but Nova only smirked and took a big bite of her wing, effectively checking herself out of the conversation.

Traitor.

"I'd say those sure are some facts," Sasha said, raising her eyebrows at Viv. "We both also play soccer. And go to NYU. And hey, I think I saw you at paintball earlier. Weird."

"Astounding how much we have in common, right?" Viv said, pushing one of the beers in front of Sasha.

"What are the odds?" Sasha asked, with friendly sarcasm. She didn't touch the beer. It wasn't like she had a problem with other people indulging in social drinking. Though it sometimes made her nervous, which she knew wasn't fair. She just couldn't switch her brain out of designated-sober-person mode. "Two single NYU soccer players sitting in the same bar after the same team building gathering? Crazy."

"Come on, Deforest," Viv complained, tipping her chin up to the ceiling. "Give a girl a break. I've been working up the nerve to ask you out since we walked in here."

Sasha checked the time on her phone. "I'm flattered it took you an entire seven minutes to do so."

"Well, I've been told I've got a lot of nerve to begin with," Viv said with a sly grin, paying no attention to Nova's stifled giggle. "I mean, seriously. Look at us. Bantering. Gelling. Plus—be honest—am I not adorable in this sweater?" She tugged at the scoop neck of her pink sweater, batting her eyelashes.

Pink was certainly a good color on Viv. And yeah, if Sasha thought about it, she had to admit she was cute. Pouty lips and a cocky dimple in one cheek. Long, dark brown hair that set off the rosy tones in her pale skin.

Sasha also happened to know that Viv had a preference for casual, no-strings-attached relationships. Which Sasha didn't care for. And anyway, she had enough trouble keeping Viv in line on the field without adding a sexual element to the mix.

"Listen—" Sasha began.

Viv leaned in and ran her hand over Sasha's bicep and up her shoulder. Sasha almost choked from holding back a startled laugh. "That jacket's pretty hot on you, too."

Sasha caught Viv's wrist and placed it gently but firmly on the table. "I'm flattered, Viv," she said again, removing the sarcasm from her voice and giving the hand a little awkward pat. "Really. But I don't date teammates. Sorry."

Viv pursed her lips into a little heart. "Boo," she said, grabbing her beer—and the one she'd offered Sasha—and toddling off toward a cluster of girls at the bar.

"Yikes." Nova sipped her drink, her eyes following Viv as she walked off. "She's a sore loser about everything, isn't she?"

Sasha huffed a laugh, wrapping her hands around her 7-Up. "She'll pick up somebody else in no time, forget all about this by the time she leaves."

"Yeah, probably," Nova said. She cut Sasha a look. "You don't date teammates, huh? Didn't realize you had a rule about that."

Sasha shrugged. "Too much hassle."

"You don't date non-teammates, either," Nova said, raising one eyebrow.

"Too much hassle," Sasha said again, narrowing her eyes. She made it a point not to get too much into her personal life with teammates. Or her friends, for that matter. The closest she got was when she was spinning yarns about her cousins back in Wyoming. And even those were carefully curated to avoid any mention of the more problematic parts of her childhood.

"If you say so," Nova said, swiping another wing.

Sasha took another for herself and tried to nudge the conversation in a safer direction. "Why do you care about my dating life, anyway?"

"I'm a busybody in my spare time." Nova grabbed a napkin from the dispenser by the wall and wiped her fingers. "I mean, I'm straight, but you seem like a catch. You're pretty. You're talented. You're funny. How do you not have a girlfriend?"

"We don't all need significant others on our arms 24/7, you know," Sasha said around a mouthful of chicken.

"Ohhhh, I get it," Nova said, nodding sagely. "You're still hung up on that Japanese chick. Kelsey, is it?"

"Kinsey," Sasha corrected automatically, bristling. Nova ought to know her name, at least. Kinsey had come to all their home games since she and Sasha roomed together last year. She often tagged along to watch their pickup games in the park, too. "And she's not Japanese. Her great-grandparents immigrated from China. And no, I'm not hung up on her," she added, belatedly realizing she was making Nova's case for her. "We're just friends."

Nova didn't seem to hear. "How long has it been? A year? Two?"

"Oh my god, Nova."

"What? You're not exactly being subtle about it. You flirt with her often enough."

"I—But that's—" Sasha floundered for an explanation Nova would buy as her ears warmed. Because Nova was right, she *did* flirt with Kinsey. A lot. She couldn't seem to help it. They'd be talking about nothing and these outrageously flirtatious lines would just hop out of Sasha's mouth. But it didn't *mean* anything. Kinsey certainly never took it seriously. She was always rolling her eyes and lobbing back playful retorts. "It's—It's not—"

"You were crushing on her last year when you had that class together," Nova said, ticking points off on her fingers, "which then got worse when she moved into your dorm—and don't tell me it didn't, Deforest, because I remember you freaking out about how you were going to convince her you shouldn't room together again this year without hurting her feelings—"

"And then I went home for summer break and got over it," Sasha said, yanking a couple napkins out of the dispenser for herself.

"Uh-huh," Nova said, clearly unconvinced. "And that's why you've been flirting with her nonstop basically since you got back?"

Grudgingly, Sasha conceded that Nova might have a point. "Okay, so maybe I still have a teeny tiny little crush. It doesn't matter. I *like* hanging out with Kinsey. She's smart and creative and tough and she's really sweet but doesn't like anyone to know it—"

"Sounds like more than a teeny tiny crush to me," Nova said, giving Sasha a smug look over her cranberry juice. "Why don't you just ask her out?"

"She doesn't like me like that. And I don't want to . . . overcomplicate anything."

"So snap yourself out of it. Being hung up on someone who doesn't like you back can't be good for you. Maybe getting a date with somebody else isn't such a bad idea."

Sasha snorted. "Yeah, I don't think so."

"I'm not saying you have to take Viv up on her offer," Nova said. "But dating someone who acknowledges what a catch you are might be good for you."

"It really wouldn't," Sasha said, trying to laugh it off.

"Why not?"

"Because . . . Okay, let me tell you something about the girls I attract," Sasha said, leaning forward. "They're flighty, or tragic, or demanding, and they don't want relationships. They want to hook up. And they figure I won't care because I'm so laid back there's no way a little casual sex would ruffle my feathers." She'd meant it to come out light and winky, but as she spoke her voice got sharp and bitter, until she was surprised at her own vehemence.

Nova's eyes widened. "Methinks I struck a nerve."

Sasha sat back in her seat, shaking off the bitterness. She was usually better at keeping her negative feelings to herself. She should work on that. "Sorry. I'm sure Viv meant well—"

"Nah, she was definitely after a hookup." Nova glanced over at Viv, who seemed to be having more success talking up a blushing sorority girl across the room. "And you're entitled to want a real relationship. But you can't be the only lesbian in New York who wants that. Why not find yourself a nice girl who'd be happy to smooch you on the regular?"

"That's the other side of the coin, isn't it?" Sasha said, rubbing her eyes. "Girls who like me are needy and tragic, and girls *I* like don't even know I exist."

Nova stretched her arms out on either side of the booth. "I don't know, Deforest. Sounds like you're stuck in a bad headspace about this. You need yourself a real girlfriend to shake you out of it."

"Sure. Easy."

"We could call Viv back over," Nova said, batting her eyelashes innocently.

"No more wings for you," Sasha said, jerking the basket firmly into her corner of the table.

Nova snickered. "Kidding. I'm kidding. Tell you what. I'll be your wingman next weekend. We'll go out and meet some people. This is Greenwich Village. You're a pretty girl. We ought to be able to find somebody you like who likes you back."

"I don't know," Sasha said, pulling at the end of her ponytail. "That's not really—"

"Just try it. Once. You *have* to snap yourself out of the unrequited crush cycle somehow. Don't keep wasting your time chasing somebody you're never going to get. It'll wear you down."

Sasha blew a breath up into her bangs. She didn't want to admit it, but she couldn't pretend Kinsey's playful rebuffs to her helpless flirting didn't occasionally sting. Just a little. But on the whole, that seemed better than if Kinsey actually took her seriously. She couldn't imagine what would happen if one day she came out and told Kinsey she'd been half in love with her for a year.

No, that wasn't right. She *could* imagine it. It just never went well. She didn't really think Kinsey would be mean about shutting her down, but she couldn't delude herself into thinking Kinsey would be anything but surprised and uncomfortable if Sasha made an actual bid for them being together. And even if she was wrong and she could talk Kinsey into giving them a try, how was that supposed to work? Dating meant vulnerability. And vulnerability meant getting hurt.

Being friends was uncomplicated. Predictable. Safe.

"It's one night," Nova pressed. "If you don't like anyone, don't give out your number. And if you hate it, you never have to do it again. I swear."

Sasha shook her head. "I don't know, Nova."

"Just think about it. A little flirting might do you good."

Sasha sighed. She clearly wasn't doing as well at repressing her feelings for Kinsey as she'd thought. It might not be a bad idea to give Nova's method a try. She wasn't committing to anything, after all.

"Yeah, okay," Sasha said, sinking down in her seat. "I'll think about it."

Alone at a wobbly table, Kinsey swept her gaze around the crowded food court and heaved an impatient sigh. The space reverberated with the sounds of conversation and footsteps, occasionally punctuated by the clatter of trays hitting tables or the tiled floor. But there was still no sign of Sasha.

Chin in hand, Kinsey picked at her slightly wilted salad with her fork, trying to ignore the tight feeling in her stomach that always seemed to come over her at lunch these days. And pretty much whenever she and Sasha had plans to meet up.

At least last semester she'd had Beatrice to act as a buffer. The three of them had gotten into the habit of meeting up for lunch on weekdays back when Kinsey and Sasha still shared a room. Often—especially when their workloads got crazy—all they did was frown at their laptops and textbooks, occasionally looking up to steal fries off each other's trays or show the other two a silly video they'd found while procrastinating.

They had a nice rhythm, the three of them. A good balance. Sasha kept the stress levels from getting too high. Kinsey made sure everyone was sufficiently fed and hydrated. Beatrice kept them focused and motivated.

And Beatrice was the audience that made sense of Sasha's ongoing flirting-with-Kinsey routine.

When Beatrice was around, Sasha's ridiculous attempts to 'seduce' Kinsey were just a running joke. Part of the rhythm. Sasha flirted. Kinsey rolled her eyes and rebuffed her. Everyone laughed. Then okay, joke over, back to whatever they were talking about before.

But last semester had blown up in Beatrice's face right before finals. She'd had too much on her plate from the get-go, and somehow more and more problems kept piling up until she was in crisis mode. She was doing much better now, but she'd taken this semester off to deal with the aftermath of all those culminating problems. And she'd been dropping hints she might be transferring to a different university in the summer.

Which Kinsey was fully supportive of. Beatrice hadn't always been great at remembering to think about her own needs, and Kinsey wasn't about to begrudge her finally doing so just because it occasionally made her feel awkward around Sasha.

Maybe awkward wasn't the right word for it. It was more like . . . standing on a high wire without a net. Shift your weight too far this way and you give in to all those untrustworthy fluttery feelings and everything goes wrong. Shift too far the other way and the jokey-mean rebuffs turn into actually-mean rebuffs and your friendship falls apart and you're all alone again. Either way—splat. Disaster.

"What're you eating salad for?" Sasha asked from about two feet behind Kinsey.

Kinsey jumped, flicking a sad wedge of tomato to its doom on the hard floor. Splat.

"Sorry," Sasha said, sliding her tray onto the table, diagonal to Kinsey. As she dropped into her chair, she flashed one of her infamous grins. The kind that could knock a person down at fifty paces if they weren't prepared. "I forget how startling my sudden appearance can be. My innate beauty and humble charm, presented all at once, can be a bit overwhelming."

"You didn't startle me," Kinsey grumbled, spearing some lettuce. The plastic fork against a plastic bowl didn't give the gesture quite the oomph she would have liked.

"Don't feel embarrassed, darling. I have that effect on everybody."

"Sure," Kinsey said. "That's why you're so good at soccer, right? Everyone just falls all over themselves to clear the way from the sheer force of your beauty."

Sasha pressed a hand over her heart. "Kinsey Han, did you just admit you think I'm beautiful?"

Kinsey rolled her eyes in an attempt to mask the weird bubbly feeling Sasha's retort provoked. Of course she thought Sasha was beautiful. She *was* beautiful. It was an indisputable fact. But Kinsey wasn't about to confirm as much when Sasha was clearly just joking around. "I walked right into that one, didn't I?"

Sasha chuckled. "Couldn't resist. But seriously, do you want my minestrone?" She grabbed a tub of soup off her tray and set it in front of Kinsey. "They were out of clam chowder by the time I got there. Plus, it's like forty degrees out. Don't you want something warm to go with that salad?"

"Here, I'll trade you," Kinsey said, lifting her own soup tub and passing it across the table. "Your chowder, nerd."

Sasha's mouth actually dropped open as she pulled the lid off. "But you don't even like clam chowder!"

Kinsey shrugged. "They've been out by the time you got there for the past two weeks. I figured I should grab it while it was still available."

You'd think Kinsey had just bought her a new car from the pure joy of Sasha's expression. "You darling, gorgeous, cantankerous angel."

"Okay, well, let's not go overboard here. We traded soup. It's barely grounds for a thank-you."

"It was thoughtful," Sasha protested, digging into the chowder. "Thoughtful gestures more than qualify for a little gushing." Her phone chimed as she spoke and she slipped it out of her pocket, a slight frown passing over her face before she locked the screen and set it on the table.

Kinsey paused partway through getting the lid off her mine-strone. "What's wrong?"

Sasha swallowed a giant spoonful of soup. "What d'you mean?"

"You look tense. And don't try to tell me it's the soup, because we already fixed that."

Sasha sagged in her chair, making a visible effort to loosen her shoulders, but her eyes were fixed on her sandwich. "It's just one of my teammates. She's trying to drag me out to this . . . thing next weekend."

"Oh yeah?" Kinsey asked carefully. It wasn't like Sasha to be cagey about soccer stuff. "What kind of thing?"

"It's dumb," Sasha said, waving her hand dismissively. "She's got this idea about me being, I don't know, lonely or something. So she wants me to go out with her to 'meet some people.'"

"Oh." Kinsey speared a fresh wedge of tomato, keeping her expression as neutral as she could. "Well . . . cool."

Sasha glanced up, her own expression unreadable. "I guess. I'm not really big on the whole bar scene."

"You never know," Kinsey said, sounding weirdly aloof. She swallowed and tried to sound more supportive. Sasha deserved a nice girlfriend. Someone who wasn't grumpy and awkward and couldn't even accept a thank-you without complaining. "Might be fun."

"Yeah." Sasha picked at her sandwich wrapper. She offered a smile, but it was a small, reflexive one. "Fun."

This would have been so much easier if Beatrice were here. Beatrice would know the right way to react, and the right things to say, and she'd have a joke ready to go if things got too weird. All Kinsey would have to do was nod and keep her face cleared of any signs of discomfort and everything would be fine.

Without the buffer, Kinsey didn't have anyone to demonstrate what a normal reaction looked like. Which might not have been a problem, except Kinsey was having such a weirdly strong negative reaction to a perfectly reasonable development. What, had she actually started to think all that flirting was anything more than friendly teasing? Even if it were true, there was no way someone as smiling and giving as Sasha would be happy with Kinsey's brand of prickly standoffishness.

"Kins?" Sasha asked softly.

Kinsey looked up, gripping her fork in her fist. Keep all her whirling feelings clenched in that fist and her face would never betray her. "Yeah?"

For two long seconds, Sasha searched her eyes, as though if Kinsey just turned her head the right way, or blinked the right code, then all the awkwardness between them would go away like a puff of smoke. Everything would go back to how it used to be, when the three of them would study and watch movies and gossip and Kinsey didn't worry so much about whether her last two friends were drifting away from her.

But Sasha shook her head, breaking eye contact as she picked up her sandwich. "Never mind. It's not important."

TWO

It was a particularly un-thrilling Monday night in Sasha's dorm. Most of her suitemates were out with friends or partners. The two others were holed up in their rooms trying to get a jump on their class assignments for the week. Sasha had taken over the couch and had her attention split between the curry she'd stopped for on the way home, the episode of *Law & Order* she'd put on the TV for noise, and a coding project for her JavaScript class which had been giving her some trouble.

Usually having more than one thing happening around her helped her concentrate, but for some reason the method wasn't as effective today. Her mind kept wandering back to the food court a few hours ago.

She didn't know why she told Kinsey about Nova's plans to get her to meet someone. It wouldn't have been that difficult to answer her question with a more generic half-truth. She could've just said a teammate was being annoying and changed the subject. Kinsey probably wouldn't have pressed her for details.

But it had felt dishonest. And yeah, sure, Sasha might be guilty of embroidering the truth when it came to talking about her life back home, and she might occasionally use humor to get out of awkward conversations, but that didn't mean she liked flat-out *lying* to one of her best friends.

And maybe part of her had wanted to see how Kinsey would react.

She didn't really believe Kinsey would instantly realize she didn't *want* Sasha to meet someone else. Or that she'd ask Sasha not to go and confess she'd secretly been attracted to her for weeks, maybe months. Sasha wasn't even sure what she would do if that happened. She *liked* how simple it was between the two of them. She liked knowing where they both stood.

Which might have been why she still felt a little shaken by what should've been a perfectly normal conversation. Because just for a second, the way Kinsey reacted to the news seemed a little . . . weird. And just for a second, Sasha had wondered if maybe . . .

But no. She was sure she'd been reading too much into the momentary tension around Kinsey's mouth. If finding clever ways to deflect Sasha's stupid one-liners wasn't enough to prove Kinsey had no interest in them being together, what did? They were friends. That was it. Obsessing over a thirty second conversation wasn't going to change that. And Sasha wouldn't want it to, anyway.

She was pretty sure she wouldn't want it to.

Sasha was chewing on her chopsticks, trying again to focus on tracking down a piece of broken programming, when her phone rang. She reached for it and swiped it open without checking the ID, assuming it was Nova or Kinsey. "Hello?"

"Sasha, hi." Her mother's rough voice traveled through the speaker and coiled around Sasha's spine. "Did I catch you at a good time?"

"Oh. Hey, Ma," Sasha said, setting the curry and chopsticks on the coffee table and muting the TV. She swallowed down the impulse to jump straight to *what's wrong?* and tried to inject a little more life in her tone. A little enthusiasm. "Um . . . Yeah, I just finished dinner. What's up?"

What's up wasn't the same as *what's wrong*, right? There was less of a *what did you do this time* implication. Nothing for anyone to get upset about.

"Well, listen," her mom said. "Things have been crazy for me lately, and I feel like I haven't seen you in ages. You didn't even come home for Christmas."

"I know. I'm sorry." She didn't sound very convincing. Jeez. She used to be better at this. Pasting on a smile she hoped would come through in her voice, she said, "Well, I'll definitely see you in a few months, right? Summer break?"

"That's actually what I wanted to call you about," Cynthia said in that excited, conspiratorial way that meant she'd devised some complicated, impossible scheme. "I've got a little extra money coming in, and I was thinking that it's been *forever* since I've watched any of your games. Not since before you started college. So I thought, hey, why don't I fly out and visit Sasha in New York next time she has a home game? Your season just started, didn't it?"

"It—Our first practice isn't technically until next week," Sasha said, her fake smile already lost.

"Perfect," Cynthia said brightly. "I can come to your first game. Won't that be great?"

"Um . . . Yeah." Sasha massaged the back of her neck, her mind bouncing erratically from lie to lie as she tried to find a way out of this. She was rejecting ideas everywhere from *I won't be able to get tickets this late* to *I don't do soccer anymore* to a desperate *You can't you can't you* can't, Ma, please.

She worked so hard to keep her life in Wyoming separate from her life in New York. She had all these rules about which stories she busted out when she needed to fake opening up to her friends and teammates. Humor close at hand in case she needed to joke her way out of a potentially serious conversation.

It wasn't hard to leave her old life behind when she didn't have to worry about it flying across the country to see her. Cynthia had been in a bad place for a while. It was only recently that she'd expressed any desire to do better. She had a job now, packing at a warehouse a few days a week. It didn't pay much, but she hadn't been fired yet, which was a step in the right direction.

Sasha knew she should be proud of her mom for trying. But it wasn't the first time Cynthia had made a few gestures toward getting her life together. All that usually happened was she'd end up right back where she was before, only angrier and less willing to change.

Maybe the New York plan would fall through on its own. It wasn't like Cynthia had a great track record for keeping promises.

"Where would you stay?" Sasha asked, squeezing her eyes shut and hoping Cynthia wasn't going to say—

"With you, baby girl. Where else?"

"You can't," Sasha said, her stomach knotting. She clutched the phone until her fingers hurt. "I live in a dorm."

"But—"

"With a roommate, Ma."

"You don't have to get pissy about it," Cynthia grumbled. "I don't think your roommate would mind if I just slept on the floor or something."

"There's no room." Her tone was too confrontational, but she couldn't seem to rein it back. "You can't stay here."

"All right, all right, I heard you the first time." Cynthia

huffed through the phone. "Shit, Sasha, I don't know what your problem is. I try to do something nice and you get an attitude? What the fuck?"

Sasha bit her tongue, pressing her hand over her nose and mouth to stop any incriminating noises from sneaking out. She used to be good at handling Cynthia. She just needed to tap into her patience. Stop being so combative and emotional and just . . . *handle this.*

"Sorry," she choked out. "I'm . . . It's great you want to come out and see me play. Really. But there's literally going to be nowhere for you to sleep if you stay with me."

Cynthia made an unhappy noise, but she didn't challenge Sasha on the space issue. "I guess we can just find somewhere else I could stay. There's hostels and stuff near you, aren't there?"

No. No *we. We* meant that Sasha would have to do all the research, all the booking. She'd probably end up having to pay for the place too.

Guilt pushed back against Sasha's negativity. Cynthia was *trying.* Right? And if she was trying, Sasha should be capable of giving her the benefit of the doubt.

"Okay," she said, forcing the words out, "why don't you start looking at flights, and—and once you've got that booked, we'll talk about lodging. Sound good?"

"Absolutely," Cynthia said, her tone swinging back into excitement. "Text me when your first game is and I'll get it set up. I'm so excited to see you, baby girl. The last time I was in New York was in the '90s, and I didn't get to see *anything* fun."

Sasha tried to picture taking her mom sightseeing around the city, juggling her course load, lunches with Kinsey, and her commitment to her team with her mom's demands on her attention. Her pulse thumped anxiously in her throat.

"Yeah, sounds great," she said, speaking too fast, voice pitched too high. "Hey, I have to hop off the phone, okay? I forgot I have this study group thing tonight."

"Study group?" Cynthia asked with a laugh. "Baby girl, you live in New York. Go out and have a little fun."

Sasha shook her head, glad her mom couldn't see. Her mom's version of 'fun' was something Sasha had spent her whole life avoiding. She'd seen what that kind of life had done to Cynthia and had no interest in following in her footsteps.

"I gotta go, sorry," she said. "I'll be late. Love you. Bye."

She didn't wait for Cynthia to respond before she ended the call. Dropping the phone in her lap, Sasha dragged her hands down her face.

She hated when her mom got these schemes in her head. When she decided she was going to get her shit together and show everyone what a good parent she was.

It wasn't like she ever followed through. Either she'd forget or the scheme would go sour. When everything inevitably fell apart, Cynthia always turned it around and made it Sasha's fault. The plan would have held if Sasha had been more supportive. If she'd had less of an attitude. If she'd kept her negative feelings to herself.

The weight of all that blame never seemed to go away. It just built and built until Sasha started to break under the pressure.

Sometimes she wished she was brave enough to tell Kinsey everything. Just to have someone to split the burden with.

But Sasha's problems with her mother had this way of coiling around her other relationships and killing them. Her friendships in New York had only been protected from that because Sasha was vigilant about how much information she let slip. Especially around Kinsey, who had an uncomfortable knack for noticing when Sasha was off her game.

Still, she found herself reaching for her phone, navigating to Kinsey's number. As though talking it out would help. As though Kinsey would *get* it.

A door opened over Sasha's shoulder and one of her suitemates dragged her feet into the kitchenette with a loud groan.

Sasha shoved her phone under her leg, smiling reflexively. "Physics?" she guessed.

"Physics," Sybil intoned, yanking open the fridge. "I need sustenance before I venture back into the fray."

Sasha hummed sympathetically and unmuted the TV, relieved that Sybil didn't seem to have overheard the call. She was definitely better off not talking to Kinsey right now, she decided. It was her mom. Her problem. She could deal with it herself.

Kinsey sat cross-legged on her bed, tapping a pencil against her knee as she waited for her mom to answer the phone. Her parents were going out of town for their anniversary tomorrow morning and Kinsey wanted to make sure they had left her the list of things they wanted her to do while housesitting.

Kinsey had insisted on taking care of the house while they were gone. Even though she'd have to drive up there and back a few times, and all that needed doing was bringing in the mail and making sure the herbs in the kitchen didn't wither. Even though her parents had told her several times that they didn't want to add to her workload and wouldn't mind getting a neighbor to do it instead.

Back when Kinsey was a homesick freshman—and even into her sophomore year—she used to drive up to her parents' house in White Plains almost every Friday night and stay until Monday morning. She would claim her parents had better washing machines, or that she could get more work done without the distractions of roommates and city noise. Any excuse she could think of so it didn't seem like she depended on her family too much.

Her parents had always seemed happy to have their only child under their roof again for a few nights a week, and never challenged her flimsy excuses. They would let Kinsey decompress and talk about how school was going, and they'd watch TV together, and steam more bao buns than the three of them could possibly finish in one weekend. Knowing she had their support made it less daunting when she had to go back to school and struggle in her usual grumpy way to make friends.

She missed it. How close they were. How easy it was for all of them to talk to each other. These days . . .

"Kinsey?" Her mom's voice was warm but held a small degree of reserve as she answered the phone. "Hi. How was your day?"

"Hi," Kinsey said, maybe a smidge too eager. "Fine. I was just calling to see if you had a chance to make a list of whatever you need done at the house while you're gone. Is—Is now okay? I can call back later if you're busy."

"We're never too busy for you, muffin. There really isn't much of a list to make, though. Just the mail and the plants. And I don't think those will need watering until we get back. You still have your key, right?"

"Of course I still have a key," Kinsey said, bringing one knee up to her chest. Her mom shouldn't have to ask, but Kinsey understood why she did. She had stopped coming home so much when she started dating Evie. Evie had never outright *said* she thought it was babyish for Kinsey to spend so much time with her parents, but it was pretty clear from her attitude.

Kinsey had only been able to convince Evie to come up with her once, and it had been a disaster. Her parents were friendly and polite but it quickly became clear that they didn't care much for Evie. Not that Evie had made any effort to endear herself to them. She was rude and withdrawn and jealous of Kinsey's attention. But Kinsey had thought she was in love. And she thought it was her job to side with Evie.

And maybe it was just easier to blame her parents for the catastrophic evening than question whether her temperamental girlfriend was the problem. Because the thing about Evie was that she didn't mind if Kinsey was cranky and sharp. She couldn't; Evie was the same way.

For weeks after that, Kinsey and her parents had operated under a tense, unspoken consensus not to discuss Evie at all. Which meant they didn't talk about much of anything.

Until Kinsey announced one day that she and Evie were moving in together.

Her parents—justifiably alarmed—had tried to persuade Kinsey to slow things down. So Kinsey—already defensive—had taken the opportunity to destroy what little remained of their comfortable, trusting closeness by initiating the worst fight in Han family history.

Kinsey had regretted that fight even before she discovered Evie cheating on her, and ever since the breakup she'd been trying to put things back together with her parents. But she couldn't seem to work out how to make them trust her again. She didn't know what to say, what to do, to get them out of this place where they were all constantly filtering themselves for fear of another argument.

"Are you sure you've got time to housesit this week?" her mom asked. "Because I can still ask one of the neighbors' kids to take care of it."

"I've got plenty of time," Kinsey said, frowning. "And the neighborhood kids would just drown your plants and probably forget to check the mail anyway. Now will you please make me a list of whatever you need done for the fridge?"

"All right, all right," Annette relented. "Here, talk to your dad while I write something up."

There was a brief shuffle and then her dad was on the line. "Hey, Kinsey. Thanks for looking after the house while we're gone."

"No problem. Do you and Mom have anything fun planned in Charlotte?"

They talked for a few minutes about her parents' plans for the trip—which parks they were going to explore, where they were staying. Her dad asked what kind of lettering projects she was working on these days and Kinsey told him about a new gig she'd picked up doing chalk menus for a pop-up restaurant based a few blocks from her dorm. Then her mom was back to confirm she had made Kinsey her list and put it on the fridge along with the phone number of the hotel they'd be staying at, and they all said their I-love-yous and goodbyes and that was it.

Kinsey fell back on her bed with a sigh after she hung up, wishing talking to her parents didn't feel so much like making small talk with her great-aunt. She just had to keep trying and maybe, eventually, they'd be close again.

And at least housesitting gave her an excuse to spend a few uninterrupted hours with Beatrice. They'd been struggling to squeeze in more than a weekend lunch every week or so, and it would be nice to be able to just hang out and watch movies for an evening.

Though it would've been better if she could've convinced Sasha to come, too.

She unlocked her phone again and texted Sasha: **Are you SURE you can't come up to White Plains tomorrow night? We could stop for donuts on the way.**

Agh! Sasha wrote back. **I wish. But I've got that thing due Wednesday morning and I don't think I'll get it done in time.**

 **Okay, fine. Let me know if you change your mind though.**

Sasha replied with a smiley face and a thumbs-up.

Making a mental note to pick up a half dozen donuts on her way back on Wednesday, Kinsey locked her phone and turned her attention to an advertising assignment she'd been putting off.

It took almost no time at all from the moment Beatrice bounced through the front door of Kinsey's parents' house for them to make a cozy nest on the living room couch, surrounded by pillows and throw blankets and movie cases and plenty of takeout and snacks. They were only half-watching the TV, too busy chatting and cracking jokes to bother with following the plots of movies they'd both seen before.

Though Beatrice was maybe spending a little more time on her phone than she used to. She had the screen open again the second the credits of *Rush Hour* started rolling, a small smile pulling at one side of her mouth.

"Texting your boyfriend?" Kinsey asked from the other side of the couch, narrowing her eyes in mock reproof.

The crooked smile on Beatrice's face gave way to a pink-cheeked, sheepish grimace as she locked her phone. "Yeah. Sorry. Am I being insufferably obnoxious?" She held her phone out. "Do you need to confiscate this?"

Kinsey didn't think Beatrice could be insufferably obnoxious if she tried. Shaking her head, she patted Beatrice's knee. "Keep your phone, hon. Tell Julian I said hi." She grabbed a handful of movie cases from the table and shuffled through them as Beatrice typed. "You got a preference for the next feature?"

"I like the buddy cop theme we've got going so far." Beatrice climbed off the couch, slipping her phone in the back pocket of her '90s mom jeans, and gathered a few empty dishes. "Are there any more of those?"

"Only fifty or so." Kinsey waved two more at her from the random handful of movies she'd just grabbed. Her dad had just about every buddy cop movie ever made. He and Kinsey used to watch them together all the time, and she'd picked up the obsession. "Whose house do you think this is?"

Beatrice snorted. "You choose a good one. I'm making more popcorn. You want anything else from the kitchen?"

"No thanks."

"Okay. Back in a sec." Beatrice padded out of the living room with the dirty bowls.

She'd probably burn the popcorn while stealing the few minutes it was in the microwave to text her boyfriend. Kinsey didn't really mind. Julian was a little reserved and occasionally rough around the edges, but he seemed nice. He obviously adored Beatrice, which gave him plenty of points in Kinsey's book. And Beatrice didn't turn into some weird shadow of herself when he was around. If anything, she shone a little bit brighter. Kinsey would never admit it out loud, but they were . . . good together. Always finding ways to make each other laugh. Always on the same team.

Kinsey was glad of it—if anyone deserved a loving, happy relationship it was Beatrice—but every now and then Kinsey would feel a little twinge. A tiny pinprick of jealousy that Beatrice had found her person when Kinsey wasn't sure she ever would.

She'd thought she had when she met Evie. That she'd found the one person in the world who could stand Kinsey's cranky tendencies.

Beatrice always made it out like Evie was the only one to blame for that relationship going so wrong. Like she'd brainwashed Kinsey into acting just like her. But the truth was, Kinsey had been drawn to Evie's dark side from the beginning. Kinsey had always been blunt and direct, and she saw Evie's cutting remarks as . . . authenticity. Honesty. Maybe it rubbed some people the wrong way, but Kinsey's bluntness could do the same. It didn't mean it was wrong. Or cruel. It was just facts, presented with none of the shuffling frills that other people used to make them more palatable.

Kinsey sifted through her dad's buddy cop movies, her stomach clenching in a hard little fist in her middle. She'd thought what she and Evie felt for each other had been love. That obsession was the same as commitment. That Evie was the one person in her life she wouldn't have to worry would leave Kinsey for someone better.

And look how that turned out.

Kinsey just didn't seem capable of showing kindness or affection. Not in a way that most people understood. Beatrice got it most of the time—but she was a bit of an oddball herself, with her freckles and her goofy jokes and her love of seriously outdated fashions in the ugliest colors she could find. How Sasha managed to take Kinsey's grumpiness in stride was a mystery. Her decision to make friends with Kinsey in the first place seemed like a weird fluke. Especially since Kinsey was such a mess when she moved into Sasha's dorm. There was no clear reason why Sasha would want to spend time with Kinsey at all.

She thought of the way Sasha tapped her shoulder with a friendly smile and a *see you tomorrow, darling* when they parted ways after lunch earlier today. And the alarming little flutter in Kinsey's stomach which made her unable to reply properly. All she'd been able to manage was an awkward *okay, bye* as she hurried up the sidewalk.

It wasn't fair. She thought she'd learned her lesson about falling in love. Why did she let her insides fizz like champagne every time Sasha glanced her way? And how could she ask Sasha to love her back when Kinsey was nothing but a prickly, defensive person?

"Hey," Beatrice said, returning with a fresh batch of popcorn and a box of Pocky sticks, "are you and Sasha okay?"

Kinsey nearly dropped the stack of movies. "What? Yes. Good. Fine. Why?" she added, staring at Beatrice in worry. "Did she say something to you?"

Beatrice set the snacks down slowly, her eyes wide. "No. Should she have?"

"No. Of course not. I don't even know what you're talking about."

Beatrice sank into the couch, pulling her ankles under her. "I was only asking because she usually comes to these things, too. I wanted to make sure you guys weren't fighting."

"No, we're—It's—No fight. We're not fighting. Everything's hunky-dory." Good god. Kinsey stuffed a handful of popcorn into her mouth to shut herself up.

"Hunky-dory, huh?"

"The hunkiest of dories," Kinsey said around the popcorn, nodding like a bobblehead. "December in the hunky dory calendar."

"Oh, sure. That's the hunkiest spot," Beatrice said, propping her chin on her hand, eyes never leaving Kinsey's face.

Kinsey took a swig of water to wash down the popcorn. They weren't supposed to be talking about Kinsey. Beatrice was the one who needed support. She *had* just been hospitalized three months ago when her problems got too big for her to handle herself. Kinsey's only issue was that she felt more flustered around Sasha than she wanted to be.

"It's just . . . different," she heard herself saying. "Without you, I mean. It's different."

Beatrice winced. "Yeah?"

"Not that you should feel bad or anything," Kinsey hastened to add. "I think you made the right decision, to change majors and—and—"

"And abandon you?" Beatrice asked, her smile sad.

"Don't feel bad," Kinsey begged. "I'm glad you're finally thinking about what you need. What makes you happy. You're kind of terrible at it, usually. I just miss you being around all the time. And I miss when we were a study tripod. When it's just Sasha and me . . . I mean, you can't hold a camera up with two spindly legs."

"You two used to hang out without me all the time," Beatrice pointed out. "You seemed fine then."

"Yeah, but . . . that was different. You were commuting down from your parents', and we were both in the dorms. So of course sometimes we'd show up earlier than you. Or you'd be the first to leave. Or we'd have nothing else to do on weekends. This is . . ." She slumped into the couch, pulling a pillow onto her stomach. "It's so awkward. She flirts with me *all the time*."

"She always flirts with you, Kins."

"Yeah, but usually you're there, too."

"You could ask her to stop, if it bothers you," Beatrice said, annoyingly reasonable. "I don't think she's trying to make you uncomfortable."

"Then what's she trying to do?" Kinsey asked, exasperated.

Beatrice gave her a funny look. "Flirt with you, probably."

"She—It's not—It's not flirting. It's a running joke."

"Is it?" Beatrice asked, cocking her head to one side.

Kinsey clutched the pillow, alarmed by Beatrice's skepticism. "Isn't it?"

"I mean . . . I guess it could be. But I always thought Sasha just likes you."

"You've heard her, though," Kinsey said desperately. "It's all ridiculous *did it hurt when you fell from heaven* nonsense."

Beatrice shrugged. "Yeah, okay, she says some pretty corny stuff, and yeah, she plays it up a little—probably because she knows you're going to deflect—but I never thought she was being insincere. With the actually liking you part, anyway."

"You're not serious," Kinsey said, horrified. "You honestly think she likes me?"

"Well . . . yeah?"

"Bee. Why didn't you say something?"

"Because I thought you were aware that when people flirt with you that much it's typically because they like you?"

"No it isn't. One of her—" Kinsey squashed the pillow over her face. "One of her soccer friends is taking her out," she confessed, hating the tremor in her voice as she spoke. "To meet people. She told me yesterday."

"Oh," Beatrice said. "As in—"

"As in looking for a date, yeah." Kinsey set her teeth, berating herself for still feeling bad about this. "So there's your proof she's not serious when she flirts with me."

Beatrice gently tugged the pillow out of Kinsey's hands. "Do you *want* her to be serious?"

Kinsey took it back and hugged it tight, trying to keep the tangled nest of emotions in her chest from exploding. Even if Sasha *had* been trying to tell Kinsey she liked her with all that flirting stuff, it didn't matter. Making plans to meet someone else meant that Kinsey had missed her chance. Sasha had probably already figured out there was a reason Evie had left. And because Sasha was a nice person, she was planning to quietly close that door before anything happened. So Kinsey's feelings wouldn't get hurt.

"I want . . . I just want everything to go back to how it was before," she said, fighting to keep her voice steady. "Before everything got so . . . complicated."

Beatrice squeezed her elbow sympathetically. "I'm not sure I can fix complicated, Kins."

"I don't suppose you've got some kind of anti-awkward potion tucked away in your bag somewhere?"

"Dang it," Beatrice said, snapping her fingers. "Left my anti-awkward potion on my desk at home."

Kinsey sighed. "Damn."

Beatrice flashed a smile, then her expression softened. "Sasha isn't Evie, Kins. It wouldn't be the same."

Kinsey didn't answer. She felt like all her remaining relationships were slipping away from her. Her best friend had a boy and a new plan for her life. She barely talked to her parents about anything real anymore. Sasha was one of the only people left who Kinsey felt she could lean on. And that was slipping away from her too. All because Kinsey was bad at showing people she actually liked them.

She flung the pillow off her and snatched up a movie at random, needing out of this conversation. "We'd better start the next movie before the popcorn gets cold."

THREE

Kinsey marched into the food court on Thursday with fresh determination. She *would* get a grip on her crankiness when it came to Sasha. Whether Sasha's flirting was a running joke or not. She certainly didn't need Beatrice around to force her to talk to Sasha like a normal human being. Kinsey was pretty sure she'd managed it before. There was no reason that should change just because there was a small possibility that Sasha's flirting may, at some point, have been half-genuine. It clearly wasn't anymore. And Kinsey refused to be a jealous mess about it.

Her resolve deflated when she didn't see Sasha anywhere. She was supposed to be at a table already. She was usually here at least ten minutes before Kinsey on Thursdays.

Ignoring the small, cowardly part of her that wanted to turn around and find a bathroom where she could hyperventilate in peace, Kinsey put her chin in the air and marched on. So maybe Sasha'd gotten stuck after class for a few minutes. Why should that make a difference?

Kinsey paid for her food, found a table, and checked her phone in case she'd missed the text explaining why Sasha was running late. Nothing.

Kinsey glowered at the phone, unsure whether asking where she was would come across as too cranky. She'd just settled on the opinion that worrying about whether she sounded cranky would only solidify the crankiness when the screen switched over to an incoming call. From her dad.

She stared at his number blankly. He was supposed to be hiking one of those North Carolina trails he'd told her about the other day. Why would he be calling her?

Kinsey accepted the call and pressed the speaker to her ear. "Dad?"

"Heya, Kins. Sorry to bother you at school. Are you—Are you busy?"

"No, I'm at lunch." She pushed her food a few inches away from her. He sounded weird. Distracted. "Why? What's going on?"

"Okay. Good. Lunch is good."

It was hard to tell, with the conversations and footsteps echoing all around her, but Kinsey could have sworn she heard a phone ringing somewhere in the background on her dad's end of the line. As though he was in an office. While on vacation. That wasn't right. She grabbed the strap of her bag, though she wasn't entirely sure what she intended to do with it. "Dad, what's up?"

"Well—First of all, the doctors say everything's going to be fine."

It took a moment for Kinsey to make sense of what he'd said. "Doctors?" she echoed. "What doctors? What happened?"

"I had to take your mom to the ER."

Kinsey's fingers went cold. "What?"

"She's fine. She's going to be fine. She was having some pain in her chest this morning—"

"Oh my god," Kinsey breathed.

"—so we drove to a hospital, just to be safe. They say—They say she had a heart attack."

Kinsey couldn't process what she was hearing. Her mom couldn't be in the hospital. She was healthy. She was titanium. She never even got the flu. How could she have had a heart attack?

"She's gonna be fine," her dad was saying. "The doctors are taking good care of her—"

Kinsey didn't remember getting to her feet. She just—She needed to do something. Anything. "Is she okay?"

"She's . . . I think so. I—Yes. It's a good hospital. They say she's going to be fine."

"Should I come down?" Kinsey asked, grabbing her bag and coat and making for the exit. She left her tray on the table. She wasn't hungry anymore. "How long does she have to stay there?"

"They're not sure yet. They're still doing tests . . ." Her dad made a faint, pained sound that went right through Kinsey's heart. But when he spoke again, it was in that same careful, neutral tone they all used since their fight about Evie. "You don't have to come down, Kinsey. You have classes you shouldn't skip. It's not life-threatening, and she's got wonderful doctors looking after her. The staff has all been really good to us. She's going to be fine."

Kinsey wished he'd stop saying that. It sounded like he was trying to convince himself it was true. "Are *you* okay?"

"Yeah. Yeah. A little shaken. But we got to the hospital in time. They'll patch her up. You shouldn't worry, sweetie."

Kinsey came to a stop on the sidewalk without any memory of stepping outside, at a loss for where to go and unable to focus long enough to figure it out. This wasn't happening. How was this happening? She should've tried harder to make things right with her parents. She'd had ten months to manage it. And now her mom was in the hospital and her dad was pretending he wasn't freaking out and they still couldn't *talk.*

She pressed an icy hand against her cheek, eyes tight shut, and tried to think of something helpful to do. "What hospital are you at? What do you need? I'll—I'll send a care package or something."

"You don't have to do anything, Kins. I know it seems scary, but everything's under control."

Kinsey swallowed a lump in her throat. Her dad sounded on the verge of a breakdown, and he still didn't want her to come down. This was how badly she'd fractured her parent's trust. They didn't even think they could count on her in an emergency.

"Okay," she said. "Okay. Good. I'm glad you've got things under control. I still want to send something. And you should let me know if there's anything I can do, okay? Or if I need to come down after all? I can skip a few classes if I have to. Mom's more important."

She got the hospital information from her dad, hastily scribbling it in the back of her planner, and made him promise two more times to call her right away if anything else happened.

She stood there on the sidewalk outside the food court after she hung up, wondering how long her heart had been beating so fast. She felt odd. Like she was inhabiting the body of someone else while she dissolved into panic deep in the back of their mind.

They say she had a heart attack.

"Kinsey?"

It had to be a mistake. Right? A mixup. She'd get a call in another minute. *Oops! It was someone* else's *mother who could've died a few hours ago. Yours is fine.*

A heart attack—

Fingers brushed her shoulder. "Kins?"

Kinsey looked up and found Sasha's deep blue eyes looking down at her, strangely serious.

"You okay?"

Kinsey started nodding, even as the barrier between her panic and stoicism began to crumble. The students walking by, the traffic on the street, swam in her vision. She swallowed. Her mom was fine. She didn't need to freak out.

"What's wrong?" Sasha said, gently turning Kinsey toward her, giving the illusion of privacy in the middle of a busy sidewalk. "Did something happen? Are you hurt?"

"I'm—" Kinsey couldn't seem to breathe right. Air rushed into her lungs in uneven gasps. "It's—It's my mom. My dad called. She had a—a heart attack this morning."

Sasha's eyebrows shot up into her bangs. "Oh, shit. Is she okay?"

"I think so. She—My dad said—" She was barely coherent. She was shaking so hard she wasn't sure she'd still be on her feet if Sasha wasn't gripping her upper arms. "They're still doing tests—"

"Okay," Sasha said, taking Kinsey's coat out of her hands. She draped it around Kinsey's shoulders and scrubbed her arms, like she needed to be warmed up. Maybe she did. She couldn't tell. "It's okay. Do you know which hospital they took her to? I'll drive you."

"You can't," Kinsey said. "They're in North Carolina. They were supposed to be on vacation for their twenty-fifth anniversary. I don't—I don't know what happened. She was fine when they left."

Sasha bit her lip, her eyes darting to the street as a frown pinched her brows together. "North Carolina?"

"Dad doesn't think it's serious," Kinsey said, wiping her eyes. The back of her hand came away streaked in mascara and eyeliner. She didn't know how long she'd been crying. She fumbled in her bag for a pack of tissues. "He didn't think I should go down. They were—They were supposed to be on vacation."

Sasha searched Kinsey's face uncertainly. "Do *you* want to go down?"

"Well . . . yeah. It's my mom. I want to see her. But—"

"Then I'll drive you," Sasha said, her uncertainty vanishing. "It's only, what, ten hours or so? I drive to Wyoming and back a couple times a year. North Carolina and back should be a breeze."

"What about—classes and stuff, though?" Kinsey hiccuped, pressing a wad of tissues to her eyes. "Don't you have—soccer stuff you have to get ready for?"

"Not until Monday," Sasha said, flashing a tentative smile. "I can afford to play hooky from school for a couple of days. It's still early in the semester. And this is an emergency. We can pack some bags and be on the road in an hour."

"Really?"

"Absolutely," Sasha said with a decisive nod. "We can look at flights if you'd rather, but it's probably cheaper to drive. And I'm not letting you go by yourself when you're shaking like a kitten. Come on. Sooner we pack, sooner we can leave."

Kinsey wasn't sure she ever verbally agreed to the plan, but she desperately wanted to see her mom, and Sasha was right. She was too worked up to be driving anywhere. She was too worked up to even argue with Sasha's determined practicality.

Sasha walked Kinsey to her dorm, keeping up a steady stream of one-sided conversation until Kinsey stepped inside. The words slipped out of Kinsey's mind as soon as Sasha finished saying them, but the sound of her voice pulled Kinsey back from the brink of panic.

She wasn't sure she could express how much she appreciated it when Sasha did this. When she noticed Kinsey was overwhelmed—by anything from school crap to holiday cooking disasters to breaking up with Evie—and just stuck close, chattering away, until Kinsey could handle things again.

She wanted to say something to let Sasha know what it meant to her, but she couldn't think of how to put it. And once they'd stepped inside her apartment, there wasn't any time left to figure it out.

"I'm gonna grab a few things from my place," Sasha said, motioning vaguely in the direction of her own suite, two floors up. "Meet you here in fifteen?"

Kinsey nodded, her chest aching. She didn't want to fly down by herself. She wanted Sasha jabbering on about her misadventures with her cousins so Kinsey wouldn't be stuck in her own head, worrying that some terrible complication would steal her mom away from her before she could get there. Before they could work through the stupid barrier Kinsey had put between them during that fight.

Sasha smiled reassuringly as she backed into the hallway. "Text me if you need anything in the meantime. Be back in fifteen."

"Sasha?"

Sasha's head appeared in the doorway again. "What's up?"

Kinsey couldn't meet her eyes. Maybe it was selfish, and maybe it made her a bad person, to ask Sasha to leave town so close to the start of soccer season. But Sasha had offered to support her. And Kinsey was too anxious to turn her down, no matter how little she felt she deserved it.

"Thanks," she croaked, the word sounding grossly inadequate.

Kinsey could feel the warmth of Sasha's smile as she replied. "Of course, Kins. What're friends for?"

"Did you actually eat anything at lunch?" Sasha asked as her van plunged into the Holland Tunnel.

Kinsey, who'd been staring out the window without speaking, peeled her eyes from the yellow lights sweeping past at regular intervals. She looked at Sasha like she'd forgotten she was there. "Lunch?" she repeated in an uncharacteristically small voice.

"Yeah. You remember lunch. The meal you eat in the middle of the day? Sandwiches are real popular in this part of the world, but it's kinda anything goes."

Kinsey shook her head, the gentle teasing appearing to bounce right off her. Then she frowned. "Did you? Eat, I mean?"

"Oh." Sasha had forgotten about lunch in the rush to get on the road. She moved her hands up the steering wheel until they were at ten and two, focusing on the cars in front of her. "No, I guess not. There's a few snacks in my bag if you're hungry," she said, thumbing toward the back seat as she slowed with the traffic. Hopefully once they got on the turnpike they could pick up a little speed. "Or I can swing by a fast food place. Should only take a few minutes out of our time."

"Maybe we should stop for something," Kinsey muttered, fiddling with her phone. "You should eat."

So should Kinsey, but she didn't seem to be in any mood to discuss her own care. She didn't seem to be in any mood to discuss anything at all.

But Sasha didn't do well with silence. Particularly when she knew a friend was getting too much in her own head. Barely ten seconds passed before she opened her mouth again. "Heard from your dad since he called?"

"Just to say they're still waiting for the tests to come in."

Sasha nodded, squeezing the wheel to stop herself from taking Kinsey's hand. She rarely saw Kinsey this overwhelmed. Even when they'd found out Beatrice was in the hospital last semester, Kinsey had been able to channel her worry into being aggressively supportive in any way she could think of. Kinsey hadn't seemed this helpless about a situation since she split with Evie Calhoun: On the walk to pick up the van, Sasha had been obligated to keep a hand around Kinsey's arm to make sure she didn't accidentally walk into traffic. Sasha had ended up doing about half of Kinsey's packing for her, too, while Beatrice talked Kinsey off the ledge on speakerphone.

It wasn't until Sasha was passing the final exit before the Holland Tunnel that she realized what exactly she was doing. And what a big, stupid gesture offering to drive her friend six hundred miles at the drop of a hat was. She'd seen a Kinsey in distress, there outside the food court, and had gone on autopilot. Which meant swooping in to save the friggin' day. For a girl who'd never been interested in her. And probably never would be.

Striker brain again. Combined with some quiet, sad need to prove herself. As though somewhere deep in her heart, where reason and logic couldn't move her, she was still more in love with Kinsey than she liked to admit. As though there was still some starry-eyed part of her that believed maybe the two of them could pull through in one piece when Sasha's home life inevitably bubbled up and threatened to destroy everything. As though one ten-hour drive would be enough to win Kinsey's heart for good. And finally prove that she meant something to somebody.

It might be pathetic, but she couldn't help it. No matter what Nova said, or what Sasha thought she *should* do, she didn't want to move on. Not yet.

"You could still drop me at Newark to find a seat on a plane," Kinsey said, breaking the silence.

Sasha glanced over, but she couldn't read Kinsey's expression. "Would you *rather* I dropped you at the airport?"

Kinsey didn't answer until the end of the tunnel came in sight, refracted sunlight dissipating the yellowish dark around them.

"I hate hospitals," she said, her voice thick.

She didn't elaborate, but she didn't need to. Sasha knew what she meant, though Kinsey—strong, proud Kinsey—would probably never admit it; she didn't want to go there alone. And Sasha wasn't going to let her. What was a few days of missed classes, when one of her best friends needed her?

"I'm with you, Kins," Sasha said, reaching over to squeeze Kinsey's shoulder. "The whole way. Whatever you need. Okay?"

Kinsey drew in a shuddering breath, then puffed it out, deflating in her seat. "Okay," she whispered.

FOUR

Sasha pulled into the first fast food restaurant she saw. She figured they would just swing past the drive-through, but Kinsey insisted they park and go inside.

"You have to actually eat something," she said as Sasha turned into the parking lot. "You won't if we stay in the car. Plus it's easier to bully you into letting me pay if we go inside."

Relieved to hear Kinsey getting back some of her usual stubbornness, Sasha didn't argue.

By the time they finished their cheeseburgers, Kinsey seemed to have gotten a grip on her panic. Getting some food in her stomach probably did most of the heavy lifting in the mood department, but Sasha had done her best to help by filling the silence with a yarn about her and her cousin Trevor getting stuck up a tree for so long Trevor's parents had started organizing a search party by the time they made it back.

Sasha didn't realize until she was partway into the story that it was one she usually tried to avoid. There was too much she had to change or lie about in order to avoid it getting depressing. Like why they were up the tree in the first place. And why it took so long for anyone to notice they'd disappeared into the dark woods. She had to do some on-the-fly editing to skim over the tricky parts, claiming she and Trevor had been out adventuring and she'd just climbed too high and got stuck for longer than she actually had. Though she worried she hadn't patched the story up very neatly.

Fortunately, Kinsey wasn't paying a lot of attention. She may have pulled herself together, but her thoughts seemed far away.

Sasha disposed of the remnants of their burgers when they were done and went to use the bathroom while Kinsey ordered a milkshake for the road. Kinsey was still waiting for the order next to a harried-looking mother at the far end of the counters when Sasha came out. Sasha caught her attention with a wave and poked a forefinger in the direction of the car. Kinsey acknowledged this with a somber thumbs-up and Sasha slipped outside.

It was nice out today. Nippy and breezy, but warm enough to make you believe spring was right around the corner. Sasha leaned against her van, inhaling the fresh air laced with french-fry grease and the faint bite of car fumes.

Maybe she should have searched harder for a different story, she thought as she watched the traffic go by. The trouble with refiguring anecdotes until they were almost unrecognizable was that the truth she'd smoothed over always seemed to stick with her afterward, pressing on the base of her skull, reminding her of everything she'd left home trying to forget.

She didn't miss Wyoming very often. She didn't miss the people she used to call her friends. She didn't even miss her family—apart from Trevor, of course. And he lived in California now. Sasha preferred the life she was making here, on her own. Where she didn't have to fight so damn hard for every little victory. Where she had more control over what happened to her.

Where her home life rarely had the chance to invade her space and ruin everything she was working toward.

Still, every now and then she missed the wide-open spaces. The sloping fields on the back of her grandmother's property. The sprawling forests. Sky that seemed to stretch on for miles. Air that smelled more of grass and evergreens than concrete and gasoline. Heck, she even got nostalgic about how careful they had to be with horse feed and garbage, in case bears decided the yard was a good place to find an easy meal. She loved New York, but sometimes it was just so . . . crowded.

One hand in the pocket of her bomber jacket, Sasha puffed out a wayward sigh and checked her phone, thinking she'd scroll through Instagram or something until Kinsey came out. Kick herself out of this funk that stupid story had put her in so she could focus on getting Kinsey to North Carolina.

But she didn't get that far. She'd missed a call from Trevor. She usually only heard from him in the evenings of days he wasn't working.

Unless something was wrong.

She glanced at the restaurant's door. No Kinsey yet. Biting her lip, Sasha called Trevor back.

"No one's dying," Trevor said, without even saying hello.

"That's a promising opening," Sasha remarked, her stomach twisting.

"I'm just, you know, trying to keep everything in perspective."

"Yeah, that makes me feel loads better. Thanks, Trev."

"Sorry. Listen—um—you haven't heard from your mom since last night, have you?"

"No," Sasha said, pressing her fingers into the back of her neck. She'd been quietly relieved her mom hadn't contacted her again since proposing the scheme to fly out to New York. In fact, she'd been doing her best to forget about the plan entirely, hopeful that the lack of communication meant Cynthia had already forgotten. It hadn't occurred to her to worry the silence was because her mom was busy getting herself into some other kind of trouble. "Why?"

"It's probably a false alarm," Trevor said. "I'm only calling because it seems like something you'd want to know."

"*What's* something I'd want to know?"

There was a beat of silence. "My mom just told me that she got in an argument with your mom—one of their big ones—and Aunt Cynthia took off for Mexico. And hasn't been answering the phone."

Sasha swore under her breath. That sounded like her mom, all right. The terrible timing included. Sasha was barely out of the gate on one rescue mission and Cynthia turned up with crisis number two. She wished she felt surprised. "She isn't hitch-hiking, is she?"

"Not that I know of. Mom said she left in her car."

"That shitbucket from the '80s?" Sasha asked, frustration sharpening her voice. "She won't get fifty miles."

"I don't think there's any reason to freak out yet—"

"When did this happen?" Sasha interrupted. It was *her* mom. She knew when she should freak out. Which she wasn't. Freaking out only made it harder to solve the problem. First step was to figure out what was actually going on.

"I don't know, a few hours ago? I just got off the phone with my mom, and she said it was early this morning when Aunt Cynthia took off."

Sasha bit her tongue to stop herself from starting on a rant. Half the time it seemed like she was the last one to hear about whatever impulsive crap her mom was trying to pull. But it wasn't Trevor's fault. And he'd called her as soon as he heard, even though Aunt Rosemary had probably already talked his ear off about her crazy sister today. He didn't deserve fielding another rant, even if he was willing to listen.

"I'll call you back," Sasha said, and hung up without waiting for a goodbye.

Nothing Trevor could do, out in San Francisco. Not a lot Sasha could do either, except maybe talk her mom out of impulsively going to Mexico. Or convince someone back home to go out and find her. And she didn't have a lot of time to do anything, with Kinsey coming to join her any minute.

Cynthia's phone went straight to voicemail. Not surprising. If Cynthia was steaming over whatever she and Rosemary fought about—usually either Cynthia's terrible taste in men or her inability to clean up her act—she'd probably turned her phone off.

"Hi, Ma," Sasha said after the beep, hoping she didn't sound too angry. Her mom didn't respond well to anger from anyone, and she seemed to resent it most from her own daughter. "Just wanted to check up on you. Call me back when you get this, okay?"

She hung up and sent a text as well, in case Cynthia didn't bother with her voicemail for a few days: **Please call me when you get a minute**

"Are you okay?" Kinsey's voice drifted over from the sidewalk three cars away. She carried a milkshake in each hand, and watched Sasha with a somewhat suspicious expression as she approached.

Sasha couldn't let Kinsey suspect anything was wrong. She'd insist on Sasha abandoning the road trip, leaving Kinsey to get to North Carolina on her own while Sasha did nothing but fret about her mom *and* Kinsey from a helpless position in New York City.

She flashed her most disarming smile, stashing the phone in her pocket, reaching for the first stupid, flirty thing that came to mind. "Better for seeing you, angel."

Kinsey scowled and the world was put to rights again. "Seriously? That line has to be as old as my grandparents."

"It's vintage," Sasha said with mock outrage as they climbed into the car.

"It's moth-bitten," Kinsey countered. She shoved one of the milkshakes in Sasha's direction. "Here, Casanova. You like chocolate, right?"

"Thanks." Sasha took the cup, touched by the gesture. "You didn't have to get me one."

"Oh yes, I did. If I'm stress-eating ice cream, you're joining me. I don't need to be feeling guilty about the calories when my mom's in the hospital."

Sasha raised her eyebrows. "Did you just play the sick-mom card to make me drink a milkshake?"

"Is it working?" Kinsey asked, mirroring the expression as she sipped her own strawberry shake.

Sasha laughed. The hoops Kinsey would jump through to avoid anyone noticing she'd done something nice. "Next time save your guilt trips for something I wouldn't do anyway." She took a gulp and dropped the shake in a cup holder to buckle her seatbelt. "All right, let's get this show on the road."

"Hey, can I ask you something?"

"Shoot."

"When you were stuck in that tree . . . where were your parents?"

Sasha paused with her hand on the gearshift. "Huh?"

Kinsey dunked her straw a few times. "You said Trevor's parents were going to organize a search party. What about yours? Weren't they worried, too?"

"Oh. Well, my mom didn't know. And my dad was never really in the picture, so . . ." She shrugged, flashing Kinsey a grin. *Not a big deal. I don't care. Neither should you.* "Guess he wouldn't have known, either."

A funny look passed over Kinsey's face. It was close to her *you're being ridiculous* frown, but with an undercurrent of worry. "You never said you came from a single-parent home."

"Well, you know." Sasha shifted into reverse and checked she was clear to back out. "That many family members living so close to me, I was hardly lacking in company. Or parental figures."

"But why didn't your mom know you were stuck up a tree for half the night?"

Sasha pretended she had to concentrate on getting out of the parking lot to stall for time. She really hadn't thought Kinsey was paying attention to her long, rambling story. Sasha could chatter about her cousins' antics for days, and she'd just latched onto the first memory that came to mind. Maybe because in the true version she'd only been out in the woods that late because her own mother had been in crisis. But she'd been careful to leave out any mention of how, at ten years old, she had snapped under the pressure of single-handedly keeping her tiny, broken family together. How, in the middle of the chaos inside, no one but Trevor even noticed her slip out the back door of her aunt's house and run out into the woods. She'd very deliberately skipped the part where she was sobbing into a tree trunk, Trevor squeezing her ankle sympathetically from another branch and doing his damnedest to convince Sasha it wasn't her fault—

"Sasha?" Kinsey asked, her voice weirdly tentative. "Why didn't anyone call your mom?"

Sasha plastered on another smile as she turned out of the parking lot. "She was . . . out of town," she said, trying a half-truth. "No one wanted to bother her. We're talking rural Wyoming here. Big ranch right on the edge of a forest. Everyone thought we'd gotten lost or been eaten by grizzlies. They probably wanted to make sure there was actually something to worry about before they got my mom involved."

Kinsey made a noncommittal humming sound. "You don't talk about her much."

Oh boy. This conversation was not going the way Sasha wanted. "I'm sure I must've mentioned her before," she said, as though she hadn't been intentionally glossing over the problematic figure of her mom in all her family stories for most of her life. "And you know how it can get when you're small and having adventures. Adults are peripheral."

"Didn't you ever have adventures with your mom, though?"

Sasha let out an oddly stiff laugh before she could stop herself. Adventures with Cynthia weren't the kind of things you whipped out for fun, folksy story time. Even the heavily edited versions. They were usually disasters from start to finish.

"You just won't let it go, will you?" Sasha said, trying to keep her tone light. "Why do you care about my mom all of a sudden?"

Kinsey sighed and turned her head toward the window. "I guess . . . I mean . . . You helped drag my zombie ass through a bad breakup when I barely knew you, I see you practically every day, you've been at my house for Thanksgiving and Christmas, and I only just now today find out your mom raised you by herself?"

"It doesn't really matter," Sasha said as she steered the van back onto the turnpike.

"Yes, it does," Kinsey said vehemently. "I should've known. That's basic get-to-know-you shit. For all I know, you've got four brothers, a dog, and an aging pony back home, anxiously awaiting your return. And I wouldn't know because I never bothered to ask! What the hell kind of friend am I?"

"Easy, there, Kins." Sasha risked a nervous glance in Kinsey's direction. This seemed like a really strange thing to get so worked up about. Maybe it was the stress of having a parent in the hospital coming out in weird ways. "You're being way too hard on yourself."

"Am I?" Kinsey demanded.

"Yeah. You are. I haven't been keeping a horde of siblings and pets from you. I'm an only child with one parent and a ton of cousins. Which you already know."

"I *didn't* know about the one parent thing, though. That's the point."

"Oh my god, not knowing about that isn't a shitty friend thing. I never talk about my mom. To anybody."

The dead silence from Kinsey's side of the car was what clued Sasha in that she hadn't brushed the topic off as neatly as she'd hoped. And that never talking about her mom was probably a pretty big indication that she had some baggage attached to the topic. Now Kinsey was going to want to know why she was keeping all that baggage to herself, and what was in it. And that wasn't an interrogation Sasha was prepared to face right now. She didn't exactly have a good track record for keeping the people she cared about around once they realized what a mess her life was.

She wondered if driving into a ditch would be sufficient distraction to make Kinsey forget about this conversation forever.

"Why don't you ever talk about your mom, Sasha?"

"I think we need some music," Sasha said loudly, pretending she hadn't heard. She switched on the radio for the noise, and then pointed Kinsey to the aux cord she could use to pipe her phone's music app through the car speakers. Which Kinsey already knew about, having driven in Sasha's van many times before. But it put another little bit of distance between Sasha and the topic of her mother—and the pent-up bitterness that always came out when Sasha talked about her. And with nowhere else to escape, verbal distance was all Sasha had to protect herself.

Kinsey sighed, but cued up a playlist on her phone and fiddled with the radio until the opening guitar riff of Heart's "Barracuda" filled the car, mercifully bringing the discussion to an end.

FIVE

Kinsey hopped out of the car when Sasha stopped for gas in Delaware, making it to the pump before Sasha could dig out her credit card. She felt bad enough for making Sasha drive her all the way to North Carolina without also letting her cover any of the expenses.

"I can pay for my own gas," Sasha objected after she'd shut off the car and joined Kinsey at the pump.

Kinsey was already punching in her zip code. "I know you *can*. But you ain't gonna. And I'm not spending every stop we make having this same argument. So get over it."

Sasha laughed and gave Kinsey a lazy salute. "Whatever you say, cap."

"At ease, soldier," Kinsey said, waving her away. "Go use the facilities or whatever. I got this."

"Fine, fine." Sasha shoved her hands in her jacket pockets as she walked away. "I'll grab you an iced tea while I'm inside," she called over her shoulder.

"Don't you dare!" Kinsey shouted.

Sasha grinned at her innocently as she backed through the convenience store's door, unperturbed by Kinsey's warning glare.

Kinsey shook her head and turned back to the pump. She didn't often ask Sasha about her life back home. She'd let herself think she knew a lot about it because of the stories Sasha was always launching into, but clearly there was more to it than an endless series of comical misadventures.

Not that Sasha showed any sign of actually wanting to unload about whatever the deal was between her and her mom. Kinsey had never in her life seen anyone dodge a topic so fast.

She was a little worried she'd pushed Sasha too hard about it. Or that her crankiness had sounded more like judgment than a clumsy attempt at support. Sasha had bounced back to her usual cheer pretty quickly once the subject was changed, but Kinsey couldn't quite shake the feeling she could've handled the conversation with more tact.

She'd just . . . never noticed Sasha needed anyone. For anything. She always seemed to have everything together.

It didn't feel like a very good excuse.

Kinsey wiped down the windshield with a beat-up gas station squeegee in a lame attempt to do *something* halfway nice for Sasha. That done, she parked the van in front of the store and headed inside to use the bathroom. As she walked inside, she ran into Sasha carrying a bag that looked like it was filled with too many snacks.

Kinsey scowled and pointed at the bag. "I'm paying you back for those."

"Just you try it, Kinsey Han," Sasha said, narrowing her eyes in a threat that was spoiled by the hint of a grin.

"Don't think I won't," Kinsey said, with what she hoped was a more threatening glare.

Sasha just laughed as she pulled the door open and slipped into the chilly sunshine.

By the time Kinsey followed her out a few minutes later, Sasha was back behind the wheel. She was massaging her neck absently, brow furrowed as she stared at something Kinsey couldn't see from her position on the sidewalk. Probably her phone again.

Kinsey didn't like it. Sasha wasn't big on serious expressions unless she was on the soccer field. And she only rubbed at her neck like that when she was either unsure or anxious.

Kinsey felt another pang of guilt for roping Sasha into this road trip. Who knew what she was having to rearrange to make this work with her schedule? At a minimum, she'd probably have to postpone that meeting-people thing with her soccer friend.

Shaking off a selfish sense of relief at that thought, Kinsey walked over and tapped on the driver's side window.

Sasha jumped, but threw on a smile when she saw it was Kinsey. She rolled down the window, phone disappearing under her leg. "What's up?"

"I can drive for a while if you have something you need to take care of," Kinsey said, planting her hands on her hips.

"Oh." Sasha shoved her phone further under her leg. "No, I'm okay."

Hmm. "Because I already told my dad we're coming down. And he says my mom's tests look pretty good. So I shouldn't be in danger of any more meltdowns in the immediate future."

Sasha's smile turned genuine. "I'm okay," she insisted. "You can spell me after dinner if you're still up to it."

"You sure? You keep checking your phone every time we stop."

"Jealous?" Sasha said, batting her eyelashes flirtatiously.

Something clicked in the back of Kinsey's mind. A hypothesis that had somehow never occurred to her. *This is how Sasha deflects questions.*

Impulsively, Kinsey leaned her forearms on the open window, holding Sasha's gaze as she invaded her space. "Should I be?" she asked, in a low, surprisingly sultry voice.

Sasha opened her mouth, but all that came out was a strange strangled sound as she exhaled.

Kinsey allowed herself a slight smolder as she leaned in another inch. "What would you do if I was?"

"I—What?" Sasha stammered, her gaze dropping to Kinsey's lips.

Something hooked Kinsey's insides, right at the base of her ribcage, and tugged. She was suddenly hyper-aware that she hadn't let anyone kiss her since Evie. Sasha was only inches away, eyes wide, mouth slightly open. Kinsey could feel the soft warmth of Sasha's breath against her face. She wanted to close the short distance between them. Wanted to find out what it would be like to be kissed by someone as sweet and gentle as her best friend.

Kinsey pulled on her bottom lip with her teeth, torn between curiosity and alarm at the turn her bluff-calling had taken, and Sasha swallowed hard, her eyes darkening. As though maybe Kinsey hadn't missed her chance after all. As though maybe Sasha *did* like her. And all Kinsey would have to do was lean in a little more and . . .

"You—" Sasha's ears turned pink and she looked away, her hand slipping off the armrest as she pulled back. Her elbow hit the gearshift. "Ow. What the—" Her tone sharpened into a warning as her eyes snapped back to Kinsey's. "What the hell, Kins?"

Kinsey straightened, dropping her arms to her sides, ignoring the disappointed thump in her stomach. She raised her eyebrows and tried to find some satisfaction—some escape from the irrational buzz under her skin—in a hypothesis unequivocally proven. "If you don't want to talk about something you can just say you don't want to talk about it."

"Wh—What?" Sasha asked weakly, still leaning away from the window.

"Quit flirting with me to get out of conversations you don't want to have," Kinsey snipped, stalking around to the other side of the car. She climbed into the passenger seat, refusing to look at Sasha, and slammed the door. "If you want me to butt out, just tell me so. Enough with the smokescreens."

Sasha didn't move as Kinsey buckled up and scrunched into her seat, pretending to be consumed with getting a playlist ready to go. She could feel Sasha's gaze on her, hear her breathing a little harder than the situation seemed to warrant.

This was so stupid. What the hell did she think she was doing anyway? She knew Sasha wasn't interested in kissing her. That was the whole point of that experiment. To call Sasha's bluff and prove once and for all that the flirting was nothing more than a way to avoid talking about anything serious.

Sasha wasn't supposed to react like that. Like she wanted her too.

And Kinsey wasn't supposed to feel hurt just because Sasha flinched. It was exactly what she'd expected. Even if it wasn't what she wanted. Sasha deserved a nice, outgoing girl. That would never be Kinsey, no matter how hard she tried. It was better if everyone just kept their mouths to themselves.

Sasha rolled up the window, and Kinsey, throat tight, reached for the radio so they'd have an excuse not to talk.

Sasha caught her hand before she could click it on, her fingers warm on Kinsey's palm. "You're right," she said quietly, eyes on the steering wheel, shoulders tight. "That's exactly what I was doing. And I can see how it'd be . . ." She blew a breath into her bangs, releasing Kinsey's hand and throwing the van into reverse. "I'll—I'll try to stop. I'm sorry."

Kinsey touched the edge of her collar with her empty hand, palm tingling. She didn't know what to say. This was as close as they'd ever gotten to an honest conversation about why things kept getting awkward between them lately. And Kinsey was afraid to poke at it, in case all her jumbled-up feelings came rushing, unfiltered, out of her mouth.

"It's not always a smokescreen," Sasha said into the silence at a stoplight, her hands at ten and two on the wheel. "The flirting, I mean. Clearly, yes, it's my go-to." She flashed a tentative smile at the bumper of the next car up. "It's kinda handy, since you always get distracted coming up with witty ways to shoot me down. But I don't actually dive behind smokescreens as often as I flirt with you. I haven't got *that* many secrets."

Kinsey swallowed, examining Sasha's profile. She wanted to ask why else Sasha flirted with her, then. But she didn't know what she wanted the answer to be. She didn't know if it would be worse if Sasha admitted it was just an ongoing bit, or if she said she actually had feelings for Kinsey that went beyond friendship. Either one seemed like it would ruin everything, one because it would hurt too much, and the other . . . the other because Kinsey wasn't sure she trusted herself not to end up hurting Sasha in the end.

Suddenly using smokescreens to avoid a topic seemed like a good idea after all. "Well, good," Kinsey said slowly. "Otherwise I'd have to conclude you were some kind of spy."

Sasha laughed, letting her hands slide down the wheel to their usual four-and-seven position. "I'll get those state secrets out of you yet, Han," she said, shaking her fist theatrically.

"Not a chance, Deforest," Kinsey said. She ignored the bittersweet pang she felt that they were back to normal. Normal was good. Normal was what she wanted.

Wasn't it?

The light changed, and Sasha nudged the van onto the ramp for the freeway. "So we're good?"

"Of course we're good," Kinsey said, swiping open her phone. She flicked through to a playlist that was mostly '80s glam rock, which seemed like the least dangerous, feelings-wise, of her existing playlists. There wasn't much romantic angst in the lyrics of "Bicycle Race" or "Mr. Roboto," thank god. "We're always good."

SIX

The hostess of the quiet diner in Virginia led them to a cozy booth in one corner. A minute later, they were giving their orders to a friendly waiter who looked a little taken aback when Sasha asked for an *un*sweet tea.

Kinsey leaned across the table when he left. "I guess that means we're officially in the South," she said so only Sasha could hear. The tension around her eyes and mouth from this morning wasn't as pronounced anymore. Sasha rested her chin on her hand, seized by the conviction that no one but Kinsey had such perfect lips.

She just . . . she always wore this vivid, red lipstick. Sasha couldn't stop her gaze from lingering too long on that color, recalling the white of Kinsey's teeth scraping her bottom lip a few hours ago. Wondering how it would feel to have those teeth nibbling her own lips. That vivid, red mouth leaving vivid, red marks on her skin—

"Nowhere else has such pervasive opinions on the right way to enjoy iced tea," Kinsey went on.

Realizing she was staring, and with no idea what Kinsey was talking about, Sasha laughed reflexively and turned her attention to the little wire thing by the wall beside her. It was the only way she could think of to keep things even semi-normal.

There was technically more distance between them now than in the car, with Sasha tucked in the booth near the wall, and Kinsey on the outer corner of the opposite bench. But Sasha didn't have to make eye contact with Kinsey when she was driving.

Sasha had never had an issue making eye contact with Kinsey before. But after that . . . whatever-the-heck-it-was when they stopped for gas in Delaware . . .

"Oh, shit," Kinsey said, digging her phone out of her purse. "I still haven't asked my dad to text me his hotel information. Sorry."

"No problem," Sasha said, being very careful to keep her gaze on the mostly empty bottle of hot sauce she was twirling between her fingers.

It wasn't like it was news to Sasha that she was attracted to Kinsey. She'd indulged in the occasional making-out-with-a-Kinsey-who-was-actually-attracted-to-her fantasy before. She'd even had an erotic dream or two, in the time since they'd met. She hadn't had a problem meeting Kinsey's eyes after *those*.

Maybe because those had been entirely hypothetical. Part of Sasha's one-sided love affair with yet another girl who could only be interested in Sasha when reduced to a figment of her imagination. Up until this week, Sasha had thought she'd done a halfway decent job of keeping her feelings for Kinsey buried. She didn't like how easily they were springing up again.

Because that *thing* in Delaware. That felt almost real. Like Kinsey actually meant to kiss her. It had taken all Sasha's willpower to keep hold of her senses and not artlessly mash their faces together, destroying her relationship with her best friend in one stupid, poorly-judged moment.

Kinsey's phone chimed, and Sasha risked a sideways peek as she read the incoming text. Kinsey pursed her lips as she tapped out a reply.

Sasha tucked her feet more securely against her seat to keep herself from stretching out a toe and tapping Kinsey's shin. She couldn't have even said why she had the impulse. She just wanted to . . . connect. Breach whatever unspoken thing between them was putting everything off-kilter.

What she *didn't* want was to examine too closely the hollow feeling that had settled in her chest after Delaware. That well-worn path of what-if. What if it *was* real? What if this time was different? What if she could just stretch out a little further and close her hand around the yearning contentment that had always seemed just out of reach?

It was a dangerous loop to get caught in, believing in happily-ever-afters. Believing you wouldn't fall if you reached too far outside of your allotted measure of happiness. And once you were stuck in that loop, the only way out again was getting your heart broken.

"What."

Sasha blinked, forcing her gaze four inches north, to meet Kinsey's narrowed eyes. "What?"

"Why are you staring at me?" Kinsey plucked at her blouse, frowning. "Do I have something on my shirt?"

"What? No," Sasha said, heat creeping up her neck as she fumbled for a lie. "I wasn't staring at anything. I . . . I think I'm just tired. I stare when I'm tired. You look fine. Great, even." Why in the hell weren't there any steak knives on the table so she could stab herself in the eye? "I wasn't staring at you."

"Okay . . . ?"

"Do you see the waiter around?" Sasha asked, twisting in her seat. "Maybe I should order a coffee."

"You sure you want the caffeine? You're talking pretty fast already."

"Am I? I do that when I'm tired, too. Listen, if the waiter comes back, order me a coffee, okay?" Sasha said, grabbing her phone and sliding out of the booth. She banged her heel against the seat as she edged past Kinsey, too focused on *not* accidentally playing footsie under the table to worry about if her feet hit anything else. "I'm gonna hit up the restroom. And don't go ordering a decaf. We still have a few hours on the road."

She didn't wait for Kinsey's reply. There was no way she'd believe all that. Kinsey knew what Sasha was like when she was tired. And it wasn't this.

The restroom was empty when Sasha slipped inside, which was a relief. She splashed cold water on her face and met her own eyes in the mirror. She looked frazzled. Wisps of hair had come loose from her ponytail like a fine, tangled net sitting atop her scalp. Some of her mascara had smudged under her eyes, making her look exhausted. And her ears were faintly pink.

Great. No wonder Kinsey was staring at her like she'd lost her mind.

"Get it together, Deforest," Sasha muttered, tearing out the rubber band in her hair. She finger-combed the flyaways smooth before retying the ponytail. "Stop freaking out. Nothing's changed. You're overreacting."

Her ears seemed unconvinced.

There was no reason to be all knotted up over a tiny incident two hundred miles behind them. Which wouldn't even have occurred if Kinsey wasn't so upset about her mom being in the hospital. Stress made people do weird things sometimes.

What in the hell was wrong with Sasha, anyway? Her own mother hadn't been answering anyone's calls all day, had probably resorted to hitchhiking after her car inevitably broke down, and all Sasha could think about was whether her unrequited crush would have kissed her if Sasha hadn't panicked.

It was better they hadn't, she reminded herself sternly. Sasha knew too well how things went when she opened herself up to people, persuaded by some fairy-tale dream that love could sweep away all the dark, clinging things in her life. In reality, the only thing that ever happened was being told, politely but firmly, that she came with more drama than she was worth. And she couldn't imagine what she'd do if she forced Kinsey to make that choice.

She and Kinsey would never work, no matter how much Sasha daydreamed. And daydreaming sure as hell wouldn't bring her mom back from Mexico. Which was what she *should* be worried about.

Halfheartedly, Sasha tried her mom again, more to ease her guilt than because she thought anything had changed in the last couple hours.

Still nothing. And somehow calling just made her feel worse.

She hung up without leaving a message and set her jaw, lacing her fingers behind her neck.

What was she doing here, exactly? There had to have been other ways to support Kinsey and get her to her family without swooping in to save the day. As though playing the hero could fool anyone into wanting her despite her problems with her own family. Despite the aching, lonely hole in her heart, desperate for something to fill it up.

Yeah. That was going to happen.

She just had to focus. Stay in control. Get Kinsey to Charlotte, stop being so damn *weird*, and maybe she could stop things from deteriorating further. Or at least refrain from grabbing Kinsey by the waist and kissing her as best she knew how.

Sasha blew a lungful of air into her bangs. "I am so screwed."

SEVEN

By the time Kinsey and Sasha walked out of the restaurant, it was dark. The somewhat balmy breeze that had enveloped them on their way in had turned nippy enough to frost their breath in the air.

Sasha had been avoiding looking at Kinsey much over dinner. And her chatter had seemed more cautious and disjointed than usual. But when Kinsey had asked her if she was okay, worried that Sasha was still upset about that whole Delaware situation, she had just offered a dim smile and claimed she was tired.

Kinsey thought it was more than that, but she didn't want to press the issue. It was no use trying to force Sasha to admit she was angry about anything. And Kinsey wasn't entirely sure talking about Delaware would do either of them any good anyway. Still, she felt like she had to make the incident up to Sasha. Even if her attempts to do so might be awkward and cranky-sounding.

"Keys," Kinsey said, holding out her hand as Sasha unlocked her van.

"Oh, that's—"

"Keys," Kinsey said again, stretching her arm out and leveling Sasha with a bossy stare. "You've been complaining about being tired since we ordered. I'm just hitting my stride."

"I'm not that tired. It's only, what, four more hours or so? No big—"

"Keys, Deforest. That's an order."

Sasha's chuckle manifested in a soft little cloud. She dropped the keyring into Kinsey's hand. "Okay, cap. If it's an order."

"That's more like it," Kinsey said, marching around to the driver's side of the vehicle.

Sasha got the map set up as Kinsey adjusted the seat and mirrors for her shorter stature, grumbling about Sasha's excessive height to keep her smiling.

As Kinsey merged onto the highway, Sasha surreptitiously checked her phone again. It disappeared under her leg a moment later and she huffed a sigh, slumping down in her seat.

"Was that your handler asking for a mission update?" Kinsey asked when no explanation seemed to be forthcoming.

Sasha snorted. "You're a tough safe to crack, Han. But . . . no. It's just a lot of nothing." She rubbed her eyes. "It's fine. I'm just . . ."

"Tired?" Kinsey supplied.

"Yeah. Sorry."

"You are *allowed* to be tired, you know," Kinsey grumbled, not liking the note of contrition in Sasha's voice. "You've done all the driving so far. And you've been keeping me sane all day. That's gotta be exhausting."

"Nah," Sasha said, waving this off. "You would've been fine without me."

Kinsey seriously doubted that. She poked Sasha's arm. "That was a thank-you, Deforest. Just say 'you're welcome.'"

"You're welcome," Sasha said dutifully. "But I think you're

giving me too much credit. You're tougher than you think."

"So are you." The words were out before Kinsey could really consider why she felt the need to say them. It just seemed like Sasha had been dodging more topics than usual since they left New York. Some of the unwillingness to talk might've been Kinsey's fault for the thing in Delaware, but that didn't explain why Sasha kept anxiously checking her phone.

"I don't know, Kins," Sasha said, adopting her lilting flirty tone. "I think I'm pretty tough. I mean, look." She flexed one bicep, patting it with her other hand. "Have you seen these guns lately? Impressive, right?"

"Put the artillery away, you nerd," Kinsey said, playfully shoving her elbow. "I'm trying to drive here."

Sasha laughed and settled into her seat, adjusting one of the air vents.

She seemed less tense after that, but she got quiet. She would perk up if Kinsey started in on a topic, but their conversations about school and Beatrice and strange billboards fizzled out quickly and led to stretches of relative silence.

Maybe Sasha *was* just tired, Kinsey fretted as the voice of the map on her phone directed her off the highway into downtown Charlotte. Sasha hadn't spoken for the last half hour or so. Her head was resting against the window, and she had gone so still she might have fallen asleep. Which made sense. Knowing Sasha, she'd probably gotten up before the sun to run around some jogging trail. If she'd stayed home, she'd be in bed by now.

But Sasha had seemed kind of distracted all day. And it had just gotten worse since that stupid Delaware experiment.

Kinsey's heart stuttered at the thought, and she gripped the wheel tight, willing her blood to remain free of that champagne feeling that kept creeping up on her.

She was still appalled at herself for trying it. She'd been worried about strong-arming sweet, accommodating Sasha into situations she wasn't comfortable with all day. And then she went and tried to strong-arm her into a kiss like some kind of monster. What on earth was wrong with her?

"Your light's green," Sasha said, her head still resting against the window.

Kinsey jumped at the sound of her voice and hit the gas too aggressively. "Sorry," she muttered.

"Just a couple more miles, looks like." Sasha sat up and adjusted Kinsey's phone on its mount on the dashboard. "You still doing okay?"

"I can make it to the hotel," Kinsey said. "You're the early bird, not me."

Sasha made a soft sound that was almost a laugh. "True. It's probably too late to see your mom tonight, huh?"

"Probably."

"It'll be nice to see your dad, though."

"Yeah," Kinsey said uncertainly. "I probably won't see him until tomorrow, either. He seemed tired when I was talking to him at dinner. I told him not to wait up."

He hadn't exactly sounded thrilled at the prospect of Kinsey coming down. Of course, that might have been due to stress, but . . .

"Don't worry," Sasha said, touching Kinsey's shoulder briefly. "She'll be okay."

Kinsey nodded, swallowing a lump in her throat. "You know what would be awesome? If everyone would stop getting themselves admitted to the fucking hospital."

"It *is* turning out to be a rather distressing trend. First Bee gets hurt, then your mom has a heart attack . . ."

"You better not be planning on coming down with the plague anytime soon. I'd lose my shit."

Sasha let out a soft chuckle. "I think that's the most romantic thing anyone's ever said to me."

There was something strange, under the typical Sasha sarcasm. A note of bitterness that made Kinsey pause. She glanced over to search her friend's face. "I know you're joking, but . . . I mean, you're joking, right?"

Sasha lifted an eyebrow. "Didn't you just answer your own question?"

Kinsey frowned at the road. "Me threatening to lose my shit if you get the plague can't seriously be the most romantic thing anyone has ever said to you."

Sasha shrugged, taking a sudden interest in an old scar that cut a backward J into the side of her hand. "Might be, actually. You'll be shocked, I'm sure, but the whole sarcastic jock thing doesn't inspire much in the way of lovesick sonnets."

"I don't see why it shouldn't. You're fun sarcastic, not annoying sarcastic. And you're not a jock, you're an athlete. A crazy good one, too."

"And yet, alas, no poets have appeared to vie for my affection," Sasha said with a halfhearted theatrical sigh, letting her head fall back against the seat.

"But your last girlfriend must have at least told you she loved you," Kinsey pressed. She didn't know why this was so important. She just hated the idea of Sasha being with anyone who couldn't do any better on the romance front than a cranky *don't get the plague or I'll lose my shit.*

She'd anticipated Sasha would lob back another piece of sarcasm, or a flirty joke, or something else calculated to put the conversation off course. Instead, she crossed her arms with a humorless, breathy laugh. "It wasn't like I thought she was the love of my life. She was a friend back in Wyoming, and she was struggling with coming out to her family. I don't think they would have had a problem with her liking girls, but she had this whole apocalypse scenario she'd worked up in her head. She wanted to be tragic, I think, and her life wasn't pelting her with enough problems. So she invented a few."

"She sounds like a hoot and a half," Kinsey groused, which at least made Sasha smile for real.

"It's all right." Sasha smoothed one hand up the back of her neck. "We weren't in a real *relationship*. I was more like a convenient booty call. I was kind of relieved, actually, when she stopped talking to me."

Something about the way she said it, like it didn't matter that someone had basically used her and tossed her aside without so much as a thank-you, made Kinsey bristle. "That's awful, Sasha. Why'd you put up with her in the first place?"

"Well, you know. No one else seemed particularly interested. And the tragic persona didn't really bother me at the time."

"That's still a sucky way to treat somebody."

"Maybe. But at least I didn't have to deal with any heartbreak when we split."

Kinsey waited for Sasha to continue, to fill in the part of the story giving her tone that undercurrent of sorrow. Just because Sasha claimed her heart didn't break didn't mean the relationship hadn't taken a toll on her. And it didn't mean that someone else hadn't broken her heart first.

But Sasha didn't elaborate. And Kinsey wasn't sure if she should probe any further. She wanted to know if that unspoken heartbreak was why Sasha stuck to letting Kinsey be cranky at her all the time instead of finding some energetic, upbeat young woman who'd swoon appropriately at Sasha's smiles, and laugh at her jokes, and tell her *I love you* every day. If only Kinsey could have been sure she could ask without her voice wavering . . .

"I think that's the hotel," Sasha said, pointing. "You better change lanes."

—ల

Kinsey put Sasha in charge of unloading their bags from the van so Kinsey could check into the hotel without having to argue about who would be paying for the room. It didn't occur to her that it might be weird for the two of them to share one room until she and Sasha were shuffling into the elevator with their luggage. She'd made sure there were two beds, after all. And it *shouldn't* be weird. They'd gotten along just fine when they'd roomed together last year. This wouldn't be any different.

Still, Sasha had gone quiet again, and Kinsey was worried she may have misjudged the situation. She peeked at Sasha sideways after she hit the button for the third floor, wanting some reassurance that Sasha was okay with this.

But Sasha wasn't looking at her. She had settled into the far corner of the elevator, her shoulder against the paneling, arms crossed, eyes fixed on a point on the floor. Her lips were pressed together, and a shallow crease had appeared between her eyebrows.

"I can—I can probably move rooms tomorrow," Kinsey said, hating the catch in her voice.

It seemed to take a second for Sasha's head to come back from wherever she'd gone and register the offer. "Oh." She met Kinsey's gaze, but there was a careful wall keeping Kinsey from guessing what she was thinking. "Okay?"

"We didn't really talk about sleeping arrangements," Kinsey said, rubbing her arm. "I don't want you to be uncomfortable or anything. If it wasn't so late I'd call my dad and get a cot sent up or something so I could stay there."

"Relax, Kins," Sasha said, the soft smile on her face at odds with her weary tone. "I realize my aura of animal magnetism might be misleading, but I *am* usually capable of keeping my hands to myself. You're perfectly safe from me."

It wasn't Sasha she was afraid of. It was the giddy feeling in her veins. It was the way her head kept going back to the moment they nearly kissed in Delaware. It was the idea caught in the back of her mind that someone ought to bump Kinsey's plague grumble off Sasha's "Top Ten List of Romantic Sayings" in a hurry—and Kinsey wanted that someone to be *her*.

She was already struggling to hold onto all the reasons that would be a bad idea. She was scared that pretty soon she'd forget them entirely and do something really, really stupid.

The elevator doors opened before Kinsey could work out how to communicate everything swirling in her head in a way that wouldn't make things worse. Sasha grabbed their bags and started off down the empty corridor, not checking to see if Kinsey followed her.

Kinsey set her teeth and lifted her chin, marching in Sasha's wake. She'd survived two months of rooming with the woman without screwing everything up. Surely she could handle a few nights in a hotel.

EIGHT

The shrill ring of Sasha's phone dragged her out of a deep sleep. She fumbled for it in the dark and accidentally knocked it to the floor. Kinsey, a barely visible lump on the other bed, made a maddening sleepy sound and turned over, dragging a pillow over her head.

"Sorry," Sasha muttered, snatching the phone off the carpet. She hit answer as she rolled out of bed and headed for the bathroom, but didn't put the phone to her ear until she'd shut herself inside. The sudden brightness when she switched on the light made her wince. "Hello?"

A voice came over the line, syrupy sweet and disconnected. "Sasha! How's my baby girl?"

"Ma." A familiar combination of relief and irritation settled on her shoulders. She sagged against the bathroom counter, pressing her free hand against her forehead. "I've been trying to reach you all day. Where are you?"

"You were always such a good girl." The words were slow and deliberate, but they still slurred together. "Such a good little girl. Not like your mama. How did a screwup like me end up with such a little angel?"

"Are you driving?" Sasha asked carefully. Her mom didn't exactly sound clean and sober.

"Can't," Cynthia said. "Pieceashit car's busted."

Thank god. "Where are you?"

"You wouldn't believe the stars out here, baby girl. I bet all that light pollution in New York means you can't see stars hardly ever. I wish you could see these ones. You'd love them. You could just fall into the sky."

"Sounds great, Ma. Can you tell me where you are?"

"Do you remember that time we took that road trip out to the coast?" Cynthia asked, her voice going dreamy. "When you were little? And we pulled off and made up names for all the constellations? Do you remember that?"

"I remember," Sasha said. She remembered sitting on a bench in a harshly lit California sheriff's office a few hours after that, too, a cup of hot chocolate that tasted like burnt coffee growing cold beside her. And the shouting, when Sasha's gran had finally arrived to bail her mom out. And the guilt she'd felt for not being able to smooth everything over before it got out of hand.

"You can see the whole galaxy out here," Cynthia said, sounding like she was drifting away. "You've never seen anything so beautiful. Pictures don't do it justice. I wish you were with me, baby girl. You'd love this."

Sasha lowered the phone, covering the mic with her hand while she took a deep breath, ridding herself of the tight feeling in her throat, the exasperation that made her want to snap at her mom just the same as everyone else always snapped at her. Sometimes it seemed like Sasha was the only person left holding onto the scraps of a foolish dream that her mom could still be saved. But she couldn't save her if she couldn't make her listen. And that required patience. Herculean patience.

It wasn't usually such a struggle to find it. But then, she didn't usually have to do this at four in the morning. After a long day of driving. With her best friend and long-time crush trying to sleep in the next room.

Get it together, Deforest.

Closing her eyes, Sasha pressed the phone to her ear once more. "Can you please try to tell me where you are?" No one would ever suspect she was trying desperately to keep her temper. She sounded like she was asking about the weather. "I want to call you a tow truck."

"I don't need a tow truck. Someone'll come by soon to help me out. Just a matter of time."

"Let me call you a tow truck," Sasha said, gripping her phone in both hands. "Please. I don't like it when you hitchhike. It'll make me feel better if I know you've got someplace to go."

The silence on the other end was so complete, Sasha worried the signal had dropped.

"Ma?"

"What did Rosemary tell you?" Cynthia asked, her tone dark.

Dammit. Some of her impatience must have come through in her voice after all. "Nothing. No one ever tells me anything."

"She's got a stick up her ass size of Texas, y'know. Hates anything that threatens her good Christian image. You should hear the way she screeches when those brats of hers track dirt onto her precious, perfect *carpeting*. Always trying to hide me in the back when her precious, perfect church friends are over."

"Is that why you took off?"

"She wanted to ship me off to rehab because she can't *deal* with me anymore," Cynthia sneered.

"Rehab?" Sasha repeated, unable to keep the weariness out of her voice. She'd lost count of how many times Cynthia had been in rehab. Sometimes it worked for a while. Most of the time she was back to her old habits within a couple weeks. Typically the family pretended they didn't notice at first. Then one of Sasha's aunts would mention a stolen twenty bucks here and there. Then her gran would complain about Cynthia's mood swings seeming worse than usual, or how she'd gotten herself fired again. Then a cousin or two would attempt a dutiful intervention. Until finally someone snapped and threatened to report Cynthia's stash to police if she didn't check herself into rehab, and the cycle would start all over again.

"She found a little weed in my sock drawer," Cynthia said defensively. "Half a joint. That's all. For emergencies."

Sasha rubbed her temple with two fingers. "I thought you wanted to get clean this time. For real."

"I've got it under control. I haven't touched any of the hard stuff all year."

Sasha decided not to point out that it was only February. Six or so weeks of sobriety was better than nothing. "That's great, Ma. I'm really proud of you. But—"

"Rosemary's an uptight little bitch. I knew I shouldn't have let her convince me to stay in her prissy, goody two-shoes house. She wants to be my goddamn warden."

"Look, none of that matters now," Sasha said. "I don't care what happened before, all I want is to get you a tow truck and a place to sleep. I don't want anything bad happening to you because your car broke down, okay? I love you."

"I love you too, baby girl," Cynthia cooed, like Sasha was four years old. Like she hadn't been defending her questionable right to keep half a joint in her sock drawer a few seconds before. "But nothing bad's going to happen to me out here. There's not a soul around for miles."

Great. So instead of getting her throat slit by a serial killer, Cynthia would be eaten alive by mountain lions. "I'll pay for the motel," Sasha begged. "The tow truck, too. You just have to tell me where you are."

Cynthia hesitated. "You won't tell anyone back home where I am, will you?"

"No," Sasha said. No one back home had the patience to deal with Cynthia, anyway. They'd probably be relieved if she was eaten by mountain lions. No more dealing with her drama. And it'd be less embarrassing for them if they didn't have to tell their friends she died of an overdose.

Sasha could fix this, as long as no one else interfered. If she could just talk to her properly—once her mom was sober and they had both cooled down a little—she was sure she could get her to go home on her own. "No, I won't tell anyone."

"Promise?"

"Promise."

"I'll pay you back, baby girl. You just keep a tally of everything and I'll get it to you real soon, okay? I swear."

"I know you will, Mama." She wouldn't. She'd forget. Just like she'd already forgotten about her plan to come see Sasha's first game. But this was how it had to be done. Pretending Cynthia was the adult while Sasha worked in the background to make their tiny, dysfunctional family appear halfway healthy to the rest of the world. It wasn't even worth feeling disappointed over. "Where did you break down?"

It took a few minutes to coax her mom to check the map on her phone and tell Sasha where she'd pulled off the highway. It wasn't exact—there weren't any mile markers nearby to help them and

Cynthia was struggling to make sense of the map—but Sasha figured out which two exits her mom had broken down between. She made her promise not to accept help from anyone except law enforcement or the tow truck, and then hung up to find a motel and a 24-hour tow service in rural Arizona.

Sasha leaned against the cold bathroom counter after she had arranged things with the tow service, her fingers laced around the back of her neck, frustration draining out of her until she just felt hollow. And lonely. She could have been surrounded by her entire extended family—all eight of her aunts and uncles, and their combined hoard of seventeen cousins—and she'd still feel alone.

None of them really understood what it was like, having Cynthia for a mom. How could they? Sasha had been glossing over the worst parts of it almost since she could talk.

It wasn't like anything *really* bad had ever happened to her. Sometimes there wasn't enough food in the house. And once in a blue moon—if Sasha talked back while her mom was in a bad mood, or if she asked a stupid question that set Cynthia off—she might've gotten slapped around a little. But being honest about it to the rest of the family only ever made Cynthia angrier and more resentful. And harder to manage.

For as long as Sasha could remember, it had been her job to hold her mom together. When things had gotten bad enough that other people started to notice—when social workers came to the house, or Sasha's gran fought for custody—it was because Sasha was losing her grip on the situation. If she'd just kept her temper under control, or lied more convincingly, or got up a little earlier to make herself a real lunch for school, she could have kept the world out and helped her mom pull it together.

It hadn't even been about a fear of being taken out of her home. Living with her grandmother put Sasha under a different kind of pressure, but for the most part it was less stressful than living with her mom. It was just that no one else ever tried to *help* Cynthia. They didn't know how to talk to her, or get her to listen. They'd given up on her.

Sasha couldn't. No matter how many times she lost her patience, no matter how much she wished—guiltily—that she'd never have to look at her mother again, Sasha was the only person left who still wanted to help her. She couldn't let go of that lifeline when her mom still needed it. Not when everyone else had walked away a long time ago.

Sasha let her hands fall to her sides, trying to rid herself of the old, sad emptiness in her chest. She wished Kinsey hadn't gone back to sleep. That she would realize something was up and come in and just . . . sit with her. Tell her everything was going to be okay. Hold her tight to remind her she wasn't as alone as she felt.

Sasha scoffed at herself. Even if Kinsey *did* come to check on her, that wouldn't happen. Sasha would probably say the first flirty thing that came to mind so Kinsey wouldn't realize she was crumbling inside. And Kinsey would roll her eyes and grumble a retort. The best Sasha could hope for would be a scowly order to go back to sleep.

Rubbing her eyes, Sasha shut off the bathroom light and shuffled out into the dark hotel room.

Except . . . it wasn't dark. The lamp between the beds was on, and Kinsey, hair rumpled, was sitting up in bed with a pillow in her arms like a teddy bear, glasses on her nose. She was adorably near-sighted, but usually wore contacts during the day, so Sasha rarely saw her in glasses.

"Everything okay?" she asked, her voice low and rough with sleep.

Sasha could only stare, caught between the profound bafflement that Kinsey hadn't irritably gone back to sleep, and the desperate, stupid urge to climb up next to her in bed and bury her face in Kinsey's shoulder for the simple comfort of touching someone else.

"I mean, it's after four," Kinsey went on, when Sasha didn't reply right away. "And you were talking in there for a while—"

"Sorry," Sasha said, rubbing her neck. "I didn't mean to keep you up."

Kinsey frowned. "You didn't keep me up. I'm trying to make sure you're okay. You've been tense all day, and now you're getting phone calls in the middle of the night? What's going on?"

Sasha let out a heavy breath as she perched on her own bed, one leg folded under her. "I'm okay," she said, setting her phone screen-down on the bedside table. "It's just family stuff. Nothing serious."

"Four in the morning family stuff?" Kinsey asked, squinting at the digital clock sitting between their beds. "Is everyone *else* okay?"

"Yeah, no one's hurt or anything. My, uh—My mom's car broke down."

"In Wyoming?"

"Arizona. Long story." Sasha ran her hands over her face. "She said she'd call back. In half an hour or so, when she makes it to the motel. So I'm sorry if my phone wakes you up again."

"I don't mind," Kinsey said, searching Sasha's face. "Do you want me to wait up with you?"

Sasha smiled even as her throat closed up. Kinsey wasn't supposed to be like this. She was supposed to be annoyed that Sasha woke her, to tell her to suck it up and go back to bed. Sasha could handle witty barbs for days. She didn't know what to do with *nice*. "Thanks. But I don't think I'm going to wait up. She probably won't actually call until tomorrow."

"Not even to let you know she made it?"

Sasha shook her head, watching her knuckles go pink as she clasped her palms together. If Cynthia remembered their conversation at all, it would be sometime tomorrow, after she'd had a chance to get some sleep and sober up. No point waiting for a call that wouldn't come.

"Well, that sucks," Kinsey said. "If she's going to wake you up to call her a tow truck, she could at least make sure you don't worry about her all night."

"It's not her fault," Sasha said without conviction. "She . . . forgets things, sometimes." She waved a hand briefly, like she was shooing a fly, and hitched on a smile as she glanced at Kinsey. "It's okay. I'm used to it."

Kinsey sucked in a breath as though to say something, but whatever it was, she seemed to think better of it. She pressed her lips together with a little shake of her head. "All right," she grumbled. "But are you gonna be okay? We can talk if you need to vent."

"I'm fine. Really. I just want to get back to sleep. Thanks, though."

"Okay . . ." Kinsey reached for the lamp, but paused with her fingers inches from the switch. Still frowning, she put the pillow in her arms aside, and before Sasha could work out what she meant to do, she slipped out of bed, perched beside Sasha, and hugged her tight.

Sasha's back went rigid in surprise. She'd been struggling to keep her feelings under control all day, and it would be so easy to let that control slip. She was afraid to move in case, once she returned the embrace, she wouldn't be able to let go.

"She'll be okay," Kinsey said, apparently unconcerned with Sasha's inability to function like a normal human being. If anything, she held on tighter. "Don't worry too much."

Sasha couldn't help herself. She looped her arms around

Kinsey's waist, hanging onto her own wrists so she wouldn't accidentally cross a line, and pressed her mouth against the thin material of Kinsey's nightshirt. Which might have been a mistake, because all Sasha could smell was Kinsey, soft and warm. She closed her eyes, tentatively allowing herself to take some of the offered comfort. Not too much—not anywhere near enough to risk depending on it later. But enough to get her through the night.

"She'll be okay," Kinsey said again when she sat back a few moments later. She brushed Sasha's cheek with her thumb, an almost unconscious gesture, her eyes soft in the lamplight.

Sasha's heartbeat staggered at the touch. She sucked in a breath, sure that in her emotionally wrung-out state, she was misreading that look in Kinsey's eyes. It was just a case of being upset and empty, of projecting an approximation of desire on a simple, innocent gesture.

Still, she could feel herself being drawn to that imagined desire like a magnet. She wanted to forget about all this stuff with her mom. Forget about the stupid get-over-Kinsey idea. And for a few minutes, pretend someone gave half a damn about her.

It took every ounce of reason and control she had left to pull away from the magnet, maybe a little more sharply than she meant to.

Kinsey blinked as though she were coming out of a dream, an expression Sasha couldn't read passing over her eyes.

But before Sasha could think of what to say to ground the incident back in reality, Kinsey moved her hand from where it had frozen between them to the top of Sasha's head, mussing her hair like she was a puppy. "All right, well. Get some sleep, kid."

Sasha huffed out a breath, part relief, part laugh, part . . . something else she didn't want to examine. "Kid? You know I'm taller than you, right?"

"So?" Kinsey stood and scooted back to her own bed. "I'm still eight months older."

"Seven and a half."

"Same difference. It's more than six, isn't it? We're only the same age for four months at a time. So yeah. Kid. That's what I'm calling you now. It's not weird."

Huh. If Sasha didn't know better, she might have thought Kinsey sounded almost . . . well . . . flustered. That was new.

Despite what a bad idea it was, and despite promising to try to cut down on the flirting a few hours ago, Sasha found herself prodding the fluster. Just to see if it held. "What's the matter, darling?" she asked, watching for Kinsey's reaction. "Worried you might be labeled a cougar, what with our insurmountable age gap of slightly over six months?"

"Oh my god." Kinsey flopped on her back and pushed her glasses up to cover her eyes with her hands, elbows in the air. "I try to do *one* nice thing."

"Because I don't mind." Sasha settled on her side and poked a little more. "I've always had a thing for older women."

"Good*night*, Deforest," Kinsey said, glaring at Sasha as she turned off the light. "You everliving nerd."

Sasha smiled faintly into the dark. That sounded more like the grumpy, no-nonsense Kinsey she knew what to do with. She must have been imagining the fluster after all.

So maybe she felt a little twinge of disappointment. At least she hadn't crossed a line she couldn't uncross.

She curled up under the covers, shaking off whatever worry and regret still clung to her. "Night, Kins."

NINE

When Kinsey woke up the next morning, Sasha was gone. It shouldn't have been that surprising—she'd only known Sasha to sleep past seven thirty when she had the flu—but Kinsey still felt a weird pang when she fumbled her glasses on and confirmed Sasha wasn't there.

Not that she was looking forward to learning whatever new permutation their awkwardness had taken after last night. That was *twice* she'd almost kissed Sasha yesterday. And twice Sasha had flinched from her advances.

One romantic dodge should've been enough to get Kinsey to lay off. She just—She didn't like how Sasha had shrugged off the idea that her mother would forget to check in with that resigned *I'm used to it*. It was that conversation about her tragic ex all over again. Like Sasha genuinely thought it wasn't a big deal when people who were supposed to love her treated her like crap.

It had pissed Kinsey off. But she doubted ranting to Sasha about her mother's crappy behavior was going to help anything.

And leaving it alone wasn't good enough. So she'd done what she would've if Beatrice was upset about something Kinsey couldn't fix for her.

And then she'd lost her head.

Of course Sasha had flinched. Kinsey couldn't be a much better romantic option than the tragic ex. Wanting to kick anybody who ever made Sasha feel worthless didn't mean Kinsey was capable of turning off the crankiness long enough to persuade Sasha she deserved better.

So maybe stop trying to kiss her, genius.

Kinsey grabbed a spare pillow, pressed it over her face, glasses and all, and let out a muffled growl.

It didn't quite get rid of the irrational fluttery feeling in her stomach, but it exorcised just enough for her to drag herself into the bathroom with her clothes and makeup bag, grumbling at herself under her breath.

Half an hour later, eyeliner perfected and a black pleather jacket pulled over her lucky lemon-print sundress, Kinsey grabbed her purse, phone, and room key and set off to find her dad. She texted the still-absent Sasha in the elevator to let her know where she was going, then slipped her phone into her bag.

Kinsey's stomach was in knots as she stepped into the corridor just a floor above hers. She found herself staring at her dad's room number after she knocked, wishing she had Sasha nearby to serve as a cheerful buffer.

It wasn't a thought she was proud of. This was *her* dad. She could talk to him without anyone's help.

Still, she chewed on her lip as she waited for him to answer the door, struggling with the feeling she should have stayed in New York. She had wanted to come down to offer some kind of support, but she wasn't sure if that support would be welcome, after the strain she'd put on the family. Maybe all she was doing coming down here was adding unnecessary stress to an already stressful situation.

Maybe she should've brought something useful with her. Like a casserole. But better than that.

Her dad opened the door, and Kinsey squared her shoulders nervously.

There were bags under his eyes, and his straight black hair was ruffled, like he'd forgotten to comb it out of its naturally gravity-defying state. But the look on his face when he saw her wasn't the forced smile Kinsey expected. He looked exhausted, yes, but also . . . relieved. He didn't hesitate a second before pulling Kinsey into a tight hug. "Hey, kiddo."

Kinsey let out a tight breath as she squeezed him back, all concerns about her reception washed away by the childish, selfish need to let her daddy assure her everything would be okay.

Which just kicked up her guilt again. She'd come down to give her parents strength, not add to their burden.

Quickly, she got herself under control and pulled away. "Is she okay?"

"It looks like the worst is over," her dad said wearily, beckoning Kinsey inside. She kicked off her ballet flats automatically, leaving them next to her dad's sneakers at the door. "She seemed fine when I left last night, and I checked with the hospital a few minutes ago and they say she's doing well. She ought to be up to visitors soon, if you're ready."

Henry looked a little lost. His eyes kept wandering around the room as though he'd forgotten something but didn't quite know what.

Kinsey thought she knew how he felt. The room looked oddly mundane for having been the recent scene of a crisis. Both her parents' suitcases were lying on the hotel dresser. Her mom's makeup was spread haphazardly over the bathroom sink. Kinsey half expected her mom to breeze through the door with an armful of hotel pastries and laugh at her two professional grumps for being so serious.

"Are *you* okay?" Kinsey asked, tapping her dad's arm to get his attention.

Henry mussed Kinsey's hair with a cursory smile. "I'm fine, kiddo. Don't worry about me."

"I'll worry about who I want," Kinsey said, frowning. "I didn't come all the way down here so you'd have to take care of *two* people. I'm here to make sure someone's taking care of *you*."

"Well, I'm your dad. And taking care of you is in the job description."

"Too bad," Kinsey said, tilting her chin up. "I'm taking care of you now. Deal with it. When was the last time you ate?"

"Um . . ." He scrunched one eye shut in a wince. "Last night?"

"And what did you eat last night?" Kinsey asked, setting her hands on her hips. A convincing liar her dad was not.

Henry scratched his temple, knocking his glasses askew before resettling them on his nose. Kinsey had inherited her myopia from her father. She'd also picked up the habit of being cranky at people to demonstrate how much you cared about them from him. Though Kinsey's attempts at this often seemed to confuse people instead of making them feel cared for. A balance her dad never seemed to struggle with striking.

"Would you believe me if I said I got room service to send up a big plate of pasta primavera?" he asked hopefully.

"No."

Henry frowned. "Drat."

"It's a good thing I came down. I don't think Mom would appreciate it if you passed out from low blood sugar in her hospital room."

"Ah, but what better place to lose consciousness than the middle of a hospital?" Henry said, nodding sagely. "I should think it shows foresight and efficiency."

Kinsey rolled her eyes at this absurdity. "We're stopping for breakfast on the way to the hospital. No arguments."

They gathered up a tote bag of toiletries and the two books Annette had brought to North Carolina with her before heading down to the hotel lobby. Kinsey had hoped to hear from Sasha again before they left, but no such luck. Sasha wasn't in the lobby as they went through to the parking lot either. Kinsey was just about to text her again to see if she was nearby or if she wanted to meet them at the hospital when a car door slammed and Sasha's voice carried Kinsey's name across the pavement.

Kinsey's pulse sparkled at the sight of Sasha's cheery smile, and for a split second she had the bizarre impulse to turn on her heel and pop back into the hotel to avoid her. Which was stupid. Why would she want to avoid Sasha? Just because she was a little jittery about her awkward attempt to make Sasha feel better last night? Ridiculous.

Sasha held up a paper bag and cupped her other hand around her mouth. "Where are you going? I brought you breakfast!"

Henry lifted an eyebrow at Kinsey. "What is this, some kind of conspiracy?"

"No one would have to conspire to feed you if you'd feed yourself," Kinsey pointed out, pushing her dad to meet Sasha. She wasn't hiding behind him, she told herself. Merely making sure he didn't run off before getting some food in his stomach.

"Hopefully breakfast sandwiches are okay," Sasha said, passing Henry the greasy paper bag. "I figured if Kinsey liked them, there was a decent chance you did, too."

Henry took the food and wrapped a stunned-looking Sasha in another one of his hugs. "They're great, Sasha, thank you."

Sasha met Kinsey's eyes over his shoulder, as though asking *what's gotten into him?*

Kinsey could only shrug, as confused as Sasha. *I don't know, he's under a lot of stress?* She'd half expected to have to convince her parents not to fret about having an extra person involved in their family crisis, so the automatic acceptance wasn't something she was prepared for.

"Thank you for bringing Kinsey down," Henry said, releasing Sasha from the embrace and patting her shoulder. "Really. I know it's a long drive, especially in the middle of a semester."

"Don't mention it," Sasha said, flashing a tentative, embarrassed smile. "I'm just glad I could do something. Your family means a lot to me."

Kinsey's stomach fluttered at the naked sincerity in Sasha's words.

Evie would have never said Kinsey's whole family meant *anything* to her. She wouldn't have slipped out early to bring them breakfast, either. Or volunteered to drive Kinsey down here in the first place. If she'd come at all, it would have only been because Kinsey begged her to. And even then, she probably would have spent the whole trip in the hotel or wandering the city by herself.

Beatrice was right. Sasha wasn't Evie. She was nothing like her. Sasha was kind and honest, despite the penchant for sarcasm. She jumped in to help her friends without even being asked. The only times she ever got close to being cruel was when she was poking fun at *herself* in an effort to make the people around her feel more at ease.

Why Sasha had decided Kinsey deserved any of that warmth was beyond comprehension. But she wanted to hold onto it for as long as she was able. She wanted to prove Sasha wasn't wasting all her kindness on someone who couldn't figure out how to reciprocate.

"Come on, I'll drive you to the hospital," Sasha was saying, ushering Kinsey and her dad toward her van. She tapped Kinsey on the shoulder as they split around the hood and pointed at her with a mock stern look. "One of those sandwiches is for you, missy."

"I'm not hungry," Kinsey said. She felt too jittery—too giddy—to eat anything just then.

"Too bad," Henry said, shoving a warm sandwich into her hands before climbing into the car.

Sasha laughed, the sound brilliant under the pale clouds. She was just so . . . good. She should have bright, happy women writing her more lovesick sonnets than she could read in a lifetime. She should be surrounded by people who loved her and knew how to show it. She should be back in New York getting ready to meet some gorgeous, smiling, affectionate woman who'd sweep her off her feet and make her forget all about that crazy, selfish ex who'd never even said *I love you.*

And instead she'd set her whole life aside just to support Kinsey and her family. Hadn't even thought about it. Even though her mom was stressing her out in Arizona. Even though Kinsey had yet to manage a thank-you that didn't sound awkward and prickly.

Kinsey yanked her door open. Sasha deserved better than whatever mess Kinsey was making of their friendship. She was just going to have to figure herself out and step it up.

TEN

Mrs. Han looked tired when the trio got to the hospital, but her smiles were as wide as Sasha remembered from the handful of times she'd joined Kinsey for dinner at the Han house. She insisted Sasha come over to collect a hug after she'd kissed Mr. Han and given Kinsey a tight embrace. She was a small woman with Kinsey's delicate features and big, dark eyes, but she gave hugs like they didn't count unless they were tight enough to crack a rib.

The doctors and nurses who came through seemed upbeat and optimistic about her prognosis. Barring an unforeseen complication, it sounded like she'd be able to go home in another day or two. Both Kinsey and Mr. Han seemed to be coping with their excess concern by fretting over whatever they could think of and giving frequent lectures against Mrs. Han neglecting her health either now or in the future.

They didn't really need Sasha at all. Which didn't seem to bother anyone except Sasha. Mrs. Han in particular kept roping her back into conversations if she'd been quiet for more than a minute or two. But Sasha still felt her outsider status more keenly every minute.

They were just such a close-knit trio. Even their lectures were delivered with an obvious undercurrent of affection. The Hans were everything Sasha always wished her own family could have been. Everything she'd given up on. That feeling of belonging. Of safety. Of easy, unconditional love. She'd stopped wishing for it so long ago she'd forgotten how much she'd wanted it. Watching Kinsey with her family was dragging all that empty desperation up again.

Not the point of this trip.

Sasha quickly appointed herself errand-runner, taking every opportunity to fetch coffee or snacks or whatever else anyone needed. Anything to get her out of there long enough to pull it together. It didn't stop her heart hurting, or stop her worrying about Cynthia's radio silence. But it meant she could check her phone for messages without Kinsey noticing.

She really didn't need Kinsey asking about her mom right now. Sasha felt too raw and out of control to trust herself not to spew all of her carefully masked frustration at the next person who looked at her sympathetically. And after that close call last night when she'd almost pulled Kinsey against her and caught her lips between her own . . . She didn't know if she could find the strength to make a rational decision if something like that happened again.

Maybe she just needed to get Trevor on the phone for a few minutes. It was much safer to vent some of her mingled anxiety and anger to him than Kinsey—who she was supposed to be helping through her own family crisis.

Sasha knew worrying about why Cynthia wouldn't pick up her phone was pointless. She was probably still asleep. It was two hours earlier in Arizona, and she'd been out late. She would turn her phone back on in another hour or so and Sasha would find out she'd been working herself up over nothing.

But it was so hard *not* to get worked up when her mom took off like this. Worst-case scenarios kept playing through Sasha's mind. Cynthia hadn't called because she'd been mugged. Or stranded. Or killed.

Or she just didn't care that her daughter might be worried.

Knowing Cynthia, it was probably that last one. Which was almost worse.

When lunchtime rolled around, Sasha volunteered to go pick up food for everyone. She just needed to get her mom on the phone to make sure she was okay. And maybe vent to Trevor for five minutes. Once that was settled, she wouldn't be such a bundle of useless nerves.

Sasha crossed the parking lot in long strides, a humid chill flushing her ears and cheeks. As soon as she thumped the car door shut, she called her mom. Voicemail. Again. She hung up without leaving a message, looked up the number for the motel, and called that instead.

"Hi, can I have Cynthia Deforest's room, please?" she asked when a curt-sounding man at the front desk answered.

"Room number?"

"I don't know. She should have checked in last night?"

There was a short sigh and the clacking of fingers on a keyboard. "Room 204," he said after a moment. "I'll put you through."

The phone rang and rang. Sasha counted fifteen of them before she made herself hang up. She slumped over the steering wheel, fingers digging into the vinyl, willing herself to stay calm. She hated how worried she was. It was just more of the same. When had Cynthia ever bothered to check in when it mattered?

Sasha tried to adopt a more forbearing outlook. If the front desk had found her room number, Cynthia must have at least made it to the motel last night. That was good, right? She'd probably just gone out for cigarettes. Or booze.

But that idea rankled too. And Sasha couldn't quite rid herself of the image of her mom sprawled unconscious on a dingy bed, a needle in her arm and no one to save her.

She was listening to Trevor's phone ring before she even knew what she wanted to say. All these confused, frustrated thoughts were stuffing her up, making it harder and harder to keep it all in. Her cousin might not know what to do about Cynthia's inability to answer a phone, but he didn't brush Sasha off if she had the occasional meltdown.

And Trevor, at least, picked up the phone when she called. "How's it going, pipsqueak?" There were kitchen sounds and voices in the background. He must be at the restaurant already. "You holding up okay?"

"Not really," Sasha said, her voice thick with anxiety and guilt. "I'm sorry, I didn't mean to bother you at work."

"You're not bothering me," Trevor said. "Chef's not even here yet. What's up?"

"I'm just . . . I'm kind of freaking out here."

"Still no word from your mom?" Trevor asked. There was a soft tap, like a door shutting, and the noises in the background quieted.

"She called me late last night," Sasha confessed. She'd only promised Cynthia not to tell anyone where she was. She hadn't said anything about keeping the phone call a secret. "I talked her into stopping at a motel, but her cell is going straight to voicemail again, and she isn't answering the phone in her room, either."

"Maybe she went out for food?" Trevor offered.

"Maybe. Probably." Sasha squeezed her eyes shut and pressed her forehead against the rim of the steering wheel. "I think she was high when she called me. It's a miracle highway patrol didn't pull her over. She could've—I mean, you know how she gets when she's pissed off. She goes completely off the rails. And I just keep thinking what if she found a dealer after she got to the motel? She says she hasn't done anything harder than weed for at least six weeks, but when she's like this . . . You know how dangerous it is with some of those drugs when you start them up again. What if she took too much and—and—"

"You're snowballing," Trevor said.

"I know. I know, but—" Sasha strangled a growl. "She said she was going to tell me that she got to the motel okay. She swore she would. And I haven't heard from her since and now I can't reach her."

"Do you want to text me the number for the motel? I can try to get the front desk to poke their heads in and see whether she's there."

Sasha rubbed her eyes. Part of her must've been hoping Trevor would volunteer to do just that. She ought to call back herself, but she didn't know what she'd do if she found out something bad had happened. Trevor might at least be able to keep his head long enough to make sure someone called 911. But . . . "I promised I wouldn't tell anyone where she is."

"Well she promised to tell you she got to the motel safe," Trevor said, with just the barest edge to his tone. "If she isn't holding up *her* end of the deal—"

"She meant to," Sasha said, coming to Cynthia's defense more out of habit than anything.

Trevor let out a long breath. "I know, pipsqueak. I just don't like when you're put into these shitty situations. If it makes you feel any better, you've got my word I won't blab about any of this. Aunt Cynthia wouldn't even have to know I was the one calling to check in."

Sasha squeezed her eyes shut. "I hate when she does this."

"I know. I'm sorry."

One corner of Sasha's mouth tugged into a tiny, sad smile. She wished Trevor didn't feel the need to make up for Cynthia's unwillingness to take responsibility by apologizing. She wished she wasn't fighting the urge to offer Trevor a similar apology. She wished . . .

But wishing didn't change anything. So she gave him the motel number and thanked him. Then she headed into Charlotte in pursuit of lunch, doing her best to put the entire sorry mess out of her head.

"I hope Sasha isn't going to miss any soccer this weekend."

Kinsey's elbow slipped off the hard wooden arm of the hospital chair she'd pulled up next to her mom's bed. "What?"

They'd been watching *Forensic Files* since Sasha ran off to pick up some food. Well—Annette had been watching *Forensic Files*. Henry had fallen asleep in a chair on the other side of the bed, his glasses askew where the back of the chair had pushed them up. And Kinsey had been staring at the screen blindly while trying to figure Sasha out.

She'd seemed almost shy since they got to the hospital. Kept making excuses to leave. Hadn't been smiling as brightly as usual. Kinsey figured it had something to do with that call last night—or the near kiss—but there hadn't been any time to pull her aside and ask about either one. She wasn't even sure if she *should* ask, with the way Sasha kept sidestepping conversations yesterday.

"Did the season start already?" Annette asked, laying a hand on Kinsey's shoulder, brow pinched in worry. "I'd hate to think she was going to get in trouble with her coach because of me."

"She doesn't have to be anywhere until Monday," Kinsey said, slumping in her seat. She already felt selfish for roping

Sasha into the whole scheme, and it was hard not to take her mom's questions as a gentle rebuke. "They already did their big preseason team bonding thing. And she volunteered to drive me," she added, crossing her arms. "I didn't make her."

"It was very sweet of her," Annette said.

Kinsey cut her mom a look, half expecting a *but*.

It was sweet, but are you sure you're not taking advantage of Sasha? It was sweet, but don't you think it would have been better for everyone if you'd stayed home?

Annette probably wouldn't be so blunt about it. Not after the way Kinsey had reacted the last time she tried to gently point out one of her mistakes. Kinsey doubted either of her parents would try to confront her about her choices directly, no matter how strongly they felt about them.

Annette smiled softly. "It's good to have you here."

Kinsey couldn't help a suspicious frown. "Really?"

"Of course, muffin," Annette said, squeezing Kinsey's arm. "Why wouldn't it be?"

Kinsey swallowed hard. She couldn't bring up the wary formality that had settled over their family after that fight about Evie. Not when her mom was in a hospital bed after scaring them all half to death. Not when her dad was so exhausted and stressed he was forgetting to eat and dropping off in uncomfortable hospital chairs. Kinsey hadn't come all the way down here to throw a tantrum and make her mom's heart attack all about her.

Instead of answering, she got out of her chair and gave her mom the best hug she could manage. "You're not allowed to have any more health scares, okay? Not ever."

"I'll do my best," Annette said, holding Kinsey tight with one arm, leaving the other hand laced with Henry's. "Don't fret, Kins. I'll be up and scaling glaciers in no time."

"Or you could *not* celebrate your escape from death by taking up dangerous sports," Kinsey grumbled, hugging her mom tighter. "Frostbite and broken limbs count as health scares too, y'know."

"All right. No glaciers. Just a quiet life of immortality."

"That's more like it."

Annette scrubbed Kinsey's back as she released her. "So," she said, a glint in her eye. "How are things with you and Sasha these days?"

Kinsey barely stopped herself from wincing. "They're . . . fine. Why?"

"No reason." Annette made herself comfortable against the pillows and fixed her gaze on the television screen, where a man with a slingshot was shooting marbles at trees. "It seems like she hasn't been around as much as she used to."

"She drove me all the way down here," Kinsey pointed out, scrunching down into her chair. "She brought Dad and me to the hospital this morning, too. She's been with us all day."

"Yes, but she also keeps slipping out. And the two of you seem intent on staying on opposite sides of the room when she's here."

Kinsey's face warmed. She was glad her mom's attention was on the TV. There was no way Kinsey's embarrassment wasn't showing in her expression. "I don't know what you're talking about, Mom."

"I just hope she doesn't feel unwelcome," Annette said, almost to herself. "I wouldn't want her to think she's in the way."

Kinsey stared. "Really?"

"Really." Annette smiled and reached out to squeeze Kinsey's shoulder again. "Sasha's thoughtful, and I'm grateful to her for bringing you all the way down. The last thing I want to do is get rid of her. I hope she knows that."

"I'll, um—I'll make sure to tell her." Kinsey had been so careful not to seek out her parents' opinions about her friends since she and Evie broke up. And her parents had been so careful not to offer their unsolicited opinions either. They were polite when Beatrice or Sasha came over, but Kinsey felt like she was always watching for some sign that her parents had noticed something wrong. Waiting for them to sit her down and point out that she'd done it again: she'd gotten too wrapped up in her feelings and missed all the obvious pitfalls everyone else could see so clearly.

She didn't expect her mom to be concerned about whether Sasha felt unwelcome. Or call her thoughtful.

"You *really* don't mind her being here?" she asked.

"Not at all. I like Sasha."

"Oh," Kinsey said, turning back to the TV, head reeling. "Okay. Great."

ELEVEN

Dammit." Sasha dropped the bag of sandwiches on the van's back seat and slid her ringing phone out of her jeans pocket. She was starting to wonder how many phone calls it would take for the damn thing to run out of battery and give her some peace.

Trevor had called a few minutes ago with what he'd found out from the motel clerk. Cynthia hadn't been in her room when the clerk poked his head in, but she wasn't half dead in the bathroom, either. One less thing to worry about. Theoretically.

Sasha wasn't optimistic enough to expect this latest call to be her mom, but she was still startled to see Nova's name on the screen. She'd been so caught up with everything else, she'd barely remembered their first practice of the season was on Monday.

She hesitated for a moment with her thumb over the reject button. But knowing Nova, she'd call again in a few minutes. Likely after Sasha was upstairs with the Hans. At least Sasha was on her own at the moment. It was as good a time as any.

Perching on the carpeted edge of the van, she answered the phone. "Hey, Nova. What's up?"

"Okay," Nova said breathlessly, "so I don't know if *you* noticed how gorgeous the weather is today, but I was talking to some of the girls and we all thought it was perfect weather for a little preseason pickup game. You in?"

"I . . . can't. Today," Sasha said, pulling at her ponytail. "You guys have fun without me."

"What, seriously?" Nova complained. "You can't be so behind on assignments you can't take an hour or two to milk this sunshine while it lasts."

Sasha's mouth twitched into a smile as she watched the thin cover of clouds gliding over Charlotte. Part of her wished she could take Nova up on the plan. Nothing helped her focus as much as getting out on the field. And boy, could she do with a dose of focus today. "Sorry. Maybe next time."

"Ugh. Fine. But you're missing out."

"I know it," Sasha said. "You kick some ass for me, okay?"

"Yeah, whatever. Hey, listen," Nova added, perking up again. "I did some research and found a few gay bars in the neighborhood that seem promising. Relatively low-key and casual, which I know is the only way to get you into a bar anyway. What do you say we meet up tonight and hit the town?"

"Oh. Right." She'd forgotten about the meeting-people plan. She didn't want to explain to Nova that she physically couldn't go because she was in North Carolina playing the hero. For the woman Nova's plan was supposed to get Sasha over, no less. "About that . . ."

"Don't tell me you're backing out, Deforest."

"It's not a good weekend for it. I've got all this stuff to take care of before Monday, and I'm just . . . I can't." She sounded cagey as hell, but she couldn't come up with a decent lie right now. She didn't want to hear Nova's opinion on exactly how stupid and hopeless this entire rescue-Kinsey idea was. "Maybe we should just forget about it."

"What happened?" Nova asked, her tone darkening. "Did Kinsey say something to you?"

"What? No."

"She did, didn't she? She said something to make you feel like you're not allowed to meet a nice girl and move on with your life."

"No, just—You know what?" Sasha could hear the edge in her voice, but couldn't seem to dull it down. "Can we let this drop, please? I hate bars, and I hate picking people up, and it's just . . . it wouldn't work."

"It's better than letting her walk all over you, isn't it? It's not fair of her to keep you on the hook like this. It's not good for you."

"And jumping in bed with a frigging stranger would cure me, right?"

"Yikes," Nova muttered. "No one's forcing you to sleep with anyone you don't want to. I'm just trying to help."

Sasha took a breath of damp, cold air through her nose. Walls. She used to have them. Where had they run off to? "I'm sorry. I didn't mean to shout at you. I'd just . . . I'd rather figure it out myself. Without forcing it."

"Well, okay, but—"

"Drop it, Nova," Sasha said, more harshly than she intended. She flinched and rubbed her forehead. "Sorry. I didn't mean . . . I just—I gotta go, okay? Talk to you later."

"Yeah," Nova said, sounding confused. "See you."

Sasha sat there for a few moments longer, fighting to find her center. She was usually better at keeping her feelings under control.

It had been a while since she'd had to deal with one of Cynthia's breakdowns, though. She was out of practice—whatever skill she had handling her mom was weak from disuse.

But she'd managed before. No reason she couldn't now. Her mom might be temporarily MIA, but she would come back to the hotel room or turn on her phone eventually. If Cynthia needed something—and she was bound to need something—Sasha would be the first person she'd try.

It couldn't be that much harder to support Kinsey while she waited for her mom to check in. Even if the Han-family-being-adorable thing kept pinching at her heart, leaving painful little bruises that only hurt more as the day went on.

They just loved each other so much. All three of them. You only had to look at them together and you could tell.

Sasha never had that. Even when Cynthia went on one of her good-mom kicks, Sasha was always bracing for the inevitable crash. And the few times she'd lived with her gran, there had been that constant feeling she could never quite make up for being Cynthia's daughter. Soccer had given her a team to belong to, but it wasn't the same thing as knowing where you fit in your own family. Knowing you had people who'd love you whether or not you made the next goal. Who'd love you even if you broke down every now and then.

She shook out her shoulders, blowing out a heavy breath. Breaking down wasn't an option. It wouldn't make her mom answer the phone and it wouldn't make Sasha feel any better. She couldn't fall apart. She wouldn't. She was stronger than that.

"Come on, Deforest," Sasha muttered, retying her ponytail. She snatched up the bag of sandwiches and hauled the van's side door shut behind her. "Keep it together."

By the time she made it back to Mrs. Han's room, Sasha had managed to pack most of her unwieldy feelings behind a smile. She'd even mentally set aside a few anecdotes that wouldn't come back to bite her later, in case she needed a quick deflection. No one would have to know how much she was struggling. Or how hard it was to be on the fringes of such a tight family.

But she caught Kinsey giving her an odd look as Sasha picked at some lettuce in what was left of her sandwich. Which meant she hadn't packed her feelings away as neatly as she'd thought.

Might be time for a run. It wouldn't be as good for her focus as the pickup game would've been, but the rhythm usually leveled her out. Gave her a chance to pull herself together.

She rolled the last of her sandwich in its paper wrapper and stood up, grabbing her keys and wallet. "Listen, I think I'm going to take off for a little bit. Get out of your hair. You can call me if you need anything."

"Why don't you take Kinsey with you?" Mrs. Han asked, before Sasha could flee. "You can keep each other company."

Kinsey choked on a potato chip and threw her mom a glare. Mrs. Han sat forward and serenely thumped her back.

Sasha felt her ears warming. "I don't—I thought maybe you'd like to have some time to yourselves," she started, rubbing the back of her neck as she edged toward the door. "I can just take myself out of the way. I don't mind."

"You're not in the way at all," Mrs. Han said, smiling warmly. It was impossible for her not to notice Kinsey's glare and Sasha's growing embarrassment, but she was doing an excellent job of ignoring both. "But since you're going out anyway, you'll do me a favor if you make sure this one here"—she poked Kinsey's wrist—"can't fret over whether my sheets are soft enough for the next two hours. I get enough of that from this one," she said, patting Mr. Han's hand.

"We love you, too," Mr. Han said dryly.

"Um—" Sasha exchanged a glance with Kinsey, part *help!*, part *what do you want to do?*

"Mom," Kinsey protested, finally recovering from her coughing fit. "Sasha's probably sick of us and is just too polite to say so. She doesn't want me to come."

"I didn't say that." The words were out of her mouth before Sasha knew she was going to say them. Her ears burned when all three Hans stared at her. "I mean, I'm not—I'm not sick of any of you. I'm just . . . I know I'm not family, so—"

"Nonsense," Mr. Han said, with a frown that was nearly identical to Kinsey's *supportive lecture time* frown. "If being a good friend to our only daughter for the last year wasn't enough to qualify you for family status, getting her down here on a moment's notice cinched it."

"Well put," Mrs. Han agreed.

"I—Oh," Sasha said, touched and confused and wary all at once. She didn't know what else to say. She didn't want to let the words sink in for fear she'd start blubbering in front of all of them.

Mrs. Han didn't give the pause time to turn awkward. She turned to Kinsey with her eyebrows raised expectantly. "Now do you have an actually good excuse not to go, or will you leave your father and me to watch *Forensic Files* in peace?"

A strange look crossed Kinsey's face as she stared at her mom. "Are you *sure* you don't want me to stay?"

"The doctors assure me I'm in no danger of dropping dead anytime soon," Mrs. Han said, prodding Kinsey out of her seat. "Even if I was, I've got your dad here to perform CPR as needed."

Kinsey frowned as she stood. "That's not funny, Mom."

"Off you go," Mrs. Han said brightly, waving Kinsey toward the door.

"Have fun, girls," Mr. Han added.

Sasha smiled at the familiar, affectionate joking, pushing down the faint sense of longing she didn't know what to do with. She slung her bag over her shoulder while a glowering Kinsey collected her things, then led her down the hall to the elevators.

"I can drop you at the hotel for a while," Sasha said as she hit the down button. "We don't have to hang out if you don't want to."

"Who said I didn't want to hang out?" Kinsey asked, crossing her arms and scowling back down the corridor.

"Yeah, no, you're right. I don't know how I missed such a blatant display of enthusiasm." Sasha grinned when Kinsey's scowl turned her way. "I like your parents. They're kind of great."

"I think they like you too." Kinsey sounded baffled.

"Hey, people like me," Sasha said, with mock defensiveness. "I'm very charming."

"I didn't mean it like that," Kinsey said, glancing at Sasha with what looked like genuine remorse.

Which *was* weird. Sasha had been expecting her to take the opening and poke fun at her. She felt odd. Like she'd stepped off a curb she hadn't realized was there.

The elevator doors opened before Sasha could figure out how to respond, and the cluster of nurses and another trio of visitors inside prevented any further conversation until they were outside in the brisk February air, walking toward the van.

"So where were you going before my mom made you drag me along?" Kinsey asked.

Ah. Hitting up the nearest park for a long run wasn't Kinsey's kind of afternoon. And she looked like she needed something fun to do, to take her mind off her mom's health for a little bit.

It took only a second for Sasha to hit on an idea she thought would do the trick of distracting both of them. "Doesn't matter," she said, twirling her keys around a finger. "We're doing something better now."

"What does that mean?"

"It means it's a surprise."

"Sasha. Just tell me. I hate surprises."

Sasha grinned as she unlocked her van. "Relax, babe. I got this."

TWELVE

Sasha refused to divulge the surprise as she drove, though she seemed increasingly entertained by Kinsey's wild attempts to guess. Kinsey was prepared for the worst—some loud, athletic activity that Sasha would love and Kinsey would be terrible at—when Sasha turned into a mall.

This didn't ease Kinsey's nerves. "Have I told you I hate ice skating?" she asked, staring at the building while Sasha circled the outer parking lot. "Also rollerblading. Also anything that requires you to strap wheels or blades or boards of any variety to your feet and has a high probability of ending with broken bones."

"*What?*" Sasha gasped, pressing a hand to her heart with mock outrage. "Kinsey Han, not particularly interested in an athletic activity? Has our entire friendship been a lie?"

"Shut up," Kinsey said, swatting Sasha's shoulder lightly with the back of her hand. "Your version of fun is romping around in the mud after a ball. You can't blame me for thinking your idea of a nice surprise is doing something that's likely to kill me. Oh god," she added, with dawning horror, "is there a paintball place in there?"

Sasha chuckled and turned into one of the long rows of parking spaces. "Could be."

"Sasha. I'm wearing a dress. You could at least take me back to the hotel and let me change into something more appropriate before you subject me to an hour of paintball humiliation."

"Be still, my child," Sasha said, putting her palm on top of Kinsey's head without taking her eyes off the road. "Upon my honor, no harm will come to you. Or your outfit."

Kinsey glared as Sasha pulled into a spot. "If it's paintball," she warned, "I'm going to kill you."

"That's kind of the point of paintball anyway," Sasha said, shutting off the engine. "You'd probably be great at it, actually. But that's not the surprise. Come on. It's not far."

Kinsey sighed and climbed out of the van. Sun dappled the parking lot through gaps in the light gray clouds overhead. Charlotte was still chilly enough to need a jacket, but the trees were greener than they'd been in New York, early spring already well underway here. The breeze ruffling Kinsey's hair carried the faint scent of new blooms and budding leaves under the more prominent scents of sun-warmed asphalt and the woodsmoke from a nearby restaurant.

Sasha had shoved her hands in the pockets of her bomber jacket as she walked ahead. Kinsey was glad to see she'd regained her usual open, self-assured posture which she'd lost back at the hospital; shoulders back, face angled toward the sky, a smile playing around her mouth. Sunlight touched her hair and shoulders like an old friend, warm and gentle . . .

Hoo boy. Kinsey couldn't have been this sappy when she and Evie were together, could she? She hurried to catch up, careful to keep at least an arm's length of space between them as they fell into step.

The surprise probably wasn't a really nice cup of hot tea, Kinsey mused, trying to steer her thoughts in a safer direction. Or even a pretzel and strawberry lemonade. If it wasn't paintball . . . A vision came to her of people on roller skates with paintball guns and she shuddered. Sasha would probably *love* that. Or—oh god, it had better not be paintball on ice. She'd die. If the ice didn't get her, the embarrassment would.

"Did you find an arcade?" she asked hopefully. "An arcade wouldn't be the worst. Or bowling. I think I could survive bowling."

Sasha snorted. "Good to know."

Kinsey made a face. "You're just enjoying watching me squirm, aren't you."

"Maybe," Sasha said, turning a bright smile on Kinsey. "You're cute when you hate everything."

"I always hate everything."

"I guess that explains why you're just so dang adorable."

"Oh my god, Sasha," Kinsey said, her face warming. "I can't even talk to you right now."

"Sorry. Force of habit," Sasha said, walking backwards through a swinging glass door. She was still grinning, though. Completely unapologetic. She held the door open and gestured inside. "Welcome to the arena, darling."

Oh. Kinsey stopped dead in her tracks. It wasn't paintball or ice skating or anything like it. It was just a bookstore. A nice, quiet, peaceful bookstore.

Kinsey let out a breath, dazed. Why had she been convinced Sasha would drag her to something awful? Sasha wasn't like that. She didn't even ask Kinsey to come to her soccer games. Half the time Kinsey had to look up the schedule on the school website to make sure she didn't miss one. Sasha never tried to make Kinsey into someone more like her. She let her be exactly who she was and—for some reason—liked her anyway.

"We don't have to stay," Sasha said, looking worried that Kinsey hadn't spoken. "There's a movie theater across the street. Or—I saw a cupcake place a few blocks back. We could—"

Kinsey cut her off with a fierce hug, which Sasha seemed too surprised to return. "It's perfect."

Sasha's ears were pink when Kinsey withdrew, but she looked pleased. "Well . . . cool," she said, lightly punching Kinsey's shoulder. She cleared her throat, pulling on the end of her ponytail. "It, uh—It looks like they've got a café. You want a tea or something?"

"*Yessss*," Kinsey said, letting Sasha lead the way. "I haven't had a decent tea in days."

Sasha insisted on buying Kinsey the biggest tea they had and got a smoothie for herself. They wandered the shelves with their drinks, chatting like they used to. Before Beatrice started talking about transferring. Before Kinsey worried so much about whether the next thing she said was going to drive Sasha away too. It was comforting, having Sasha nearby, laughing at Kinsey's dry remarks, free from some of the tension she'd been holding in her shoulders since they left New York.

"We should bring your mom back a book or two," Sasha said, plucking a fresh novel off the shelf she was sitting against. They'd been reading the back covers to each other for the last ten minutes or so. Sasha manned the cozy mysteries, and Kinsey the romances across the aisle. "Some of these sound awesome."

"She'd like that," Kinsey said, watching Sasha's free hand absently roll her nearly empty cup on its edge. She had this way of moving that was so . . . deliberate. Lithe. Even when she wasn't thinking about what she was doing. She just had this subtle grace about her. It was something about the confidence of her posture, the ease of her smile. It was the shape of her hand when she tucked her hair behind her ear . . .

Kinsey bit her lip as an image came to her, unbidden, of Sasha's fingers in her own hair, drawing her in for a long, sweet kiss—

"You okay?" Sasha asked, going still.

Kinsey gave herself a firm mental shake, retreating behind a frown. "What?"

"You were looking at me funny."

Fantastic. Kinsey sipped the remnants of her tea, repressing a wince when cold, gritty dregs hit her tongue. "Sorry."

"Still worried about your mom?" Sasha guessed.

"Kind of." It wasn't why she'd been staring, but it was true. There was no reason to think her mom wasn't well on her way to recovery, but Kinsey was still shaken by the scare. And it was easier to talk about that than admit the track her imagination had taken a few moments ago.

She sighed, slumping against the hard shelf at her back. "I keep wondering if it was a bad idea to come down," she confessed.

"Really?" Sasha asked, tilting her head to one side with a little frown. "Why?"

"All I'm doing is stressing them out," Kinsey said, lifting her shoulders. "You're being more helpful than I am. I'm just . . . sitting around complaining about the sheets."

"Well, sure," Sasha said. "That's how your family says you care. I'm sure your mom knows that. Your dad does it too."

"My dad doesn't sound mean when he does it."

Sasha still looked confused. "Neither do you."

"Okay, but you're . . . immune from taking things personally or something."

"I don't know about that," Sasha said, pulling her knees up

and looping her arms around them. "But I really think you're being too hard on yourself. Why would having you around stress them out?"

Kinsey crossed her arms, fixing her gaze on a book on the lowest shelf across the aisle. She hadn't really talked about the big Han fallout with anyone but Evie. She'd been too wrapped up in her own self-righteous indignation at first. And too ashamed of how she'd handled it after they broke up. Too scared that confessing to being that much of a proud, stubborn idiot would drive away the two friends she had left.

But for some reason she didn't feel the same old dread when she thought about telling Sasha now. And after everything Sasha had done for Kinsey in the past few days, she felt she owed her the truth.

"We kind of had a fight last year," Kinsey said. "About Evie. It wasn't anything they did," she added hastily. "They were the best when I came out. The best. No pushback. No grumbling. I think they might have worked it out before I said anything, because they didn't even need time to process. They were just one hundred percent on board and supportive.

"But then I started dating Evie, and we just . . ." She huffed. "I don't know if Bee ever told you this, but being with Evie made me a little shit."

"I don't believe that," Sasha said at once.

"You should," Kinsey said emphatically. "I was terrible. I just—I thought she was so *authentic*. So *real* because she didn't bother being polite or trying to spare people's feelings." She clenched her teeth, still mad at herself for thinking that meant she'd been in love. For using Evie as an excuse to push everyone away.

"My parents tried *so hard* to be okay with her," she said. "They really did. But they were worried about me. They thought she was

controlling, and that I was losing my personality to the relationship. And . . . I mean, they were *right*, but I couldn't see it. I didn't
want to see it. So when they—very gently, I might add—tried to
point out that maybe Evie had a few flaws . . ."

Sasha winced. "Didn't go so well?"

Kinsey mimed a bomb going off, complete with sound effects.
"I lost it. Any shitty thing I could've said, I said it. A couple times
over. They'd never really accepted me, they only had a problem
with her because she was a girl . . . That sort of thing. I even
threatened to elope and never speak to them again if they didn't
back off."

Sasha let out a low whistle.

"I didn't mean most of it," Kinsey said. "Not really. But by the
time I got over myself and realized what a mess I'd made . . . I
couldn't figure out how to put us back together. I still haven't figured it out. And I'm just worried they're more concerned about
not setting me off again than making sure Mom's getting better."

Sasha picked up her smoothie and cupped her hands around
it, eyes on its bright green straw. "For what it's worth," she said
slowly, "I haven't noticed anything that would support that theory. They're not acting like they think you'll explode at any second.
They seem really happy to see you, actually. Anyone looking at
you can tell you all love each other a lot. More than most families
I know about." The corner of her mouth ticked up. "Even when
you're complaining about sheets."

Kinsey watched her face, distracted from her family problem
by the odd waver in Sasha's voice. The flicker of a smile hadn't
quite concealed the sadness in her downcast eyes.

She didn't know what to say. She only knew enough about
Sasha's mom to guess their relationship was strained at best,
but she hadn't thought it was bad enough for Sasha to question

whether her mom *loved* her. Even at the lowest point of her relationship with her own parents, Kinsey had taken their love as a given.

Setting her jaw, Kinsey plucked her tea off the floor and crawled over to Sasha's side of the aisle. She plopped down next to her so they were shoulder to shoulder, ignoring the way Sasha tensed up.

Sasha laughed nervously. "Hi?"

"There's a draft over there," Kinsey lied archly. Sasha might not want to talk about her mom, but that didn't mean she didn't need support. All Kinsey knew how to provide was the bossy variety, but that was probably better than nothing.

"Okay . . ."

"Never question a draft, Deforest. It's not polite."

"I wouldn't dream of it." Sasha didn't sound any less confused, but Kinsey felt her relax, and when she spoke again it was with a glint in her eye. "Though if this is just a ploy to be near me, darling, all you had to do was ask."

"Oh my god." Kinsey rolled her eyes, though she couldn't summon true irritation. On some level, she understood that pretending this was a joke was what Sasha needed to be okay with accepting the comfort. "What's wrong with you?"

"Well," Sasha said, flicking the lid of her drink with her thumb, "I *can* be a bit of a flirt."

"You? Never."

A grin played at the corner of Sasha's mouth. "I've also been known to romp around in the mud after a ball. For fun."

"Shocking."

"And . . ." Sasha glanced in both directions before leaning in and speaking in a low voice. "This may come as a shock. Not a lot of people know this." She took a deep breath. "I sometimes indulge in sarcasm."

"You are such a *nerd*," Kinsey said, giving Sasha a little shove with one finger.

Sasha laughed as she shrugged out of the way. "That, too."

Kinsey picked up a book from the little pile beside her. She should just let it go. Allow the conversation to move into the slightly ridiculous and enjoy the normal while it lasted. But something about sitting on the floor side by side made her feel reckless. Maybe it was pushing her luck, but . . . "Can I ask you something?"

"Shoot."

"Why did you decide to be friends with me? I was a mess. You should've run for the hills."

"I thought you were hot," Sasha said in a dry lilt.

"Sasha," Kinsey complained. "Come on. Seriously."

Sasha shrugged, stretching her legs out in front of her. "I don't know. You always seemed so . . . strong. And you're smart and funny. Plus you seemed like you needed a knight. I like charging in and saving the day." She paused, an almost imperceptible hitch, before she went on. "And I liked you. Still do."

Kinsey tried to catch her gaze, but Sasha was picking at the last of her drink with her straw. Her expression was impossible to read.

Kinsey couldn't help remembering that conversation in the car about Sasha's ex. And their talk last night. Too many people had let Sasha down too many times. Kinsey didn't want to stay within their ranks any longer. *Someone* ought to let Sasha know she mattered. And she felt just reckless enough to try.

"Do you want to know why I wanted to be friends with you?"

"You thought I was hot?" Sasha asked with a flirty smile, predictably trying to flip the conversation out of the heartfelt and into the sarcastic.

For once Kinsey flipped it back. "Because you sat with me when I couldn't get off the ground, and you kicked my butt into gear when I could but didn't want to. Because you gave me space to figure myself out, and you were always there when I needed you. Because when you're not being sarcastic, you're one of the kindest people I know."

Sasha searched her eyes, motionless except for the rise and fall of her chest and the wary flick of her gaze.

"And because I liked you," Kinsey said softly. She couldn't tell if she was revealing too much, or not enough. "Still do."

Sasha let out a short breath, turning to her drink. "Stop saying nice things. It's weird."

"Yeah, well . . ." Kinsey sat back, scowling at the book in her hands. "Maybe it shouldn't be."

THIRTEEN

As Sasha drove back to the hospital, Kinsey stared out the window, tapping a knuckle against the glass in time to the music. Neither of them said much, but the quiet didn't feel strained or full of things that shouldn't be said. It was the kind of lull nearly a year of friendship had earned them. Something easy. Comfortable.

Which was starting to make Sasha worry. In the back of her mind, she could feel herself rationalizing away her need for all those rules. All those walls. As though maybe for once it wouldn't ruin everything if she was honest about some of the problems weighing on her. As though Kinsey staring her down in that bookstore and saying she liked her meant more than it really had.

It would've been so easy to believe that. So easy to take the tiny flash of vulnerability she thought she'd seen in Kinsey's eyes and assign it world-changing significance. She needed to shake off the what-ifs circling her head before she did something stupid.

Maybe she should get that run in after all.

Sasha turned down the music when she'd parked in front of the hospital, but didn't shut off the engine. She needed space to get her head together before she lost her ability to think rationally. Plus, she was still hoping to reach her mom. Which she couldn't try if she didn't carve out a few minutes to herself before visiting hours were over.

"Don't forget the books," she said, as Kinsey unfastened her seatbelt.

"Got 'em." She grabbed the bag from between their seats, but stopped with her hand on the door handle. "Hang on. Aren't you coming?"

Sasha shrugged. "You guys have it under control."

"You're not in the way or anything. My mom told me specifically she likes having you around."

"I like being around. But I've got something I need to take care of. I'll come back in time to pick you and your dad up for dinner."

Kinsey narrowed her eyes. "Are you okay?"

"Me?" Sasha hitched on a smile, maybe a beat too late. "Sure. Fine and dandy."

Kinsey's frown only deepened. "You don't look fine and dandy. Is it your mom? Didn't she ever call you back?"

Jeez. Was she that transparent? She rubbed a hand over her neck. "It's . . . fine. It doesn't matter."

"Yeah it does," Kinsey said, her chin lifting slightly. "*You* matter, Sasha."

Sasha made a breathy sound that she hoped sounded more like a laugh than getting the wind knocked out of her. *You matter.* Where in the hell did that come from? "God, Kins."

"You do," Kinsey insisted.

Sasha shook her head. She was supposed to be able to control her feelings—or at least joke them off—enough that no one could notice when something was bothering her. No one was supposed to be able to see through the facade and notice she was hurting. And here was Kinsey, seeing the pain anyway and not balking, but seeming to offer the acceptance Sasha was so scared to ask for.

But it was just another what-if. And Sasha knew better than to let herself believe her what-ifs ever led to happily-ever-after.

"Just because you're playing knight for me doesn't mean I can't hold you up, too," Kinsey pressed. "I won't crumble if you tell me what's wrong."

"I know." Sasha swallowed the knot in her throat and met Kinsey's gaze. "But I might."

And she couldn't let herself. Not now. It wasn't just about being there for Kinsey. If Sasha let herself vent, she wasn't sure she'd be able to stop. And no matter how good Kinsey's intentions might be, at some point she was sure to reach the limit of her sympathy. There was too much—none of it pleasant, none of it easily shrugged off if Sasha let herself dwell on it for long. Kinsey wouldn't prove to be the exception just because Sasha wanted her to be.

Though god, did she wish she was wrong.

For a moment Kinsey said nothing. Her dark eyes simply bored into Sasha's, as though she already knew everything Sasha couldn't express and was deciding whether or not to call Sasha's bluff. Sasha felt her chest tightening with fear that Kinsey was angry she wasn't being honest enough, or cheerful enough, or strong enough—

Then Kinsey's expression set into stubborn determination and she leaned across the car and pressed a kiss to Sasha's cheek.

It was just a soft, swift brush. Barely a breath's worth of pressure. But Sasha was overcome by the scent of her—the coconut of her shampoo, the trace of lavender from her clothes.

Her heart stopped. She didn't dare move as Kinsey retreated to her side of the van once more. She didn't trust herself not to grab Kinsey and kiss her—hard—until their lips went numb.

"You don't have to talk if you don't want to," Kinsey said. "But I'm happy to listen, if you think it'd do any good."

"Kins . . ." Sasha whispered, her voice as brittle as dry, dead leaves. She wanted to believe things would be different if she told Kinsey everything. That she wouldn't shut Sasha down like most people did. That she wouldn't flinch from the empty longing hidden away in Sasha's heart. She wanted to be brave enough to shake off the fear and tell Kinsey everything. But she just . . . couldn't. "I'm . . . I can't. I'm sorry."

"Don't be sorry," Kinsey said sternly. "I'm just letting you know I'm here if you change your mind. Okay?"

Sasha nodded, unable to speak.

Kinsey nodded once in reply. Then she reached over and squeezed Sasha's wrist. "Thank you. For today. It was perfect." Her fingers lingered a moment, thumb sliding against Sasha's palm.

Sasha had to withdraw her hand into a fist to keep herself from trapping Kinsey's fingers and asking her to stay.

Kinsey slipped out of the car with her things and shut the door. She turned once to wave before the next row of cars hid her from view.

Sasha ran her hands over her face once Kinsey was out of sight. She had to pull it together before she forgot what she was supposed to be doing and started believing Kinsey's gestures were anything more than expressions of friendship.

A good run. That's what she needed. A muscle-aching, lung-stinging, head-clearing run. Then she wouldn't be so susceptible to these stupid what-ifs.

Kinsey struggled not to knock her head repeatedly against the side of the elevator as it ascended to her mom's floor. Her stomach was tight, and she felt vaguely giddy, and she had that *feeling*

again. That stupid-making, champagne-in-her-blood feeling she used to mistake for love.

And part of her didn't even care. She *liked* that feeling, dammit. And she liked Sasha. A lot.

So she didn't like talking about her mom. Kinsey might not either, if her mom routinely got herself in worrying situations in the middle of the night and couldn't be bothered to check in the next day.

She was just irritated that she hadn't noticed how often Sasha talked about herself like she didn't have the right to expect love or support from anyone. It made Kinsey furious at the people in Sasha's life who'd made her believe she wasn't important.

Herself included. Sasha shouldn't look so baffled and uncomfortable when Kinsey tried to be nice. She *wouldn't*, if Kinsey hadn't spent the better part of the last few months swatting away Sasha's ridiculous pick-up lines. All because Kinsey couldn't handle the bright, fizzy feeling the pseudo-flirting provoked.

She couldn't say she was handling those feelings any better now. Trying to do better in the nice department only seemed to freak Sasha out.

Especially when Kinsey felt the need to cross the unspoken boundaries they'd both been very careful to maintain. What did she think she was doing, kissing Sasha in the car like that?

But *someone* should show Sasha a little love now and then, shouldn't they? And Kinsey didn't want it to be some faceless vision of beauty. She wanted it to be *her*.

Kinsey chewed on her lip as she stepped out of the elevator. A more rational person probably could have *said* something to demonstrate their support. They wouldn't have gone and *kissed* her, however innocuous a kiss on the cheek happened to be. Not when there was no precedent for friendly kissing in their relationship. Not even kisses blown across the room in jest.

It had felt like the right thing to do at the time. Even after the way Sasha had fallen over herself trying to get away from Kinsey's advances in Delaware. And the way she tensed whenever Kinsey hugged her.

Thing was, she wasn't so sure Sasha's evasive maneuvers were simply because she didn't *want* affection. Kinsey had a pet theory that maybe Sasha just wasn't *used* to it. Her crazy ex certainly didn't sound like the cuddly type. And Kinsey had to question whether Sasha's mom had been big on displaying affection, based on the scraps of information Kinsey had gathered about her over the past couple of days. Sasha had seemed awkward when Kinsey's parents hugged her too, so it wasn't necessarily that she had a problem with Kinsey specifically.

Kinsey paused in the hallway outside her mom's room, taking a moment to put that line of thought out of her head.

She wished she could work this through out loud, though. If this was before their fight, she could have spilled her guts to her parents, and they'd help her sort out her feelings. Give her some advice. Because Kinsey obviously didn't have the least idea what to do about any of this.

She was huffing out an irritated breath, her back against the wall, book bag dangling from her fingers, when her dad walked out.

He stopped short and blinked, gaze flicking from the books to Kinsey's face to the corridor beyond her. "No Sasha?"

"She dropped me off," Kinsey said, swinging the bag aimlessly. "Had to take care of something."

Her dad scratched his temple, watching her, then pointed back the way Kinsey had come. "Join me for a walk to the vending machine?"

"Shouldn't someone stay with Mom?"

"If something happens, the doctors will know," Henry said. "Also, she told me to take my time getting back. It's *possible* all our loving concern is getting on her nerves."

Kinsey made a face. "Shoulda thought of that before she went and had a heart attack, shouldn't she?"

Her dad's smile was tired but sympathetic. "Come on," he said, starting back up the corridor. "You can pick out whatever you want."

"Okay," Kinsey grumbled.

She followed him to a windowless alcove off one of the waiting areas and leaned against an ancient coffee dispenser. When her dad asked her if she wanted anything, she just shrugged.

"Feeling okay?" he asked, glancing at her sideways as he fed some money into a snack machine.

"Fine. You?"

"Also fine."

"That's good." She swung the bag so the books tapped against her shin. "Hey, Dad?"

He pressed a final button and turned to her as the machine released a bag of chips. "Yes, Kinsey."

She kept her eyes on the slow pendulum dangling from her fingers, trying to figure out how to break out of the never-talking cycle. Maybe all she had to do was take a deep breath and jump. But jumping directly into more or less the same subject that started the cycle seemed like a bad idea, so she went for something that would give her plausible deniability. "How did you know you were in love with Mom? Like really in love with her?"

He fished out the change and reinserted the coins to make another selection, but didn't answer right away.

Kinsey probably could've come up with a more subtle question. She held her breath, afraid he was going to ask why she wanted to know, or—worse—give some half-answer because he didn't want to point out that the common denominator in all of Kinsey's failed relationships was Kinsey herself.

"Well," he said slowly, "I suppose it was a lot of little things. I loved her laugh from the beginning, and I loved how silly she could be. I loved that I didn't need to tell her when I was joking, because she just knew." He paused, adjusting his glasses. "But I think the moment it really hit me was the moment I realized I didn't have to pretend with your mom. And she didn't have to pretend with me. We were better when we were together. Once I figured that out, there was no going back."

Kinsey nodded, swinging the bag to her other side before she gave herself a bruise. What he said tracked. That was basically why they'd objected to Evie—because they'd been *worse* together.

She wanted to think she and Sasha were better together. But she couldn't quite shake the fear that she wasn't the kind of person who could make *anyone* better. No matter how much she liked them and wanted to be there for them. She didn't have a great record for sustaining healthy, open relationships. She hadn't even been able to keep from wrecking things with her parents.

Henry handed her the sleeve of cookies he'd just retrieved from the machine. "Everything okay, kiddo?"

"Yeah," Kinsey said. "Just . . . thinking."

"Okay." Her dad gave her a one-armed hug and a rough kiss above the ear. "I love you."

Kinsey let her head rest on his shoulder, imagining for a moment there wasn't a wedge between them. "Love you too."

Sasha hadn't come back to the hospital until visiting hours were almost over. She didn't seem as worried as she had for most of the day, but Kinsey couldn't help wondering if she was just doing a better job of hiding it. Sasha said goodbye to Kinsey's mom, since she had to take off the next morning, then took Kinsey and her dad to dinner. Sasha acted chipper enough as they ate, answering Henry's questions about school and soccer with her usual smiling humor.

Kinsey had started to hope that Sasha's easy laugh meant she'd actually managed to work out her family stuff while she was gone. But the moment they left Henry in the hotel elevator, Sasha went quiet again.

"You ever get ahold of your mom?" Kinsey asked as they stepped through the door of their room.

"I think her phone battery died," Sasha said, avoiding Kinsey's gaze as she hauled her duffel bag from the floor onto the foot of her bed. Before Kinsey could reply, though, she changed the subject. "Are you still planning to get a lift home from your folks?"

"That's what we said," Kinsey said, perching on the end of her own bed. "Unless—Unless you want the company tomorrow. It's a long way to go on your own."

"You don't want to leave your mom before they discharge her," Sasha said, tossing Kinsey an understanding smile. She shoved a spare phone charger and the shirt she'd worn yesterday into a corner of the bag. "I'm used to long solo road trips anyway. Don't worry about me."

"Yeah, okay." She *didn't* want to leave before the local doctors cleared her mom to go home, but letting Sasha drive all the way back to New York by herself didn't sit right either. "I don't suppose your coach would understand if you missed the first practice of the season?"

"I doubt it. We got bumped up a division last season and she'll be pissed if we're not all at a hundred and twenty percent from word go." She paused partway through taking out a fresh set of clothes for tomorrow, glancing at Kinsey. "Unless you still need me here. I can handle a few lectures if you do."

"I don't *need* you," Kinsey said, crossing her arms. "I'm not going to become a puddle of dysfunctional emotion if you aren't within arm's reach at all times."

Sasha issued a soft laugh and pressed a hand over her heart. "You always say the sweetest things."

Kinsey's mouth twisted to the side. She knew Sasha was only teasing, but she still wished she'd expressed herself in a less cranky way. She wanted to be the kind of person who could write lovesick sonnets by the bushel, whose first instinct wasn't to show affection by complaining. She wanted Sasha to trust her enough to talk about her family stuff.

"What I meant," she ventured, kicking at a tiny knot in the carpet, "is I *do* want you to stay. But only if you were sure you wouldn't get in trouble. You've done so much already, and I wouldn't want you to feel bad about going tomorrow because I'm trying to make out I can't, you know, *exist* without close supervision."

"I know what you meant, Kins," Sasha said. "I've known you long enough I can usually work out when your grumbling is actual irritation and when it's just your way of being friendly. You don't need to explain yourself to me."

Kinsey blinked at her as her heart did a strange little flip. "I guess."

But Sasha didn't seem to realize she'd said anything significant. She finished gathering her things and shut herself in the bathroom to get ready for bed without another word.

Kinsey tried turning on the TV to distract herself from the stupid fluttery feeling spreading from her stomach to the tips of her fingers, but it wasn't helping at all, and she switched it off again the second Sasha came out of the bathroom in a soft-looking tank and a pair of sweatpants.

"I don't mind if you leave that on," Sasha said as she climbed into bed.

"There's nothing good on anyway," Kinsey mumbled, tossing the remote aside and grabbing her own pajamas.

By the time Kinsey was ready for bed, face scrubbed, teeth brushed, a too-big men's teeshirt pulled over her head, Sasha appeared to be asleep. Kinsey paused at the edge of the bathroom hallway, resting her head against the corner. Sasha was all scrunched up at the edge of the bed, her brow slightly pinched. Still more troubled than she wanted to let on.

Kinsey wished she knew how to make Sasha trust her with her worries. But months of shutting her down every time Sasha tried to flirt had probably killed that possibility a long time ago.

Kinsey just couldn't seem to stop herself from hurting people with her thoughtlessness. She just . . . She really didn't want to do that to Sasha anymore. She wanted to find a way to prove she cared about her. In a way that Sasha would understand. She wanted to believe she could be a better person for the sake of someone else. That if she let herself fall in love with Sasha, they would have the kind of relationship Kinsey had always hoped for but never thought she deserved.

But the only way she could think of to open that conversation wouldn't help in the slightest. Despite all the times Sasha had flinched from her over the past two days, all Kinsey wanted to do was curl up next to her, coax her awake with gentle kisses. Soothe away the things she wouldn't talk about with slow caresses. *You can talk to me. You're important to me. I won't hurt you.*

Kinsey sighed. If she tried it, Sasha would probably fall out of bed in shock. And she'd be freaked out enough to go sleep in the car or something. And that would be it for their friendship.

She walked past Sasha's bed and climbed into her own, shutting off the light so Sasha could sleep. Kinsey wasn't tired yet, but she could work on a lettering project on her tablet in the dark for a few minutes to wind down.

Lettering in the dark was something she'd started doing shortly after she'd moved into Sasha's dorm room. Sasha had always told her she didn't mind the lamplight, but she never actually relaxed out of that tightly wrapped bundle until after Kinsey shut it off.

Another instance of Sasha acting like it was normal for people to treat her like dirt. All while doing everything she could to help a near stranger through a breakup. Even asleep, she'd made Kinsey feel better. Sitting up in bed with only the dim glow of her tablet to see by, accompanied by the soft, steady rhythm of Sasha's breath a few feet away, had comforted Kinsey's broken heart in a way she hadn't fully appreciated at the time.

Though she was having a hard time concentrating on her project now. Her gaze kept wandering to the dark bundle on the next bed that was Sasha, and she kept listening for the soft sound of her breathing, as though if she listened hard enough she could make out everything Sasha didn't want to say.

But she couldn't read Sasha's mind no matter how hard she listened. Eventually she gave up, fishing out her earbuds to listen to music as she inked, until—a long while later—she nodded off to sleep.

FOURTEEN

The sky was an uninterrupted gray. The grass and weeds were brown and as high as Sasha's waist. They bent in the breeze, brushing against her elbows like spiderwebs, pushing her toward the rusting hulk of a trailer interrupting the horizon line. Dry, trampled earth circled the trailer, ending only inches from Sasha's feet.

She was back home—but it didn't look like anywhere she'd lived growing up. The trailer was too old and run-down and dominated too much space in her vision. There were pieces of reality here and there—the gray blinds in the kitchen window, the chipping tan paint on the door, the glint of sun against a shiny spot of rusted chrome trim—but not in any of the right combinations. She only knew it was home because it *felt* the same.

She didn't want to be here. But she didn't know which way would take her back. Everything was the same flat, brown field in every direction.

Before she could panic, she noticed a figure sitting on the trailer's front steps.

Her mom. Barefoot and gaunt, with dirty-blond hair hanging in limp curtains around her face. She was turned away, watching something on the far horizon.

Ma, Sasha tried to say. But her mom didn't hear. Or maybe Sasha hadn't spoken.

Something moved in the grass at Sasha's feet. It slithered past her, a thin black vine stretching across dry earth. Sasha tried to call out to her mom again, to warn her, but the word wouldn't leave her throat. The vine climbed the trailer steps and coiled around her mother's ankle.

She didn't seem to notice.

Sasha wanted to rush forward and help, but she might as well have been made of stone. All she could do was watch as the vine looped around her mom's torso and wrapped itself around her arms. It wound so tight Sasha could see welts forming on her skin. And still her mom didn't react.

Sasha fought to shout a warning—to run to her and tear the vines off—but she couldn't take a step. Couldn't even eke out a whisper.

The vine raised its head and Sasha realized that it wasn't a vine at all. It was a snake, thin and sharp and deadly venomous. It showed its fangs in a terrible grin and sank them deep into her mom's forearm.

Ma!

Her mom turned her head from the horizon at last, her eyes already glassy. Lifeless.

Sasha tried to scream, but there were snakes around her, too. Stopping her from moving. So tight around her chest and throat she couldn't breathe—

"No!" Sasha broke out of the dream, away from the twisted, hot sheets, before she was fully awake.

She gasped for air like she'd been running too long, digging her fingers into her scalp and pressing her back against the cool wall.

She let herself make a small noise in her throat, just to reassure herself the inability to speak hadn't followed her into wakefulness. *Just a dream. Calm down.*

"Sasha?"

A light switched on, blinding and devastatingly welcome. It burned away the most vivid images, replacing them with the reality of rumpled comforters and blocky hotel furniture.

"What's wrong?" Kinsey asked, swinging one leg out of bed. "What happened?"

"Just—Just give me a minute," Sasha begged, pressing the heels of her hands against her temple until it hurt. It was just a dream. A choking, awful dream that wasn't shaking off as quickly as she wanted. She'd been worrying too much about not being able to reach Cynthia all day. That was it. It didn't mean anything more than that.

Focus, Deforest. Hard carpet under her feet. Firm wall at her shoulders. Cool air prickling her arms. Yellow light stinging her retinas.

And Kinsey sitting motionless six feet away, probably annoyed her sleep had been interrupted over nothing.

"I'll get you some water," she said abruptly.

Sasha listened as Kinsey padded into the bathroom and ran the tap for a few seconds. Focusing on that helped her as she found her center and started to slow her breathing.

"Here," Kinsey said when she returned.

Sasha swiped the back of her hand over her eyes, trying to rid herself of the last clinging images of the dream, and took the water without looking at Kinsey directly. "Thanks," she muttered, and gulped most of it down.

"Sure." Kinsey stayed at the foot of the bed, leaving the narrow pathway between the wall and the bed open, as though she sensed Sasha wouldn't react well to being boxed in just now. "You wanna tell me—"

"What time is it?" Sasha interrupted.

Kinsey glanced at the digital clock that sat between the beds, crossing her arms. "'Bout three."

Jeez. "Sorry I woke you up."

"It's all right," Kinsey said, lifting a shoulder. "I was sort of awake anyway."

"Late night lettering?" Sasha guessed, her voice hitching.

"Why, was your nightmare about a resurgence in popularity of Comic Sans?"

Sasha let out a strange sound—a sort of high, fluttery thing that made her sound like a crazy person. "What gave it away?"

"Most of my Comic Sans nightmares happen at three in the morning, too."

Sasha could feel Kinsey's eyes on her face, though she still couldn't look at her.

For a few breaths, neither of them spoke. Then Kinsey reached out and took the glass out of Sasha's hands. "All right, hon," she said briskly, laying a hand on Sasha's elbow to usher her back to bed. "Lie down."

Sasha planted her feet, a childish fear of finding that dream again if she got back in bed making her freeze. "I don't—"

"Lie down." Kinsey leveled a glare at Sasha and pointed a forefinger at her. "Under the covers, please."

"Counteroffer," Sasha said, staring at the tangle of sheets with the same trepidation she might have felt if Kinsey suggested she barrel-roll into a grizzly den. "*You* go back to bed and I'll run laps around the parking lot until the sun comes up."

"No deal." Kinsey walked between their beds and set the water on the nightstand. "Bed, Deforest." The stubborn set of her jaw softened when Sasha didn't move. "I won't let the outdated typefaces get you, I promise."

Sasha swallowed and tugged at the corner of the sheets. Stalling.

This was stupid. She was an adult. She shouldn't be this freaked out over a meaningless dream.

She yanked the bedding straight with her teeth clenched and slid her legs under the covers, folding them under her. "There. I'm in bed. Now you can go back to sleep in good conscience."

"That's sitting." Kinsey put her hands on her hips. "This isn't going to work if you don't cooperate."

"*What* isn't going to work?" Sasha asked, gripping the edge of the sheets with one hand. She wasn't sure she liked that defiant look in Kinsey's eye.

"I only know of two ways to get rid of bad dreams. And since you don't want to talk about it, then we'll have to try plan B."

Sasha's mouth went dry. "Which is what?"

Kinsey gave her a hard little look as inscrutable as a bird's. "Cuddling."

Sasha gaped, but before she could work out if she was joking, Kinsey shut off the light.

"Did you just say—"

"Shut up or you'll make it awkward," Kinsey said, climbing under the covers.

Not joking, then.

"Kinsey," Sasha began weakly.

"It's not weird," Kinsey insisted, despite all evidence to the contrary. She was wriggling around as though fighting to pull her shirt down, they'd never shared a bed before, and Sasha was afraid to move in case she lost her reason and did something really, really stupid. This was all *kinds* of weird.

"Kins—"

"It's what you do when you're little and you have a bad dream, right?" Kinsey plowed on. "You climb into your parents' bed for cuddles, and the nightmares don't come back because you know they're going to keep you safe. Will you lie down already?"

"Kinsey, *stop*," Sasha snapped, shoving the covers off and pushing her back against the headboard. No one kept Sasha safe but herself. It had always been like that, and it always would be. Cuddling her crush in her bed in the dark wasn't going to change anything, so why pretend? "I can't—I can't—"

Kinsey switched the light on. Sasha wished she'd left it off, so she wouldn't have to see the hurt on her face as she slipped her glasses back on. "Can't what?"

"I—" Sasha pressed her fingers against her too-hot cheeks, gaze on her knees as she tried to find the words that would explain the impossibility without ruining everything. "Look, I don't want to fuck up our friendship, but—but I need you to quit doing this affectionate shit. You can't tell me you like me, and not be upset when I wake you up at three in the morning, and say I frigging *matter*—"

"You don't want me to be nice to you?" Kinsey asked, her lip pulling up in confusion.

"*No*," Sasha said, spreading her hands in an empty, helpless kind of shrug. "No, Kins, I don't. I *know* you don't like me the same way I like you. And normally that's okay, because that's just what I do. There's some glitch in my brain where the only people I ever like are people who I have zero chance with. And it's fine. Whatever. I'm used to it. But when you start doing things like— like acting like you're gonna kiss me, or climbing into bed with me . . . I mean, it makes me think maybe you—maybe—" She let out a small sound, burying her face in her hands. *Shut up, Deforest, you're making it worse.* "I'm sorry. I know you're trying to help, but it's—it's—"

"Sasha." Kinsey shifted closer and circled her fingers around Sasha's wrists, drawing them away from her face.

Sasha tensed, hands curling into loose fists. She was caught between the need to get as far away from Kinsey as she could and the sharp hunger for more. It paralyzed her.

Kinsey searched her face, her brow pinched. "What if . . . What if I *wanted* to kiss you?"

Christ. Sasha had thought it was painful when her clumsy attempts at seduction were shot down one after another. This, though. This was so much worse. Every scrap of affection Kinsey threw her way didn't ease the hunger, it just tore her apart.

She withdrew her wrists from Kinsey's fingers and hugged herself. "Don't," she whispered, her voice rough. "Please don't lie to me right now."

"I'm not—" Kinsey huffed, scrubbing her own arm, gaze on the wall. Then she straightened her shoulders, lifting her chin as she leveled a stubborn glare at Sasha. "Okay. Cards on the table? I'm a jerk."

It was a statement so out of left field, Sasha's mind went blank. "No you're not."

"Yes I am. I'm not good at talking about things, and sometimes I'm cruel when I don't mean to be, and you could do a *lot* better than me. But I do so like you. I think about kissing you all the time. And jerk that I am, I hate the idea of you kissing anyone else."

Sasha shook her head, afraid of letting that speech seep in. She had to have misunderstood. Or misheard.

Kinsey touched the back of Sasha's hand tentatively, her eyes big and direct behind her glasses, brow pinched. "I like you, Sasha. A lot. A whole damn lot. Clearly I'm shit at showing it, but it's true. I want to kiss you. I want to be with you. And I've just been too scared to say anything, because . . . because I don't want to get in the way of you finding someone less . . . terrible."

It was like Sasha had slipped into one of her daydreams. Everything Kinsey said was so at odds with what Sasha thought she knew, she didn't know how to process it. But when Sasha reached out and brushed Kinsey's cheek, soft and cautious, her skin was warm and real under her fingers. And she was watching Sasha with this careful earnestness in her warm, dark eyes. Sasha didn't know how, but she seemed to mean everything she'd said.

"You're not a jerk," Sasha murmured. "You're not terrible. You're smart and creative and . . . and gorgeous. And under that cranky shell of yours, you've got such a big heart. There's no such thing as better than you. Even if there was, I wouldn't want her."

"Not even if she was always cheerful and liked paintball and wrote you sonnets every day?" Kinsey asked, searching Sasha's eyes as though she really expected her to say *oh, dang, you're right. I take it back.*

Sasha shook her head, canting towards Kinsey instinctively. "She still wouldn't be you, Kins."

Kinsey's lips parted and she drew in a breath as though to speak. But she didn't say anything. She leaned into the last small space between them and brushed her lips against Sasha's.

It barely counted as a kiss, it was so careful—they could have set it aside as a fluke, a mistake. But something in Sasha broke apart under that gentle pressure. All her careful control, all her sturdy walls, came crashing to the ground. And she didn't even care.

She let out a sound like she'd had the wind knocked out of her and pushed her fingers into Kinsey's hair, drawing her close, kissing her until she couldn't breathe.

She was dimly aware she was kissing too hard, going too fast, but she couldn't make herself slow down. She'd been hurting too much for too long. Pretending it didn't matter if she had to keep everything she felt hidden from view. Trying to make herself believe it didn't bother her to feel so alone. She was desperate to try to fill up at least a small portion of her hurting, empty heart. To fully express at least one of those things she'd kept buried so deep for so long. No matter the consequences.

But Kinsey, bless her, didn't try to stop it. Her kisses seemed almost as urgent as she climbed into Sasha's lap, melding their bodies together, even as her fingers caressed Sasha's shoulders, quiet and soothing. Her curves were warm and soft under Sasha's fingers. Kissing her was better than anything she could have imagined. Because this Kinsey—the real Kinsey—touched her, too. Played her like a song, seeming to take pleasure in every sound she could coax out of her, every shiver and groan.

"Kins," Sasha begged, her fingers digging into Kinsey's hips. "Tell me to stop." They'd already blown past the line they'd held for so long, and she couldn't think clearly enough to figure out where the new boundaries were. She knew it was too much to ask for, but she wanted as much of Kinsey as she was willing to give. Not just tonight, but forever.

Kinsey pressed a kiss to the corner of Sasha's mouth. "I don't want you to stop," she murmured in her ear. "Do you?"

"Hell, no," Sasha breathed. She brought Kinsey's mouth back to hers for a long kiss. Then she rolled them both back on the bed.

Kinsey was beautiful, laid out under her like this. Her black hair spread out like a halo, eyes half-lidded behind her glasses. She always looked different without the '40s bombshell makeup. Not younger, really. Not even vulnerable. Just . . . softer. More open. Kinsey could've taken on the world single-handedly no matter what she was wearing, but like this . . . Sasha couldn't explain it. It made her feel like Kinsey wouldn't mind if Sasha was there to back her up.

It was too much.

"Sasha?" Kinsey asked, tugging at the edge of Sasha's shirt. "What're you waiting for?"

She couldn't answer. There was so much she wanted to say, but she didn't know how. No words existed that were big enough to express everything in her heart. *Don't disappear. Tell me I matter.*

I love you.

I'm scared.

"This is usually the part where I wake up," she finally managed.

She thought she'd done a reasonably good job of keeping the grit out of her voice, but something in the way Kinsey looked at her changed, as though she'd heard it anyway. Sasha felt her shoulders tense, bracing for the pushback she'd grown to expect if she ever let her feelings through.

But Kinsey's fingers were gentle as she cradled Sasha's face between her hands, and there was no anger in her eyes. "It's okay," she said. "It's okay, hon. We can slow down. We've got time."

Sasha swallowed against the tight feeling in her throat. The way Kinsey touched her, the heady things she said, the fact that they were tangled up together in bed in the middle of the night—it was overwhelming. She couldn't absorb it all. It was easier to duck her head and press a slow kiss to Kinsey's jaw. That didn't require much thinking.

Kinsey sighed and turned her mouth to Sasha's again, pulling her in as they kissed, slow and deep. Sasha's shoulders began to relax as Kinsey's hands stroked her back, and her racing mind eased off the gas as they slowly explored each other's mouths.

They were both breathless when Sasha finally made herself pull back, feeling it was cruel to both of them to continue if she was still too nervous to do anything more. But she couldn't make herself go far. She rested her forehead against Kinsey's, sharing the same air, not wanting to break the connection just yet.

"My god, Sasha," Kinsey breathed in a voice like a purr. Her fingers trailed up and down Sasha's side lazily. "Where'd you learn to kiss like that?"

Sasha smiled and pushed herself up on her elbows to get a better look at Kinsey's face. Her eyes were soft and hazy behind her crooked glasses. Sasha gingerly adjusted them so they were no longer askew, letting her thumb linger along the plane of Kinsey's cheek. It still seemed incomprehensible that she'd allow it. That instead of an eye roll or a frown, Sasha was given a contented sigh and a final, sweet kiss.

"So does that mean we're still . . . we're still good?" Sasha asked, searching Kinsey's eyes. "You and me?"

"Yeah," Kinsey said, frowning. "Of course. What, you think I'd make out with you for half an hour and then ditch you the next second?"

"No," Sasha said, rolling onto her back and staring at the ceiling. She took a deep breath and looked at Kinsey sideways. "Maybe. Just a little."

Kinsey propped herself up on her elbow to look Sasha in the eye. "Well, I'm not gonna. Okay? I like you. You're thoughtful and sweet and . . . and don't let this go to your head, but you're a phenomenal kisser. I mean . . . my god."

Sasha snorted, her ears warming. "You're not so bad yourself." She grazed the back of her fingers over Kinsey's wrist, after all that, too shy to meet her eyes.

Kinsey caught her fingers and threaded them with her own, a little miracle.

"You're lovely," Kinsey said, gazing down at her like she meant it. "Just . . . lovely."

"Don't say things like that," Sasha said, offering a crooked smile so Kinsey wouldn't take her too seriously. "I'm having a hard enough time believing this is really happening without adding a whole other layer of compliment-based surrealism to the mix."

Kinsey glared. "You're lovely and you matter and I care about you," she said. "People being nice to you shouldn't be surreal, Sasha. I might be blunt and cranky, but I like you and I'm going to tell you so. And you're just going to have to deal with it."

Sasha didn't know what to say to that. She didn't want to destroy this fragile happiness because she couldn't get a grip on her own feelings. She tugged on Kinsey's hand until she lay down, head on Sasha's shoulder. Kinsey was here, and real, and she said she liked her. Maybe that was enough.

"Can I ask you a favor?" Sasha ventured, cautiously running a strand of Kinsey's hair through her fingers.

Kinsey tilted her head up to press a warm, reassuring kiss under Sasha's ear. "Anything."

She shut her eyes tight, so scared to ask for more, so afraid to be alone. "Stay," she whispered. "Until I fall asleep. Just this once."

Kinsey gathered her up, holding her close. Keeping her safe. "I'm not going anywhere, hon."

FIFTEEN

The first thing Kinsey noticed as she found her way to wakefulness the next morning was the warm, foreign weight on her shoulder. The second thing was that the skin under her fingers wasn't her own. Blearily, she reached for the bedside table and slid her glasses on, moving slowly so she wouldn't disturb Sasha.

From the quality of the light peeking around the curtains, it must be early still. At least by Kinsey's standards. It was probably late for the early bird folded under her arm, but Kinsey made no move to wake her. Sasha should have a chance to sleep in for once. Get a little reprieve from the stress she wouldn't talk about, while she still seemed untroubled by bad dreams.

The two of them had sprawled out during the night, though they were almost as tangled now as they'd begun. Sasha's head was tucked against Kinsey's shoulder, one hand resting against her ribs under her rucked-up shirt. Their legs were tangled under the covers, ankles hooked together. Sasha looked so peaceful, so lovely. It was enough to melt anyone's heart.

Kinsey wanted to hold onto this moment for as long as she could. She didn't know the next time she'd get a chance to admire Sasha like this without making her feel like she had to deflect the attention with a series of self-deprecating jokes.

Gently, Kinsey moved a few rogue strands of hair out of Sasha's face. Whatever anxieties had followed her into dreaming last night seemed to have lifted. That tension Kinsey had noticed after they came back from dinner had eased from her features. The fan of her pale eyelashes was delicate and graceful. Kinsey could count every last one of the tiny freckles scattered across her nose and cheeks.

She caught herself tracing the curve of Sasha's browbone with her gaze and bit her lip, a little warning voice in her head telling her she was being too sappy again. Who laid around in bed obsessing over the beauty of an eye socket?

But Sasha was just so . . . lovely. It wasn't just that blue-eyed blonde, traditional-western-beauty-standard thing she had going on. It was the way she threw her heart into whatever she was doing. The way she took pains to make people feel comfortable and included. The way her whole being lit up when she was happy. It was everything about her. From her eyebrows right down to her shining, lovely soul.

Not that Sasha would hear it if Kinsey tried to say as much.

Kinsey wasn't sure how it had taken her so long to notice Sasha's aversion to compliments. Maybe it had been because Kinsey didn't offer them very often. And when she did, they were usually buried in the middle of a grumpy threat, which made them easy to dismiss.

She was determined to do better from now on. She wasn't going to make a mess of this relationship. She couldn't.

Not that she was entirely sure how to go about keeping that resolution.

Sasha stirred, drawing Kinsey closer as she inhaled, and Kinsey's heart trilled in response. Sasha's thumb moved against her ribs and she paused, eyes fluttering open. She tilted her face to meet Kinsey's gaze, confusion creating a thin line of tension in her forehead, her shoulders stiffening under Kinsey's hand.

"Morning," Kinsey said, trying to keep the nerves out of her voice, careful not to tighten her hold on Sasha. She didn't want her to have a delayed freak-out and bolt just because Kinsey couldn't work out how to handle the situation gracefully.

"You're still here," Sasha said, her voice raspy with sleep.

"Still here," Kinsey agreed in a tone that was so matter-of-fact it was almost curt. Yikes. *Dial it back, Kinsey, you want her to trust you.* "Why? Did you want me to leave?"

Sasha didn't seem upset by the complete lack of seduction in Kinsey's voice. If anything, she relaxed. "No," she said. "I'm just... I'm . . ." She brushed her thumb over Kinsey's ribs again, leaving a ripple of gooseflesh in its wake. "So you're—You're good? You're not freaking out? Or having second thoughts or . . . I mean, this is a strange city, and you're under a lot of stress because of your mom, so I'd—I'd get it, if—"

That was quite enough of that. Giving up any idea she may have had of pretending she didn't have morning breath for the next few weeks, Kinsey pressed a hard, sure kiss against Sasha's mouth.

Sasha tensed, but only for a moment. She made a soft, relieved sound in her throat, sliding her palm down Kinsey's side to rest against her hip as she returned the kiss.

"No freaking out," Kinsey said, holding Sasha's gaze. "No second thoughts. Screw that strange city stuff. I'm in this if you are."

For a moment, Sasha had that same anxious, vulnerable, waiting-to-be-hurt expression from last night. "Really?"

"Really," Kinsey said with as much conviction as she could muster. She might be struggling to capture the kindness and warmth she wanted to show, but she was stubborn. Maybe if she dug her heels in often enough, she could hold them together by sheer force of will.

"Okay." Closing her eyes, Sasha took a long breath and nestled closer. "What time is it?"

Kinsey briefly considered saying *fuck the time* and trying to convince Sasha to stay in bed for another hour or three. But it was still a long drive back to New York, and Sasha would have to get up early tomorrow. And Kinsey's dad was going to want to head to the hospital soon. She had probably kept Sasha to herself for too long already.

She fumbled for the nearest phone and tapped it awake one-handed. It happened to be Sasha's, and Kinsey noted with a flash of irritation that the lock screen gave no indication of any missed calls or messages—seemed like her mom still hadn't called Sasha back. Kinsey pushed the irritation aside, reluctant to bring up a reason for Sasha to start stressing herself out again.

"Just after nine," she reported, slipping the phone back onto the table. "You'll probably want to get going soon, huh?"

Sasha creaked out a groan of protest. "No. But I should."

"Five more minutes, then," Kinsey said, wrapping Sasha in a tight hug, face buried in her hair.

She felt Sasha smile against her collarbone as her arm looped around Kinsey's waist. "Aren't I cutting off your circulation?"

"I don't mind."

"You will pretty soon."

"Wanna bet?" Kinsey challenged.

Sasha chuckled. "Against you? Never." She kissed Kinsey's throat before rolling onto her back and stretching her arms out in front of her. "Are you sure you're okay catching a ride back home with your parents? I can stay awhile longer."

"No you can't." Kinsey resisted the urge to nuzzle under Sasha's arm. Instead, she sat up, pushing her glasses up her nose. "First practice of the season, bright and early tomorrow morning. You have to be there."

"Yeah, I guess so." Sasha sighed, dragging herself out of bed and padding over to the dresser. Her movements slowed as she opened the zipper on her bag. For a moment she didn't move. Then she set her shoulders the way she might if she was about to kick off an important play and crossed back to Kinsey, lifting her chin with gentle fingers. "I'm in this too, by the way," she said, her eyes big and blue and more vulnerable than seemed possible. "I'm not the best at being genuine, but I like you like crazy. I want this to work."

"Then we'll make it work," Kinsey said, like it was that easy. One decision made in a hotel room miles from home and they'd be together forever.

"You say that now," Sasha replied, a thin smile pulling at her lips even though her eyes were sad. "You haven't discovered my fatal flaw yet."

"I don't believe you have one," Kinsey said firmly. "We've known each other a long time, and the only negative thing I can think of to say about you is you suck at taking compliments."

That earned her a sheepish but sparkling grin. "I can work on that." Sasha pressed a kiss to Kinsey's forehead. "I should get ready. Stick around to see me off?"

"Doy."

Smiling, Sasha hesitated another moment, as though she was trying to decide whether to say something more. Kinsey held her breath, waiting, but Sasha only kissed her lightly and went back to her bag.

It didn't take long before Sasha was showered and packed and ready to head out. Kinsey checked the room thoroughly three or four times to stall the inevitable, but it was no use. Sasha had done an excellent job packing up most of her things the night before, and even if she *had* missed something, Kinsey could just bring it with her when she followed in another day or so.

"I wish we could go back together," Kinsey said, giving Sasha a long hug. Enjoying the fact that Sasha actually returned the embrace for once, if still somewhat gingerly.

"Me too," Sasha said, giving her a gentle squeeze before drawing back. "But you need to be here for your mom. I'll be okay. And hey, as soon as you get home we'll go out and eat or something."

"Like a date?" Kinsey asked, a little thrill of anticipation fluttering around her ribcage.

Sasha chuckled, her gaze flicking shyly to the carpet. "Like a real, live, genuine date." She paused at the door, slinging the heavier of her two bags over her shoulder, keys secure in one hand. "I'll miss you," she said, her ears turning ever-so-slightly pink.

"Not as much as I'll miss you," Kinsey said, joining Sasha at the entrance and pulling her in for one last kiss.

Sasha's hand spread over her back as she returned the kiss, quiet and slow. Little bubbles spread under Kinsey's skin with that touch until she fizzled all over.

"I'll call you when I get in," Sasha promised in a low voice, fingers lingering on Kinsey's waist. "Let me know if you need anything. Moral support, someone to vent to . . . anything. Okay?"

"Back at you, Deforest. I mean it." Kinsey caught Sasha's fingers and gave them a tight squeeze. She didn't want her to go.

This kissing thing was so new. And it felt so fragile. She knew it was silly, but part of her was worried whether it would last if they wouldn't see each other again for a few days.

She gave herself a mental shake and reluctantly released Sasha's hand. "Drive safe, hon."

"You got it, babe," Sasha said with a grin and a quick salute. She scooped up the last bag and with one final smile over her shoulder, she was gone.

SIXTEEN

Sasha had to pull into a small gas station after only an hour or so on the road. Two of the six pumps were out of order, but Sasha just circled cheerfully around until she found one that worked. As she stood by her van, watching the numbers tick away the gallons, she caught herself whistling along to a pop song blaring through the overhang speakers and checked herself with a laugh. She just couldn't seem to stop smiling.

It was like she'd tumbled into a different plane of existence overnight. Like she'd traded places with a Sasha Deforest who didn't worry about her mom being AWOL, and who didn't feel guilty for not worrying, and who could kiss Kinsey whenever she wanted. A Sasha who had everything she wanted right in front of her.

Even the weather was perfect this morning. Clear and bright, with spring softening the sharp edges of once-naked trees, clouds big and high and fluffy, and a pleasant nip in the green-smelling air.

The whole morning was almost too good to be true. This kind of feeling might have normally made her nervous. Like she was caught in the kind of fairy-tale thinking that made her more prone to mistakes. More prone to getting hurt.

But Sasha wasn't a lonely, powerless sixteen-year-old anymore, head filled with baseless dreams and her heart exposed. She had learned to take care of herself since then. To protect herself. She'd learned how to handle her mother's drama without letting it affect her life as acutely. She wasn't going to forget herself and dump too much information on Kinsey's shoulders too fast. Which meant she didn't have to worry what Kinsey would do with that information.

And just then, she couldn't truly believe Kinsey *would* push her away, even if Sasha slipped up. Not after the way she held her last night. Not when the image of Kinsey's stubborn frown this morning was so fresh in Sasha's memory. *I'm in this if you are.*

A smile played across Sasha's face as she popped into the convenience store to grab a water and something to snack on. She loved the way Kinsey scowled whenever she was being earnest. She loved her bossy confidence, and she loved when it gave way to a brief moment of fluster at the oddest provocation. Sasha was more than just half in love with her now. Sometime between leaving New York and sharing a bed last night, Sasha had fallen head-over-heels, no-holds-barred, irrevocably in love. And for once she wasn't worried about whether her feelings would make things too complicated between them, or whether she was opening herself up to getting hurt. She was in love with a girl who seemed to be falling for her, too. And who had been her closest friend for nearly a year. How could that possibly be a bad thing?

She tossed her newly-purchased pack of donuts in the passenger seat when she climbed back in the car, and checked her phone. Kinsey had texted her while she was inside with an update: Mrs.

Han was just waiting for the okay from one last doctor, which was expected by the end of the day. They were planning to stay one more night and then follow Sasha to New York the next morning.

I'm glad, Sasha replied, grinning at her screen. **Mostly because your mom is better. Partly because that means I get to make out with you again soon.**

It was a strange little thrill when Kinsey replied with a handful of winking kissing emojis instead of the eye roll emoji Sasha half expected. She told Kinsey she was getting back on the road and couldn't reply to anything else until she stopped for lunch, ending the message with a few kissing emojis of her own.

She started up a playlist Kinsey had made her last summer and was twisting around to reverse out of her parking spot when the music faded to let her ringtone through. She turned back to look at the screen and froze with her hand on the passenger headrest. She didn't recognize the number, but it looked like the same area code as her mother's motel in Arizona. An anxious pang made her smile falter as reality pushed back against her fairy-tale cheer.

She had *just* made some kind of peace with the idea that she wasn't going to know what was going on with Cynthia again until the news made its way back through the family grapevine. And she wasn't sure she was prepared to get wrapped up in another crisis right now.

But what if her mom was in real trouble this time? Sasha might be the only person who her mom believed would be willing to throw her a lifeline. It was her responsibility to pick up the phone and try to help.

Wasn't it?

"Fuck," Sasha muttered with no small amount of guilt. Clenching her teeth, she threw the gear into park and snatched her phone off its dashboard mount. "Hello?"

"Hey, baby girl," Cynthia said brightly. "How are you?"

Sasha bit her tongue as irritation flared in her chest. It didn't sound like her mom was in trouble at all. It sounded like she pictured herself calling Sasha up from a tropical vacation instead of whatever lowlife party she seemed to be at. There was some kind of action movie rat-a-tatting in the background, mixed with the rowdy chatter of the inebriated.

A male voice that sounded closer to Cynthia than the others said something Sasha couldn't decipher. Cynthia giggled in response. "Shut up," she said in a too-loud whisper. "Sasha, baby, listen—"

"Where have you been?" Sasha interrupted, more bite in her tone than she wanted. "You were supposed to call me back two days ago." She knew, distantly, that she wouldn't be able to get her mom to listen if she could hear Sasha's impatience. But she was struggling to remember why it was so important to make her listen.

"What?" Cynthia asked. "Oh. Yeah. Sorry, I forgot. Listen, baby girl, I need to ask you a favor."

"A favor," Sasha repeated. She clenched her fingers around the phone, fighting to find her usual patience. "A favor, after you call me high in the middle of the night, stranded in the desert because you decided it was unreasonable for Aunt Rosemary to ask you not to keep joints in the house when two of her kids are in high school. A favor, after you worry me sick for *days* because you couldn't even bother to call me when you got to the damn motel."

"I forgot, Sasha," Cynthia said, in the closest approximation of a mom-voice she'd ever been able to manage. "Give me a break."

"How could you *forget*?" The words rushed out of her like pressurized steam. She didn't care about convincing her mom to go home anymore. The only thing she wanted was for Cynthia to understand how much it hurt when she broke her promises. "I've spent the last two days worried you'd *died*, Ma. I've been killing myself trying to find out what happened to you. I asked you—you *promised*—to call me so I knew you were safe. Just one simple thing I wanted you to do for me. One tiny phone call so I wouldn't have to worry. And all you have to say for yourself is you *forgot?*"

"Fuckin hell," Cynthia said. "I said I was sorry, didn't I? It wasn't on purpose or anything. You know I'm not great at remembering things like that."

"You promised," Sasha said, her throat tight. "You *promised*, Ma." She didn't know how else to make Cynthia understand this mattered. It wasn't just this promise she was upset about. It was every promise Cynthia had made since Sasha was a kid. Promises to get clean, promises to be a better mom, promises that their shitty lives would improve just as soon as this or that or the other. Every one of them broken the moment they came out of Cynthia's mouth. Just *once*, Sasha wanted her to take a little bit of responsibility. To understand how those broken promises affected the people around her. To feel some kind of remorse, however small.

"I don't know why you're getting so worked up about it," Cynthia grumbled. "It's not like you're fuckin daughter of the year with how often you call me. When was the last time you called just to say hello?"

It felt like a door slamming in her face. And the worst part was, it wasn't surprising. This was what happened when Sasha tried to make her mother hear her. When she made herself vulnerable and said how she really felt instead of hiding behind a mask of patience and detachment. Cynthia got defensive and lashed out, twisting reality until she was back in her comfortable position as the tragic victim. It was stupid of Sasha to expect anything else.

"Yeah," she said, gathering sarcasm around her like it could stop her from caring. "Sure. It's my fault. My fault you never answer your phone, my fault you're fucking high all the time—"

"That's enough, Sasha Marie," Cynthia said, flexing her poor imitation of a mom-voice again. "I'm your mother and I won't have you talk to me like that."

Sasha let out a wild laugh. It was either that or cry, and she didn't want to give Cynthia the satisfaction. "Seriously? You want to play the mom card *now*? What exactly was this favor you needed again? Party running out of steam, is it? You were hoping I'd fund another pot-and-booze run for your shitty new friends?"

"It's not for that," Cynthia said, sounding like a petulant teen. "I'm almost out of money for food. You want your mother to starve?"

Someone—sounded like the same man Cynthia had shushed before—stifled a laugh. There was a light whacking sound, as though Cynthia had smacked him to shut him up.

"I already sent you two hundred bucks, Ma. That was supposed to be enough to get you home."

"Oh, come on, Sasha. Who cares what it's for? It's not like you'll miss it, the way you hoard cash."

Sasha raked her hair back from her forehead, digging her nails into her scalp. Cynthia couldn't even be bothered to lie anymore. Couldn't even invent a plausible emergency when petitioning her daughter for drug money.

And why should she? Sasha had never told her no before. She'd always been too scared. Because what if something happened to her? What if she really didn't have enough money to eat? What if this was the one time she committed to getting clean and sober? What if Sasha put her foot down and it made Cynthia so mad she did something stupid? Got herself arrested again? What if she overdosed and it was Sasha's fault?

She'd given Cynthia money—even when she didn't feel good about it—because there was always that hope in the back of her mind that she'd listen this time. Get help. Get clean. Start taking responsibility.

But dammit, Sasha was so tired of being the parent. Cynthia was supposed to be the one looking out for Sasha, not the other way around. And instead her mom was treating her like a bank. The easiest person to manipulate into giving her money with no repercussions. Because Sasha was the last idiot clinging to the idea that one day Cynthia would transform into a good, reasonable, loving person.

"No," she said softly.

There was a short pause, punctuated by a burst of drunken jeering in the background. "What was that, baby girl?"

"I'm not sending you any more money, Ma." Sasha expected her voice to waver, the words to hurt. But she just felt flat. Numb. "The money I wired you earlier was supposed to get you home. I told you that. If you spent it on something else, then . . . then I guess that's your problem."

"Sasha," Cynthia said, sounding baffled. She offered a nervous laugh. "Come on. You can't be serious."

"Yeah, Ma. I'm serious. I won't be your bank anymore. I can't. I *can't.*"

There was a short, tense silence. "Well fuck you, too," Cynthia snapped. And with a loud click, the line went dead.

Sasha stared at the screen for a long moment, chest tight. For the last twenty-one years, she'd been holding onto the idea that there was a clean, sober Cynthia under the addict. A Cynthia who wasn't so unpredictable, who could be reasonable and responsible when she had to be. A Cynthia whose addiction didn't always win out over her love for her daughter. She used to cling to those rare moments of fun and affection with her mom as proof that *somewhere,* deep in Cynthia's soul, she was at least *trying* to show she loved Sasha.

But all those excuses . . . They weren't working anymore. Every happy memory she had with her mom was tainted by the selfishness and illogical whims of an addict. A surprise trip to the coast had been more about spiting Sasha's gran than mother-daughter bonding. Extravagant dinners out were always followed by weeks of canned veggies and instant noodles from food banks and local churches. Proud promises to come to all of Sasha's games were quickly forgotten, while Sasha scrambled to find rides with cousins and friends just so she wouldn't miss too many practices.

Sasha dropped her phone in her lap and braced her shaking hands against the steering wheel. She wanted to keep believing Cynthia could change. She wanted it more than anything.

But she couldn't. Those last few words before she hung up had carried more truth than any of her promises. If her mom had ever loved her, it was pushed down so deep it almost didn't matter. And Sasha couldn't keep on pretending otherwise.

Sasha waited for the pain to hit, for her heart to break. It seemed earth-shattering, to come to the conclusion your mom didn't love you. But she only felt hollowed out. Like she'd known for a long time and simply hadn't accepted it.

Of course she'd known. She'd just been too weak to admit it to herself. She'd spent her childhood scrambling to pick up the slack so no one would realize their lives weren't as normal as everyone else's. And the only thanks Cynthia ever gave her was to keep depending on Sasha to fix the things Cynthia set out to break.

With trembling fingers, Sasha fumbled her way to Kinsey's number. Kinsey had said to tell her if she needed anything. And just now there was nothing Sasha needed more than to hear a friendly voice.

She didn't pick up. The phone rang a few times and then went to voicemail.

A recording of Kinsey's voice told her brusquely to leave a message. But Sasha didn't know what she wanted to say. Or what she wanted Kinsey to do. She shouldn't have called—

The beep sounded in her ear before she could persuade herself to hang up. "Uh. Hey, Kins. Um . . ." She cleared her throat, trying to remove the rasp from her words. "Sorry. It's not important or anything. I just . . ." But she couldn't explain. She didn't know how. She was too upset to lay it all out in a way that wouldn't make it sound like she was being too sensitive.

And what the hell was she doing, trying to dump some stupid fight on Kinsey's shoulders when she should be allowed to focus on supporting her parents? She knew how important it was to Kinsey to be there for them right now. The last thing Sasha wanted was to get in the way of that.

"Never mind," Sasha muttered, blinking away the sting of tears. "It's nothing. You just take care of your mom. I'll . . . I'll talk to you later."

She hung up and watched the blank screen of her phone, wishing Kinsey would call her back, afraid to answer if she did.

But it didn't matter. Kinsey was busy. She wasn't going to call. No point dwelling on it. No point dwelling on any of it.

So what if Cynthia didn't give a shit about her? Sasha had already proved she didn't need her mom to survive. That was how she was riding a full scholarship to NYU; by not letting her mother dictate her life's trajectory.

Sasha sucked in a breath and cranked the music up to drown out her thoughts. One fight wasn't going to make her crumble. She was stone. She was iron. She didn't need anyone.

Least of all her mother.

"Get it together, Deforest," she muttered, slamming the gearshift into reverse.

It took a while before Kinsey had a chance to call Sasha back. Right after Sasha had texted that she was getting back on the road, a doctor had come in to say that he was clearing Annette to go home. Kinsey and her dad were still double- and triple-checking that it wouldn't be a health hazard to drive home the next day when Kinsey's phone rang. She had silenced it quickly, assuming Sasha had called her by mistake. She didn't realize Sasha had left a message until almost an hour later, when she was following her parents back to the car, her mom's overnight bag slung over her shoulder.

She slowed, letting her parents pull ahead as she listened to the message. A pit settled in her stomach the moment it began. Sasha's voice had none of the blushing joy that had been there when she left this morning. She sounded like she was trying not to cry.

Ignoring Sasha's insistence that whatever made her leave the message wasn't important, Kinsey called back immediately. If something was making her cry, it was important. Sasha hardly ever cried.

It went to voicemail after a few rings. Sasha had never texted while driving in her life, but she didn't usually mind calls, so long as she had her hands free. Maybe traffic was just really hairy at the moment?

"Hey," Kinsey said after the beep. "I only just got your message. We checked my mom out of the hospital, so we're heading out to get lunch and then we'll probably go back to the hotel. But you can call me whenever, okay?"

"Kinsey?" Henry raised a hand from beside the car up ahead in a kind of shrug that was family sign language for *what's going on?*

Kinsey made an undefined flapping motion with one hand. "I gotta go. But seriously, call me whenever. I promise I'll pick up next time. And I'll see you tomorrow night." She wanted to say more, but she didn't know what. *Don't cry* seemed too bossy, even if she didn't mean it like that, and *love you* was too frightening. "Drive safe, hon" was the best she could do. Hanging up, she slipped her phone into her purse and hurried to catch up to her parents.

"Everything okay?" Annette asked with a smile, touching Kinsey's shoulder as she joined them.

"Fine," Kinsey said, careful to keep her voice light. "Just . . . Just a lead on a freelance gig. Nothing serious."

Annette nodded, though there was something in her expression that made Kinsey think she didn't buy the story. Kinsey wasn't entirely sure why she didn't tell her the truth. Both her parents liked Sasha. It wasn't anything like when Kinsey had brought Evie home. She just didn't know how to tell her parents about her and Sasha when it already felt like things between the two of them were deteriorating. After less than a day of them getting together.

Kinsey tossed the overnight bag in the trunk as her parents got into the car. She'd just have to check up on Sasha later, once she had a few seconds alone. And maybe that would be enough to convince Sasha that Kinsey wanted to help with whatever was stressing her out like this.

She hoped it would be enough.

SEVENTEEN

Two of Sasha's suitemates were sitting on the couch in front of the TV when she pushed through the door that night.

"Hey, Sasha. Good weekend?" one of them asked, still absorbed in whatever she was scrolling through on her phone.

"Fine," Sasha said, glad she didn't have to hitch on a smile to prove it. She didn't think she had any smiles left, with that fight with Cynthia still playing through her head. She didn't know whether she more needed a shower or to just crash on the first softish, mostly-horizontal surface she could find.

She wrestled her bags into her empty room—her roomie must be out—laid eyes on her bed, and decided she was too tired to shower. After brushing her teeth and changing into a shirt and pajama pants that didn't have that gritty travel smell, she fell into bed. She stared blankly at the ceiling, fighting to keep her breathing even, battling the crush of bad memories which had been pushing in on her since that conversation with Cynthia: Searching the stands for her mom even though she knew she wouldn't be there. Dreading coming home from school because she never knew whether her mom would be in a bad mood. The dozens of times she'd been forced to apologize for some imagined slight because she knew digging her heels in only meant getting into blow-out arguments.

Even when Cynthia wasn't around, Sasha could never escape the responsibility of taking care of her. Her time at school was a bizarre combination of distancing herself from her mother and lying to cover for her. She tended to stay on the fringes of her friend groups, not wanting anyone to get close enough to see the cracks in the facade.

Pressure was building behind her eyes, pricking the back of her nose. She made herself take a long, slow breath, counting it out to the rhythm of her heartbeat.

She didn't understand why she couldn't just . . . pull it together. This wasn't the first time she and Cynthia had argued. Compared to some of their screaming matches when Sasha was in high school, one little *fuck you* should've hardly registered.

Her phone chimed on her bedside table, and Sasha reluctantly checked the screen, guilt tugging at her conscience when she saw it was another text from Kinsey.

Hey. Just got back to the hotel. I'm alone if you want to talk 🖤

Sasha dropped the phone on her chest, teeth clenched. She had been struggling all day to seem like the normal, cheerful Sasha who had left Kinsey at the hotel this morning. She couldn't bring herself to pick up the phone when Kinsey had called her about the voicemail, and she'd been careful to just text at lunch and dinner. It was easier to pretend she was okay if she had a few extra seconds to craft a reply and didn't have to worry about her voice giving her away.

Though from the cautious tone of Kinsey's texts, she'd noticed something was wrong anyway.

Sasha didn't know what to tell her. She couldn't admit she'd had a fight with her mom. Kinsey may have offered to let Sasha vent, but . . . Sasha didn't want to put her heavy, confused feelings on Kinsey's shoulders.

She couldn't. Every time she thought about it, she just remembered the summer she turned sixteen, and she couldn't go through with it.

Summers were almost always rough at home, and that year had been no exception. Cynthia was on one of her downward spirals and kept picking fights over trivialities. Sasha couldn't even escape to Trevor's place for a break from the pressure because he was away at culinary school. She had gotten a job at a department store until school started again, half so she had an excuse to be out of the house, partly with the idea of saving up to buy a car so she wouldn't be dependent on rides and a semi-rural bus system to get her where she needed to be.

She'd only been working there for a few weeks when Madison started in the same department. Madison was a couple years older with these stunning brown eyes and a bubbly laugh. And— maybe best of all—she knew nothing about Cynthia's reputation, meaning she treated Sasha just like anyone else.

It took no time at all before Sasha found herself nursing an awful crush. Made all the worse when Madison started playfully flirting with her whenever they crossed paths. Pretty soon, Sasha's shifts at the department store with Madison were the only things keeping her sane.

Then Madison had kissed her at the bus stop one night in the balmy July air. And it had seemed like a fairy tale. Finally her princess had found her. Finally she would be swept out of the messy parts of her life into a life where she didn't have to fight so hard every day. Finally she'd have space to be happy and healthy. Before she could think better of it, Sasha's head had been filled with daydreams. Of getting out. Of happily-ever-afters. Of never looking back.

Until one miserable, hot day two weeks later when Sasha discovered that her mother had spent the money for the electric bill on drugs. Again. And she expected Sasha to use her measly savings to get the power turned back on. Which meant no car. Which meant being stuck begging for rides to soccer practice for another year. Right when it was most important that Sasha make every last practice so she could get the hell out of Wyoming.

Sasha had been so angry, she didn't even care when the screaming began in record time. She was so sick of it. The lying. The manipulation. Being asked to solve all these stupid problems that she shouldn't even be thinking about yet. She couldn't stand being under the same roof as her mother anymore.

So she took off for Madison's.

Sasha had barely waited for Madison to invite her inside before she was unloading every horrible moment of her summer in an unstoppable rush. All her frustration, all her anger, all her ruined hopes.

She knew almost as soon as she'd started her rant that she'd miscalculated. She'd been so desperate for a fairy tale, she'd let herself become completely deluded. The wide-eyed look Madison gave her as the truth tumbled out was one of poorly concealed horror, deepening by the second.

And why wouldn't she be horrified? Madison had been after an easy summer fling with the cheerful, unruffled Sasha she knew from work. Not a difficult romance with some kicked puppy of a kid who dissolved into tears in her living room over her screwed-up mother.

Madison had been polite when Sasha finally ground herself to a halt. But it was clear the damage had already been done. Her voice was cool as she suggested Sasha would see things differently once she'd calmed down. Her smile was distant and flat. There were none of the ready assurances Sasha had half expected. None of the fairy-tale solutions she'd hoped for. Just one more person who flinched when Sasha tried to open her heart to them.

Sasha had left a few minutes later, too hollowed out to even feel hurt by Madison's obvious relief. She hadn't been surprised at her next shift when she discovered Madison had left the department store for another job. Or when Madison never contacted her again. After all, Madison hadn't been the first person who glimpsed the parts of Sasha's life she usually kept hidden and decided she wasn't worth the trouble.

Sasha scrubbed her hands over her face, frustrated that the memory still upset her. What did it matter if she got her heart broken when she was sixteen? That was years ago. Get the fuck over it.

She just . . . she didn't know how to talk to Kinsey when all she could think about was that stupid mistake with Madison. And that stupid fight with her mother this morning. And she was so scared that, even if she could articulate everything she was feeling in a calm, reasonable way, Kinsey would equate the fight to the argument she'd had with her own parents and try to persuade Sasha to be the better person. Find some kind of compromise.

Sasha didn't have any compromises left in her. Because with Cynthia, *compromise* was nothing more than Sasha shutting her mouth and letting everything she wanted or needed get trampled. And for what? It had never made Cynthia take responsibility. It had never made her listen. It had only ever given her more and more leeway to do whatever she wanted, regardless of what it was doing to anyone else.

But how could Sasha possibly explain that to someone like Kinsey? Someone who thought expecting your parents to protect you from nightmares—or anything else—was a universal experience? Someone that tough and perfect?

Even if she could explain it . . . she didn't want to make another miscalculation. She couldn't handle that. Not now. Not after that perfect kiss. Not when there was still a chance—if she could just get her feelings under control—that they could actually make this relationship work.

If she could've been sure the guilt wouldn't eat away at her all night, she might've given up trying to talk to Kinsey at all. She was too emotional. Too raw. But she'd promised to call when she got in. Actually talking was out of the question when she was so close to breaking, but she had to say *something*.

Taking another deep breath, she wrote out a text haltingly, each letter a struggle: **Hey. I got in a few minutes ago. All in one piece. Pretty tired tho. Call you tomorrow?**

She watched the little dots on Kinsey's side of the screen appear and disappear for a few seconds, rubbing her forehead with two fingers, not sure how Kinsey would take the change of plans. Sasha knew she was in dangerous territory. Kinsey already seemed suspicious, and Sasha was doing a piss-poor job of keeping her walls up, even over text—

Sure, hon, Kinsey replied. **Everything okay?**

The screen blurred as tears filled Sasha's eyes. "Dammit," she whispered, shoving them away. She almost wished Kinsey's reply had been prickly and brusque. That Kinsey would sound annoyed at her for being weird all day. That simple, understanding question made Sasha want to call her after all and spill everything. *Everything.* That awful argument, the stress of worrying about her mom all the time, the hundreds of little digs and disappointments

that had torn her to pieces until she was only holding herself together with sarcasm and willpower.

She wanted to believe Kinsey was different, that she wouldn't
be so easily scared off by Sasha's troubles. But experience had
taught Sasha to keep her troubles to herself. And it wasn't a lesson
that was easily unlearned. Especially after she'd had such a stark
refresher this morning. If her own mother couldn't hear her, why
should Sasha expect anyone else to?

I'm fine, she managed. **Just tired.**

**I'm not surprised. You've been running through my mind all
day** 😊😊😊😊😊

Sasha let out a startled bark of laughter through the tears. **omg**

I know I know, Kinsey wrote. **Kill me now.**

It was beautiful, Sasha replied. **Truly.**

Sasha didn't know how Kinsey could tell she needed a laugh,
but she loved her for it. More fiercely than she thought possible.

Hating how robotic her texts had looked all day, and still
wishing she could find the courage to tell Kinsey everything—no
matter how risky—she added, **I miss you.**

I miss you too 🤍🤍🤍 **I'm coming home as soon as I can.**

Sasha replied with a lone heart, not knowing what else she
could say. She was too wrung out. Too defeated. She just wanted
to crawl through the phone and curl up next to Kinsey. Feel the
reassurance of her embrace, breathe in her familiar, homey scent.
No explanations. No struggling to find words. Just quiet comfort.

I'm holding you to your promise when I get back, you know,
Kinsey wrote.

Which promise?

Real live date, remember? I've got a place in mind already.

Sasha smiled softly. She could almost see Kinsey's no-nonsense expression, hear the crisp tone of her voice. **Of course you do.**

It's going to be the most epic first date in the history of first dates. Prepare to have your socks blown off, Deforest.

I wouldn't expect anything less from you, Han. ♡

♡♡♡♡♡ **Get some sleep. We'll talk tomorrow.**

Okay. Night, Kins. ♡♡

Sweet dreams, nerd 😴

Sasha shut off the light and rolled toward the wall, pressing her phone to her aching chest. Eyes tight shut, she tried to glean some residual comfort from the memory of Kinsey's touch, the feel of her lips. But it felt as distant and surreal as any of her old daydreams. And so much more fragile.

Things would look better in the morning, she told herself. She would have soccer practice and classes to distract her until Kinsey came back. And maybe by then she wouldn't be so bothered about all this stuff with her mom. And they could just move past it without needing to talk about any of it.

Maybe it was wishful thinking, but it was the only thing keeping her from falling apart. So she dragged the idea around her like a blanket, hiding herself from the world until she fell into an uneasy sleep.

The hotel room seemed too big without Sasha's sparkling laugh to fill it up. Kinsey sat on the bed with her legs crossed, staring at the place where Sasha had slept only last night, wishing she was that close again. It was so much easier to read her when Kinsey could watch her body language or note the subtle shifts in the tone of her voice.

That voicemail from this morning still bothered her. So did the way Sasha had pretty much refused to acknowledge anything was wrong since then. And the reserved, careful wording of her texts. There was none of that playful undercurrent Kinsey was used to. Barely any of the friendly teasing and sarcasm that typically flavored their conversations. And that *I miss you* sitting alone in the middle of the screen read like a plea for help that Kinsey didn't know how to answer.

She bit her lip as she scrolled back to this morning and read through the texts between them again, worried this had all started because of something she'd said. It wasn't unheard of for Kinsey to be unintentionally hurtful. But she couldn't find anything that seemed like a real problem. She'd technically threatened Sasha once, but only as part of a demand for her to arrive safely in New York. And Sasha had replied with a *roger that* and a thumbs-up. So that probably wasn't it. Right?

She wished Sasha had called so she could hear her voice, know for sure that everything was okay. She wished she had another car so she could drive to her right now. Kinsey wasn't strictly needed here anymore. Her mom had displayed no signs of a relapse since they left the hospital this morning, and Henry could probably handle the drive back home himself.

Though Annette wasn't exactly following doctors' orders to take it easy as closely as her husband and daughter would have liked. It was only by Kinsey bullying her mom into sitting back down with forceful distractions that Henry had been able to pack without interference this afternoon. Kinsey couldn't imagine her mom would be any less eager to overextend herself tomorrow. Sasha's schedule on Mondays was packed, too, so Kinsey probably wouldn't be able to talk to her properly until almost dinner time anyway. And even if Kinsey had access to a second vehicle, she wouldn't want to stress her parents out more by up and leaving for New York in the middle of the night. Especially when *this girl I like is acting weird and I need to go talk to her* sounded an awful lot like the excuses she used to make for Evie.

It wasn't the same, she told herself firmly.

But that didn't mean she'd be able to explain the difference to her parents.

"I hate this," Kinsey grumbled, dropping her phone on the mattress. She couldn't help fretting that Sasha was only acting like this because of her. It wasn't like Sasha to be this withdrawn. And the only difference Kinsey could see between today and yesterday—when Sasha had at least been able to talk to her normally, even if she sometimes dodged a topic or two—was that kiss.

But Sasha had looked so sure when she said all those things about not wanting anyone else. And she'd seemed genuinely worried this morning when she thought Kinsey might want to backpedal out of the relationship. And the way she'd held Kinsey last night, the way she drew kisses from her like she'd never get enough—like nothing else mattered . . . Kinsey hadn't imagined that. She was sure of it.

So what happened?

Maybe Kinsey had pushed things too far too soon last night. Maybe she shouldn't have started that kiss. Or at least hadn't tried to rip Sasha's clothes off immediately. No wonder Sasha had tried to attribute the whole thing to Kinsey being stressed out. If Kinsey had just stopped for two seconds to *think* about what she was doing . . .

She pushed her glasses into her hair and scrubbed her hands over her face. Why was she so bad at this?

She needed perspective. Beatrice was usually good at that. Picking up her phone, she switched over to Beatrice's number and wrote, **Are you still awake?**

As she waited for a reply, she returned to scrutinizing Sasha's texts. As though a new message might have appeared since the last time she looked at them, explaining exactly what she needed to do to fix this—

I'm awake, Beatrice wrote.

Thank god. **How early do you have to be up tomorrow?**

I don't. Got the day off. Why? Wanna talk?

Are you free right now?

Kinsey's phone jingled two seconds later. "Hey, Kins," Beatrice said brightly when Kinsey answered. There was music playing quietly in the background. Kinsey thought it might have been Fleetwood Mac. "How are you holding up?"

"I don't know. Okay." Kinsey chewed on her lip, not sure where to start. The last time they'd talked about Sasha, Kinsey had been pretty adamant about *not* going for it. She wasn't entirely sure how to account for the change in attitude.

Most of her brief exchanges with Beatrice for the past few days had been health updates about her mom. She might as well start there. "Um . . . My mom's doing a lot better. She got discharged this afternoon."

"Hey, that's great! Is she gonna be able to travel soon?"

"Yeah," Kinsey said. "We should be back in New York tomorrow night."

"That's a relief."

"Yeah." Kinsey picked at a thread in the hotel bed's coverlet, thinking of Sasha, alone and unwilling to talk. Thinking of that lonely *I miss you* she didn't know how to fix—

"Okay, what's the catch?" Beatrice asked.

Kinsey grimaced, her face warming. "What do you mean?" she hedged.

"You just sound awfully morose for someone delivering good news. Which means something's up. So what's up?"

Sometimes Beatrice was just too damn perceptive. For a second, Kinsey considered coming up with something else to talk about. But she'd called because she felt lost. She couldn't fix that unless she explained what the problem was. So she dragged in a deep breath, thought *screw it*, and blurted, "SashaandImadeout."

There was a full second of silence. "*What?*" Beatrice squeaked.

"We made out," Kinsey said on a groan. "Last night. It just kind of . . . happened."

"Does that mean you're together?"

"Yes?"

Beatrice squealed. "I'm so happy for you two!"

"We kissed, Bee. It's not like we're getting married. I don't—" Her throat closed against voicing the fear, but she made herself say it anyway. "I don't know if we're going to make it to next week."

"Why not?" Beatrice asked, her pitch falling to something closer to normal. "You've always been great together."

"I don't know, I'm just . . ." Kinsey pressed the palm of her hand against her forehead. "I feel like . . . like I'm missing something. Like when you leave the house and you're sure you left something behind but you can't remember what it is. Except it's not a thing it's . . . it's the reason this is going to fall apart."

"Okay, but . . . that sounds like nerves to me. You were kind of blindsided when you and Evie broke up last year. I wouldn't be surprised if that was making you a little paranoid."

Kinsey wanted her to be right—that the only reason she was seeing all these potential problems was so she couldn't be surprised when Sasha decided to leave her for someone better. But Beatrice hadn't heard Sasha's voicemail this morning. Or witnessed the change in her attitude since.

"You don't know it's nerves," Kinsey said, hoping her anxiety was sufficiently masked by her dry tone. "Maybe I'm precognitive now."

Beatrice snorted, but from the sturdy conviction of her reply, she wasn't fooled for a second. "You're not precognitive. And unless you two had a fight you haven't told me about, I'm pretty sure you're just scared about starting something new with someone you really care about."

"I just don't want to screw up," Kinsey said desperately. "And I feel like something's wrong. Sasha's been stressed out about some family thing all weekend and she keeps dodging the topic when I try to ask her about it."

"Maybe she didn't want to add to your stress while you were visiting your mom?" Beatrice suggested.

"Maybe. But she left me this voicemail earlier today where she seemed kind of . . . I don't know. Not herself. And she said she was going to call me when she got home tonight, but she texted instead. And she's been evasive about what's wrong all day. And I can't tell if it's just her family stuff, or if she's second-guessing wanting to be together, or if she's tired, or if—if I did something wrong and she doesn't want to tell me—"

"Or she's scared, too."

Kinsey's heart fell. "Because she doesn't want to be with me?"

"No," Beatrice said patiently. "Because falling in love is scary. Because believing someone else when they say they care about you is scary. Because you made a big change to your relationship and you don't know what's going to happen yet. It's perfectly reasonable you might both be worried about screwing up. It doesn't necessarily mean you *will*."

"I guess." Kinsey rubbed her eyes, trying to let Beatrice's confidence carry through the phone and bolster Kinsey's flagging optimism. But she couldn't help laying out all the evidence contradicting her best friend's reasoning. The only relationship she'd ever had which she *hadn't* royally screwed up was her friendship with Beatrice. Which seemed more like a fluke than anything. And probably had more to do with Beatrice's insistence on seeing the best in people than Kinsey figuring out how to play nice.

"I just don't want to screw up," she said again, voice tight. "I don't think I could handle it if . . . if . . ." She blew out a breath, annoyed at herself for stammering. "I can't do another breakup, Bee. Not with her. I just can't."

"Oh, Kins," Beatrice said sympathetically. The soft music behind her had changed to Janis Joplin singing her soul out in a melody that made Kinsey want to cry.

"For what it's worth," Beatrice said, "I believe in both of you. You're going to work it out. Before you know it, you'll be the most adorable power couple in the tri-state area."

"Really?" Kinsey asked in a small voice.

"Really. You're good together as friends. There's no reason that wouldn't still apply."

"Okay," Kinsey said, hoping Beatrice was right. Wishing Sasha hadn't left without her. She sighed hugely, doing her best to adopt some of Beatrice's positivity and believe there was nothing more to Kinsey's concerns but unrelated paranoia. "If you say so."

EIGHTEEN

In the chaotic bustle of getting out of the hotel before check-out the next morning, Kinsey didn't have time to text Sasha. She'd slept later than she meant to and had to scramble to get ready and pack her own things, skidding to a stop at the front desk to turn in the keycards with about thirty seconds to spare. Outside, she'd been recruited to keep her mom from rearranging the luggage her dad was loading into the trunk. Then she'd been arguing with her dad about which of the two of them should drive the first leg of the trip—both were making cases for why the other needed more rest—and scolding Annette back into the passenger's seat whenever she tried to settle the matter by volunteering herself.

Kinsey won the bid to drive them to breakfast, which was more like brunch by the time they sat down, but was forced to hand over the keys when she couldn't suppress a yawn as they waited for their pancakes. It wasn't until her dad was merging onto the highway forty minutes later that Kinsey had a chance to actually read the text sitting in her notifications since she woke up.

It was the only thing Sasha had written her all day: **Heading out to practice. I'll text you when I can.**

Kinsey glanced at the time in the corner of her screen and frowned. Practice should've ended a few hours ago. But Sasha had back-to-back classes on Mondays—she should be in one of her computer science classes right now—so Kinsey shouldn't be too worried about not hearing anything since.

Though it did seem a *little* weird that Sasha hadn't texted her again when practice let out. Kinsey was used to getting regular updates on soccer practices and games, often told in the same goofy, rambling style Sasha adopted when telling stories about Wyoming. It was unusual for her to not say *anything*.

Maybe she was just feeling shy. Or worrying that Kinsey hadn't replied yet.

Well, they couldn't *both* be flipping out and acting weird. They'd never get anywhere.

Kinsey set her jaw and tapped out a short text saying she and her parents were finally on the road and what time she thought they'd be back. **How was practice?** she added. **Good?**

She couldn't expect an answer until Sasha's next class ended. But she didn't have time to worry about it. Her mom, busy flipping through their radio options, had just discovered an old country ballad that was so twangy, Kinsey and her dad both screamed in horror.

"Mom!" Kinsey protested. "Change the station!"

"Why?" Annette asked innocently, turning it up. "Don't you like it?"

Henry winced as the vocalist perpetrated a flat, nasal slide. "Not particularly, dear, no."

"This is why you're not allowed to emcee the music." Kinsey flicked to a better playlist in her music app. She was thrilled her mom was acting like her old, silly self, of course, but not quite thrilled enough to endure much more of this song. "Switch it over to my phone."

"All right, all right," Annette said as she changed the stereo setting. "I don't know what you two have against a good old country song."

"Nothing at all," Henry said. "But that wasn't a good old anything."

"It sounded like he was singing about beans," Kinsey said, which made her mom giggle.

"Oh my dearest, darling can of beans," Henry sang, imitating the caterwauling with alarming accuracy. *"The finest beans I ever have seen—"*

By now Annette was cackling so hard she was gasping for breath. She swatted at Henry's shoulder, her other arm wrapped around her belly. "Stop making me laugh! I'm going to break a rib!"

"Laughing is good for you," Kinsey said as the beat of Foreigner's "Juke Box Hero" came through the speakers. She'd picked a playlist that was half '60s girl groups and half '80s bops, fairly confident that would keep the whole car happy. "There's an entire cliché about it. Clichés can't be wrong."

"And she didn't want to be a doctor," Henry said dryly.

Kinsey made a face at the back of his head. He was joking, of course. Her grandparents were more prone to fretting about how she'd make money with her graphic design degree than her parents had ever been. And even her grandparents' questioning came from a place of love. They wanted her to succeed so she could have a good life, and they couldn't see a clear way forward if college threw her into the "real world" with nothing but an arts degree.

But Kinsey's parents had always backed her career choices, however crazy they sounded to anyone else. When she'd expressed interest in the arts as a kid, they made sure she had opportunities to explore that further. They encouraged her to take any art or design class she could find, bought her all kinds of books on the subject, accompanied her to a half dozen campuses as she debated where to get her degree. All while keeping up a front of *go get 'em* support that was so constant, Kinsey had never thought to question it. If they harbored any concerns about her success, they'd never let on. Not even during the worst of the Evie crisis. They'd even gotten her grandparents to back off when they occasionally felt the need to hint that Kinsey wasn't as *focused* as they'd like.

"Do you ever wish I *had* gone into medicine?" she asked.

Annette giggled, apparently still tickled by Henry's song. She looked so much more like her normal self, now that she wasn't under the harsh hospital lights. The color was back in her face and her voice didn't sound tired and deflated anymore. "After you nearly fainted in tenth-grade biology when you had to slice open a worm? I don't think you and medicine would get along too well."

"Law, then," Kinsey said. "Or—I don't know—business. Something more practical."

Annette shook her head, turning to meet Kinsey's eyes over her shoulder. "I don't think you'd be very happy trapped in a courtroom or an office, either."

"Graphic design *is* practical for you, Kinsey," Henry said. "If anyone has the gumption to launch their career single-handedly, it's you. As long as you're passionate," he added. "You never got very far with anything you didn't care about."

"That's true," Annette said. "And I don't think you're very pas-sionate about business, are you?"

"No."

Annette held out a palm as though to say *there's your answer.* "You'd probably just run back to your pretty, hand-drawn letters the first chance you got."

"Probably," Kinsey said.

She wondered, though, how Sasha's mom felt about her career choices. Since they met, Sasha had seemed so confident and steady. And talented. Even if you knew nothing about soccer but what you'd skimmed on your phone five minutes before the game, you could tell she had something special going for her. When she stepped on that field, it was *hers*. And she made her whole team better for it. Of *course* NYU had offered her a full-ride scholarship. Of *course* she was captaining the team to better rankings than they'd had in years. It seemed impossible that anyone would have ever questioned her.

But Sasha also had a tendency to be almost *too* humble about her skill. She rarely talked about what she hoped to accomplish after college. Kinsey never doubted that Sasha was good enough to make any pro team she set her heart on, but the way Sasha talked, it almost seemed like she expected her soccer career to end as soon as she graduated. Which might have been a symptom of not having enough support at home. No one to turn to if she was worried about going in the wrong direction who could say *yes, you're on the right track, I believe in you.* No one to catch her if she fell. To kiss the bruises and help her back on her feet.

Kinsey checked her phone as her mom turned up the volume to better sing along with Bonnie Tyler, half hoping Sasha had texted her back, even though she probably hadn't seen the message yet.

Nothing new. Which shouldn't be troubling, since Kinsey was pretty sure Sasha wouldn't have another free moment until her lunch break. Still . . .

Is everything okay? she started to type. But she got only a few letters in before deleting the text. There was still a good chance she was reading too much into Sasha's lack of communication because of some kind of unresolved angst about the split with Evie last year. She'd probably get an entire rundown of the morning once Sasha sat down to lunch. *Be cool.*

She started and deleted two more texts—**You'll call me at lunch, right?** and **Just say hi or something so I know you're alive**—but they looked too brusque even to Kinsey. She slumped in her seat, watching the shapes of half-naked trees flash against rolling, white clouds.

There was no question that Sasha made Kinsey happy. She just wasn't so sure she was the kind of person who could make Sasha happy. And Kinsey didn't know whether Sasha would speak up if something was wrong. Sasha was quick to come to the defense of her friends, but she sometimes acted like she'd lost the motivation to stick up for herself.

Setting her teeth, Kinsey wrote out another text and hit send before she could lose her nerve. **You already know this, but I like you. And I miss you. Just in case you were wondering** 🩶

She locked her phone once the message had been delivered and tried to turn her attention to whatever her parents were talking about. Sasha would text her soon.

And even if she didn't, Kinsey would be home by tonight. It was only a few more hours. Surely they could both hang on until then.

NINETEEN

Morning had done fuck-all for Sasha's outlook on life. She'd woken up with an unsettled, restless feeling in her stomach and a sharp knife of pain at the base of her skull. What little sleep she'd managed to get was peppered with bad dreams that lurked in the corners of her mind like predawn mist, even after she got outside into the bracing, cold air.

Running plays with the team should have been enough to clear her head. She'd always been drawn to the chaotic order of a game. The quantifiable measures of success. There was no room for guilt when all she had to do to fix a mistake was run the play again until she got it right. No room for second-guessing herself when the only objective was to get the ball into the goal. No room for troubled relationships when her only function was to be one piece of a complicated machine.

But she hadn't been able to get her head in the game. She was unfocused and irritable and she kept screwing up—overshooting simple passes, losing track of the ball at the worst moments—which was screwing everyone else up, too. The team kept giving her these *what's with you* looks that made her feel like a freak. It was a relief when Coach finally sent them back in to shower, chanting an unconvincing *we'll work on it* as they filed past.

Sasha avoided talking to anyone as she changed into her street clothes. She used to be better at keeping up a bright, cheery facade no matter what. So what if she was fighting with her mom? What else was new? Get a frigging grip.

She was fumbling the last of her things out of her locker, trying to focus on her breathing so she wouldn't succumb to the full-on meltdown pressing in on her chest, when Nova caught up to her.

"Okay, look." Nova leaned a shoulder against the locker next to Sasha's. Her hair was slicked into a neat bun except for a few dark whisps curling along her hairline. "We're all entitled to bad days every now and then. Even you. It's not the end of the world."

Sasha clamped her teeth together, pretending she hadn't heard. Better to block everyone out now and apologize later than lose what little control she had left and get herself delegated the team charity case. She grabbed her wallet and keys and slammed the locker shut before stalking toward the exit.

"Hey, wait up," Nova said, hurrying after her. "What's with the mood, Deforest?"

"It's nothing." Sasha pushed through the locker-room door onto the sidewalk, flinching when the wind hit her face, dragging at her hair, pushing its chill under her collar and up her sleeves.

"It's gotta be *something*," Nova insisted, hitching her bag higher on her shoulder as she fell into step with Sasha. "First you blow off the pickup game, then you bail on drinks, then I find out you weren't even *home* all weekend—"

"Who told you that?" Sasha demanded, coming up short as she lobbed a glare at Nova.

Nova's eyes narrowed as she studied Sasha's face. "I stopped by your dorm after the pickup game to see if you wanted to get something to eat with me and some of the girls. Your roommate said you'd taken off. Didn't expect you back until last night."

"So?"

Strangely, Nova smiled. As though she was in on a secret. "So why didn't you just say you'd met someone when I called? I wasn't going to be weird about you shacking up with a cute girl for a few days. That was the whole point of taking you out, wasn't it? So you could meet someone you like."

"I didn't meet anyone." Sasha buried her hands deep in her pockets and started to walk away. "I had an emergency thing. Out of town."

She didn't get far before Nova grabbed her sleeve and pulled her to a stop. "Emergency thing?" The levity in Nova's expression had vanished. "What kind of emergency?"

"A personal one. It's dealt with."

"A Kinsey emergency?" Nova guessed, the corners of her mouth turning down in disapproval.

Sasha yanked her arm out of Nova's grip as pain pierced her skull again. "Yes, Nova. A Kinsey emergency. Is that a problem?"

"I thought we talked about this," Nova said, lowering her voice. "How is shooting your social life in the foot to help her every time she bats her eyelids supposed to get you over her?"

"Maybe I don't *want* to get over her," Sasha snapped, her own voice rising. She didn't care that she couldn't keep a lid on her emotions anymore. It was only a matter of time until this happened, right? Until she lost control and everything she'd built for herself fell apart. Might as well get it over with. "You can stand there and glower and tell me it's doomed all you want. It's not going to change anything. I like her. I care about her. If she needs me to help with a family emergency at the expense of a freaking pickup game, then I'm going to freaking help her. So get the hell off my back about it."

Nova scoffed, drawing herself up to her full height, shoulders squared. "Excuse me for having the nerve to want you to be with someone who doesn't make you this defensive and crazy."

"Yeah," Sasha bit out. "Thanks for the support, buddy. I really appreciate all the high-and-mighty lectures."

"Whatever, Sasha." Nova flipped a dismissive hand as she strode away. "You want to trail after some girl like a puppy for the rest of your life, you go right ahead. See if I care."

Sasha choked back another retort as a half dozen of her teammates burst out of the locker room door in a cloud of laughter. Threading her fingers behind the spike of pain in her skull, Sasha marched off. Away from Nova, away from her head-splittingly giggly teammates, away from everything.

But *everything* was so much harder to escape when she was smack in the center of New York City. There were people everywhere. Swarming in and out of subway stations, blaring their car horns, crowded into cafés and shops and apartments clear up to the sky.

A little voice in the back of her mind kept telling her to text Kinsey again. But the thought of faking a good mood for her just made Sasha feel penned in. Every time she'd interacted with anybody since she left Charlotte, it had gone wrong. She couldn't imagine she and Kinsey wouldn't end up arguing too. Kinsey already seemed impatient that Sasha wasn't being open enough. And Sasha had lost her ability to play everything off like it didn't matter.

She just couldn't get enough space to figure herself out. To shake off all the negativity buzzing in her head and make sure her walls were securely in place. She was a lousy soccer player, an irritable friend, a neglectful, evasive girlfriend . . . And she couldn't get that last argument with her mom out of her head. No matter how hard she tried to think about something—*anything*—else, it just kept going in a miserable, guilt-ridden loop.

I don't know why you're getting so worked up about it.

It's not like you're fuckin daughter of the year.

Well fuck you, too.

Sasha tried to throw herself into her classes to escape it. But the packed classrooms didn't ease her sense of being penned in. Her professors and classmates kept giving her strange looks too. Like the apocalypse had come upon them all because Sasha couldn't smile through a shitty day.

She'd never wanted so badly to just . . . be someone else. Get out of her own head for a few hours so she didn't have to *think* so much.

Which was how she found herself walking into Winnie's that evening. The interior of the bar was too warm. It smelled like spilled beer and the decades-stale smoke clinging to the ancient wallpaper and upholstery. Students milled around the hightops and jostled each other next to the pinball machines in the back. All the booths were taken and there were only a few stools left at the counter. Students' shouts and laughter nearly drowned out the pop music coming in through the speakers.

Sasha set her shoulders and wove her way to the less packed end of the bar. She'd been hoping Winnie's would be quieter on a Monday night. Though given how the rest of her day was going, the crowd seemed about right.

Maybe it would be better this way. She could fade into the background, just one insignificant body among the throng. As long as she could get her hands on a damn drink, what did it even matter?

"What can I get you?" the bartender asked once she'd managed to catch his attention.

"Just—Just give me whatever's on tap." Sasha rubbed the painful spot at the base of her skull. "And a shot of the strongest, cheapest stuff you got."

The bartender stared at her for a moment, like even *he* thought she was acting weird. And she couldn't possibly be the first emotional college student to ever order alcohol.

"I'm twenty-one," Sasha said impatiently, slipping her wallet out of her pocket and showing him her ID.

He scrutinized it before shrugging and handing it back. "Coming up."

Cynthia's voice pushed through the din as the bartender moved to the nearest tap: *Well fuck you, too.*

Pressure was building behind Sasha's eyes. She covered her face with her hands, trying to will it away. It wasn't like she *expected* her mom to care about her. Most of Sasha's life, she'd had to look out for herself. She just—She'd always thought she'd grow into the enormous responsibility that was taking care of Cynthia. That one day she'd wake up and realize the crushing weight had become something . . . manageable. Something she could handle.

But it never got lighter or easier. It was crippling her. Every time Cynthia called, she shoveled on another responsibility, another obligation, until Sasha folded. Until she was pinned to the ground, ribs cracking, scrabbling for a way out before it crushed her.

And still there was part of her that wanted to put her shoulder to it and try again. Even though she knew she didn't have the strength anymore. If she ever did.

For some reason she saw Kinsey's face behind her eyelids, a familiar, stubborn frown on her face. *You're lovely and you matter and I care about you.*

Sasha's throat closed. It wasn't true. She didn't believe Kinsey was lying. She was just . . . wrong. Kinsey didn't see the desperate, lonely wraith shivering in the depths of Sasha's heart. She didn't see all the aching, empty space Sasha hid behind smiles and sarcasm. Whoever she was talking about when she said those words was as imaginary as any of Sasha's daydreams.

"Beer and a shot of tequila," the bartender said, sliding the pair in front of Sasha, along with a slice of lime on a plate.

"Thanks," Sasha muttered.

The guy hesitated for a moment, then produced a bowl of pretzel rods from under the bar. He set the bowl in front of Sasha before walking down the bar to take another order, oblivious to the glare she aimed at his back.

Her gaze fell to the two glasses in front of her. Nothing else she'd tried all day had been able to shut her brain off. And she needed to shut down fast, before Kinsey came home and Sasha ruined everything.

She held her breath and threw the shot back before she could talk herself out of it. She nearly coughed it right back up. It tasted like nail polish remover and dirt.

"Fuck," she wheezed, grabbing the lime slice, which at least got the worst of the chemical taste off her tongue. She could feel the effects of the alcohol already, crawling into her skull and along her shoulders. Maybe it wouldn't take her as long to get drunk as she'd thought. And since she didn't recognize anyone in the bar, she wouldn't have to worry about people judging her or asking her a lot of questions she didn't have the strength or humor to answer right now.

"Hey, Deforest!"

Sasha inwardly cursed her bad luck as Viv Collins wedged herself into the space next to her stool, fingers linked with the sorority girl Sasha had seen her talking to last week.

Viv flashed her dimples with cheerful arrogance. "Since when do you hang out at Winnie's?"

Sasha dragged the beer closer. Why couldn't she get five minutes to herself? "What do you want, Viv?"

"We're meeting up with some of Rosalie's friends," Viv said brightly. "Just thought we'd come over and say hi. Have you met my girlfriend Rosalie?" Viv beamed as she tugged her date closer and looped an arm around her waist. She didn't wait for an answer before going on. "Rosalie, this is our captain Sasha Deforest."

"Hi," Rosalie said, smiling shyly.

"Hey," Sasha said, throwing a perfunctory wave in her direction. It was all she could do not to bark at the both of them to leave her the hell alone.

"You wanna come sit with us?" Viv asked, still glowing. "You can save me being the odd jock out."

"As *fun* as talking you up to your girlfriend's friends sounds," Sasha said acidly, "I think I'll pass."

Viv blinked, smile vanishing, like she'd only just realized something was off. Then she turned her dimples on Rosalie. "I'll grab us drinks if you want to save me a seat."

Sasha gulped down a few swallows of her beer, pretending not to notice their parting kiss. She really didn't need this right now. Viv "Casual Relationship" Collins being all bubbly and excited about having a girlfriend when Sasha was pretty sure she'd already ruined her relationship with Kinsey by refusing to answer her texts all day. She hadn't even been able to look at them. She'd already fought with too many people today. And she couldn't handle losing Kinsey too, just because she couldn't pull herself together.

"What are you so grouchy about anyway?" Viv asked, leaning against the bar as Rosalie disappeared into the crowd. "You aren't seriously still moping about practice this morning, are you? So we sucked. We always suck first day back." She brightened, showing off her dimples with a sly grin. "Remember last year, when Joy

Danvers had to go to the health center because she nearly knocked herself out running full-tilt into the goalpost?"

"I thought you were ordering drinks for your girlfriend," Sasha snapped.

Viv pursed her lips, a little furrow appearing between her eyebrows. "Are you here by yourself?"

"What if I am?" Sasha took another long draft of beer. It didn't taste as bad as the tequila. It took longer to travel to her brain, though. And neither drink was doing anything to ease her headache. If anything, it was getting worse.

Viv was still frowning at her, but there was this . . . uncertain vulnerability in her eyes. As though Sasha had let her down unexpectedly. "Listen," she said, "just come sit with us. You shouldn't drink alone. That's like . . . Girl Drinking Code 101."

"Butt out, Viv," Sasha said, not bothering to keep the bite out of her voice.

Viv's eyes narrowed, but she turned away to get the bartender's attention. She didn't say anything when Sasha asked for another shot after Viv had ordered a couple of cocktails. She only gave Sasha a long, worried look which she ignored.

Viv braced her palms against the bartop when the drinks arrived, drumming her fingers on the lacquered surface. Then she pointed to a booth in the corner. "We're over there if you change your mind, okay?"

"I won't," Sasha said, and downed the tequila.

Shaking her head, Viv took her drinks and walked away.

Everything Sasha knew about drinking had led her to believe it was something you did when you wanted to stop your thoughts from spinning. It was supposed to numb you. Or at least make you care less. It was supposed to turn you into somebody else.

But all two shots of tequila and a beer had done so far was trap her. The piercing headache she'd had all day was worse than ever.

Her body felt weird in a way she didn't care for. All her worries and insecurities pressed closer than before. She barely had enough self-control left to stop herself from blubbering into her beer.

No crying, Deforest. No fucking crying.

She thought she heard her phone chime and fumbled it out of her pocket. Another text from Kinsey. Something about how far from home she was.

Sasha swiped away the notification before she could read it properly. She just couldn't handle it. It was too much pressure. Kinsey might be angry at her for not replying, but it still seemed better than letting her see what a wreck Sasha had become since yesterday morning.

She found herself navigating to Trevor's number. He'd be at work by now, busy getting dinner service rolling. He wouldn't be able to reply for hours. But he was the only person who might still be in her corner if she couldn't find a way to get herself together.

She didn't know how to say *don't leave me* without sounding crazy. So instead she wrote, **If I quit school forever and turned up on your doorstep, could I crash on your couch?**

The answer came sooner than she'd expected. She'd barely set the phone down when the screen lit up again with his reply. **My couch was MADE for cousins to crash on. Crisis or no.** And then a few seconds later: **But you're not going to quit school because you're the best gosh darn soccer player who ever graced US soil. And good soccer players stay in school so pro teams can snatch them up.**

Sasha pressed her lips together, fighting to type out the words with clumsy fingers and blurred vision. **Unless it turns out they suck and nobody wants them.**

You don't suck, Trevor wrote back promptly. **What's wrong, pipsqueak?**

Sasha imagined telling him about how things had ended with Cynthia yesterday. But all she could envision was her own uncertainty and guilt talking back at her. *She's your mom. Don't you want to have a relationship with her?*

She blinked hard, forcing back tears. The whole point of drinking was to make herself stop feeling every little hurt. Dredging them all up via text wouldn't help a damn thing.

It wasn't like Trevor wouldn't listen. But trying to untangle her twisted, conflicted feelings into coherent sentences felt impossible. Breaking down wouldn't change her mom, after all. It wouldn't put her back on solid ground. All it was likely to do was try Trevor's patience.

Just in a mood, she typed. **Bad day.**

She shoved her phone in her pocket before Trevor could answer and ordered another shot. Alcohol wasn't giving her more relief than anything else, but waiting to sober up seemed like an insurmountable problem. She winced as the shot burned its way down, pushed her fingers hard against the sharp pain in her skull as nausea washed over her. Hopefully it meant she'd black out soon.

She used to be *so good* at keeping herself under control. A quick smile here, a little flirting there, and she could fool everyone into thinking she was impervious to wanting anything more complicated than winning the next soccer game.

And then this week . . . It was like she didn't care about keeping herself in check. Managing her expectations. Like she actually thought a few kisses and a smattering of belligerent understanding could save her from the clinging parts of her life which had always held her back.

Stupid. To waste her time yearning for a reality that belonged to someone else. Someone who had her shit figured out. Who wasn't a desperate, needy pit. Who wasn't so delusional she thought a few thousand miles could dissipate the compulsion to manage her mother.

Sasha pressed her hands over her face, hating the crush of bodies around her, the loud blend of music and slamming pinball machines and meaningless conversations. Hating herself for coming here in the first place. She didn't have enough room to move. There was nowhere she could go to escape. What she wouldn't do for a vast, wild forest right now—

"There you are." The voice was familiar, but Sasha couldn't place it.

The room spun as she turned to get a look at the woman perched on the stool beside her. Nova.

Sasha sagged over the bar top, forehead pushed against the heels of her hands. "Come to yell at me more?"

"I don't know yet." Nova picked up Sasha's beer and examined it. "Jesus, Deforest. What happened to you being the self-designated soccer mom?"

Sasha dragged her beer back in front of her. "Piss off, Nova," she said, her words blending together. Her lips and tongue didn't seem to want to operate at the same pace. She gripped the sturdy handle of her beer . . . glass . . . thing . . . and finished it off in two gulps.

"How many of those have you had?" Nova asked.

Sasha held up an index finger. The room hadn't stopped spinning. If anything, the spins were getting tighter. It was taking most of her slipping concentration to keep herself from falling off the barstool.

"Just one?" Nova asked, steadying her with a firm hand on her elbow. "What are you, the world's lightest lightweight?"

"May've been a couple shots too," Sasha muttered, shrugging Nova off.

"Tequila," Viv said, appearing at Nova's shoulder. "Three of 'em since I've been here."

"You called her?" Sasha asked, turning an unsteady glare on Viv, who flinched guiltily.

"She was worried about you," Nova said. "I can't say I blame her. You look wasted."

Sasha held up a different finger.

Nova looked unimpressed. "What are you doing, Sasha? This isn't like you."

"What d'you know 'bout . . . what I'm like?" Sasha asked. The words came out piecemeal, in fits and starts. She hated this. The spinning room. The thick, bristly feeling in her head. Not being able to talk like she wanted to. She didn't sound angry or threatening. She just sounded drunk. She sounded like her mom. "You don' know shit. Why don't you jus' . . get lost and leave me alone?"

Nova's lips thinned, but she seemed to decide to let the jab go. "I think it's time we got you home."

Sasha wanted to object, but mostly for the sake of objecting. She was too tired and miserable to fight anymore. Anything to get out of this shithole and back to her own bed. She scrabbled some cash onto the bar and slid, unsteadily, out of her chair. "Fine. Let's go."

Eyes on her phone, Kinsey dropped her bags by the desk in her room. She must have refreshed the texts between her and Sasha twenty times since her parents dropped her off in front of the dorm a few minutes ago. She'd even resorted to restarting her phone in the elevator, on the off chance that Sasha *had* replied to any of the half-dozen messages Kinsey had sent over the course of the day and it had somehow gotten lost in the ether.

But no new messages appeared, no matter how Kinsey scowled at them.

She'd been half hoping she would meet Sasha in the lobby or find her waiting in the hallway outside Kinsey's apartment, anxious to explain that she'd dropped her phone down a sewer grate or lost it on the bus. Kinsey didn't understand why else Sasha would have gone dead silent.

Unless she'd realized Kinsey wouldn't be any good for her and wanted out.

Kinsey set her phone on her desk and shook out her hands. The easiest thing to do would be to just go upstairs and get Sasha to talk to her face-to-face.

But worry was making Kinsey irritable. She didn't want to start the conversation being prickly and rude before Sasha even got a chance to explain.

Pacing her room wondering if Sasha had already realized she wanted someone better wouldn't help either, though. All in all, she'd rather Sasha tell her now that she'd made a mistake. Then at least Kinsey would know where they stood.

Taking only her phone and keys, Kinsey walked back to the elevators down the hall. Worst that could happen was Sasha's suitemates would say she was asleep and Kinsey would have to wait until morning to talk to her.

She bounced on her toes as the elevator shuddered upward, trying to get rid of some of the frenetic, nervy energy crackling through her. Everything was going to work out fine, she told herself. She just had to be patient. And maybe a little stubborn. Any stray connection her brain was trying to make between checking on Sasha and walking in on Evie sleeping with another girl was nothing but fear talking. Even if Sasha *did* want to break up, she wouldn't try to hurt Kinsey in the process. She wasn't that cruel.

Kinsey puffed out a breath when the elevator doors let her out onto Sasha's floor. Hoping she'd cleared her expression so she didn't look too abrasive, she marched into the hallway—

—and faltered to a stop when she registered the scene that greeted her.

Sasha was standing—swaying, really—in front of her apartment, fumbling with her keys. One of her soccer friends stood at her shoulder, a hand hovering near the small of Sasha's back, as though ready to catch her if she fell.

And no wonder. Sasha looked sort of . . . wilted. Disheveled and upset. Like gravity was dragging her down.

Kinsey didn't know what to make of it. If she didn't know better, she would've thought Sasha was drunk. Which was impossible.

"Just let me," the other woman was saying. Kinsey couldn't recall her name. It was something weird. Celestial. The woman reached for the keys, but Sasha jerked them away, staggering into the doorframe.

"No," Sasha said thickly, pressing her forehead against the door. "I don't need you. Go away." She shoved her key at the lock and lost her grip. The keys hit the floor and Sasha let out a breathy growl that ended in what sounded an awful lot like a sob.

Kinsey's defensive confusion gave way to a kind of pragmatic fix-it mode that she usually only deployed when Beatrice needed someone to drag her out of the tangle of her own lists. "What's going on?" she asked, starting forward to help.

Sasha's friend—Nova, Kinsey finally remembered—looked around first. Her lips thinned. "Nothing. She's fine."

Sasha met Kinsey's eyes for only a split second. Sasha's were rimmed in pink and a faint smudge of mascara. "Fuck," she breathed, sagging against the door with both hands over her face.

Kinsey froze, at a loss for how to proceed. She wanted to bundle Sasha up and keep her safe. Fight off whatever had her this upset. But she wasn't so sure that Sasha hadn't come to this because of *her*.

She took another cautious step forward. "Sasha—"

"She's fine," Nova said, crossing her arms and putting herself between Sasha and Kinsey. "You can go along back home."

Kinsey's fingernails dug into her palms. "She doesn't *look* fine," she snapped. "She looks drunk."

"Yeah. I don't suppose *you* have any idea why she might want to drink herself blind."

"'Cause fate, that's why," Sasha said, before Kinsey could retort. Her voice was so muffled and strained it was barely audible. "'S gravity. You can fight it all you want. You won't win. One day everything's gonna collapse. What's the point trying to stop it?"

Kinsey glanced at Nova, but from the worried look she was giving Sasha, Nova didn't know what she was talking about either.

"Sasha?" Kinsey said, slipping past Nova unchallenged and scooping the keys off the floor. She touched Sasha's sleeve gingerly. "It's okay, hon. Let's just get you inside. You'll feel better once you sleep this off."

Sasha shook her head, but Kinsey didn't know if she was rejecting the help or the idea that sleep would make her feel better. She wouldn't uncover her face, and her breath was coming in uneven gasps.

"I'll help her in if you get the door," Nova said.

"Okay," Kinsey said, thankful for the offer. Even if it was from someone who'd been inexplicably hostile not ten seconds ago.

Kinsey unlocked the front door and held it open while Nova, who was closer to Sasha's height, supported her across the threshold. None of her suitemates were in the common area, which was probably for the best. Kinsey hurried ahead to unlock Sasha's bedroom door and switch on the light.

While Nova took charge of bundling Sasha into bed, Kinsey headed back to the kitchenette, willing herself to stay in fix-it mode. She found a tin of trail mix with Sasha's name written in marker on the lid and grabbed a sports drink from the fridge.

By the time she came back, Sasha was curled in a ball on her bed, both hands pressed against her forehead. She was still wearing her jacket, though Nova must have talked her into removing her shoes. Nova stood by the other bed with her hands on her hips, lips thin, eyes worried. Her eyebrows lowered when Kinsey came in, but she kept her mouth shut.

Kinsey decided to ignore her. Take care of Sasha first, *then* deal with Miss Hostility. She set the trail mix on Sasha's bedside table and cracked open the Gatorade.

"Okay, listen up." She guided one of Sasha's hands away from her face and pressed the bottle into her palm. "You're going to drink this before you go to sleep," she ordered. "No arguments."

Sasha stared up at her, saying nothing, eyes unfocused and bright with unshed tears.

Kinsey touched her overly warm cheek. *It's okay, hon.* "The whole thing. You hear me?"

"Mm-kay," Sasha croaked.

"Okay. You start hydrating. I'll be right back." She pressed Sasha's shoulder and turned back to Nova. "Talk to me outside for a second?"

Nova shrugged. "Fine."

Sasha gripped Kinsey's hand before she could leave. "Kins . . ."

Kinsey squeezed Sasha's fingers, trying to reassure her. She'd never seen Sasha this miserable before, and she didn't know how to reach her, how to protect her from whatever it was that had driven her so far into herself. "I'm coming right back. Don't worry."

"I'm sorry," Sasha whispered, the words cracking apart.

"It's okay. You're okay." Kinsey wished Sasha would talk to her. Let her help. She dropped a kiss on the back of Sasha's hand, not caring if Nova was glowering at her from the doorway. "Just concentrate on finishing that Gatorade. I'll come check on you in a minute."

Kinsey followed Nova into the empty common area, pulling the bedroom door mostly shut behind them. "What happened?" she asked anxiously, keeping her voice low. "Sasha never drinks."

"I am aware," Nova snipped, matching Kinsey's volume. "I *have* known her longer than you."

Kinsey swallowed the first sharp comeback that jumped to her throat. Reaming Nova out might work out some of the worry swirling in her chest, but it wouldn't tell her what happened to Sasha. "I don't know what your problem is with me, but do you think you can put it on hold for five minutes? I just want to help. Same as you."

"Do you?" Nova challenged. "Because from where I'm standing, all you've been doing since you met her is walk all over her."

Kinsey bristled, her fists clenching at her sides. "I'm sorry?"

"You should be. Sasha might be the most genuinely good person I've ever met. And I don't like it when people take advantage of her."

"You think she did this because of *me*?" Kinsey demanded, trying to fend off her uncertainty with more anger. She had thought—if she just tried hard enough—she could turn herself into the kind of person who could make Sasha happy. She had been trying not to think about how Sasha had only seemed to feel worse since they got together. But if Nova had seen it too . . .

Nova put her hands up. "All I know is she never pulled anything like this until she came back from a weekend of dealing with *your* problems."

Kinsey's heart sank, the fight going out of her. "Is that what she said?" she asked, voice flat. "That she was drinking because of something I did?"

"Well, no. She . . ." Nova glanced at the bedroom door, concern clouding out some of her bravado. "I don't know why she was drinking. I wasn't there when she started. First I heard of it was Viv Collins texting me to come pick Sasha up ASAP. Viv didn't know why she was drinking, either. And the most I've been able to get out of Sasha about it is a couple of 'piss offs.'" She tugged on her ear. "Look, I just . . . Sasha's been hung up on you forever. And you put anyone in a situation where they're hung up on someone who's not interested—especially someone like Sasha, who's already so hard on herself—they're going to get hurt. Maybe you just can't see what it's doing to her, but I think it's pretty shitty of you to keep making her hope you might one day change your mind about how you feel about her. Sasha deserves better than that."

"I'm—" Kinsey folded her arms, teeth clenched. "I know. I . . . I'm not leading her on, though. At least . . ."

Nova searched her face, frowning. "You got together over the weekend."

Kinsey nodded miserably. Even Nova believed Kinsey was destroying her relationship with Sasha with her thoughtlessness. And how could Kinsey tell her otherwise, with Sasha curled up on her bed, drunk and near tears, in the next room?

Nova sighed, eyes closed. "She didn't tell me that," she muttered. "All she said was—I don't know. She seemed upset about something this morning, but when I tried to talk to her about it we just got into a spat. About you, actually. It . . . wasn't great. But I didn't think it was bad enough to make her tailspin like this."

Kinsey ran her hands over her face. This wasn't solving anything. If Sasha wasn't talking, the only thing to do was make sure she got to sleep okay. They wouldn't be able to figure anything else out until she was feeling better, anyway. She tried to switch back into fix-it mode. "Do you have soccer tomorrow?"

Nova shook her head. "Next practice is Wednesday."

One less thing to worry about. "I don't like the idea of leaving Sasha here alone. I can stay with her until her roomie shows up. Keep an eye on her. I won't take advantage of her," she added hastily when Nova frowned.

"No, I know." Nova took a deep breath and held Kinsey's gaze. "She really cares about you, you know. And she deserves to be with someone who cares about her just as much."

"I know."

"Just be good to her," Nova said, turning on her heel and making for the door. "You hurt her on purpose, you're gonna have to deal with me."

TWENTY

Sasha hadn't made much progress on the Gatorade when Kinsey slipped back into the room. The sports drink sat on the bedside table next to the untouched trail mix. Sasha was sitting up, but she was pressed into the corner, curled around a pillow, her face buried in the pale yellow cotton.

Kinsey paused by the door, briefly seized by the conviction she was already too late. There had been just one tiny window of opportunity to make things work between them, and Kinsey had screwed it up and missed it.

Irritably, she shoved that idea away and squared her shoulders. "Okay, Sasha," she said, snatching the Gatorade off the bedside table and offering it, stiff-armed, to Sasha. "No more excuses. If you don't get some water or something in your system you're going to feel like shit tomorrow."

"I don't care," Sasha murmured into the pillow.

"Well, I do," Kinsey said stubbornly. "You're gonna take care of yourself, missy, or I'm gonna do it for you."

Sasha only curled up tighter.

The sports drink fell to Kinsey's side. Clearly the brusque order method wasn't working. It was stupid to have tried it.

She perched gingerly on the edge of the mattress, one leg tucked under her, no longer sure if she could do anything to help. The way Sasha was acting, maybe it would've been better to ask Nova to stay with her. Nova was the one who managed to bring her home. And Sasha hadn't seemed so hell-bent on hiding her face before Kinsey turned up.

"Sasha," Kinsey breathed, trying to make her voice softer. She reached out cautiously to touch Sasha's sleeve with the backs of her fingers, hoping to soothe her out of that defensive ball. Sasha didn't flinch from her, at least. "You wanna tell me what happened?"

"Were you not aware I get blackout drunk on Monday nights?"

The sarcastic deflection thing was hardly new, but the dark, miserable tone certainly was. Kinsey didn't understand how this could've happened. She thought they were actually making some progress yesterday morning. That Sasha was starting to believe her when she said she cared about her. And now she was more closed off than ever.

"Sasha. Look at me." Kinsey tugged at the pillow and Sasha let her pull it away from her face.

She was flushed pink from her ears to her nose, and her eyelashes were damp. She wouldn't meet Kinsey's eyes. She kept her gaze lowered as she hid her mouth against her knees.

"Come on, Sasha," Kinsey tried, an edge of desperation slipping into her tone. "Talk to me." She nudged Sasha's knee with the Gatorade until she accepted it. "You never drink. Something must have made you want to start, right? So what was it?"

Sasha scraped her nail over the Gatorade's lid, saying nothing.

"Is it—Is it us?" Kinsey asked, trying to keep the worry out of her voice. She didn't think she was very successful. "Is it me?"

Sasha's eyes snapped up to look at her properly for the first time all evening. "What? No. God, Kins, no. Never. How can you ask that?"

Kinsey puffed out a shallow breath of relief. "Then what is it, hon?"

Sasha wet her lips, blinking hard as her gaze fell to the drink in her hands. She finally took a few sips, though maybe only as an attempt to avoid the subject.

"Sasha," Kinsey whispered. She crawled up beside her, loosely mirroring Sasha's posture, and lightly tucked a stray wisp of wheat-blond hair behind her ear. "Let me help you," she begged. "Tell me what's wrong. Maybe I can do something."

"You can't," Sasha said thickly. A tear escaped and stuttered down her face, unchecked. "Nobody can. It's . . . *dammit,*" she choked out under her breath, dragging her fingers back through her hair. "You want to know what happened? I had a stupid argument with my mom. She wanted me to give her money and when I told her no, she said—" Sasha let out a strangled kind of sob, but only tensed when Kinsey tried instinctively to lay a hand on her shoulder.

"She's a junkie, you know," Sasha said, expression half hidden by the arm she kept between them like a shield. Her voice was choked with tears, but her inflection was strangely hard. As though she wanted to use the words to push Kinsey away. "My mom. Has been, on and off, my whole life. That's why she was asking for money. So she could get high instead of going home."

Kinsey didn't know what to say. She knew Sasha didn't like talking about her mom, but she'd thought . . . She wasn't sure what she thought. Nothing as bad as this.

"People don't know what it's like," Sasha plowed on, seemingly unsurprised by Kinsey's silence. "Trying to keep your family going when you have to fight for every moment of normal. When your family isn't even really a family. And you're pretending so hard to make it look like one anyway." She moved her hand from her hair to cover her eyes and Kinsey realized she was shaking. "I was always supposed to cover for her. Always. Because if I said anything—if I got anyone else involved, I was ratting her out. Ruining our so-called *family* because I was too weak to put up with a little instability."

"Oh, Sasha," Kinsey breathed, putting her arms around Sasha's shoulders and holding her tight. She didn't know what else she could do. She felt so useless. Her family was whole and functioning and unconditionally loving, even at their worst. It sounded like Sasha's family had been none of those things. No wonder she didn't believe Kinsey could help her.

Sasha let out a sob that broke Kinsey's heart. "I can't do it anymore, Kins. I *can't*. Every single thing I ever did was *despite* her. *Despite* all the moving. *Despite* being passed around between my mom and my gran like an ugly houseplant—"

"Stop that," Kinsey said firmly, turning Sasha's face towards her and holding her gaze with all the stubbornness she had in her. "You're not an ugly houseplant. You're a lovely, talented, precious human being. Anyone who doesn't see that can go fuck themselves."

Sasha didn't seem to hear. She searched Kinsey's eyes as though they were living on different planets, as though Kinsey might disappear at any moment. Her fingers traced a shallow curve on the back of Kinsey's hand like a question she couldn't decipher . . .

Then she turned back to her knees, expression blank, body tensing.

"Sasha—" Kinsey began.

"I almost killed her," Sasha said. "My mom. When I was ten."

Kinsey froze, not sure she'd heard Sasha right. "What do you mean?"

"I didn't mean to," Sasha said, her inflection so flat it was almost a monotone. "I was . . . We were living in this shitty trailer on the back of my aunt's ranch, and my mom didn't like that I was up at the house all the time. She used to complain about it every time I came home. Mostly just dumb shit. She'd accuse me of gossiping about her, or she'd get upset because she thought my aunt and uncle were implying she couldn't take care of her own kid because they'd made sandwiches for everyone for lunch. One day she got off on this rant about . . . I don't know. Something about Aunt Rosemary trying to turn me against her. And I couldn't take it anymore. She was shouting all these lies and I *knew* it was stupid, but I couldn't help it. I was so angry. Before I could stop myself I was shouting back that at least Aunt Rosemary never blew the food money on vodka.

"I should've just kept my mouth shut." Sasha pushed tears out of her eyes. "We only ever fought like that when I lost my temper. If I'd just let her get the rant out of her system it would've been fine. She got real mad after I said that. Hauled me outside and got this rusty old pair of wire cutters from the shed. She said if I was going to disrespect her, she was going to make damn sure I wouldn't disobey her. And she broke the chain on my bike. Cut it to pieces so I couldn't fix it. Shut me in the shed with the bike and the wire cutters and told me she'd come get me when she was good and ready."

Kinsey didn't know what to do. Or how to fix something this big. She found Sasha's hand and threaded their fingers together. "Did she hurt you?"

Sasha stared at Kinsey's hand as though she didn't know what she was supposed to do with it. "Not really," she said. Which wasn't a *no*, Kinsey noted with a rush of protectiveness. "I was more angry than anything. I was just . . . I was so sick of it. Her getting these stupid grudges in her head and taking them out on me. So I waited until I was sure she'd gone back in the trailer, and then I broke the window and climbed out. I still have a scar from the glass," she said, turning her hand to show the old scar slicing across the side of her palm.

Kinsey traced the thin, backward J lightly with her fingers. She'd always assumed the scar had been from an accident during a soccer game. Or some adventuring mishap while Sasha was running through the woods with her cousins. Kinsey's heart ached at the idea of ten-year-old Sasha being forced to break out of a shed. Why hadn't anyone stepped in to get her away from her mom? Couldn't any of her aunts and uncles see what was happening? Kinsey swallowed the emotion in her throat and brought Sasha's hand to her lips, even though it was far too late to kiss the wound away.

Sasha's eyes flicked up to meet Kinsey's, wary confusion written on her face. Kinsey didn't know how to convince her she wasn't looking for an excuse to leave. Except to stay right here, holding her hand tight.

"What did you do when you made it outside?" she asked softly.

Sasha dropped her gaze, brushing Kinsey's knuckles with her thumb. "I left," she said. "I didn't care what Ma said. I didn't care I had to walk a mile and a half to get up to the house. I wrapped the cut in the edge of my shirt and just . . . left. My aunt patched up my hand when I got there. And she gave me one of my cousins' old shirts to change into while she tried to get the bloodstains out in the wash."

"Didn't she do anything?" Kinsey demanded. "About your mom?"

Sasha's expression didn't change as she gave a tiny shrug. "I didn't tell her. I said I'd hurt myself falling off my bike."

"Why? Maybe she could've helped."

Sasha shook her head, shoulders going up another inch. "No one ever helped."

Kinsey's jaw tightened. Someone should've done something. Rescued Sasha before she ever got locked in a shed for standing up for herself. Before things got so bad she stopped hoping for anyone to save her.

"I didn't want to go back," Sasha went on in her lifeless monotone. "I almost asked Trev to ask his mom if I could stay the night. But I was afraid I'd get in more trouble if Aunt Rosemary called home and found out I was supposed to be grounded. So after dinner, I walked home.

"It . . ." Sasha's voice faltered, and she drew her fingers out of Kinsey's grip and wrapped both hands around the neglected Gatorade. Her face went blank, her eyes hollow. "It was dark. The radio was blaring. I tried calling for her, but nobody answered. I thought she might've been so mad she'd run off with a boyfriend or something. But when I checked her bedroom, she was passed out cold. Needle in her arm. Wouldn't wake up, no matter how hard I shook her or how loud I shouted."

"Oh god," Kinsey breathed, stomach clenching.

"I couldn't find her cell anywhere to call for help," Sasha continued, as though she hadn't heard. "So I ran for the house. Trevor ran out first, no shoes or anything. His dad came out with the shotgun right after him. I must've been screaming, but I don't really . . . I don't remember it. I remember I couldn't breathe right. I remember thinking no one was moving fast enough. I remember Trevor had to repeat almost everything I said before my aunt and uncle could understand. As soon as they realized what happened, my aunt went inside to call 911, and my uncle got in his truck and drove up to the trailer."

Kinsey swallowed the urge to demand why no one had

insisted on driving Sasha home in the first place. They might've spared her finding her mom like that. At the very least, there would've been someone there who could have taken charge of the situation. Someone who wasn't ten years old and scared of losing her only parent. But Sasha was struggling to get the story out already, and Kinsey didn't want to interrupt just to make her feel like she had to defend the only people who were there to help her.

"They wouldn't let me do anything." Sasha's voice was breaking, but she pressed on stubbornly. "I got shunted into the kitchen, away from everybody but Trev. People kept showing up to the house. Family mostly. The police were there at one point. None of them would tell me what was going on. All anyone would say was . . . was I should stop worrying, and I'd done all I could, and it would work out in the end. Bullshit you tell kids when you don't want them to get upset. I was sure she was dead. And it was my fault."

"Oh, Sasha, no." Kinsey gripped her shoulder. This was why Sasha said she'd almost killed her mom? Because she'd put off going home after a fight? "No, hon. It wasn't your fault in the least."

Shaking her head, Sasha scooted down until she was curled up on her side, back pressed against the wall. "That story I told you about me and Trev getting stuck in that tree?" she said tightly. "We weren't adventuring. I was going crazy in that house, with everyone lying to me. So I just walked out the back door. Across the yard and the vegetable garden and into the forest in the dark. Trevor was the only one who noticed. He was the only one who— the only one who followed me out there. I . . ." A sob interrupted her, and she buried her face in her hands, weeping.

Kinsey might have no idea how to chase away all the demons of Sasha's past, but she couldn't just sit there and watch her crumble. She moved the Gatorade to the bedside table and lay down next to Sasha, pulling her close. "Come here."

Sasha wrapped her arm around Kinsey, fisting her hand in the cotton of her shirt. "I can't do it anymore," she sobbed, her voice muffled against Kinsey's shoulder. "I can't. I don't care if she's my mom. I don't care if no one else will take care of her. I can't do it. I'm breaking my back trying to save her, and she doesn't even care. She only ever talks to me when she wants something from me. And I can't. I can't."

Kinsey pressed her mouth against Sasha's fever-warm forehead. "I'm sorry, hon," she said hoarsely, wishing there was more she could say. More she could do.

"I tried so hard," Sasha said with this awful helplessness. "I tried so hard and it still wasn't enough."

"It's okay," Kinsey murmured, stroking Sasha's trembling back. "It's okay, hon. I'm right here."

Sasha shook her head, but didn't respond. All Kinsey could do was hold her and mutter useless nothings in her ear, trying to soothe away the tears, to persuade the tension running through her to ease off.

No wonder Sasha went for the conversational self-eject button whenever her mom came up. She sounded even worse than Kinsey had guessed. How could anyone think they could get away with treating Sasha like that? With leeching away her smiles and determination until she was reduced to *this*?

Kinsey wished she was better equipped to . . . *do something.* Sasha had always been so good at picking Kinsey up when she was down. She'd been her defender, her confidant, a constant support.

Kinsey just wanted to reciprocate. To make Sasha feel cherished. Important. Like affection and kindness were the norm, and not something to flinch from, as though love was only a pretty wrapping for an emotional pipe bomb.

But Kinsey had none of Sasha's warm, ready sympathy. None of her sweetness. All Kinsey had was cold bluntness that was more likely to make it sound like she was picking a fight than expressing affection.

She continued stroking Sasha's back as the tears subsided, until her shoulders relaxed and her breathing became even and shallow. Until her fingers released their vice-grip on the back of Kinsey's shirt and she had drifted into sleep at last.

Kinsey bit her lip. She wasn't willing to disentangle herself from Sasha. She doubted her presence could be doing much good, but she couldn't leave Sasha alone now, and risk her waking up to someone else abandoning her.

Even if Kinsey seemed like the worst possible person to help with this kind of situation. She wasn't a particularly nice person. And she had a knack for torpedoing all her relationships at some point or another. She cared about Sasha and wanted to protect her from anything that would hurt her—but what if Kinsey was one of the things Sasha needed protection from?

She shoved that thought away quickly. If she just . . . listened, and kept digging her heels in, maybe she could keep Sasha from blocking her out anymore. And maybe they could still make it through this little rough patch in one piece.

She brushed a kiss against Sasha's forehead, careful not to wake her. "I love you," she whispered on a breath so soft she barely heard herself. She wanted to say it. Even if Sasha would probably freak out if she heard it. Even if she wasn't yet sure enough of herself to make a promise that big. Even if it didn't seem anywhere near enough.

She thought she felt Sasha sigh, but she didn't wake.

Kinsey pulled the comforter over them as best she could and reached back to switch off the light. Before long, she had joined Sasha in sleep, both of them cuddled up together in the narrow bed.

TWENTY-ONE

A blast of music from the bedside table dragged Sasha out of sleep. She fumbled for the source of the noise to make it stop, confusedly reaching over another form in the gritty dark. It took her a moment to realize it was Kinsey, her coconut-scented hair like ink over the pillow.

Kinsey grunted softly and snuggled closer. Sasha couldn't figure out what she was doing in her bed. Or why she was sleeping in a cotton blouse instead of one of her out-sized teeshirts. Sasha had slept in her clothes too. Jacket and all. Her mouth tasted like a subway platform in July, and she had a headache like a spike between her eyes. She couldn't fathom why. Nor did she care. Nothing was as pressing as making her alarm shut up.

She dragged her phone off the nightstand, thumb poised over the screen—

—and froze. It wasn't her alarm making the god-awful racket. It was a phone call. She didn't recognize the number.

Her stomach soured. She struggled to sit up, disengaging from Kinsey's sleepy embrace with more urgency than tact. "Ma?" she croaked, pressing the phone to her ear.

"Sasha?" Cynthia's voice was higher than usual and thick with tears. There were voices in the background, but they didn't have the loud, emotional quality of junkies conversing. The cadences were low and professional. "Hey, Sasha. Hey, baby girl."

Sasha was going to be sick. She snapped on the lamp, wincing as the light shot through her head, too bright after the darkness of what had to be the small hours of the morning. Kinsey's arm was still around her hips—she grunted again with a frown as Sasha removed it and fought her way out of the tangle of sheets.

"What did you do?" Sasha asked as her feet hit the thin, cold carpet.

"'S going on?" Kinsey grumbled, turning onto her back and rubbing a hand over her eyes.

Sasha held up a finger—*not now*—and scanned the floor for her shoes. She needed room to move. Pace. Run, if it came down to it.

If she could just make it to the stairwell—

Cynthia sniffled in her ear. "It wasn't my fault."

"What. Happened," Sasha demanded, each word forceful, unforgiving.

"I *asked you* to give me a little bit of money. I was going to pay you back—"

"Ma," Sasha snapped. She couldn't find her damn shoes. Kinsey was sitting up in bed now, scowling sleepily at Sasha, hair in tangles. "Enough with the excuses. Just tell me what happened."

"We got picked up by the cops."

She felt as though she'd stepped out of time, into a place where everything was gray and lifeless. Including her.

Of course. Of fucking *course*.

Sasha gave up looking for her shoes and knelt to rummage in her bag for a pen and some scratch paper. The movement made her feel sick and dizzy, made it harder to hang onto the disinterested practicality she needed to get through this conversation, but she did her best to push through it. "What are the charges?"

"Charges?" Cynthia echoed.

"What did they arrest you for, Ma?" Sasha asked, too loud, too harsh.

Kinsey's head snapped up. "What?"

Fuck.

She ripped out a page from the back of a notebook. Just block Kinsey out. Deal with the fallout later.

"Possession," Cynthia said. "And armed robbery. And . . . And aggravated assault. The 7-Eleven clerk is saying I pistol-whipped him. But he's a—"

Sasha slapped her phone face down on the floor and dug her nails into her jeans. This wasn't the first time her mom had been arrested. She'd been busted for possession before, plus a DUI or two and a few counts of shoplifting. Usually it just meant fines or a few weeks in jail. All part of the cycle.

But armed robbery and aggravated assault—what the hell was she thinking?

"Sasha," Kinsey whispered, sliding one foot out of bed. "What's going on?"

Sasha shook her aching head. She couldn't handle Kinsey and Cynthia at the same time. She could still hear her mom making excuses through the speaker. It was too faint to parse the exact words, but she knew the drill. It was her new friends' fault for leading her astray. It was her sister's fault for being an uptight bitch and driving Cynthia out of the house. It was Sasha's fault for refusing to wire her money for her motel party fund.

Because Cynthia didn't have a *choice*. Someone else had put the weapon in her hand. Someone else had dragged her to the scene. Someone else threatened her if she didn't go along with the robbery.

"Sasha?" Kinsey knelt on the floor a little distance away and reached for her hand.

Sasha jerked away, grabbing the phone again before Kinsey could touch her. "Where are you?" she demanded, interrupting Cynthia mid-sentence.

Cynthia told her, still sniffling with self-pity. Sasha didn't recognize the name of the county, but that didn't mean much.

"You have to get me out of here, baby girl," Cynthia said. "It wasn't my idea."

Sasha ignored the blame-shifting, knowing she'd only end up in another fight if she followed that tangent. "Did they set bail yet?"

"They won't do that part until tomorrow. Podunk town's too small for a night court."

"Anyone have a guess, then?"

Cynthia hesitated. Maybe trying to work in another complaint. Maybe stunned that Sasha wasn't in the mood to humor her. "Cops are saying it'll probably be around fifty grand."

Sasha copied this down too, her pen carving deep grooves into the paper. Fifty grand. All she had in savings was a couple thousand, carefully squirreled away from working summer jobs back home. Even if she *could* find the funds and wherewithal to figure out some kind of solution, she couldn't stomach the idea of throwing Cynthia another lifeline. She couldn't do it anymore. "I'm calling Gran."

"You can't," Cynthia said at once. "You promised you wouldn't."

"Either I call Gran or you can get used to Arizona prison," Sasha snapped. "You should have called her first anyway. Where in the hell am I supposed to come up with fifty grand, Ma? I'm a frigging college student."

"You think she gives a shit about me?" Cynthia asked, the self-pity turning bitter. "She'd sooner let me rot down here than get off her high horse long enough to help me."

"Then I guess you better start groveling. Because I'm not dealing with this anymore."

"Sasha—"

"No, Ma. Just—Don't talk to anyone without a lawyer." She hung up before her mom could reply and dropped the phone on the floor to press her hands over her face. As though that would be enough to stop her brain from pulsing against her skull and give her a chance to think.

"What happened?" Kinsey asked.

Sasha squeezed her eyes shut. "Nothing. It's fine." She didn't want to open them and see the dawning horror in Kinsey's eyes. She should've tried harder to get out of the room. She should never have answered that call—

"It's obviously not fine," Kinsey said in a cool tone that stiffened Sasha's spine. "People don't tell their mothers not to talk to anyone without a lawyer if everything's fine."

Struggling to breathe properly, Sasha made herself look Kinsey in the eyes. She must have been holding on to a distant hope of finding a measure of understanding there, because the careful distance she saw instead was a blow.

"What are you doing here, Kinsey?" she asked, surprised at the detached tone of her own voice.

Kinsey blinked. "You don't remember?"

"No," Sasha said. A few hazy memories were coming back to her—of fighting with Nova, and walking into Winnie's, and texting Trevor—but none of them explained how she got home. Or how Kinsey ended up in her bed.

Kinsey searched her eyes, as though she was trying to figure out exactly how much she should say. "You were—You'd been drinking. And you were really upset. I was worried about you so I—I thought I should stay until your roommate came back. I didn't feel right leaving you alone."

Oh, hell. Pieces of last night slammed into place as Kinsey spoke, each image worse than the last. Nova dragging her out of the bar. Kinsey and Nova bickering while Sasha struggled to get the front door open. And Kinsey sitting on the bed, her expression growing more and more alarmed as every horrible secret Sasha had been fighting to keep poured out of her mouth.

Sasha lurched to her feet, shame and regret pushing in from all sides. She'd always worked so hard to keep her weird family shit from invading her life in New York. Made extra sure that Kinsey never got a hint that she wasn't as put together as she made it seem. She'd never wanted Kinsey exposed to the dark, tangled mess of resentment and helplessness buried in her heart.

So fucking much for that.

"Sasha—"

"Just—Just don't talk to me for a minute," Sasha said, raking her fingers back through her hair and pacing to the far end of the room. Maybe she could still figure out how to save this. Maybe if her head would stop pounding, she could come up with a way to persuade Kinsey not to decide Sasha wasn't worth the drama. But her thoughts were cramped and broken, and no matter how much air she dragged into her lungs, she wasn't getting enough oxygen.

Get it fucking together.

Kinsey blew out a frustrated breath. "Sasha, come on," she said, the impatience in her voice growing more pronounced with every word. "How am I supposed to help you if we can't talk about it?"

"Let it go, Kins," Sasha begged. "It doesn't matter."

"Yeah, Sasha, it does," Kinsey said, getting to her feet with more grace than Sasha had. "Of course it does. You said you wanted me. You said you wanted us to work. But how is that supposed to happen if you won't even try to meet me halfway?"

"What halfway?" Sasha cried, her thin control cracking into anger. Or panic. She didn't know which. There was no realistic scenario in which Kinsey was blasted with all these horrifying revelations about her past and still wanted to be with her. There was no scenario in which her lattice of normalcy wasn't already collapsed and burning around her. "What do you think the compromise is here? We make out one time and suddenly I owe you my entire life story? Every shitty thing that's happened to me is fair game for you to poke into? Is that what this is?"

Kinsey's nostrils flared as her frown sharpened. "No. I'm trying to *help*, Sasha. That's all I've been trying to do for the past three days. But how do you expect me to do *anything* if you won't tell me when something's bothering you?"

"You wouldn't get it," Sasha said desperately. "How could you possibly get it? You had a childhood out of a freaking picture book. All I had was a junkie mom who blamed me for all her problems and an extended family who didn't want me enough to do anything about it. Where the fuck is halfway supposed to be?"

Kinsey's hands curled into fists at her sides. "You might think my problems are vapid, but at least *I'm* capable of letting people in without needing to get drunk to do it."

Sasha couldn't find any of her humor, any of that seemingly limitless well of patience she'd developed to deal with Cynthia. All she had left was the worst kind of sarcasm. "Yeah. No, you're right. You're completely right. Tell me, how exactly were you planning to 'help?' Do you know of a rehab in the western United States my mom hasn't already been to? Maybe you have fifty grand in your sock drawer to cover her bail? Or were you thinking you could just make it all go away with a chat and a good fuck? Sure. That'll fix me. Trauma cured. Halle-fucking-lujah."

Kinsey drew herself up until even through the rumpled clothes and the smudged, faded makeup, she looked like a vengeful goddess. "So all that stuff about not wanting anyone else, all that stuff about wanting us to work, that was just . . . what? Another one of your stupid deflection moves? You were too scared to tell me to back off about your mom so you faked being into me until I got off your case?"

"What more do you want from me, Kinsey?" Sasha was loud enough by now that she was in danger of waking up the girls on the other side of the wall, but she couldn't bring the volume down. "Me telling you my mom overdosed when I was a kid wasn't honest enough for you? Or is it just that I'm not reacting to finding out she attacked some poor cashier with a gun in a way you think is *appropriate*?"

"You could try just *talking to me*," Kinsey shot back.

Sasha let out a humorless laugh, turning her gaze to the ceiling. She hated that laugh. She hated everything that came out of her mouth, caustic and fake. "Yeah. Because you're the one fucking exception, aren't you? You can fix me by just *believing* in me hard enough. Like I'm some bullshit cryptid in your fairy-tale life."

"You were the one who started flirting with me, remember?" Kinsey snapped. "I didn't ask to be friends with you. I didn't ask you to like me. If what you just said is how you really feel about me, then why the hell are we even together?"

Kinsey's words seemed to suck all the air out of the room. It was just the same old thing—*cut yourself open for us, Sasha, and show us what's underneath. You can trust us.* Whenever Sasha believed it was true, believed she could let down her guard and they'd keep on caring about her afterward, it only ever got thrown back in her face.

She knew she shouldn't keep looking for someone to sweep her off her feet. No one ever looked out for Sasha but herself. Why in the hell had she ever thought it would be different this time?

It was too close in that room. Too small. Too hot. She needed space. Lots of space. Somehow she found her shoes, half hidden under the desk, and yanked them on despite the blank white noise in her head and the chill in her fingers. "Okay," she said, her tone weirdly calm. "Fine. Have it your way."

Kinsey growled, dragging her hands over her face. "Sasha—"

"No, it's fine." Sasha snatched up her wallet and keys on her way to the door. "You want to break up? Done. It's not like this was ever going to work anyway."

"I didn't—Just wait a second," Kinsey said, catching the edge of Sasha's jacket and pulling her around. She was still scowling, but something had deflated in her posture and her eyes were wide and guarded. "Where are you going?"

"Doesn't matter." She shrugged Kinsey off and yanked the bedroom door open. "Somewhere else."

"Sasha, wait," Kinsey said, starting after her. "*Sasha.*"

"Leave me the fuck alone, Kinsey," Sasha ground out, throwing one last glare over her shoulder.

Kinsey stopped in her tracks, her eyes full of angry accusations. Sasha tore her gaze away before any more guilt could hit her and shoved into the hall, slamming the door behind her.

TWENTY-TWO

The protection Kinsey's anger had lent her started to crumble the second she stepped into the darkness of her apartment's common room. She couldn't understand how it had gone so wrong so fast. How she could have gone from holding Sasha close and wanting to protect her to shouting accusations at her a few hours later.

She had wanted to *help*. That was all. Sasha had to realize that bottling up her frustrations wasn't doing her any good. She had to know that Kinsey was the last person who would pass judgment on her for venting about her mom.

But then Sasha was yelling at her. And Kinsey, taken off guard, had done what she always did when she felt the least bit threatened: she lashed out, escalating the argument with every tiny insecure thought she'd had in the last twenty-four hours until Sasha finally had enough.

She kept seeing Sasha's face when she was talking to her mom. The fury hardening her usually gentle expression. The unforgiving force in her usually patient, cheerful voice.

It had scared her. She'd never thought Sasha was capable of losing her temper. Even when Sasha told her she'd argued with her mom when she was ten, Kinsey hadn't really believed it. She'd assumed it was misplaced guilt or something. That Sasha remembered her side of the argument being worse than it was because she'd dealt with the OD by taking the blame herself. For chrissakes, Sasha barely even got pissed off when refs made calls she didn't agree with during important games.

Realizing Sasha had a very real limit to her seemingly infinite store of sympathy and patience had thrown Kinsey into a near-panic. Because if Sasha had a breaking point, then it was only a matter of time before Kinsey managed to push her to that place, too. And how was she supposed to cope with that? Knowing she could push the sweetest, most patient, most understanding woman she'd ever known into hating her?

It's not like this was ever going to work anyway.

Kinsey remembered the scared, whispered *I love you* she'd breathed in Sasha's ear last night and her face burned. How could she have talked herself into thinking Sasha's only hangups were being wary of affection? Sasha had been trying to tell Kinsey it wouldn't work from the beginning. All the times she'd flinched from gestures of affection, all the times she'd asked Kinsey to stop being nice . . . They were warnings. Just because they were attracted to each other didn't mean they made a good team.

Why hadn't Kinsey listened?

She slid down the door, her hands limp in her lap. She ought to be relieved. It wasn't like she could've turned herself into the empathetic, understanding woman she'd wanted to be for Sasha.

She should have never asked Sasha to look past her brusque tendencies and want to stay with her forever. It was easier to break up now than it would've been after another six months of pretending away their problems. There was nothing substantial holding them together, after all. Never had been. Just cranky frowns and bad pickup lines.

But even as she thought it, she knew that wasn't true. Sasha always had this knack for turning up the moment Kinsey needed her. Sometimes it was as simple as helping Kinsey shake off the stress of visiting her mom in the hospital by whisking her away to a quiet bookstore for a couple of hours. Sometimes it was holding her up and blocking out the rest of the world while Kinsey had a meltdown. Or rescuing her from a public fight with her ex with a well-timed whistle.

Sasha was always there to make Kinsey feel better with her rambling tall tales, ready to laugh at Kinsey's dark, needly humor until she didn't feel quite so sharp anymore.

Kinsey drew in a shuddering breath as she remembered the press of Sasha's fingers against her skin, the slide of her tongue as they kissed. Her voice soft and cautious, her eyes earnest and solemn as she touched Kinsey's cheek. *Under that cranky shell of yours, you've got such a big heart—*

Kinsey let out a raspy growl and shoved the memory away. She'd *tried* to make things work. She'd fucking *tried*. If Sasha couldn't even talk to her when she was stressed out, that was her problem, not Kinsey's. And if she wasn't prepared to work on that, then . . . then good fucking riddance.

She insulated herself in threadbare vindication, blocking out the hurt, blocking out the childlike confusion, blocking out the memory of Sasha's hardened expression as she left.

Anger was easier to cope with. If she was angry, she could march on. If she was angry, her heart couldn't break.

And if it did anyway, she could bury it deep under her fury, where not even Sasha could see it.

Problem fucking solved.

Rage got Kinsey showered and dressed a few sleepless hours later, but it wasn't doing much for her ability to apply eyeliner. Her hands weren't steady enough to get the wings even, no matter how much she swore at them under her breath.

It was probably good that the rest of her suitemates had cleared out by the time Kinsey finished showering or she would've been swearing at them, too. Which might have made her feel better. It would've distracted her from going over the last twenty-four hours again and again in excruciating detail. Maybe it would've also made enemies out of girls she had up to that point successfully avoided alienating, but who cared what they thought of her anyway?

She hated how helpless she felt. She hated how she kept catching herself on the verge of tears. She hated how much her chest ached when she so much as thought Sasha's name. She hated how much she just . . . *missed* her. The way Sasha's ears turned pink when she was caught off guard. The timbre of her voice when she did that half-joking flirting thing. The way she'd somehow understood what Kinsey really meant under all her cranky comebacks.

At least she had up until last night.

In the bathroom mirror, Kinsey saw tears welling in her eyes and she flinched back, glaring at her reflection with contempt. She'd wanted to project strength and independence today. To guild herself with confidence so anyone who saw her would know she wasn't someone to be messed with. She'd left her quirky patterns in the drawer, instead choosing a high-waisted pencil skirt and a plain white blouse. Doing her makeup was supposed to be the finishing touch on the message: *I don't need anyone to validate me. I'm just fine on my own. And if the rest of the world has a problem with that, they can go fuck themselves.*

But Kinsey didn't see any of that attitude reflected back at her. All she saw was a confused, hurt little girl playing dress-up.

"Screw this," she said in a broken voice, throwing the eyeliner in her makeup bag in disgust. Snatching the bag off the counter, she turned on her heel and stormed back into the common area toward her bedroom.

She was only halfway there when a sharp knock on the apartment door brought her up short.

A spike of hope that it might be Sasha punctured her carefully maintained anger. Maybe she had changed her mind and wanted to make up.

Or maybe she'd come to make sure Kinsey understood they were really over.

But it wouldn't be Sasha. The knock was too brusque to be hers. It was probably just someone locked out of their apartment across the hall.

Another round of banging and a muffled voice through the door ruled that option out. "Come on, Kinsey, open up."

Definitely not Sasha's voice. Kinsey didn't let herself examine the reason her heart fell at the realization. Clutching her bag, she marched over and stretched up to look through the peephole.

Nova stood in the hallway, black curls cascading from under a knit hat, lips pressed together as she scowled up the hallway. She must have found out about . . . earlier. Otherwise what would she be doing here?

Feeling she'd rather snap at someone than cower in her room, Kinsey blew out a breath and yanked open the door. "What."

"Is Sasha with you?" Nova asked, almost before Kinsey could get the word out. For a moment, Kinsey could've sworn she didn't look pissed off so much as . . . worried? Nova hadn't unbuttoned her jacket as most people did by the time they got out of the elevator, and she still wore her gloves. One hand gripped the strap of her backpack like it was a parachute.

"No," Kinsey began, surprise making her forget her half-formed plan to be as absolutely scathing as possible. "Why?"

"Please tell me 'no' actually means 'yes, but she wants you to piss off.'"

"It just means 'no,'" Kinsey said. The way Nova was looking at her made her stomach knot. She pulled the door wide to let Nova by. "She's not here. Look for yourself."

Nova gave her a small nod of thanks as she strode inside. "Sasha?" She poked her head into both the small bathrooms. When that proved fruitless, she raised her voice, looking around the living area and kitchenette as though she was going to start checking the cupboards in a minute. "I swear to god, Deforest—"

"She's really, honestly, not here," Kinsey said, letting the front door close and retreating to a corner of the couch. "Didn't you try hollering at *her* place first?"

"Of course I tried her place first," Nova said, spreading her arms in exasperation. "If she was there, do you think I'd be talking to you right now? The hell happened to you keeping an eye on her, anyway? How do you lose track of your own girlfriend?"

"She's not my—" Kinsey stopped, furious she couldn't get the words out effortlessly. They sounded fractured and hoarse, as though she was going to cry. Which she *wasn't*.

Nova's expression was icy. "You broke up with her?"

"I—She was the one who walked out," Kinsey said, crossing her arms. She might have technically put breaking up on the table, but Sasha hadn't exactly fought very hard to stay together. She hadn't fought for them at all.

"Bullshit," Nova said, though she looked uncertain. "Why would she do that? She's basically been in love with you since you turned up in her humanities class last year."

Kinsey had to turn her face away as the treacherous urge to cry blurred her vision again. Maybe it *was* all her fault. Maybe all she did in her relationships was poison them with her unfeeling, hostile defenses. But Sasha was the one who started the yelling. Sasha was the one who walked out. If she'd really been in love with Kinsey that long, why was it so easy for her to just . . . give up?

Nova puffed out a breath and paced to the far end of the kitchen with her hands on her hips. When she turned to face Kinsey again, she seemed to be making a concentrated effort to appear more patient. "Look, I'm not going to lie and say I don't kind of want to shake you right now, but I've got more to worry about than whether you've been a dick to my friend. Sasha isn't picking up her phone. And she didn't answer me when I shouted through her door, either. I haven't heard anything from her since last night and I'm getting worried. And if you ever cared about her at all, I'd think you'd be worried, too."

"Don't tell me I never cared about her," Kinsey growled. "Don't you dare."

Nova was unfazed by Kinsey's stormy expression. "So help me find her."

Kinsey hesitated. The likelihood of Sasha actually going missing was infinitesimal. She was too steady for that. She'd probably just skipped her first class to go for a run and she'd forgotten to charge her phone. Or she was screening Nova's calls because they'd fought about her and Kinsey dating and Sasha didn't want to hear an I-told-you-so. Or she was nursing a hangover over a coffee from the cheap café down the block.

But that look Sasha had given Kinsey when she left last night kept coming back to her. Sasha had never been so much as irritated with her, and all Kinsey had been able to take in was how angry she looked. Kinsey wanted to believe that Sasha was blowing Nova off because she was still angry, but there had been something in her eyes and in the tone of her voice last night—a kind of fragility—that made Kinsey think it wasn't that simple.

As angry and unfeeling as Kinsey wished she could be right now, when it came down to it, it wasn't as easy to just *stop caring* about one of her best friends as she would have liked. Sasha probably didn't want to see her—Kinsey didn't want to see Sasha right now either—but if she was going to go around turning up missing they'd both have to suck it up until someone found out where Sasha was.

Growling, Kinsey got to her feet and marched into her room.

"What are you doing?" Nova walked over and stood in the doorway, gripping the doorjamb with one hand.

"I've got a spare key to her room," Kinsey said, rummaging through her desk drawers. "For just-in-case." She spotted the Statue of Liberty keychain peeping from under a tangle of earrings and snatched it up. Kinsey had dragged Sasha to a tourist shop a few blocks from Washington Square Park to get matching keychains after they swapped spare keys to their new dorms. To commemorate the occasion, she'd said.

They must've spent an hour in the tiny store, turning over the paperweights and notebooks and little stuffed animals, chatting about nothing and everything. After a few minutes, Kinsey had started a game with herself to see how often she could get Sasha to laugh. She lost count after twenty or so . . .

Kinsey shrugged the memory off with a frown. "We should make sure she's not in her room first. Then we can get a search going if we have to."

"If she was in her room, she would've told me to piss off when I was up there before," Nova muttered.

Kinsey ignored her as she led the way to the elevators down the hall, barely pausing to slip on a pair of flats on her way out. She had to be systematic about this. If Sasha was in her room and just too angry or whatever to answer people when they shouted through the door, then that would be the end of the search. And Kinsey could snap at everybody for dragging her into a non-problem and throw Sasha's spare keys on her desk and march back downstairs. She'd even let herself have a good cry about it.

If Sasha was missing . . . Well, then Kinsey already had a list of places to check before anyone had to get hysterical.

She pounded on the door of Sasha's suite when they got upstairs. One of Sasha's suitemates opened the door, all frazzled, nervous energy.

"If she's in there, she's not answering," Sybil said as she ushered Kinsey and Nova inside. "Do you think she needs an ambulance?"

"Absolutely not," Kinsey snapped. It had seemed like Sasha had slept off most of the effects of the alcohol by the time her mom's call woke them up. So she wouldn't have alcohol poisoning or anything like that. She *better* not.

Stomach twisting, Kinsey knocked twice on Sasha's bedroom door. "Hey, Deforest!" she called. "If you don't want me breaking the door down, you better say something."

Kinsey held her breath, listening, but not a sound came from inside. Not even the creak of a chair.

"I'm coming in," she announced as she shoved the key into the lock.

She pushed her shoulder against the door, her scowl firmly in place—

She stopped cold, one hand still on the doorknob. Sasha had been robbed. The drawers of her desk were ransacked, her things scattered over the floor.

Except . . . her laptop still sat on her desk, exactly where it had been last night. And her roommate's side of the room was as spartan as always. It couldn't be burglars if nothing had been taken. Which meant . . .

"She's not here," Kinsey said stupidly, turning back to the other girls for help.

Nova came to stand next to Kinsey in the doorway. "Jesus," she breathed. "When did this happen?"

"I don't know." Kinsey picked her way into the room, careful not to step on any of the papers or clothes strewn around. "Her bags aren't here. She had a duffel and her backpack with her when we were in North Carolina. Her duffel was hanging on the hook on the wall there," she said, pointing to a naked stretch of wall on the other side of the room. "And her backpack was right there by her bed . . ."

Nova tapped her phone screen a few times and held it to her ear. "Did she say anything to you about taking off?"

"No." Kinsey stood frozen in the middle of the room, utter helplessness washing over her. She didn't know where to start looking if she couldn't reasonably confine the search to the immediate neighborhood. If Sasha had packed a bag she could have headed anywhere.

"Straight to voicemail," Nova said, ending the call.

"Fuck," Kinsey said, staring at Nova like she somehow knew where Sasha had gone.

But Nova looked as baffled as Kinsey was. "Yeah," she said, arms limp at her sides. "Fuck."

TWENTY-THREE

An ominous thunk from the engine drew Sasha's attention to the van's dashboard gauges. She'd been too busy concentrating on the road and the too-loud radio to remember to keep an eye on anything but her speedometer. But while she was distracted, the van had been overheating. The second she glanced down, the engine light came on with a soft ding.

"Dammit," she whispered, easing off the gas as a faint smell of burning rubber drifted through the vents. She switched off the heat while she was at it, though she knew the preventative measure wouldn't help much at this point. If she could just make it another two miles to the next exit—

The engine's stuttering growl informed her that wasn't going to happen.

"Fucking fantastic." Sasha punched on the hazard blinkers and pulled off the road.

As soon as she came to a stop, she threw the gearshift into park and killed the engine. The radio cut out, letting through the hiss of the settling engine and the hum of cars whizzing past. It wasn't enough to drown out her thoughts anymore. Sasha slumped over the steering wheel, eyes tight shut, head aching, trying not to let this one additional problem overwhelm her.

She'd managed to walk back inside her dorm to get her things, after all. Even though there had been a chance Kinsey would still be there, waiting impatiently with her arms crossed, eyes flashing, ready for round two. Even though Sasha wasn't sure what she would have done if she couldn't get out of there without interference. She hadn't had much control left, and she knew it wouldn't hold if Kinsey questioned her again.

But Kinsey was long gone by the time Sasha came back upstairs, fingers still chilled from being out in the gritty cold for too long. There had been no trace of her anywhere except a faint smudge of mascara on the pillow.

Sasha had turned the pillow over and shoved her wallet and the contents of her dresser into her backpack and duffel bag. She didn't put any thought into what she was bringing. As long as she had her wallet and ID, she could replace everything else.

She almost left her phone behind. Part of her had wanted to crush it under her heel and never look at it again. No one could make her mom's arrest Sasha's problem if they couldn't reach her.

But she'd promised Cynthia to tell Gran about the arrest. Loath as Sasha was to have anything more to do with either of them, she wasn't going to be able to rid herself of the responsibility until it had been passed on to someone else.

So she texted her gran the information Cynthia had given her, ending the message with **I don't care how you handle this. Just keep me out of it.**

Then she'd powered her phone off and shoved it into the depths of her backpack. She wasn't going to be the family fixer anymore.

And if going incommunicado for a few hours was the only way to prove that, then so be it.

She'd been doing all right from then until now. If *all right* meant *shutting down so hard you can't feel anything.* Once she'd made the decision to leave—and once her phone was off—it had been easy enough to pack her feelings away and just go. She didn't know the most efficient route to San Francisco, but it didn't really matter yet. So long as she was heading west, that was a question she could resolve later. So was the question of what she was going to tell Trevor. Just because he was theoretically willing to put her up didn't mean he'd be happy to hear she'd fucked up her life this spectacularly in such a short amount of time.

She'd have to turn her phone back on if she was going to get a tow truck, though.

As long as she didn't look at any of the messages that were no doubt waiting for her, she thought she could still keep it together.

Sasha dragged her backpack into her lap, poking through it. It was almost all clothes, plus a couple of textbooks she hadn't bothered to remove. She hadn't even brought her computer.

Brushing off a weird twinge of guilt at her thoughtlessness, she found her phone and started it up.

A dark icon of an empty battery flashed on the screen for a moment and then it went black.

"Shit." She tried again, but it was no use. It was dead. *"Shit."*

Tossing her phone on the passenger seat, she dug through her backpack again. Surely she wasn't so completely irresponsible she hadn't even picked up her phone charger on the way out. Even her *mom* could manage that much.

It wasn't there. She shoved the backpack to the side and twisted around to drag her duffel out of the back. No cord there, either.

"Dammit, dammit, *dammit.*"

Dropping the duffel bag in her lap, she clenched her teeth and braced her hands on the steering wheel, locking her elbows. She wasn't helpless. She could figure this out. There was a gas station at the next exit. If she let the engine cool for a few minutes and tried the old water-for-coolant trick, she'd probably be able to make it there without the car exploding. And if it didn't look like that would work, she could just walk. That wouldn't be a big deal.

This was a solvable problem. No need to have a meltdown about it. Just fix it.

She popped the hood and climbed out on the passenger's side. The wind was a shock to her system after the warmth of the van. The cold found every inch of exposed skin and seeped through her jeans and shirt like they were nothing. Zipping up her coat, she grabbed her gloves from the passenger seat and slammed the door shut. Hopefully there'd still be some heat left when she got back in.

The hood was warm beneath her gloves when Sasha lifted it, releasing a plume of steam into the air. She didn't know much about cars, but she'd been driving her van to Wyoming and back for three summers. She could patch most problems long enough to find a mechanic.

A quick inspection confirmed that her coolant tank was empty. Probably due to a leak they hadn't noticed the last time she took the van in for a tune-up.

It wasn't great, but it wasn't bad enough to resort to walking yet. She left the hood open and went back to the car to wait for the engine to cool off before she tried anything else.

She busied herself with other tasks for a while—excavating a half-empty water bottle from under the back seat, shedding her coat and sneakers for a few seconds to pull on a sweatshirt and a second, thick pair of socks from her bag—but within a couple of minutes she didn't have anything else to do but watch the steam rise from around the hood.

Sasha tried counting out the seconds to keep herself occupied. Then counting the cars speeding by. Then, desperately, reciting coding algorithms to herself, line by line. But nothing worked.

She just couldn't stop thinking about Kinsey. It was like she was sorting through their entire relationship in her head, trying to rid herself of the painful parts so they couldn't hurt her anymore.

But the memories she turned over in her mind were all painful. Not because they were tainted with broken promises and instability, but because they were perfect: The way Kinsey got so protective when she'd asked Sasha about her ex. The way she looked at her as she listed reasons she'd wanted to be friends. Her brisk, no-nonsense prescription for cuddles after Sasha had a nightmare . . .

She wished they'd never kissed. Remembering Kinsey's fingers caressing her skin like she was something special—remembering the way she said Sasha mattered with that stubborn, fight-me glint in her big, brown eyes—it just made it harder to let go.

People being nice to you shouldn't be surreal, Sasha.

Sasha scrunched down in her seat, arms wrapped tightly around herself as she stared out the window. The thorny, gray weeds sweeping up the slope on this side of the highway blurred together through the tears in her eyes.

She used to love feeling isolated from the rest of the world. When she was a kid, being alone—unattached—had been an ideal. She used to seek out lonely places on the back of her gran's property, or in the far corners of her aunt's ranch. She'd spend hours sitting on old fence posts, knees scraped up, the house out of sight, with no one but birds and squirrels for company. No one around to hear if she shouted out all her anger. No one to shush her if she didn't muffle her sobs.

Not that she did either very often. Usually she'd just try to get the squirrels to take seeds and dried berries from her fingers. Or coax caterpillars onto her outstretched palm. Or lie in the grass and watch the clouds creep across the sky, imagining if she stayed still enough for long enough, the chaos back home would have time to settle. And by the time she dragged herself back to civilization, she'd have a normal life.

When that wasn't enough, she used to take her bike and ride out over the fields and into the forest, as far as she could. She'd pretend every last tie binding her to her home snapped, one by one, the further she went. *Snap.* No obligation to be at school tomorrow. *Snap.* No obligation to put on a brave face for Sunday dinner with the extended family. *Snap.* No obligation to take care of her mom anymore.

The birds never eyed her worriedly and asked how often her mother bought new clothes. The trees never accused Sasha of sabotaging them out of some imagined slight. She didn't have to worry about whether there would be strange people in her house when she got home from school. Or getting screamed at for flushing her mom's stash after finding it hidden in an old cereal box in an otherwise empty pantry.

Out under the big sky, with grass whipping her legs and the wild woods reaching up the nearest mountains, there had been nothing for Sasha to worry about except herself.

But she had none of that tentative peace with her now. She didn't just feel isolated. She felt . . . lost.

Maybe it was because she was stranded next to a highway in the middle of Pennsylvania with no way to call for help. Maybe it was because she hadn't gone far enough yet to snap the cord attaching her heart to Kinsey's.

Maybe it was just because the one tie she was trying to escape was the one cord she'd never wanted to sever.

She'd known she'd been living someone else's life, those two beautiful days they were together. It was inevitable it would all come crashing down. Love was never going to be enough to save her. She'd lost her future with Kinsey the moment she stopped watching how much of herself she was revealing.

Sasha's fingers drifted to her cheek where Kinsey had kissed her because she had noticed something was wrong. When she'd pressed her wrist and said she mattered with that stubborn set of her chin. As though she intended to bully Sasha into believing it.

It was pushed out almost at once by the vivid, horrible image of Kinsey standing by the edge of Sasha's bed, her hands in fists, eyes hard, demanding to know why they were even together.

Sasha dragged her sleeve across her eyes before the building tears could escape. She couldn't keep thinking about this. She just needed to get it the hell together and focus.

Grabbing the water bottle, she stumbled out of the car to check the engine. She'd never had so much trouble keeping a lid on her emotions before. It was bullshit she couldn't clamp them down now.

"This is bullshit," Kinsey snapped, riffling through the scattered papers on Sasha's desk with shaking fingers. "I can't believe she'd pull something like this without leaving a fucking *note*."

Nova, conducting her own search of Sasha's bedside table, didn't respond. She seemed to believe Kinsey's half-coherent ranting was purely rhetorical. Either that or she'd just tuned Kinsey out. Now that it didn't look like Sasha was in need of immediate medical attention, Nova seemed much calmer.

Or maybe she was only calm by comparison, because Kinsey was freaking the fuck out. She kept thinking about when Beatrice got hurt a few months ago, about how she'd only heard about it hours later, after Beatrice's brother thought to call her. Only who would think to call Kinsey if Sasha had an accident and was in the hospital?

She threw down the useless papers in her hands and grabbed a fresh stack—old syllabi, mostly—searching for Sasha's handwriting in a hidden corner, some tiny message saying where she'd gone. All she found was a correction in purple ink of a due date from last semester and a couple of shapeless scribbles.

"What the fuck was she thinking?" she burst out, slapping the papers on the growing pile of things she'd already searched.

"There's nothing out here," Sibyl called from the other room. She poked her head in and held up a green Post-it. "The only thing I could find is this note on the fridge saying she'd be gone last weekend."

"Nothing here, either," Nova said, while Kinsey abandoned the futile desk search to take the sticky note from Sibyl.

Hey, girls! I'm gonna be out for the weekend. Be back Sunday. Help yourselves to the Thai leftovers. —SASHA

See? What was so hard about leaving a note in a visible place so concerned people could find it? It was common courtesy.

"This is bullshit," Kinsey said, her voice cracking.

"Should we call the police?" Sibyl asked. Again.

"Because a twenty-one-year-old woman took off?" Nova asked. "Under her own steam, too, as far as I can tell. Her phone, her wallet, her car keys are all gone. Looks like she took most of her clothes, too. I don't like that she left without saying anything either, but there's nothing illegal about it."

"This is *bullshit*." Kinsey fumbled with the lock on her phone and typed out a text to Beatrice. **Have you heard from Sasha in the last 12 hours or so?** Then she sent another. **Text me back asap. This is important.** And another. **911**

"Maybe she just went to spend the night with whoever she was with over the weekend?" Sybil ventured hopefully.

Kinsey rounded on her. "*I'm* whoever she was with over the weekend."

"Oh." Sibyl shrank into the doorway. "Sorry."

Nova made a soft disapproving sound in the back of her throat.

Kinsey's phone chimed before she could decide whether Nova's reaction was worth picking a fight over. Beatrice.

Sorry. Last text I have from her is from 5 days ago. Why 911?

I can't find her, Kinsey wrote back. "This is—"

"Bullshit," Nova interrupted impatiently. "Yeah. I get it. What are we gonna do about it?"

Kinsey scowled. "And you standing there judging everyone is a good use of time?"

"Maybe not, but neither is stomping around and cursing."

"Guys, come on," Sybil put in wearily. "We're all worried. Fighting won't help anything."

"You—"

Kinsey's phone rang in her hand and she scrambled to answer it, whatever she'd meant to say already forgotten. Her heart fell when she saw Beatrice's name on the screen. "She's not picking up for you either?" she guessed as she answered.

"No," Beatrice said. "Her phone must've died or something. It didn't even ring. What happened, Kins?"

"I don't know," Kinsey said, furious to discover her voice was breaking. She sank down on the desk chair, trying not to be aware of the two other women watching her. "We kind of . . . Something happened and she took off. I can't reach her by phone and she didn't leave any notes and she's just not here. Nobody's seen her since last night. I hoped . . . I hoped maybe she'd have called you."

"I haven't heard anything. I'm sorry."

Kinsey blew out an unsteady breath. This was bullshit. What the fuck did Sasha think she was doing, vanishing like this? Without even telling *Beatrice* when she was coming back?

She didn't even want to consider the possibility that Sasha *wasn't* coming back. That couldn't be an option. She wouldn't let it be.

"Have you tried contacting her teammates?" Beatrice asked. "Maybe they know something."

"They don't," Kinsey said, glancing at Nova, who had tactfully moved to the doorway to speak quietly with Sybil. "Nobody's seen her. Nobody. I don't even know where to start looking."

"Okay." Kinsey could hear the worry in Beatrice's voice, but she was back to her practical planning tone in another instant. "Okay. Don't freak out. Sasha doesn't just disappear. She probably . . . went on a run or something."

"And took a bunch of clothes with her?"

"Oh. Maybe not. But she's gotta be somewhere, right?"

"Theoretically."

"Do you need me to head down to help you look?"

Kinsey pressed her hand against the bridge of her nose, trying to set aside the panic and the hurt and the confusion and find a rational course of action. It would take at least two hours for Beatrice to make the trip down. Longer, if she had to wait for a train. If they couldn't find Sasha by then . . .

But they *would* find Sasha by then. They just would. There was no other option.

"No," she decided. "You . . . you stay where you are. Maybe she headed up to see you. Someone should be there if she did."

"Okay. Don't stress, Kins. I'm sure she's fine. We'll find her in no time."

"I hope so."

"I know so. Keep me updated."

"You too." Kinsey hung up and checked her text messages again, half hoping she'd missed a notification. But there was nothing. Of course there was nothing.

"This is bullshit," she said, dropping her phone in her lap. "Why didn't she tell anyone where she was going?"

"I'm trying her on Instagram," Nova said, busy tapping at her screen.

"How do you expect her to see it when her phone is off and her laptop is sitting right here?" Kinsey asked, more because arguing gave her a sense of purpose than anything.

Nova shot Kinsey a glare. "Ever heard of an internet café?"

"I think it's a good idea," Sibyl said quickly. "If you post something on one of her photos, then if someone else knows where she is, they might see it and let us know she's okay."

"It won't work," Kinsey said, but no one paid attention to her. She switched back to Sasha's number in her own phone. As though pulling up her contact information would open a magical line of communication that didn't require screens.

Sasha was always so steady. Predictable. *Together.* How could she have left without saying *anything*?

"This is bullshit," Kinsey whispered.

TWENTY-FOUR

Kinsey and Nova divided forces after it became clear that searching Sasha's room wasn't going to turn up any useful information. Nova recruited one or two of her teammates to check anywhere Sasha might have gone nearby while Kinsey, her stomach in a knot of dread the whole way, went to check on Sasha's van.

It wasn't a surprise to find it missing from the garage where Sasha rented a space during the school year, but it brought Kinsey up short. Until she laid eyes on the empty space, she'd been able to keep some kind of lid on the swarm of anger, hurt, and frenetic, anxious energy buzzing inside her head. Not a very good lid, maybe—but the possibility that Sasha had simply gone to crash with one of her soccer friends for a few days had been enough to keep Kinsey from flat-out panicking.

With that lid all but gone, Kinsey turned on her heel and marched back to her own car without checking in with Nova. She couldn't keep wandering around New York pretending there was still a chance they'd find Sasha sitting on a bench in Washington Square Park, or holed up on one of the couches in the study area in the dorm's basement. Clinging to one final hope that Sasha had just gone upstate to talk to Beatrice, Kinsey drove north, keeping an eye out for broken-down vans on the side of the road.

Traffic was light going out of the city so early, and no one was broken down on the stretch of highway going north to Beatrice's house at all. Sasha's van wasn't parked outside Beatrice's apartment block, either—Kinsey circled the block twice just to be sure. Sasha was just . . . gone.

Anger wasn't keeping Kinsey's anxiety at bay anymore, and even if she thought she could calm herself enough to drive back to the city, she didn't know where else to look that Nova and the other girls weren't already checking.

Sasha wouldn't want Kinsey to find her anyway. So it didn't matter.

Kinsey slammed out of her car and climbed the steps to Beatrice's apartment with her keys grasped so tight they dug grooves into her fingers. She didn't know what else to do except ask Beatrice for help. Beatrice was the master of organization. She'd have Kinsey's messy, contradictory feelings plotted on a graph or in some kind of itemized list in no time.

Gritting her teeth, Kinsey rapped on the door. The faint sound of '70s music inside stopped. A few seconds later, Beatrice swung the door open, her eyes wide and worried. "Hey, Kins. What are you doing here?"

Kinsey's fingers ached from gripping her keys, but she didn't relax. She couldn't or she'd burst into tears. "I needed to talk to you. Is that okay?"

"Of course," Beatrice said, standing back to let Kinsey pass. "It's just Julian and me at the moment. Everyone else is at work. Did you hear from Sasha yet?"

"No." Kinsey stepped inside the apartment where Beatrice lived with her parents and brother, barely taking in the familiarity of the space. Beatrice's fluffy gray cat was dozing on one of the two couches crammed around the coffee table in the living room. The kitchen table taking up most of the small eating area was scattered with pens and highlighters, papers that appeared to be mostly junk mail, and Beatrice's laptop, which was currently being scowled at by her boyfriend.

Julian looked up as Kinsey walked in, half-closing the computer. His sleeves were pushed up to his elbows, showing a smudge of blue ink above the twisting black lines of the smoky tattoo that wound up his left arm. "Hi, Kinsey," he said, glancing at Beatrice, who shrugged.

"Sorry," Kinsey said, her gaze flicking between them. "Hi. I should've called. I'm interrupting your . . . whatever you're doing."

"Nothing exciting." Julian shut the laptop and pushed it a few inches away. "Trust me, interruptions are welcome."

"We were due for a break anyway. And you don't have to call to come over, Kins." Beatrice perched on the chair next to Julian's and patted the empty one beside her. "Have a seat."

"Do you want something to drink?" Julian offered, standing up. "Tea? Coffee?"

"Got anything stronger?" Kinsey asked, sliding into the offered chair.

Beatrice wrinkled her nose apologetically. "Just cooking sherry. My mom's a little funny about keeping alcohol in the house."

"Never mind." Kinsey slumped over the table. Adding *more* alcohol to this mess was a bad idea anyway. "Coffee is fine."

"Coming up," Julian said. He squeezed Beatrice's shoulder as he made for the kitchen, and she smiled up at him. "Thanks, babe."

Kinsey clenched her teeth, willing herself not to break down. She'd been holding her anger close, hoping it would override the hurt, but that small little gesture, the easy intimacy between Beatrice and Julian, just reminded her of everything she'd thrown away.

It wasn't like she hadn't seen them like this before. It had just never bothered her when they were all at lunch or getting coffee or hanging out or whatever.

Maybe because Sasha had always been there too. To chat with on the way there, to distract Kinsey from any fleeting sense of loss on the way back. Without Sasha to fill in the gaps, Kinsey found she wasn't sure where she was supposed to fit in Beatrice's life anymore. The tight bond they'd shared—when Beatrice still came to lunch every day, before she had someone better to shake her out of her list-oriented tunnel vision—felt like it was coming apart at the edges. Like it had been disintegrating for weeks and Kinsey had just been too selfish to notice or do anything to patch it.

She could feel tears pricking her eyes and tried to blink them away before Beatrice could see.

But very little ever got past Beatrice. She squeezed Kinsey's forearm reassuringly. "Don't worry. She'll turn up, Kins. I know she will."

Kinsey shook her head, making herself focus on just getting the logistics out. The only thing she needed to deal with right now was what to do about Sasha. She couldn't let herself get wrapped up in this insecurity thing with Beatrice or she'd end up losing her, too.

"Her van's gone," Kinsey forced out. "And she took most of her things with her. If she isn't here, then . . . then . . ." The truth settled over her with grim finality. She'd been so caught up trying to stave off her anxiety at the idea of never seeing Sasha again, she hadn't ever considered the most obvious conclusion.

She sagged in her chair, the fight going out of her in a whoosh of air. "She's going home," she said with dull conviction.

"To Wyoming?" Julian asked from the kitchen.

"California," Kinsey said in the same lifeless tone. "Her favorite cousin lives in San Francisco."

"But that's—" Beatrice shook her head, brow pinched. "Hang on. That doesn't make sense. You two *just* got together. Why would she take off for California without telling you?"

Kinsey tugged absently at one of the open booklets on the table, still not sure she wanted to get into explaining the fight. She didn't want to think about it anymore. She didn't want Beatrice to confirm what Kinsey was so scared of turning up if she examined last night's argument too closely. That everything Sasha had said about her was true: Kinsey was too demanding, too judgmental, too impatient, too damn *angry* to ever make things work—

A streak of highlighted text on the paper in front of her registered through her blind stare. Kinsey frowned at the booklet, giving it a closer look. It wasn't junk mail like she'd thought. It was a course catalog. Marked up in Beatrice's handwriting. Two courses were highlighted on the open spread, and there were little sticky flags marking other pages. Kinsey flipped to the cover, her stomach clenching. "You're transferring to Syracuse?" Her voice sounded strange in her ears, rough and forceful.

"Oh. Um." Beatrice took the catalog and shoved it under a notebook. "Maybe? I mean, we've been talking about it. Julian just got into the art program there, and it's the place he wanted, and I was going to have to start over anyway, since I'm not doing the marketing thing anymore, and you and Sasha are going to graduate soon, which means I'd have another year or two of doing the commute thing by myself if I stayed at NYU, and . . . I don't know, I thought it was worth looking into."

Kinsey clenched her teeth as she fought back tears. She'd guessed Beatrice was going to transfer out of NYU—she'd *known* this was a possibility—but she'd always imagined it would be to somewhere nearby. Within a two or three hour drive from the city. Syracuse was almost five hours away from Greenwich Village. How were they supposed to keep up the already-difficult-to-sustain twice monthly lunches at that distance? Or was this just Beatrice's gentle way of getting Kinsey out of her life without needing to actually argue about it?

"Nothing's set in stone," Beatrice said, wrapping her arms around her middle, the way she did when she found herself in direct conflict with someone else. She hadn't ever done that with Kinsey before. Kinsey only knew what it meant because it had always been the first sign that Beatrice might need backup.

If there was one relationship in her life she thought was relatively stable, it was her friendship with Beatrice. The only thing they ever butted heads about was whether Beatrice was paying attention to her own emotional wellbeing. It was impossible to get upset with her about anything else, and she saw too much good in people to be bothered if Kinsey was occasionally extra cranky. But now she was just . . . leaving. Without any warning. And Kinsey didn't even understand what she'd done wrong.

"It's fine." Kinsey stood, snatching her purse from the table with cold fingers as she made for the door. An indefinable buzzing filled her head and chest, swarming through her until she was shaking all over. She shouldn't have come here. Not when she was feeling like this. "Do what you need to do. Have a nice life."

Chair legs scraped the linoleum as Beatrice got to her feet. "Kins—"

"It's *fine*," Kinsey snapped, pivoting to face Beatrice. "You think it's news to me that no one wants to be around me for longer than it takes to find someone better? I know I'm abrasive and mean. I know I suck at convincing anybody I like them. It's not exactly a big shock that you'd rather be with your fucking *boyfriend* than keep putting up with my bullshit. My own parents would probably swap me for a nicer daughter if they could. I don't even blame you for having enough. I couldn't even stop myself from—from screwing everything up with Sasha." Her voice, which had already been rough, cracked apart on Sasha's name, letting through a rush of wrenching, angry, awful tears.

"Oh, Kins." Beatrice darted over and wrapped Kinsey in a tight hug, as though Kinsey hadn't just been screaming at her. Julian hovered in the kitchen doorway, seemingly unsure of how or whether to intervene. "I didn't mean to make you feel like I was trying to ditch you. That's not what I want at all."

Guilt hit Kinsey square in the chest. Beatrice was the last person in the world who deserved to be snapped at for trying to point her life in a better direction. "I'm sorry," Kinsey blubbered into her shoulder, selfishly leaning into the embrace. "I'm sorry, Bee. I'm just—I'm—I'm—"

"It's okay. You're upset. You get prickly when you're upset. I know that."

"I just exploded at you and swore at your very nice boyfriend," Kinsey said hysterically. "That's not prickly, that's grounds for never talking to me again."

Julian lifted a shoulder. "I've been called worse."

"That doesn't make it okay," Kinsey said, pulling back a little to wipe tears from her face. "I don't know what's wrong with me."

"Okay, stop," Beatrice said gently, a stubborn glint in her eyes. "Nothing's wrong with you. You've been crazy supportive while I figured myself out these past few months. I've lost count of how many times you saved me from getting too overwhelmed or helped me course-correct when I got stuck following the plan instead of going in the right direction. You think one little outburst is going to make me want to stop talking to you forever? Yeah, I don't think so."

"I still shouldn't have yelled at you," Kinsey hiccuped. "I'm sorry."

"Apology accepted." Beatrice ushered Kinsey briskly onto the nearest couch. "Just take a deep breath and let's figure this out. What's going on?"

"I don't know." Kinsey sniffed, trying without much success to pull herself together. "I just—I wanted to help and it all just spun out of control so fast—"

Beatrice grabbed a box of tissues from the cluttered coffee table and pressed it into Kinsey's hands. "You and Sasha had a fight?"

"We didn't just fight, we broke up." Kinsey dug out a couple of tissues and pressed them to her eyes. "I don't even know why I'm crying about it. I figured this would happen. I mean, we make a terrible couple. She's . . . Well, she *cares* about people, for one. I don't think she's ever met someone she couldn't have a friendly conversation with. And I'm just . . . I'm an angry, prickly disaster who hates everyone."

"That's not true."

"Yes it is. Why else would everyone keep leaving me?" Kinsey asked, grabbing another wad of tissues. "You're taking off for Syracuse—which is fine but . . . and . . . and Sasha . . ." She ground out a frustrated half-scream, furious she couldn't just spit it out. "I don't know why I thought I could be good enough for her. I wasn't even good enough for Evie."

A thin line appeared in the center of Beatrice's freckled forehead. "Kinsey, Evie cheating on you didn't have anything to do with you being good enough. She was a manipulative narcissist who tried to dump the blame on you instead of taking responsibility for her crappy behavior. That's one hundred percent on *her*. Not you. And honestly? Screw her for making you feel like that."

Kinsey stared, shocked into silence by hearing sweet, understanding Beatrice make such a vehement speech about anyone.

"But one bad breakup doesn't mean you're . . . I don't know, destined for perpetual loneliness or something," Beatrice went on. "Especially when this *I'm so awful and uncaring* self-assessment is such a load of crap. You might be slow to warm up to people, but once you do, you're constantly checking in and doing nice things without even being asked. Just because you don't give yourself credit for that kind of thing doesn't mean the rest of us don't notice. Sasha included." She sighed and rubbed her forehead. "Which is maybe why I'm having trouble wrapping my head around this whole breakup thing. It doesn't make sense."

"Yeah, I don't get it either," Julian said, reappearing from the kitchen with a pair of steaming mugs. "Sorry," he added as he passed the first one to Kinsey, who realized belatedly that she was glaring at him. "I know I don't know either of you that well. But you always seem like you're on the same wavelength. What would you have to fight about?"

"Exactly," Beatrice said as she accepted the second coffee. "The worst arguments I've ever witnessed between you two are when Sasha goes a little too self-deprecating with the humor and you take her to task about it. Which barely counts. So your personalities aren't identical. So what? You're the good kind of opposites."

"Complimentary," Julian agreed, perching on a cleared edge of the coffee table.

"Right," Beatrice said, nodding. "Sasha keeps you from getting too sullen, and you—"

"Keep Sasha from being too happy?" Kinsey asked miserably.

Beatrice blinked. "No, Kins. You stop her from being too down on herself." She set her coffee down next to Julian and touched Kinsey's arm again. "What happened, exactly? Everything seemed fine yesterday."

"I thought everything *was* fine. But she . . ." Kinsey let out a breath. She was going to have to explain the fight sooner or later.

Might as well get it over with. "She's just been dealing with personal crap all week. She was keeping me out of the loop for most of it, but then she got this . . . call. At like three in the morning last night. And she got so . . . just . . . *angry.*" She met Beatrice's gaze, silently pleading for her to understand the magnitude of what had happened. "You know how she is. It's *really* hard to ruffle her feathers. Everyone else could be trying to form a mob and she'd be standing there at a maximum of mild irritation. She *never* snaps at people. Not like that. It freaked me out. And I just wanted her to—to talk to me. And I was scared. And I guess I pushed her too hard because then we started shouting at each other and before I could even process how we got there, she—she walked out."

She'd been shoving that fight out of her head all day with little success, but now there was nothing she could do to mitigate the press of grief and regret that settled on her shoulders as she heard her past self getting frustrated and defensive, watched Sasha throwing out accusations with her back to the wall, restless and tense. *Because you're the one fucking exception, aren't you?*

"I thought being together was what she wanted," Kinsey said. "I thought . . . I thought she liked me. But she just left. And I don't think she's coming back. And I don't know how it happened."

Beatrice gripped Kinsey's wrist, though she seemed at a loss for what to say.

Kinsey had wanted to be the kind of person Sasha could be with. The kind of person she could trust. Who could make her feel safe. How the hell did she screw up so badly?

"Are you sure she wanted to break up with you?" Julian ventured after a few seconds.

"Exactly what part of her taking off for California to get away from me after a fight says *let's stay together* to you?" Kinsey asked.

"Well, okay," Julian said. "But . . . I mean, I've tried the cut-and-run thing once or twice. It's usually more of a panic move than anything."

"You did say she's been struggling with other stuff all week," Beatrice said. "What exactly did she say when she left? Do you remember?"

Kinsey shifted in her seat, staring determinedly at the still-nearly-full mug in her hands. Of course she remembered. She remembered every last word they'd flung at each other. But suddenly she wasn't so sure that she'd actually *listened*.

Sasha had asked her, right before things spun out of control, to give her a little bit of space. Just a minute of quiet. Everything about her posture—the stiffness of her shoulders, the way she prowled to the far side of the room, her fingers pressed into her scalp—should have been more than enough to signal that the last thing she needed was to be yanked into a fresh argument with her insecure girlfriend.

Kinsey had just dragged her into one anyway, too preoccupied with her own worries about the relationship to realize Sasha was just as scared as she was. Maybe more. Kinsey wasn't the one backed into a literal corner, her whole body tight as a wire, eyes pleading, as she spat out everything she was afraid of.

She remembered Sasha waking up in her arms the morning after they kissed; the guarded wonder in her voice when she said *you're still here*. Like she expected Kinsey to ditch her at the first opportunity.

She remembered Sasha saying she didn't want to talk about her worry over her AWOL mom in case she crumbled. She remembered how she had flipped out when Kinsey crawled into her bed after she had that nightmare. Because she couldn't seem to process Kinsey being nice to her. Or wanting to be with her.

So when Kinsey stood there and made it sound like she wouldn't have looked at Sasha twice if she hadn't been the one to push for the relationship . . . No wonder Sasha hadn't fought back. Kinsey was just telling her exactly what she'd been expecting to hear from the beginning.

It wasn't even true. Kinsey had only blurted it out because she was scared that Sasha was pushing her away. And the only way she thought she could handle that possibility was if Kinsey was the one to give the final shove.

Which was exactly what Sasha had learned to expect from people who were supposed to care about her—that they'd feign affection right up until they didn't see a use for her anymore. And then they'd throw her away and blame her for everything that had gone wrong.

Kinsey stood up in a haze, feeling like she needed to do something. But she was completely blanking on what she *could* do. All she knew was she couldn't sit there any longer, pretending she hadn't just royally screwed things up with the woman she loved. Kinsey would never be a sunny, paintball-loving extrovert, but maybe she didn't have to be, so long as she could figure out a way to make things right. Though how she was supposed to do that when Sasha was off the grid was beyond her.

"I don't know how to fix this, Bee," she said. "Her phone is off or dead. I don't know where she is or if I could catch up to her. Even if I could, I don't think she'd want to hear me out. I've always been better at breaking things than putting them back together. But I want to try. I *have* to try." She huffed out a breath. "I just . . . don't know how I'm supposed to find her."

Beatrice got to her feet too, one finger raised absently, her eyes adopting that dreamy look she got when she was thinking. "You know," she said, "I might actually be able to help with that."

TWENTY-FIVE

Sasha eventually limped the van to a tiny body shop tucked behind a run-down strip mall. Most of the floor space was taken up by the garage—the waiting room was minuscule and felt even smaller because of the reception desk and the expensive-looking coffee machine dominating most of the space. The gas station clerk who had given her directions had sworn up and down that Holly was the best, most honest mechanic in the state.

Not that Sasha could follow Holly's diagnosis enough to tell. The mechanic was gray-haired and squat, with an intimidatingly competent, direct manner. And she talked much faster than Sasha's still-slightly-hungover, emotionally-fried brain could keep up with.

What Sasha *could* gather was the problem with her van was worse than a little coolant leak. "How long is it going to take to fix?" she asked, gripping the edge of the counter.

"It'll be a few days, probably," Holly said, resting her hands on her ample hips. "Depends how fast I can get the parts in."

Sasha clenched her teeth against a stupid urge to burst into tears. It was just a minor setback. She could handle this.

"No chance of patching it up today?" she asked, struggling to keep her voice even.

Holly twisted her mouth to one side, sizing Sasha up as she considered. "I might be able to buy you some slow-going driving time—that means no highways—by the end of business. But I wouldn't feel good about it. Where are you headed?"

"I don't know." Sasha rested her elbows on the counter and pressed her hands over her face. The plan—such as it was—had been to crash with Trevor. So she could stop fighting so hard. So she could figure out what to do now that she'd ruined everything with Nova and Viv and probably her whole team. Now that she'd destroyed her relationship with Kinsey.

But waiting for Holly to examine her van had the unfortunate side-effect of giving her time to think. And thinking just made her less sure of what to do next. There were too many thoughts crowding her head to see a clear way forward in any direction.

"How old are you, kid?"

Pull it together, Deforest. "Twenty-one," she said, lowering her hands but avoiding the mechanic's eyes.

"Thought so. My nephew's about your age. Got someone to pick you up?"

"Not really." She'd forgotten to look for a phone charger when she stopped for directions, so even if she found a pay phone, she was limited to calling the handful of people whose numbers she knew by heart. Nova didn't have a car, so she was out. Trevor obviously couldn't do anything but worry. Beatrice would be willing to help, but she also got stressed out when she was put in the middle of other peoples' conflicts, and there was no way to explain why Sasha was stranded in Pennsylvania without putting Beatrice in the middle of the . . . of the breakup.

That just left Kinsey. And calling her was unthinkable. What would she even say? *Hey, Kins. I know I just fucked up our entire relationship, but would you mind swinging out to rural Pennsylvania to get me? My car broke down while I was fleeing to California.*

Yeah. That would go over *real* well. The three-and-a-half-hour drive back to the city would be especially fun. And that was assuming Kinsey didn't hang up on her before she even got to the request.

"My phone's dead," Sasha explained when Holly's scrutiny intensified. "I'll just . . ."

Without removing her gaze from Sasha's face, Holly grabbed the office phone and plonked it on the counter by Sasha's elbow. "If my nephew was stuck without a ride in some batty woman's car shop, I'd wanna know. No matter what." Jamming a furry hat over her short, gray hair, the woman turned for the door to the garage. "I'll start working on that leak. You need anything, shout. I'll check back in a half hour."

Holly shut the door to the garage behind her before Sasha could formulate a reply.

She stared at the EMPLOYEES ONLY sign fastened to the door, her hands bracketing the bulky phone uncertainly. She could just call for a cab to take her to the nearest motel and leave it at that. The mechanic wouldn't have to know.

Or she could call Trevor. If family gossip had gotten to him about her text to Gran, he'd probably have tried to reach her. He'd be worried that she wasn't answering.

And god, did she just want to know that there was at least one person in the world who wasn't fed up with her and her problems.

The ring of his phone sounded rough through the old plastic receiver. She closed her eyes as she counted them. He wouldn't pick up until she left a message explaining it was her. She was sure he wouldn't. Sasha was the only person in the family with a compulsion to pick up the phone for strange numbers.

The third ring cut off abruptly, and even though she'd tried to prepare herself for this, her heart fell.

But instead of a mechanical voice instructing her to leave a message, a harried-sounding male answered, "Hello?"

"Trev?" His name came out in a thin, high rasp. She sounded like an emotional chain smoker. Not like herself at all. She swallowed the lump in her throat and tried again. "It's—It's Sasha."

"Oh thank god," Trevor breathed. There was a soft thump, like he'd dropped onto the couch in relief. "Are you okay? Are you hurt?"

"No. I'm . . . I'm okay."

"No one's been able to reach you all morning. I was about to start calling hospitals to see if you'd gotten run over by a taxi."

Sasha rubbed her knuckles across her forehead. "I'm sorry."

"No, it's fine. I'm just glad you're okay." Trevor paused. "You *are* okay, right?"

"Yeah, I'm just . . ." She went on in a rush, like if she talked fast enough she could stay ahead of the emotion in her tone. "I didn't know what to do. Ma called me and everything was going wrong and I guess I just couldn't handle it anymore. So I started out to see you. But then my car broke down. And I couldn't call a tow truck because my phone's dead and I left my charger in my dorm. And also my laptop. And pretty much everything else." She winced. Saying it out loud made her decision to leave sound like such a childish impulse. "I didn't . . . I guess I didn't really plan this out very well."

Trevor sighed. "Sasha."

"I know," Sasha said. It wasn't the first time feeling cornered had made her want to run without any thought to the consequences. Trevor had every right to be impatient with her for pulling this kind of thing again. "It was stupid. I'm sorry. I should've handled it better."

"Don't apologize, pipsqueak," Trevor said gently. "It's okay to ask for help."

"This isn't asking for help, Trev. This is—This is fucking everything up and running away because I can't deal with having a dumb fight with my mom. I just—I—I actually . . ." She swallowed and forced herself to breathe. "I don't know. I thought maybe I was going to catch a break this time. And maybe I could stop fighting so hard to be a normal, functional person. And instead I just—I blew it all up."

"What are you talking about? What your mom does isn't your fault. It's never been your fault."

"It's not just that, it's . . ." Another memory of the night before slotted into place—Kinsey telling her fiercely and without hesitation that Sasha was lovely and talented and . . . and precious.

It hadn't taken long at all before Sasha proved her wrong.

Huffing a shaky breath, she took the base of the phone to the edge of the counter so she could sink into one of the plastic chairs crammed against one wall. "Do you . . . Do you remember me telling you about my graphic designer friend?"

"Miss Kinsey Han, queen of dark humor, adorable human being, lettering genius, and unrequited love of your life? *That* graphic designer friend?"

Sasha heaved a heavy sigh. "Is there another one?"

"What did she do?" Trevor asked, an edge to his voice. Like Kinsey was a kid who'd been harassing Sasha on the playground.

"Nothing," Sasha said helplessly. "It wasn't her, it was me. She was . . . She said she liked me too. And she wanted to be with me. And I tried to make it work. I wanted to make it work. More than anything. But I just—I couldn't deal with it."

"You couldn't deal with the love of your life liking you back?"

"No. I couldn't. I can't, Trev. I couldn't even keep it together for two days. And I knew it wouldn't last. I *knew* it. But I didn't care because . . . because it was Kinsey. I thought maybe it would be different. I thought I could just . . . stop caring if I was fighting with Ma over stupid shit and get over it. I thought that would be enough." She slouched in her chair, letting her head fall back against the wall. "I thought I was better at this."

"Better at what?" Trevor asked skeptically. "Not caring?"

"We only started fighting because I lashed out first. None of this would have happened if I had been more careful about keeping how I felt to myself. If I had just kept my mouth shut about how much I wanted her. At least before she kissed me we were friends. Now we're . . . we're *nothing*." Her voice broke on the last word and she raked her hair back with her free hand, not bothering to check the tears spilling down her face any longer. "I'm so stupid. I really thought it was all going to work out. I thought I could actually be a normal, happy, well-adjusted person for her. And instead I just fell apart and told her everything. Ma being a junkie, and how she overdosed . . ."

"Neither of which have ever been your problems."

"But they *are*. My whole life has been about pretending I'm fine, pretending everything is normal, pretending it doesn't matter if my mom never cared enough about me to get her life together. And then Ma called to make me bail her out again and Kinsey heard basically the whole thing and I just—I couldn't keep pretending anymore. And I flipped out."

"Sasha—"

"Kinsey's just . . . she's so tough," Sasha said over him, needing to get this out. Knowing she couldn't manage it if Trevor started feeling sorry for her. "She doesn't take bullshit from anyone. And her family is so close. Even when they're fighting, she and her parents would do anything for each other. Why would she want to be with me? With my shitty little family. And my shitty little attempts at make believing it doesn't matter. When inside I'm so broken I don't know how to put myself back together anymore."

"You're not stupid and you're not broken," Trevor said sternly.

"I feel broken," Sasha whispered.

Trevor just let out a long, soft breath.

Sasha had really hoped that talking to him would make her feel better. Or at least help her make sense of the tight, confused feelings knotted around her chest. But she just felt like more of an idiot. There was a reason she had constructed all the rules about which childhood stories were safe and which were off-limits. There was a reason she kept herself to herself whenever she could help it. It prevented her from opening her heart and feeling like . . . *this*.

She would have never let herself keep crushing on Kinsey for so long if she ever thought she'd had a real chance. Falling for women who wouldn't look twice at her was how Sasha had learned to protect herself from having her heart shattered again. If she knew what to expect—nothing—she couldn't be disappointed. No one could hurt her if she was already hurting. Not enough for it to matter. Certainly not as much as she was hurting now.

Why did she ever let herself believe she was strong enough to leave that protection behind?

"You're not broken, Sasha," Trevor said into the silence. His voice was calm and sure and comforting in its familiarity. "You're a fighter. You always have been. It's what makes you a force to be reckoned with on the soccer field. It's how you got yourself a pick of athletic scholarships with only a fraction of the emotional and financial support most athletes need to get anywhere. That fighting spirit taught you things that helped you pick yourself up when most people would've given up. It taught you how to focus, and how to manage a lot of shifting priorities, and how to deal with the immense amount of pressure you've always put on yourself. Not just on the field, but at home, too. Being a fighter helped you survive, and helped you bootstrap your way out of Wyoming.

"But maybe it also taught you a few things that aren't so helpful anymore."

Sasha sniffed, dabbing tears from her cheeks with her coat sleeve. "What do you mean?"

"I mean you don't have to make believe it doesn't bother you when people hurt you," Trevor said. "You're allowed to be bothered. You're allowed to feel hurt. Your feelings matter, Sasha."

Sasha made a small, involuntary sound in the back of her throat. It was too close to what Kinsey kept telling her in North Carolina. *Just because you're playing knight for me doesn't mean I can't hold you up, too . . .*

"I mean it," Trevor insisted. "Maybe the only way to survive when you were little was to deal with your feelings by pretending you didn't have any. And maybe it really did protect you when you didn't have any other options. But you can't keep thinking like that forever. Not when it's starting to mess with the good things in your life."

"You mean Kinsey?"

"You tell me, pipsqueak. She's your lettering genius."

Sasha shuddered out a breath. She'd always told herself that dealing with her mom required patience, but it wasn't really patience that got her through those conversations, was it? It was training herself to go numb on cue. To shut off. So Cynthia's cutting remarks couldn't actually hurt her.

But being numb didn't prevent the bruises from forming. It didn't stop all the little blows coming in. All it did was make her really good at lying about how bad things were getting.

At least—it used to. Ever since she moved to New York, she'd needed that numb practicality less and less. Without the burden of managing her mother's moods 24/7—of always preparing for another battle, another cut to her heart—she'd had space to spread out. It became easier to laugh. She started caring more. She stopped filtering her opinions so much.

She still wasn't great at expressing how she felt. Most of the time, when she wanted to say something real, she had to come at it backwards, turning it into sarcasm or an easily dismissed, corny one-liner.

Only . . . Only it wasn't a tactic that always worked on Kinsey. She had this way of fixing Sasha with that intense, no-bullshit stare and getting the truth out of her anyway.

It should have been terrifying. Sasha had spent so much of her life never letting anyone see her. Never letting anyone catch a glimpse of the pain she kept locked away in the darkest corner of her heart. She barely let *herself* acknowledge that hurt.

But something about the way Kinsey challenged Sasha's deflections made her want to be brave enough to break through the walls and protections she'd put up around her heart. Being around Kinsey—who cared about people so fiercely but tried so hard to prevent anyone noticing how kind and warm her heart was—made Sasha feel like it might not be so dangerous to let her guard down. Like opening up and being unafraid might actually make her happier.

Maybe what she needed wasn't a fairy tale princess to sweep her off into the sunset. Maybe all she'd ever needed was someone who was willing to wait up with her when she was stressed out. Who'd come to sit shoulder-to-shoulder with her because some of her confused, complicated grief over her mom had bled through her defenses. Who looked her in the eye and kept reminding her again and again how much she mattered. Someone who would unquestioningly back her up when she had to make a tough decision. Someone like Kinsey.

She pressed her eyes shut against a wave of guilt. "I don't know if it matters whether she was a good part of my life, Trev. I've never flipped out like that at anyone except maybe my mom. She won't want to take me back. I'm not sure she'd even want to hear an apology."

"Are you going to let that stop you from trying?"

Sasha tugged at her ponytail. She didn't believe Trevor was asking because he didn't want to give up his couch, or even because he was disappointed in her for how she was handling her meltdown. If she told him right now that going back just wasn't an option, he wouldn't push her to change her mind. He'd tell her it was okay and help her figure out what to do about the van. He'd even book her a flight to San Francisco. By the time she got there he would have the couch made up and the fridge stocked with her favorite snacks. And he wouldn't mind if it took her a couple of weeks to pull herself together enough to start figuring out what she was going to do next.

But that wasn't what she wanted. It wasn't the person she wanted to be. Giving up when things got tough was something her mom did. Not Sasha. How many games had she played when the first half was so bad it seemed easier to concede than keep getting their asses kicked? Had she ever let herself give up then? No. She'd shaken it off, regrouped, and she'd gone out there and *fought back.*

She knew she'd fucked up with Kinsey. She didn't expect one apology was going to make up for the way she'd treated her yesterday. But Sasha's options now were to either give up on everything she'd ever fought for or grit her teeth and get back in the game. And she didn't think she could forgive herself if she quit now.

She sighed. "Would you be devastated if I put off crashing on your couch awhile longer?"

"Only a little bit," Trevor said. She could hear the smile in his voice. "Mostly I'd be proud of you."

Sasha let out a noise that was somewhere between an awkward laugh and a sob. "Really?"

"Super proud."

Sasha was too overwhelmed to know how to respond, but she felt the corner of her mouth pulling up in a small smile.

"Let me know how it goes with Kinsey, okay?"

"Okay."

"Love you."

Sasha's ears warmed, but in a nice way. "Love you too. And—Trev?"

"Yeah?"

"Thanks. For yelling at me."

He snorted. "Anytime, pipsqueak."

Sasha took a deep breath after she hung up. Once her eyes were dry, thanks to a hand towel she found shoved into her backpack, she zipped up her coat and stepped outside. An old stereo was playing crackly blues music in the back corner of the open garage, the tinny guitar accompanied by rummaging sounds and occasional throaty hums.

"Holly?" Sasha called, picking her way toward where her van was sitting with its hood open.

The mechanic appeared from around the hood and grabbed a rag from a bench to wipe her hands. "Figure out where you're headed yet?" she asked, turning the stereo down.

"Yeah. Back . . . Back home." Sasha rubbed her neck with one hand. "Um . . . Do you happen to know if there's a bus station nearby that'll get me to New York?"

TWENTY-SIX

Kinsey chewed her lip as she sped over the Delaware River into Pennsylvania. She had never been so thankful for Beatrice's insane organizational skills as when she'd emerged from her room with a thin folder containing nothing but slips of paper detailing the emergency contact information for all her friends and family. She had collected numbers and addresses for everyone from Julian's twin sister and Kinsey's parents to Beatrice's brother's former roommate. Buried in the middle of all those papers was the contact info of Sasha's favorite cousin.

Kinsey had stared at the San Francisco address in a haze, trying to work out exactly how crazy it would be to fly all the way out there and wait for Sasha to arrive. And whether that was more or less crazy than jumping in her car with nothing but what she already had with her and hoping to catch up before Sasha got that far.

But Beatrice, fortunately, had been practical enough to insist they call Trevor first to find out if he knew any more than they did. Kinsey didn't think she should be the one to talk to him, in case Sasha had already told Trevor about their fight, so Beatrice volunteered to take care of it. Trevor had called back shortly after Beatrice left a message explaining their concern. She had scribbled down some notes in the back of the Syracuse course catalog as they talked.

After she hung up, she'd relayed the broad points of what Trevor had told her: Sasha had called him a few minutes ago from a number with a Pennsylvania area code to say her van had broken down and 'talk through some things'—he hadn't gone into any more detail than that. He was sure she was safe and unhurt, and thought she'd decided to head back to New York. But he didn't know how long it would take to get her van repaired.

Kinsey had been ready to march out the door right then and there. At least Pennsylvania was a smaller area to search than the entirety of the continental United States. But Julian, who had been looking up the phone number Trevor gave them, stopped her before she could hurry out the door.

"It's a body shop in Buckhorn," he said, turning the laptop around to show the map he'd found. "If she just called her cousin, she's probably still there."

Kinsey grabbed Beatrice's notes and punched the body shop's number into her phone. It rang a few times and then switched to voicemail. "Dammit."

"No answer?" Beatrice asked, looking worried. "You don't think she left already, do you?"

"No idea." Kinsey slung her purse over her shoulder and pulled up the map on her phone. "You said this place is in Buckhorn, Pennsylvania?"

Kinsey's map was telling her Buckhorn's only body shop was almost three hours away. It might be stupid to drive three hours only to find out Sasha had already left, but she couldn't wait around Beatrice's apartment trying not to scream for not knowing any longer. The situation reminded her too strongly of the story Sasha told her of running into the woods when she was ten because she was too overwhelmed to cope anymore. If there was even the slightest chance Sasha was still stuck out there, someone ought to go after her. *Kinsey* ought to go after her.

"You two keep trying that number and call me if you find anything out," she said. "I'm going to head out there."

Beatrice had popped out of her chair to give Kinsey a quick hug and wish her luck, and then Kinsey was hurrying down the steps to her car.

She hadn't turned on any music for fear she'd miss the voice of her map telling her which exit to take, or a call from Beatrice declaring she'd tracked Sasha down at last and had talked her into staying put until Kinsey could get there. But she hadn't heard anything in the hour or so since she left the apartment.

What if no one was answering at the body shop because they were usually closed on Tuesdays? Or because Sasha had been hurt and taken to a hospital? What if Beatrice *had* found Sasha, but she'd made her swear not to tell Kinsey anything because Sasha never wanted to see her again?

"Come on, Deforest," Kinsey muttered, glancing from the map on her phone to the long stretch of highway in front of her. She was driving as fast as she could without guaranteeing herself a ticket, but there were still miles to go. "Just hang in there for a little while longer."

She jumped at the deafening blast of her ringtone—she'd pumped up the volume so she couldn't fail to hear it—but it was only her mom.

Her stomach knotted. For one wild moment, she thought her mom had discovered that Kinsey had skipped out on her classes this morning and wanted an explanation. Then she remembered that she'd promised to check in with her parents this morning. She'd completely forgotten about it after last night. Her mom was probably just worried about her.

Berating herself for the oversight, Kinsey answered the call with a quick swipe of her thumb. "Hi, Mom." Her voice was strained, but when she tried to fix it she only sounded irritable. "How are you feeling?"

"Like I could crush rocks with my bare hands," Annette said. "I've never felt so healthy in my life. I did five entire push-ups this morning, you know. I could've done more, except your father cruelly distracted me with breakfast."

"I've been trying to tell her to take it easy," Henry called from somewhere in the background. "She thinks I'm being overprotective."

"You should listen to Dad," Kinsey said. She was actually glad for the distraction. Persuading her mom to chill on the feats of strength was something she knew how to do. Which was more than could be said for figuring out how she was going to convince Sasha to come home. "We already know you're Supermom. You don't have to prove it with excessive exercise."

"Since when are five push-ups excessive?" Annette asked, a laugh in her voice.

Kinsey's eyes flicked to her phone screen. It struck her that she hadn't heard this level of open humor in her mom's voice in a long time. Not before they fought about Evie. Since when had she earned their trust back? She was still just as prickly as she'd ever been. She'd even forgotten her promise to call them this morning.

"Kins? Are you still there?"

"Yeah," Kinsey said hoarsely. "I'm here."

"What's the matter?" Annette asked. Kinsey could tell from the slightly tinnier sound of her voice that she'd switched to speakerphone so her dad could hear too.

Kinsey opened her mouth with every intention of giving some half-truth to explain her tone—that she was just happy her mom was doing better, maybe, or she was having a rough morning for unrelated reasons—but instead she blurted out, "I'm sorry I didn't listen to you about Evie."

"Oh," Annette said, sounding faintly surprised.

"You were trying to warn me I was dating a controlling jerk and I didn't want to listen because I knew you were right and I didn't want you to be. I mean—what the hell is wrong with me, trying to hurt you any way I could think of just because you were—very rightly—concerned about how my girlfriend was acting?"

"Well, we shouldn't have ambushed you, either," Annette began.

"Are you kidding?" Kinsey demanded. "You were trying to help and I threatened to never talk to you again. I was the crazy asshole throwing a tantrum. I was the one who wrecked everything. I mean, isn't that why we've been stuck in this stupid holding pattern ever since? Because I ruined everything?"

"Is that what you thought?" her mom asked. "That we've been holding that fight against you all this time?"

"How could you not?" Kinsey said, gripping the steering wheel until her knuckles blanched. "I was awful just to spite you and I never even apologized after I realized what I'd done—"

"I can't say I blame you, after the way we handled it," her dad put in. "I'm pretty sure I would've reacted the exact same way if my parents had tried to get me to break up with my first love."

"We shouldn't have tried to interfere," her mom said. "All we did was make you feel like you had to choose between us and your girlfriend when we should have been telling you that we were on your side no matter what. No wonder you didn't want to come to us after you two broke up. You probably thought we'd gloat instead of giving you space to grieve."

"But . . . you were right." Kinsey stared at the back of the semi she was keeping pace with while she talked, trying to process this new version of events. She'd always assumed they'd stopped talking to each other because she'd gone too far during that fight and her parents were understandably wary of setting her off again. It had never occurred to her that they thought *they'd* screwed up. Which was ridiculous. "You were trying to warn me about her because you loved me. If I had listened, maybe I could've—"

"Do you know what my biggest objection to you and Evie dating was?" her dad interrupted.

"She gave me an excuse to treat everyone like crap?"

"She was always trying to make you feel like less than what you are," Henry said. "You're such a smart, driven, caring young woman. I consider myself extremely lucky to have you as a daughter."

"Really?"

"Of course, Kins. But something about being around Evie seemed to make you think you weren't good enough. Like you had to scramble to keep her affection. That's not how you treat people you love."

Kinsey swallowed the knot in her throat. "Screaming at them for trying to point that out isn't that great either, though."

"Neither is ambushing them with parental disapproval when they're already feeling vulnerable," Annette said. "We never held that fight against you, you know. We just . . . We thought you might be gun-shy about letting us know about any new relationships in your life after we ambushed you. We figured you'd be more willing to tell us about you and Sasha if you saw we weren't going to pounce on you again."

Kinsey had to play back the last part of that speech in her head to make sure she'd heard right. She had been pretty careful about not mentioning the whole making-out-in-Charlotte thing. It had been so new. She'd wanted to give it a few days to make sure nothing was going to happen to warrant another intervention. And then Sasha had started acting weird, and then the whole thing last night . . . So where was that *you and Sasha* thing coming from? "What did you say?"

"Well, I mean," Annette began, sounding slightly defensive, as though Henry was glaring at her. "You're not the most subtle pair in the world. Sasha's always at our house on holidays, you talk about her all the time, you go to her soccer games despite never having enjoyed a single sport in your life before you met her. And she made sure you got to North Carolina even though she had to miss a few days of classes *and* drive back on her own on Sunday. Tell me that isn't girlfriend territory."

"I—But—*Mom*," Kinsey spluttered. "We're—We're not—"

"Really?" Annette asked, sounding entirely unconvinced. "Huh. Guess we were wrong."

"*Way* wrong," Henry said. "The way you've been talking lately, I thought you were building up the courage to announce your engagement."

"*Engagement?*" Kinsey yelped.

"You kept talking about relationships and the future," he pointed out. "I thought you were at least ratcheting up to pop the question."

"But—You can't—Exactly how long did you think we were secretly dating?"

"Since summer break?" her dad guessed. "Maybe a little longer?"

"I mean, you watched the World Cup with her over the phone, Kins," Annette said. "And *enjoyed* it. What were we supposed to think?"

"Mom, just because I'm gay doesn't mean I can't also be *friends with girls.*"

"I know, muffin. But you don't . . . light up quite the same way when Beatrice comes over."

Kinsey opened her mouth to object, but all that came out were a series of incoherent squawks.

"I think I broke our daughter," Annette muttered.

"I guess our imaginations got out of hand," Henry said. "If you and Sasha aren't dating, you aren't dating. No judgment."

"No, that's—I just—" She huffed out a breath. She could've come up with a way to reroute the conversation. Even if she caught up to Sasha in Buckhorn, she wasn't sure if this last-ditch effort to get her back was going to work. No one would fault her for not wanting to get into the entire fiasco with her parents while the outcome was uncertain.

But she was sick of never talking to her parents. And she was sick of hiding behind old arguments to justify keeping such a big part of her life from them. And she didn't want to be another tragic ex in Sasha's life who kept her like a dark secret instead of the lovely, precious person she was.

"Okay, yes, fine, I like her," she blurted out. "But we never actually talked about it until a few days ago, and now we're—We broke up."

"Oh, honey," her mom said. "I'm so sorry. What happened?"

"She was upset and I handled it in the worst possible way and now I'm trying to get to some dinky town in Pennsylvania before she gets her car fixed so I can apologize and try to convince her to come home with me. And please don't tell me it's a stupid plan. I know it's a stupid plan, but it's the only one I've got. And I'm not turning around," she added, stubbornly digging her fingernails into the vinyl of the steering wheel. They could fret about how many classes she was missing and whether it would mean her GPA taking a hit all they wanted. She didn't care. This was more important.

"Who said you should turn around?" Henry asked, with a kind of false outrage that reached through the speakers like an affectionate nudge to her shoulder.

"Yeah," Annette said. "I like Sasha. She's a sweetheart. She laughs at my jokes, too. Which is more than I can say for either of you two grumps."

"And she makes you happy," Henry said. "Doesn't she?"

"Really happy," Kinsey croaked, thinking of Sasha's teasing grin when she flirted, of the earnest look in her eyes when she told Kinsey she didn't want anybody else, of the way she made Kinsey feel like herself—as though that was enough—just by being there. She was hit again by how much she missed her. And how stupid she'd been to let her walk away so easily.

"Then go tell her that," Henry said.

Kinsey huffed out a weak laugh. It had been a long time since she'd been brave enough to ask for her parents' support, and to get it so easily was such a relief she almost started crying again. "Don't worry," she said, merging into the fast lane. "I'm gonna try."

TWENTY-SEVEN

Sasha held out her hand as a small, nearly translucent flake of snow drifted down, just inches from her nose. It landed in the center of her glove and melted instantly. Another snowflake landed on the tip of her thumb, a little bigger than the first. By the time the third flake had melted into her glove, she was surrounded by whirling snow.

Everything was quieting already. The occasional snatch of conversation from the truck stop behind her seemed further away. The hiss of overpass traffic softened to a hush.

A cold bench in a small dog park behind a truck stop wasn't exactly the wild, empty places of her childhood, but it was better than sitting in the drab, stuffy bus terminal up the street. The park itself was mostly deserted apart from the occasional curious squirrel, so at least she didn't have to talk to anyone while she waited for the next bus to New York.

Holly had given Sasha a ride to the bus terminal in her vintage Mustang, refusing to take payment for the favor. She'd only grunted with a pleased sort of frown when Sasha thanked her. Unfortunately, when she walked into the bus terminal, Sasha found out her options for getting home weren't extensive. She'd missed the flurry of buses that left for Philadelphia and New York City in the early morning, and there hadn't been anything else heading east until almost three in the afternoon. Which would at least get her home sometime today, even if it wouldn't be until late.

With a few hours to kill before she could leave, she'd walked up the street to the truck stop to grab some lunch and a few snacks, plus a charger for her phone, a crossword book, and the two least romantic paperbacks she could find.

The plan had been to head back to the bus station to find an outlet and revive her phone. But she didn't want to deal with whatever notifications were waiting for her there. And the bite of wind across her face had been more enticing than the idea of shutting herself into the well-heated terminal. Eventually she'd have to grit her teeth and field whatever pushback her refusal to handle her mom anymore initiated in the rest of the family. But it didn't have to be right now. It didn't have to be today.

A thin layer of snow was forming on the bench around her. She should head back. The sun had granted feeble warmth for the last hour or so, but the temperature was dropping rapidly as clouds rolled in. And she really should try to find a place to charge her phone, even if she couldn't bring herself to turn it on just yet.

Taking in a breath of chilly, damp air, she put away the unread thriller she'd been leafing through and stood, slinging her duffel bag over one shoulder and her backpack over the other. She walked slowly, watching lacy patches of snow decorate the weedy, brown grass beside the road.

There was a drive-through and another gas station across the street, and what looked like a storage facility beyond those. A few hundred yards the other way, empty lots turned into farmland

and rolling hills. Somewhere beyond those was the Manhattan skyline. And Sasha's cramped, friendly dorm. And Kinsey, just two floors down . . .

Sasha wondered if any of the notifications waiting for her were from Kinsey. It didn't seem likely. Not after what happened between them last night. Kinsey probably hadn't even realized she was gone.

Which was probably good. Sasha still wasn't sure how to explain why she'd flipped out in a way that made sense, but it seemed like it would be easier to do if no one had noticed she was missing yet.

Her hair was damp and her ears and nose were freezing by the time she reached the bus terminal's parking lot. Snow was falling thick enough to start building up in earnest, settling in a white layer over the small cluster of cars parked out front.

On all but one of them. A black sedan that looked chest-tighteningly familiar was parked crookedly a couple rows back. The snow hitting the roof and hood was still melting when it touched the surface.

Sasha came to a halt on the sidewalk. Her duffel bag fell from her shoulder. It couldn't be Kinsey's car. How could it be her car? It might have the same scratch in the left headlight, and the same parking sticker in the window—and even the same pompom-and-felt peach charm hanging from the rearview mirror—but it couldn't be her car. It was impossible. Even if Kinsey had realized Sasha was gone, even if she'd somehow figured out where she *was*, there was no reason for her to—

"*Hey!*" The word cut through the whispery snow, sharp and tough. Sasha knew that voice even before she laid eyes on the speaker.

Her heart caught in her throat. Kinsey couldn't be here. Yet there she was, bursting out of the swinging glass doors of the terminal, a breeze sweeping her feathery black hair off her scowling, beautiful face.

"The *least* you could do when you cut and run is stay in one place," Kinsey said as she stalked up the sidewalk, eyes flashing. "How the hell is anyone supposed to find you if you can't stay fucking put?"

Maybe she should have been concerned about the hard look on Kinsey's face, but Sasha was too preoccupied with processing her sudden appearance to take in anything else. "Kinsey?" she breathed. "What . . . How did you . . ." She had no idea where to start, or what to say. All she wanted to do was gather Kinsey up and hold onto her, to press her face into that soft, dark hair and breathe her in, to find Kinsey's mouth with her own and persuade her to give them another chance . . .

She had just enough reason left to understand what a bad idea that was, and started to take a step back so she wouldn't try it anyway—

Kinsey's hand darted out and closed around Sasha's palm, tight as a vice. "Don't you dare," she said, voice rough, eyes pleading as they bored into Sasha's. "Don't you dare tell me it's too late, Sasha Deforest. Not after I came all the way out here to bring you home."

"Kins," Sasha whispered in a voice like cracked earth. She gripped Kinsey's fingers despite herself, despite wanting to conceal the aching, empty *need* that wanted to latch onto that offhand promise of home and never, never let go. "I don't—I don't understand. After I flipped out at you . . ."

"You thought I'd just let you run out the back door thinking no one cared enough to come after you?"

Sasha didn't know how to respond to the careful stubbornness she saw in Kinsey's eyes. She dropped her gaze to their interlocked hands, guilt compressing her chest. "I'm sorry," she whispered. "I didn't mean to worry anybody. I just couldn't . . . I guess I had this idea in my head that I could keep all the crap with my mom away from the good parts of my life. And if I kept them separate, the bad parts wouldn't have a chance to wrap around the good things I had and kill them. I . . ."

Sasha blew out a shivery breath, trying to work out how to explain it. She'd expended so much energy trying to *avoid* talking about her issues with her mom. She wasn't really sure how to distill the multitude of little blows into a few comprehensible sentences.

"You have to understand," she said slowly. "Growing up with my mom, I couldn't really say how I felt about anything without it turning into a battle. It was always easier to pretend I didn't care. Make everyone believe nothing really bothered me. That way I could tell myself it didn't hurt when things didn't pan out the way I hoped. It made me feel like I had some kind of control over my life. I couldn't do anything about my mom's mood swings or whatever disaster her decisions had created, but I could control how I reacted. And I guess I've just been digging myself deeper into the sarcasm reflex ever since.

"But I can't do that with you," she said, tentatively lifting her gaze to meet Kinsey's. "You have this way of . . . of finding the weak spots in my defenses and getting through."

"I'm sorry," Kinsey whispered.

"No," Sasha said quickly, pressing Kinsey's fingers. "No, it's— It's—" She took a deep breath, searching the falling snow for a way to explain this. "I've been so careful for so long. I had all these rules and defenses set up in my head so I'd be safe from getting hurt again. And then you showed up in my living room last year and turned me upside down. In the best possible way.

And it got harder and harder to remember why I had to be so careful. Because I don't *want* to keep you out, Kins. I want to talk to you about stuff, even if it's hard. I want you to see me. But I'm also . . . I'm scared you'll take a look around, realize what a mess I am, and walk out forever. And I can't . . . I've never . . . I've never cared about anybody as much as I care about you. And that scares me so much. Because I can't tell myself it wouldn't hurt to lose you. And I don't know how to convince you I'm not too screwed up to deal with. Especially after . . . after last night."

Kinsey searched her eyes, an indefinable softness in her expression. Slowly, she reached up and brushed her thumb across Sasha's cheek. "You know what I see when I look at you?"

Sasha shook her head, throat too tight to answer.

"I see a courageous, talented woman with the biggest heart and the most joyful laugh I've ever encountered. *Ever.* And that's something you held onto despite anything that might have happened to you before I met you. Anyone who sees *that* and wants to walk away can go fuck themselves."

Sasha let out a pained breath, leaning her forehead against Kinsey's. "Kins," she breathed. She wished she had words for the emotions squeezing her heart—the lingering fear, the yearning hope, the mingled affection and regret.

"It was stupid of me to ask you to meet me halfway," Kinsey said. "You've always met me exactly where I was, no matter what I was going through. I couldn't even give you a minute to breathe. And don't you dare try to make excuses for me," she added when Sasha opened her mouth to do exactly that. "We wouldn't have fought if I hadn't pushed you to open up before you were ready. You wouldn't have left if I hadn't made it sound like I didn't even want to be with you. I *do* want to be with you. I *like* when you flirt with me. I like just talking to you. I like *you*. Scars and late-night family crises and all."

"Kins—"

"I know I'm a cranky, sharp person," Kinsey interrupted. "And I'm not going to claim I know what it's like to grow up in a bad family situation like you did. But I . . ."

She took her fingers from Sasha's to cup her face in both hands and look her in the eyes. Her frown wasn't angry so much as . . . vulnerable. "It matters to me whether you're around or not. It matters a lot. I can't imagine going through the rest of my life without even being able to call you. Without being able to make you laugh. Without having you around to—to swap soup with and goof off with and sit on the floor sharing a tub of ice cream with. You make me so happy, Sasha. Just having you in my life makes it so much better. I just want a chance to try to make you happy, too."

Sasha's hand drifted absently to Kinsey's waist. Though the snow was falling fast and thick around them, the space between them felt protected and warm. "But you do make me happy, Kins."

Kinsey's frown turned suspicious. "What, you enjoy being scowled at now?"

A soft smile tugged at Sasha's mouth. "Maybe. It's kind of . . . peaceful, when it's coming from you."

"Peaceful?"

"Yeah. Or . . . reassuring, I guess? You've got this one particular scowl that means you believe so hard in what you're saying, you'd fight anyone who tries to argue. And when you frown like that and tell me things like . . . Like when you said I mattered and you cared about me . . . I knew you meant that."

"That's still true, Sasha." Whether it was a conscious choice or not, Sasha didn't know, but Kinsey's expression shifted to the exact scowl she'd been trying to describe. "And I'll keep on repeating it as long as you need me to, because it's not going to change. I like you. I care about you. And you matter. You *matter.* Always and incontrovertibly."

Sasha swallowed, pressing her eyes shut, her fingers lightly, lightly beckoning Kinsey closer with the barest pressure against her side. She felt the warmth of Kinsey's breath against her face as she came to her, wrapping her in a sure embrace.

Sasha's arms went around Kinsey's waist, wanting to hang on with all she had, still scared to hang on too tight.

"It might take some work before I get good at the being-genuine thing," she muttered into Kinsey's neck. "Or even get mediocre at it. And I don't blame you for getting frustrated that I wouldn't talk about what was going on with my mom last night. If you don't want to be around me until I figure myself out, then I get it. I know I'm a mess."

"No, you're not," Kinsey said softly.

Sasha made a sound that was supposed to be a laugh but didn't quite make it. "I'm pretty sure I am," she said, forcing herself to let Kinsey go. Kinsey slipped her hands into Sasha's as she stepped back, her grip firm, as though she was worried Sasha would bolt if she severed contact.

"I—I pretty much decided to cut my mom off," Sasha confessed, her gaze on the top button of Kinsey's blouse. She deserved to know that much, at least. Even if it meant another argument, even if Sasha couldn't make her understand why it needed to be done. "And I'm not really sure how the rest of the family is going to take it. My phone's been dead since I told my grandmother I wasn't go-ing to deal with my mom anymore."

"You do realize that *them* being dicks doesn't make *you* a mess, right?" Kinsey asked.

Sasha blinked at her. "It doesn't bother you?"

"What doesn't bother me? Your family putting you in a position where you think they're all going to turn on you the second you stand up for yourself? Yeah, Sasha, that bothers the hell out of me. Your mom's problems should have never been on you to fix."

"No, not—I just . . . I thought . . ." She searched Kinsey's eyes for the censure she was so sure had to be there. For some hint that she thought Sasha was making a bad decision. But apart from a hint of vengefulness that was probably directed at Sasha's family, Kinsey mainly seemed confused. "It wouldn't bother you to be with someone whose junkie, alcoholic mom is in jail for armed robbery? And whose family might not want to talk to her anymore because it was supposed to be her job to take care of that kind of thing?"

"No," Kinsey said simply. "That's bullshit. I don't care who or what your mom is. I don't care if the rest of your family are idiots. I only care about who you are. And in case you forgot again, *I like you.*"

"Really?"

"Hell, yes, Sasha. I wouldn't say it if it wasn't true. Plus, you can always share my family. I know it's not the same, but there's more than enough support and love to go around. My parents already adore you. They actually seemed disappointed when I had to break it to them we weren't secretly engaged."

Sasha's eyebrows lifted. Maybe some snow had gotten in her ears, because what Kinsey said couldn't have been what Sasha heard. "I'm sorry, secretly *what*?"

Kinsey's cheeks, which were already flushed from the damp cold, went a few shades darker. "Oh. Um." She cleared her throat and tried—failing spectacularly—to seem nonchalant. "I sort of told them about . . . us. They were utterly unsurprised because they thought we'd been dating for months already."

"They—They did? Why?"

"I don't know," Kinsey said with a flustered shrug, taking her hands from Sasha's. "Something about how I never stop talking about you and apparently I light up in a very specific way when you walk in the room and I guess you're only allowed to watch soccer now if you're head over heels for one of the players—"

"H—head over—"

"I hope it was okay that I brought it up with them," Kinsey said, her forehead crinkling as she crossed her arms. "We never talked about what we were telling people. If you'd rather they didn't know we're together yet, I can—I can try bullying them into pretending they don't, I guess?"

Sasha huffed out a bewildered laugh. She brushed a lock of dampened, black hair behind Kinsey's ear. "God, I love you."

She hadn't meant to say it. The words just slipped out, too big, too true to keep to herself any longer.

But before Sasha could start worrying about whether it was too soon or too late or just plain unwelcome, Kinsey's eyes glittered, a sigh of relief relaxing her shoulders. "Thank goodness," she breathed, pulling Sasha in by her coat pockets.

Sasha grinned as their lips met, her uncertainty uncoiling from around her spine. This was what she'd been running after, all those times she fled into the woods. Not isolation. Not a different life. Just someone who saw beyond the sarcasm and accepted her for who she was. Someone who was in her corner no matter what. Someone who made her feel like she'd finally found a home.

"Oh!" Kinsey ducked back halfway through a kiss, a look of horror on her face, fingers still hooked in Sasha's coat pockets.

"What?" Sasha asked, tensing.

Kinsey scowled. "I love you, too."

Sasha stared. And then she was laughing, a big, bright belly-laugh she couldn't have stopped if she wanted to. She planted kisses all over Kinsey's face, love and joy flooding through her, filling her up until she was positively overflowing. "Thank goodness."

EPILOGUE

Four months later

Kinsey yelped and grabbed the support rail at the edge of the ice skating rink as one foot slipped out from under her. She managed to stop her fall before landing on her ass, but only just. And she was pretty sure any attempt to get both skates firmly on the ice would only result in another tumble.

Sasha scraped to a graceful stop in front of her, eyebrows raised. "You okay?"

"Why did I let you talk me into this, again?" Kinsey asked, clinging to the rail.

Sasha grinned. "Because you love me. Obviously."

Kinsey puffed out a long-suffering burst of air, unable to keep up her frown. "It *is* remarkably hard to remember I hate skating when you're sparkling at me like that."

Laughing, Sasha offered a hand up. "Just hold onto me, darling. I won't let you fall."

"You underestimate my inability to sport," Kinsey said, scowling as Nova did some kind of jumpy spin thing at the far end of the rink.

You'd think the fact it was nearly summer would mean there would be no ice rinks to go to. But *no.* Freaking White Plains had to have a big indoor rink just a few miles from Kinsey's parents' house.

The worst part was this was actually Kinsey's idea. She couldn't let Sasha's birthday pass without getting her friends together and doing something she liked. Even though spending a couple of hours trying not to break any bones on slippery ice sounded distinctly like torture to Kinsey. Sasha would enjoy it, and so would the rest of their friends, so Kinsey could make herself enjoy it too. Or at least enjoy the fact that the rest of them were enjoying themselves.

She had sort of hoped she could get away with sitting on the sidelines with a warm drink and cheering everyone on. But on the way in, Sasha had asked if she was going to actually rent a pair of skates with that slightly teasing dare in her eyes. Kinsey, without thinking, had protested that of course she was. She couldn't regret it because saying yes made Sasha beam. And what did a little incompetence matter, when it earned Kinsey that smile? Fifteen minutes on the ice *probably* wouldn't kill her.

Setting her teeth, Kinsey gripped Sasha's fingers with one hand, keeping the other on the rail. It took some scrabbling and another near-fall, but eventually she got both feet under her.

"There you go," Sasha said brightly. "You're nailing step one of skating."

"What, standing up?" Kinsey asked. "You're sweet, but I'm not sure how long that one's going to last."

Sasha squeezed her hand. "Don't worry, I've got you. Try bending your knees a little."

Kinsey bit her lip as some of the other girls glided past, calling out a jumble of friendly greetings and good-natured taunts. Sasha laughed and ordered them to behave themselves, her grip on Kinsey's hand not wavering for an instant.

Knowing she couldn't cling to the rail without moving all day, Kinsey unmoored herself from the bar. Her skates instantly tried to escape again. She flailed, searching blindly for the security of the railing, and found Sasha's free hand instead.

Kinsey's shoulders sagged in relief. "Thanks."

"I told you I wouldn't let you fall," Sasha said with an encouraging smile. "Do you want to try actually skating now?"

"I guess," Kinsey grumbled. "Just promise me this isn't going to turn into paintball on ice."

Sasha chuckled. "Paintball on ice? Is that a thing?"

"I *hope* not," Kinsey said, horrified that Sasha would look so excited by the idea.

Sasha glided half a step closer and lowered her voice. "I didn't see any paintball guns lying around the locker area, so I think we're safe. Come on." She tugged gently on Kinsey's hands as she started skating backwards, towing Kinsey along after her.

"You are disgustingly good at this," Kinsey complained as she struggled to keep her feet parallel.

Sasha's smile just widened. She bumped a kiss to Kinsey's lips. "Thank you, darling. Now try actually moving your feet."

Kinsey scowled, but Sasha's hands were steady, and there really was no saying no to that grin.

It was nice to see the smiles come so easily these days. The first few weeks after Sasha decided to cut her mom off had been rough on her. She'd had to work through a lingering sense of guilt over the decision, made worse when she actually did get some pushback from some of her relatives. They just couldn't seem to understand why Sasha had finally dug her heels in.

Fortunately, the pushback didn't last long. As soon as Trevor found out about it, he'd taken it upon himself to run interference with the rest of the family. Whatever he told them, it worked. A few of the naysayers actually reached out to apologize, and the rest at least had the decency to let the subject drop.

After that, it seemed to get easier. Sasha still woke out of the odd nightmare, but she'd started taking them as signs she needed to vent, and the more she talked, the less the dreams bothered her—and the more she smiled. The relief of not having to worry about the next time her mom called overtook the last remaining guilt, and slowly, slowly, Sasha had blossomed into a woman more shining and brilliant than ever.

"Don't look now, my dear, but you're skating." Sasha withdrew one hand and deftly moved to Kinsey's side.

"Don't let go," Kinsey warned, gripping Sasha's remaining hand as she awkwardly made some forward progress.

Sasha squeezed her hand back. "I wouldn't dream of it."

Skating wasn't so bad as long as Sasha was holding her hand. Kinsey was aware she probably looked like a newborn foal next to Sasha's athletic grace, but she really didn't care. Her hand was secure in Sasha's fingers, and she was the reason Sasha was smiling, and nothing else mattered.

She actually felt a twinge of disappointment when they had to get off the ice for a few minutes so they could send the little truck thing around the rink.

"Are you two coming to grab anything at the snack bar?" Nova called from the bench where she and a handful of other girls were pulling off their skates. Kinsey wouldn't say they were best of friends these days, but Nova had come around when Kinsey brought Sasha back from Pennsylvania. They got along about as well as could be expected for two women who didn't share many interests.

"Maybe in a minute," Sasha said with a wave, gently tugging Kinsey toward an empty bench.

"You can go get something if you want," Kinsey said softly, pressing her shoulder against Sasha's as they walked. "You should hang out with your friends some, too. I'm the one who gets to take you home."

"Yeah, but you're going to get tired of skating in a few minutes, and I don't think I want to stop holding hands just yet."

"I don't either," Kinsey protested. "That's the best part of the whole skating thing."

"Well, I'm glad we're on the same page, then," Sasha said, brushing her thumb against Kinsey's palm.

Kinsey didn't have time to reply. Beatrice, who'd been running late, turned up to attack both of them with hugs and to chat for a few seconds before running back to find Julian and rent their skates.

With most of the crowd at the snack bar, the benches around the rink quieted until the most prominent sound was the motor of the machine creeping across the ice like a giant snail, leaving deadly smooth ice in its wake. The handful of people who'd hung back were either standing at the side of the rink or sitting on benches out of earshot, chatting or stretching.

Kinsey poked Sasha's arm to get her attention. "Enjoying your birthday?"

"Yeah, I am," Sasha said, a note of surprise in her voice. "I mean, any time I can get you to strap wheels or blades or boards of any variety to your feet is going to be a great time."

"Well, that's a given. I'm such a disaster I *have* to be entertaining."

"You're not a disaster. You're a sweetheart." Sasha drew her closer and kissed her, one of the just-because kisses that Kinsey loved. "Thank you for planning this for me. I don't have a great track record with birthdays going smoothly. And you've made this one just . . . perfect."

Kinsey squeezed Sasha's hand protectively. She knew ranting about how people treated Sasha wouldn't help much in this scenario. It helped *sometimes*, but only if Sasha was taking up guilt that didn't belong to her. Which didn't seem to be a problem today.

It took Kinsey a moment to settle on something better to say. "This is going to sound cheesy," she began, "but I'm glad you were born. And that you somehow found your way to me. You're the most lovely, wonderful, big-hearted person I've ever met. I'm so thankful I get to know you." She rested her palm above Sasha's heart, feeling its steady beat and holding her gaze. "I love you, Sasha Deforest. Every single particle."

Sasha didn't flinch. She didn't deflect. She didn't even break eye contact. She just pulled Kinsey closer, her smile soft and luminous. "I love you more, Kinsey Han."

A warm, bubbly feeling settled under Kinsey's skin as she lifted her chin. "Not a chance, Deforest," she said, her lips brushing Sasha's as she spoke. "Not a chance."

ACKNOWLEDGMENTS

I think first thanks are earned by the people who kept me sane through the craziness that was 2020. In particular, Mom and Dad for being relatively calm about the entire thing; Brae and Jordan for all the game nights and *Rock Band* torture and terrible media consumption; and Lila and Connor for the cuddles and cuteness (and occasional affectionate maulings). It was a year of high anxiety and I think we all handled it pretty well. High fives all around!

I'm forever thankful to the folks who wade into my early drafts and poke at all the iffy bits until I relent and fix them. Neil and Lola read portions of the early chapters and set me straight on a few soccer terms. Jordan and Brae both beta read the first draft with an actual end on it and helpfully yelled at me about Kinsey until I figured her out. Jayne Davis zipped through an early draft, provided lots of great suggestions, and pointed out the problem I couldn't seem to identify in the last handful of chapters. Melinda Perzy, as always, was great at catching any wonky character beats or misplaced emotions, all the while being ridiculously encouraging. My mom is always quick to proof for me (usually multiple times) and say nice things about my writing skillz (I know she's biased, but it's still nice to hear!). An enormous thanks to all of you! This book wouldn't be nearly as good without your input.

ABOUT THE AUTHOR

Rachel Stockbridge is an indie romance author based in central California. She's a lifelong accidental nomad with a Bachelor's Degree in Electronic and Acoustic Composition (yes, really) and an ever-growing collection of books, Post-its, and art supplies. She believes everyone deserves a happy ending and a healthy dose of humor in their lives, and endeavors to write stories that provide a bit of both.

When she's not writing, you can often find her crafting, making art, dabbling in hand lettering, playing music, or running D&D campaigns.

ALSO BY RACHEL STOCKBRIDGE

Next Stop Love

When a shared commute brings two struggling twenty-somethings together, they start to wonder if love might get them back on track.

PAPERBACK: 978-1-7352494-0-7
EBOOK: 978-1-7352494-1-4

The Map to You

A sweet, sarcastic college soccer player and a scowling, secret-softie graphic design major embark on a road trip that could change their friendship forever.

PAPERBACK: 978-1-7352494-2-1
EBOOK: 978-1-7352494-3-8

Sign up for Rachel Stockbridge's mailing list at
newsletter.rachelstockbridge.com/themaptoyou
to be the first to know when she publishes a new book!